W9-AKS-432

A GAME MEN PLAY

Fiction by Vance Bourjaily

The End of My Life
The Hound of Earth
The Violated
Confessions of a Spent Youth
The Man Who Knew Kennedy
Brill Among the Ruins
Now Playing at Canterbury

Nonfiction by Vance Bourjaily

The Unnatural Enemy
Country Matters

The Dial Press
New York

A GAME MEN PLAY

A NOVEL BY

VANCE BOURJAILY

PUBLISHED BY

The Dial Press
1 Dag Hammarskjold Plaza
New York, New York 10017

Manufactured in the United States of America

First Dial printing

Design by Holly McNeely

A limited first edition of this book has been privately printed.

Library of Congress Cataloging in Publication Data

Bourjaily, Vance Nye.
A game men play.

I. Title.
PZ3.B6672Gam [PS3503.077] 813'.5'4
79–19660
ISBN 0–8037–0092–X

For Philip

A GAME MEN PLAY

His deck chair was a bale of hay. The horses he was taking to New Zealand wouldn't need it before the trip was over. It was grass hay, mostly timothy. He had set it by the rail at the stern of the *Vesterålen,* and when he walked towards it along the deck it was always a surprise to see the rectangle of brown-green land color against the bright, blue and white sparkle of the ocean. He liked to sit there, after lunch, reading, looking forward now and then towards the stalls, where the horses slept standing up, or back and down at the ship's wake.

One afternoon he read, in a scholarly collection of classic nursery rhymes:

When I was a little boy
I had but little wit,
'Tis a long time ago
And I have no more yet;
Nor ever, ever shall
Until that I die,
For the longer I live
The More Fool am I.

Then he reread it and smiled, and raised his eyes past the wake and over the Pacific to the eastern horizon. There were footsteps. Pietr, the midshipman, knelt on the bale beside him:

"One penny for your thought?"

"I wish I had a thought worth a penny," Chink Peters said.

"But you have an expression. Coming on the deck, I was seeing your face."

"I read a nursery rhyme."

"What rhyme?"

"One for children. We call them Mother Goose."

"Please may I see?" Pietr took the open book and read the rhyme carefully. It took him a while. "Oh yes," he said, passing the book back. "Then please, what is a More Fool?"

"One degree less than a Most Fool, I guess," Chink said. "Or at least I hope it is."

THE MORE FOOL

When the Diefenbach sisters were killed, he wired their dad from San Francisco:

Is there anything at all that I can do?

He added his phone number and the old familiar name, *Chink.*

He didn't know whether he expected a reply. He didn't know whether or not he hoped for one. He hadn't seen Mary and Wendy Diefenbach, nor their father, Wally, whose title was now Ambassador-at-Large, for eleven years. But he was as full of rage and love, and of a malarial loathing for mankind which came and went chronically, as if the girls had been his own and he and Wally still friends.

The news had come on evening television, unillustrated except by the mustached face that read it: Two young women, daughters of a notable American family, had been found murdered in New York, in the ground floor apartment of a remodelled Greenwich Village brownstone house. They were Wendy Diefenbach, nineteen, and her sister Mary, twenty, heiresses of the great meat-packing fortune.

A solitary man, C. K. ("Chink") Peters spoke to the picture machine aloud, as if it were an animal:

"Get out of here."

He turned the control that blackened the screen, keeping only the voice:

Wendy was found first, partly clothed in a nightgown and dressing gown, her feet bare, the victim of repeated stab wounds in the back and stomach.

Barefoot Wendy dead, he thought. She never would wear shoes.

The young woman who discovered the body, occupant of an adjoining apartment, had thought the older sister, Mary, out for the evening. But when police arrived to investigate, they found Mary, too, drowned in the bathtub. The sisters had been students at The New School.

The professional voice began to read its next story, and Chink Peters hit the little knob that turned off the set. There was nothing else to hit and no one, only the silenced machine, to speak or to cry out to. He gave it a name:

"You ought to try undertaking, Cronkite. With that voice you could be a big success."

He left his housekeeping room and went down onto the street.

Once North Beach had been the Italian part of San Francisco. Now it was the tourist part, and this block of it a street of small jittery restaurants and clubs. Across the street, between a gay bar and a topless one, was a cigar store that sold pornographic books and magazines. It sold newspapers too. He crossed and bought an evening edition, but the story wasn't in yet.

He folded the paper, placed it in a trash basket, crossed the street again, climbed back up to his room, and used the telephone to send his wire to Wally Diefenbach, care of the U.S. Delegation to the United Nations. He made himself a sandwich, looked at it, and dropped it into the garbage sack under the kitchen sink. He made instant coffee with tap water and turned on the radio. By the time he had moved across the tuning band, finding only music and a night baseball game, the coffee was tepid. He sipped it, poured out the rest, rinsed the mug, and poured it half full of gin.

The mug was white French china, with a painting transferred onto it, in lavender, grey, and sand, of a tall, shaggy mushroom, with its French and Latin names, *coprin chevelu* and *Coprinus comatus*.

Chink Peters was a man who preferred beer to wine or liquor when he drank for pleasure. The gin was on hand for hospitality. Its smell reminded him of chloroform, but drinking it did not anaesthetize his horror or his sense of helplessness.

He went back down onto the street, and waited outside the cigar store for ten o'clock and the tall, red, doorless van which brought the first edition of tomorrow morning's paper.

Now the story was on page one, in ink so fresh it smudged his fingertips. He moved under a streetlamp, and saw that there were pictures. They were blurred laser photos of the two victims, and a clear print of someone called April Dorsey, twenty-three, an actress.

April Dorsey, returning from an evening acting class, had noticed that the door to the Diefenbach sisters' apartment was partly open. She had knocked, looked in, and seen no one at first. She had stepped into the room and seen blood on one white wall, enough more on a yellow velour sofa to turn its cushions orange, and then, beyond the sofa, nineteen-year-old Wendy's butchered body, lying on the floor.

The story said that April had screamed but later, when he knew April, Chink wondered if she really had.

After phoning the police from her own apartment, the story said, April Dorsey had returned to the doorway of the Diefenbach sisters, the police having asked if she was sure Wendy was dead. April stood in the vestibule, watching the body, until she heard the arrival of the police at the outer door and went to open it for them. The interne who accompanied the detectives gave April a tranquilizer, and left her with another occupant of the building. She was Olive Dahlke, twenty-six, a junior executive. The other tenants in the remodelled house, all of them women, were another actress, a teacher, and the widely published young poet Lydia Paul.

The police had examined Wendy's body before searching the apartment, and found it to be sexually mutilated.

"Oh, God, Lieutenant, look at that."

Chink Peters did not say this aloud, standing under the blue-white, buzzing streetlamp, reading his newspaper, but he had known many policemen and could hear them.

"Jesus fucking Christ."

"Didya ever see anything like that before, Doc?"

"Get out of the way."

"Let the goddamn photographer set up, willya?"

"Jesus Christ."

"All right, let's check the place. Keep your fucking hand off the light switch, idiot."

The search group looked into the dining room and kitchen, the paper said. They went down a short hall, and into the paired bedrooms. When they opened the door to the connecting bathroom, they saw Mary's body. She had been bathing, running water they guessed, so that she would not have heard whatever sounds were made in the living room. The tub was nearly full of water and bloody soap bubbles. The faucet handles had been used to turn the bathwater off, and were blood smeared, too. All this was Wendy's blood, washed from the killer's hands and wrists, for there were no wounds on Mary's body. Mary had been drowned. There was a deeply stained towel, which the killer had apparently used to maintain a grip on the slippery face and shoulders, in order to hold them under the bubbles.

The police spokesman supposed the killer had meant to wash and started for the bathroom, not knowing there was anyone there. The spokesman was Police Lieutenant George Pappas. Lieutenant Pappas said the sound of running water, which secured the victim, would have been the killer's warning.

Chink Peters stared at the center photograph, and tried to make the face that of Mary, whom he'd called Mike and last seen when she was nine. A twenty-year-old now; or yesterday. With, it seemed, not the short, bobbed summer hair of childhood, ends sprouting out under the black velvet brim of a hunt cap, for riding, but with long dark hair for floating.

He could feel the tug of water at his scalp.

The hair floated in the scented bubbles around her face, no longer freckled but a young woman's face. Her arms and shoulders floated gently, her hips and knees rising slightly in the mild, warm swirl as the tub filled between her feet. He could feel them lift. And as the bathroom door pushed open towards her?

"O Wendy, lovely, lovely bath . . ."

In the steam a man's face formed. Red wrists and hands came clear. In spite of hearing the water, he was as startled to see her, whole and living after what he had just done, as she was him, but he recovered faster than Mike Diefenbach, water-warmed, drowsing, hardly beginning to understand and know fear, Chink prayed, when the red hands clutched their towel, found her chin, and pressed down against the water's buoyancy.

The hands gripped and held until there was no more movement, turned off the water taps, and went away.

Chink Peters was shaking when he finished reading the story, and his eyes were wet. He wiped at them with his wrist, and began to walk, discarding the newspaper in the same trash basket into which he had put the first. Then he stopped, went back, and got the paper out again. Carefully, with the point of the small blade on his pocketknife, he cut around two of the photographs and lifted them from the page, then once more discarded the rest of the paper and with it the picture of April Dorsey, twenty-three, an actress. He folded Mike's and Wendy's pictures together and put them in his billfold.

He walked up Telegraph Hill, past Coit Tower, turned west, went downhill, then up, then down again, using alleys, until he reached the Bay front. He went along it, past the marina. When he got to the Presidio he thought of going south, to Golden Gate Park, where he had already run for an hour, earlier in the day. Fear of an encounter, and not of what might happen to himself but of what he might do to someone who accosted him, caused him to turn north instead, and out across the bridge. On the bridge he was aware that fog had turned to drizzle and started wetting through his khaki pants, blue flannel shirt, and canvas shoes. He began to run. He went steadily to somewhere around Fort Baker before he turned and started walking and then running back again. When he reached the door to his room, he had covered eight or ten miles, a small-boned, hard, dark-haired, forty-eight-year-old man of unusual strength, with a nervous animal's need for constant exercise.

It was just after two in the morning when he let himself back into the room, doubtful that he was tired enough even yet. He sat forward in an overstuffed armchair with a threadbare red slipcover, holding another half mug of gin, wishing he could just go to sleep, and before the gin was gone had his wish.

The phone rang next morning at six-fifteen. It was nine-fifteen New York time. He was not surprised to find himself still dressed and in his chair. Improvised sleep had been a common occurrence earlier in his life, and seemed to fit the coming back into it, at long remove, of violence and dismay.

A woman's voice asked if this was Mr. Peters, and he said yes.

"Can you hold for Ambassador Diefenbach?"

Wally's voice replaced the woman's immediately. "Chink? Is it really you?"

"Hello, Wally. What a terrible way to be back in touch."

"Thank you for the telegram."

"You must be getting hundreds."

"Mostly the phone. It's hard to refuse when it's Europe or Asia. God, Chink, calls from every place I ever worked."

"Is there something I can do, then?"

"Are you free? To come to New York?"

"I'll be on the first plane."

"Let me see about it, Chink. What are you doing, anyway?"

"Waiting for a boat."

"To where this time?"

It wasn't asked for politeness, though Wally Diefenbach was a courtly man sometimes. It was for distraction, Chink thought, so he spoke more fully than he might have ordinarily.

"New Zealand. I found some thoroughbreds for a breeder, and I'm supposed to take them down for him. Racing stock. Four brood mares and a stud."

"Horses."

"I can find someone else to go."

"Horses, Chink?"

"It's what I seem to come back to."

Then Wally started sobbing. Horses had been their last connection. They had been involved in many things together, starting early in the Second World War, but at the last they had been neighbors in Virginia, riding companions, horseshow competitors, and at just that time Chink had begun training the little girls, Mike and Wendy, on a pretty pair of Connemara ponies.

"Do you have someone, Wally?" he asked. "Besides the whole world? A wife, or a friend?"

Wally said yes, he was married again, and Adrienne was being wonderful, she was with him now in the office. Then he said:

"The police here are being as kind as they know how to be. Even the newspeople."

Chink understood. "You want a buffer."

"We'll have the travel office get you a plane seat. You're really willing, Chink? There's nobody else in the world I'd ask."

Chink said he could handle his own reservation. Wally said it would be a kindness if Chink would let him have the U.N. people do it. This came as close as anything could that morning to making Chink smile. It was as if his price, in Wally's mind, were the difference between a tourist-class ticket, bought personally, and a first-class one, charged to the United Nations, to be reimbursed by whoever wrote the Ambassador's checks these days. This would not be a clear thought in Wally's mind, only the kind of assumption he'd always made.

Chink said, "Sure. Okay, Wally."

Wally asked him to stay near the telephone.

It was not yet seven o'clock, too early to call the New Zealand horse breeder at the Jack Tar Hotel. Chink made a list of people who might be happy to take his place on the boat with the horses. He didn't start trying to phone any of them because he didn't want to tie up the line.

He took off his clothes, took a shower and shaved, put on his raincoat for a dressing gown, and boiled a pale egg. He ate, moved the phone as close to the bed as the cord would reach, lay down, and went back to sleep. It was nine when the phone rang again. A woman's voice asked for the lady of the house. Chink said there wasn't one, and the voice asked him please to answer three test questions in order to win the first volume of a set of encyclopedias. It was a timid voice, some temporary woman worker, a housewife or a student. He imagined her sitting on one of a row of stools in a phone bank, with a quota of calls to make for the minimum wage and a day of abuse. Chink said no thank you as gently as he could.

The phone rang again as soon as he'd hung up. This time it was Wally's new wife, who was called Adrienne.

"Mr. Peters. First I want to thank you very much for being willing to give up a wonderful trip to help us. It's so very kind of you."

"It was a routine trip, Mrs. Diefenbach."

"Well, you see, they've found the man!" It was an eastern school voice, full of rush and hush, stressed rhythm and arbitrary emphasis. There'd been another of Wally's wives with a voice like that, who had first been Mrs. C.K. Peters. "That is, they're quite sure they have, so the worst is really over now."

"They found him?"

"Yes. In the river. Drowned. Apparently he ran all the way to the docks and threw himself into the river. He was all scratched on the arms, and some police officer made a very bright guess and took the fingerprints."

"Who was he?" Chink asked.

"Nobody really. Nobody at all. A little Venezuelan man."

"Is Wally better?"

"He's still terribly shaken, of course, but the worst is over, the police and the reporters. The White House called and the President talked to Wally and I know that helped. Wally's doing something quite brave, now. You see, there are five other girls who live in that apartment house, and Wally owns it. He's there now, talking with some parents, and he asked me to call you back. And well, wish you *bon voyage*, after all."

"All right. Thanks."

"He bought it just last year. So that Mary and Wendy would have a nice place . . ."

She didn't finish the phrase: *a nice place to live.*

". . . one of the girls, April. I don't know her last name, but she was so brave. Oh, and lovely and fresh, like one of those high school girls. She marched right down with the police to see the man's body, like a good soldier, and she knew him. They all did. The girls in the house. An illegal immigrant, a folksinger or something the girls had been trying to help . . ."

Chink Peters glanced, while he listened to her, at the list of horse people he'd made but not phoned. He picked up the list and slowly crumpled it, feeling no anticipation but some relief. He looked out the window, through the fog, at the street, where the bars were still mostly closed, the trash uncollected.

Hangover Street, he thought, and said: "Good-bye, Mrs. Diefenbach. Thank you for calling." Their tragedy was far from over, but the menace and harassment were, for now, and he felt undeservedly fortunate that he would be moving, not back east over the wasting land, but west through clean ocean air.

"Jack Tar Hotel. Good morning."

"Mr. Fairleigh, please. Room Fifteen-Oh-Four."

Fairleigh came on the line, and said: "I've been trying to ring you. Your phone hasn't been half busy, has it?"

"Sorry."

"Whoever she is, better phone her back and say ta-ta. Our beamish boat is at the dock."

"Early, isn't it?"

"Came in last night. They have their main cargo from Seattle. Just stopping by here to get the nags, so they're ready to load us, soon as ever."

"I'll rent a car and go out to Stockton," Chink said. "Do you want to come?"

There was a pause, and then Fairleigh said: "Well, actually, the horses are in the van right now and on the way."

Chink picked up the crumpled list of names, and began to smooth it out. "I said I'd start with them from the stable, Mr. Fairleigh."

"Yes, but you see, Visalia is a good deal farther off than Stockton, isn't it?"

"Visalia?"

"That's the place. Yes."

"You've bought different horses."

"So true. I just happened to run into something, old boy."

"We closed a deal in Stockton."

"Not quite we didn't, did we? Let me tell you what I've found, all on my own."

"Hold it," Chink said.

"Excuse?"

"Hold it. Wait a moment, please."

He looked at the list of names, and decided to start reading it slowly, over the phone. He'd found good animals in Stockton, at a fair price, spent more time than he was paid to, traded on his reputation. Now he looked out through the fog again, at the street. There was a huge garbage truck, its silver-ribbed box streaked with liquefied soot, in front of the cigar store which sold pornography.

"You have shipping papers for the horses you bought?"

"Absolutely. Pedigrees, vet certificates, track records, export licenses, the lot. I'll bring them to the dock."

"I'd like to see them now," Chink said.

"Whatever for?"

"I'll be there in fifteen minutes, if it's convenient. If it's not, please say when it will be."

The living room of Fairleigh's hotel suite smelled of sex and scotch whiskey. The drapes and carpets were brick colored, the walls salmon pink. There were reproductions of Degas ballet dancers hanging on them. Chink looked at the bill of sale.

"You bought these horses from Henry Zimmer?"

"The four mares at six hundred dollars each, and the young stud for a thousand. Not bad, eh? They were closing out the stable, and I happened onto it."

"It wouldn't be Henry's stable, Mr. Fairleigh, unless they're taking horses in motel rooms these days."

"Oh, he said that, of course. Perfectly straightforward man. Perfectly agreeable. He'd bought from the previous owner, and now had to get them off the place quick. My good luck."

"Henry's very agreeable," Chink said. "So's the veterinarian who signed these health certificates. Buy him a drink and he'll agree to anything."

"Oh, come along with it, Peters."

"Throw in a couple of Santa Anita winners, too."

"Are you trying to say the vet's not licensed, or what? Are you losing a commission perhaps, old boy?"

"He's still licensed, I imagine. Sometimes his winners win, too. His practice is all at the track. Not Santa Anita. A little track. He manages to get the saliva tests done." Chink stood up. "A commission, Mr. Fairleigh?"

"Sorry, Peters. Sit down, sit down. In any case, they're a splendid lot of horses. You've got my word on it."

"I see."

"Do sit down. Here, look at this. The stud. Had two starts at the winter meeting, won them both."

Chink took the piece of paper Fairleigh held out and walked to the window with it. It was a description and track record of a horse named Vasco. "Lame?" he asked.

"Shoulder, and it's sound now."

"Seventeen hands already."

"Oh, he'll be a big one."

"And still a baby. People who run two-year-olds ought to be run themselves."

"That's what Henry Zimmer said. Exactly."

"Hooray for Henry."

"Look here. Let's get things straight."

A woman's voice from behind the closed door of the bedroom of Fairleigh's suite called, "Darling?" Fairleigh ignored it.

"I simply ran into Zimmer at an auction," he said. "We got along nicely, and he invited me out to the stable. His friend had just sold the place, right, and Henry'd bought what stock was left to help out. Realized he was in over his head, and wanted badly to resell. So I had my chance. I'd have been a fool not to take it. Went for a look-see and said yes, right there in the barn."

"Sure. And let's see what happened, just before you said yes, Mr. Fairleigh. You were bargaining, and just then another man arrived. He's about five foot ten, with red hair, and he's called Rosey. Rosey Hodges. Rosey was quite angry with Henry Zimmer, wasn't he?"

"Oh, I say."

"Rosey yelled, 'Henry Zimmer, you promised me first bid on these horses.' And then Zimmer lost his own temper, didn't he? And said, 'You lied to me, Mr. Hodges. Didn't I make it clear these are for private sale only? You're a goddamn dealer. I'd shoot them one by one before I'd let them go through your sale barn; now get out of here.' "

"You don't need to go on," Fairleigh said, almost whispering.

"You supposed I wouldn't know? How would they have worked it next? Let's see. Rosey stormed out. Henry went to the can. Rosey slipped in again fast, and offered you a hundred dollars more a head if you'd make your deal and then resell to him."

There was a pause, and then Fairleigh said, getting his voice back, but very quietly: "It was only fifty, Chink. A hundred on the stud."

"Yep."

"As soon as my check cleared, the bastard backed out, of course."

"I'm sorry."

"There's nothing I can do, is there?"

"Not that I know of." Chink sat down again, opposite the man. "Make the best of it."

"They're a good enough lot. At least I think they are."

Chink reached for the rest of the papers. "Let's see. Maybe you'll luck out."

There was an X-ray report on one of the mares, which seemed to show her sound. Another had been pinfired, but that wouldn't affect her as a brood mare. He wished there were an X-ray report on the young stallion's shoulder. He wished the stallion were old enough to have had all his immunizations. There'd been equine encephalomyelitis around Visalia. The mares were all vaccinated for it, anyway.

Vasco, the stud, was by Pelota, who was a son of Jai-alai; those were two good horses. And all the mares had been bred to an old stallion named General Whitesides. Apparently Henry Zimmer's friend, the stable owner, had once owned General Whitesides. Chink thought better than most people did of the old horse, but was surprised he was still standing. He was a stud Chink might once have liked to own himself.

The woman's voice from the bedroom asked Fairleigh if there was any more coffee.

"You'll have coffee, Chink?" Fairleigh asked. "Please?"

"Sounds as if the lady wants some."

"She's only a tart."

It hit Chink so exactly like a blow that his hands clenched, and he made himself stay sitting so that he wouldn't start to shake again.

A moment before, feeling sorry for Fairleigh, he'd been going to return the man's money and help arrange for someone else to take charge of the horses on the boat.

Now he stood, went to the door, took the handle for something hard to hold on to, and said: "I'll see you on the dock."

"What's the matter, Chink?"

He left without answering. By tomorrow morning he would be out of sight of land.

He had ordered some veterinary supplies. He took a cab to the sales office, found that his order was ready, and arranged to have it delivered to the dock in a wooden crate.

He went to a bookstore near the University to buy books for the trip. He wanted to try reading *Dead Souls* in Russian, and found a facing-page translation. The book had been his father's favorite, and Russian the language of their household in New Jersey, but Chink had not read Russian in some time. German was easier for him, but classic German literature didn't interest him and he could find no books he hadn't read by the postwar novelists except in English.

He hadn't read much history in a while, either, though it had been his college major. He took pleasure in buying himself a good secondhand set of Runciman on the Crusades. At the art table he bought a discounted portfolio of Ingres's drawings, and a picture book about New Zealand which happened to be there. He bought some current novels he'd heard of, in paperback, and then went to the poetry shelves to look for a recent university press collection of English nursery rhymes.

He found it and, though he did not care greatly for poetry, found himself picking from the shelf an anthology of work by young, contemporary poets.

He didn't understand why he was doing this until he saw the name Lydia Paul in the table of contents, and even then was puzzled as to why the name meant something to him.

Then he recalled that he had read it last night in the newspaper, in the list of women residents in the Greenwich Village brownstone and, unwillingly, feeling that he could not refuse it, bought that book as well.

Walking to his room to pack, he thought: Father loved Pushkin, Lermontov he lived by, but nosy Gogol's *Dead Souls* was the finest, funniest, truest book anybody ever wrote.

Tony Peters, Chink's father, also thought Dostoevsky a bore and Tolstoy a nut. Turgenev, he conceded, was a gentleman, and Chekhov, the grandson of a serf, had turned out very well.

That was the range of his literary opinions except that every year or so, in the winter, he would try again to read a novel called *Oblomov*, and give up after a hundred pages. In English, Tony read what he needed to, with no great difficulty and no great pleasure.

His name to start with was Anton Petrovich Kovici, and he thought of himself as White Russian. Actually Anton was born in Siberia. The grandparents, Chink's great-grandparents, were the White Russians, and apparently helpless to manage the land after their serfs were liberated. Anton's father was Peter Ivanovich Kovici, one of four grandparents Chink Peters never knew. Peter Ivanovich hadn't been able to run the place any better than his parents could without serfs, and soon lost it. It must have been quite a place.

Peter Ivanovich took his family to Siberia in the 1890s, where Anton Petrovich, later Tony, was born. There Peter was a famous failure as a customs officer. The legend, as told in New Jersey, was that smugglers would make vast detours in order to get inspected by Peter Ivanovich and his team, all of them incompetent, incorruptible, cheerful, and generous.

"He was never promoted once!" Tony Peters would say with pride. "What a bureaucrat he was." Father had those very bright blue eyes, Chink thought, and could stop traffic with his smile.

But in spite of Peter's failure, the family connections must have been in pretty good shape. Anton, later Tony, the youngest son, got a commission at eighteen, and was posted as a cadet to the Siberian Cossack *voisko* at Omsk. He meant to spend his life as a cavalry officer.

Besides the package of books, Chink Peters, back in his room, packed a duffle bag with stable clothes, grooming tools, his Dehner boots, a sweat suit, and the canvas shoes. He zipped the duffle. He opened and placed on the bed a very old leather suitcase.

Grandfather's generation must have been, he thought—not quite saying it to the brown herringbone suit he was folding, his only suit—something like the sons and daughters of Southern slave-holders, after the Civil War, except there'd been no military defeat to blame it on, the dislocation, no gall to cherish, no hopeless dream of rising up to drink to, but I guess they found some other things to drink to.

He folded and packed a pair of dark grey flannel pants, like the ones he had on, a camel's hair hacking jacket, a heavy sweater and a light one.

They moved their bewilderment east, he thought, not west, and if some kept going, their California was Kamchatka, where they didn't bask in sunsets on Pacific beaches but stared east at cold dawns, over the ice floes in the Bering Sea.

He closed the suitcase and gave in.

What can Lydia Paul be doing now, he thought, and April Dorsey? God, where are the bodies now, the torn, stained body, and the smooth, sad, clean one, Wally, Wally, shall I come anyway to New York? I have been told, so politely, not to, ship ahoy.

He picked up the duffle, the package, and the suitcase. Except for a twenty-year-old Hermès saddle, his Newmarket boots, and a few more books which he'd left with the steward at the Bay Equestrian Club, he was carrying everything he owned. What was left in the gin bottle stayed behind in the housekeeping room, along with two cans of beer and most of a bottle of Worcestershire sauce. Hoping the next tenant would find it attractive, he left the French china mug in the center of the kitchen table, with its image of a tall, shaggy mushroom in lavender and grey and sand.

The ship was new. It had a grey-blue hull with white trim. Its name was *Vesterålen*. He went on board, found his cabin, tossed his gear on a bunk, and went aft to see where the horses would be.

Fairleigh was there, talking with the purser.

It was a Norwegian freighter they'd chosen for the voyage because it had twenty stalls in it, designed for dairy cattle. It had a semicircular wooden deck area, opening off a wide compartment door that led into an alley between the stalls. The wooden area was actually teak decking over metal deck plates, forty feet wide across the straight part, and followed the line of the hull around the stern. It was meant for passengers as a lounging area. Chink and Fairleigh had engaged it as exercise space. There was a sun deck up one level for the passengers. The *Vesterålen* accommodated eight, but would be carrying only six this trip, two singles and two doubles.

"Nice, don't you say?" Fairleigh hopped up and down on the teak, being comical. "Decent footing. Teach 'em rumba."

Chink didn't feel like smiling. "Have you seen the stalls?"

"First-class. Finest staterooms on the boat. Have a look."

Chink nodded, and went in through the compartment door. The horses would have to lift their feet over the eight-inch sill and duck their heads at the same time, heading in and out.

There were ten stalls on either side of the alley, the stalls formed by lattice-metal partitions bolted to the deck. Two on the left had hay, feed, and barrels of sawdust for bedding in them. On the right, five had been kept clear. There was cargo stowed in the other stalls on both sides, though none was really full, and there were more crates in the alley.

"No," Chink said.

Fairleigh and the purser had followed him in.

"What's the matter, Peters?"

"We were offered box stalls. That means stalls big enough for a horse to turn around in."

"You have the deck space," the purser said. His English was pretty good. "Plenty to exercise. And the stalls are long."

"You guarantee calm weather?" Chink asked. "A horse goes down in one of these, there won't be room to get back up."

"What can we do?" Fairleigh asked. "Only suitable ship we could find."

"The alley," the purser said. "I call the boatswain. We clear the alley. All right." He was a brown-eyed, chesty man, with dark skin, and wore a short beard.

"We can take out every other partition on the right," Chink said. "That's five big stalls."

"The hay?" The purser pointed. "The horse food. Two stalls more already."

"They're okay. You don't have to clear the alley, but use the far end so we don't block the door of the last stall. I'll need this end for crossties."

"For what?"

"It's a way to hold the horses for treatment and grooming. I'll need rope."

"Carpenter on shore," the purser said.

"I can rig it," Chink said. "I can take out the partitions, too. Did the carpenter take all the wrenches on shore with him?"

"You pay, Mr. Fairleigh?"

"How bloody much?" Fairleigh asked.

"I'm going to change clothes," Chink said.

"See here, Chink . . ."

He stopped, and looked at Fairleigh. He still didn't feel anything like smiling.

"Very well," Fairleigh said. "All right, Peters."

When Chink got back, there were three men rearranging cargo. They'd cleared the first of the narrow stalls. The rope and wrenches were waiting for him.

Fairleigh had left. The purser was still there, watching the work. He smiled and nodded at Chink.

"Very good," he said. The bristles on his beard gleamed, and the buttons on his uniform. "I love horse so much, too."

Chink nodded back and picked out a wrench.

Ah beautiful purser, he thought. Ah purser my own. What a beautiful purser you are.

The stalls were ready, and he had started rigging the first cross-tie, when a young officer, a midshipman who introduced himself as Pietr, came to say that the horse van was on the dock.

"Four horses!"

"I think there's five of them, Mother."

"Right on the boat with us."

"Going to New Zealand, the sweet things."

The other five passengers had boarded in Seattle. Four consisted of two retired couples in their late fifties, from De Kalb, Illinois, who travelled together constantly, they said, by freighter, anywhere. Asia, Africa, Europe, South America, you name it. It was a wonderful bargain because you always had a clean place to stay on board, no extra cost, and food you could trust. The fifth was a young woman teacher, going to New Zealand for an exchange year.

The two De Kalb men seemed bleary from being out the night before in San Francisco, of which they spoke suggestively, asking Chink if he wasn't sorry to be leaving such a town. Their wives wore bright dresses and tennis shoes. The younger woman wore jeans, clogs, and a paisley halter.

The sun had come out, and there was a shine from the dark oil in the wooden dock planks. The slip across from the *Vesterålen* was empty, and a weak swirl of tide moved dull green water towards the piers.

The slats on the trailer part of the twelve-horse van were bright red, with designs of white curlicue at the top and bottom. Against the blue-grey hull of the *Vesterålen* it had the look to Chink of a circus wagon, making the little scene nostalgically gay. It lifted his spirits only for an instant, though, for Fairleigh, the purser, and the ship's captain were all there, standing by the door of the big red cab which read "Bledsoe Horse Transfer" in white scroll, and the purser cried out, officiously: "Now, Mr. Peters. Now, Mr. Peters."

"I haven't let them start unloading without you, Chink," Fairleigh said.

The door into the trailer was in the center of the side away from the ship. It had been slid open, and a ramp placed and fastened at the base of the opening. A boy of about seventeen came down the ramp, and said, "Hello, sir."

"You the driver?" Chink asked, shaking hands.

"I'm from the stable," the boy said, starting to smile and then looking at his feet. He looked up again. "The driver's gone to eat. I always wanted to meet you, Mr. Peters. I've seen you ride lots of times."

"Thank you," Chink said, and smiled. "If you had charge of a rig like this, would you go eat and let someone else unload it?"

"No, sir." The boy shook his head emphatically. Then: "Is everything ready up there?" He indicated the ship.

"Let's go."

"Shall we get the stallion out first?"

"It's your load. Tell me what you want me to do."

The boy's name was Lewis. He had nice, big freckled forearms. Lewis led the way up the ramp, into the trailer. Except for one, the horses were standing quietly in the shadows, and from the smell and warmth of their sweat and fresh droppings, Chink took a certain comfort. It was the stud doing the pawing, tied in a tight stall towards the front. Chink went to his head, put a hand on the big, curved neck, and felt trembling.

"You can go ahead and take him out if you want," Lewis said.

"Have trouble getting him on?"

"No. He followed the mares all right. But he raised heck all the way down."

"Take one of the mares first," Chink said. "So he doesn't think he's being separated. I'll bring him right after you. Vasco?" He was stroking the horse's neck. "Vasco, boy? Rough trip?"

It seemed to him Vasco wasn't so much frightened as uncomfortable. He undid the tie, snapped on a halter rope, keeping his free hand on the neck that was rippling now rather than trembling, and opened the stall gate.

Lewis went out with a mare, and Chink followed, leading Vasco, ready to have the big horse try to surge past and, when that didn't happen, ready to have him rear when he saw the water and the people.

Instead, Vasco stumbled on the ramp and jumped sideways off it and onto the pier. Chink jumped with him, keeping light pressure on the halter rope.

"Easy, Vasco, easy." The big colt skidded, slewed partway around, and stopped, head up, breathing hard, nostrils flared. Chink saw what was wrong.

"Shall we keep going?" Lewis asked. "Right on board?"

"Whoa," Chink said. "Look at this guy's feet. How long since he was trimmed?" Vasco's hooves were grotesquely overgrown, splaying laterally and uneven. He might have been able to stand in a dirt-floored stall or out in pasture, but on a hard, level surface he had no control.

"The trainer quit last February," Lewis said. "I've been the only one there."

"Sure your horse raised heck. He can't balance."

Now Chink looked at the feet of the mare, a little black-nosed bay the kid was holding. "That mare's not shod, is she?"

"All the mares are, Mr. Peters. I've been asking Mr. Zimmer to get the blacksmith."

"Can someone hold this boy for me?" Chink asked. Fairleigh came over and took the stallion's halter rope. Chink moved to the mare's near side and picked up the front foot. Her name was Sweet Lorraine.

"This shoe's been on four or five months," he said, and, to Lewis, who was still holding her: "Didn't your trainer pull the shoes when he bred her?"

"The trainer was gone. It was just the owner and me, and see, he'd sold his old horse, General Whitesides. And it was a couple of weeks, he wanted to use him before the new people got him."

"Was there much left of General Whitesides to get?"

"Did you hear something?"

"Never mind," Chink said. "Put her back up on the van, and bring the others down, one by one, would you please?"

"Are they all right, Chink?" Fairleigh asked.

"They will be, I hope," Chink said. "I like your stud. He'll be a horse. The bay mare's thin. Let's see the others."

The captain and the purser, who'd been conversing in Norwegian, stopped when they saw Sweet Lorraine being led back into the van. The captain shouted something, turned, and walked away.

The purser said: "He thinks the horses are so beautiful. Is proud to have them for his ship, but now hurry, please. We have the short gangplank fixed, as for cattle."

"I know," Chink said. "I'm glad we don't have to sling them."

"So not delay?"

"They're not ready," Chink said.

Lewis was coming down the ramp now with a second mare, a slender grey who would be Rebel Deb. Even before Chink picked up the first foot, he could tell by the smell that the hoof had thrush in it.

"What needs doing?" Fairleigh asked.

"Besides trim your stud? Pull the shoes off these mares, and trim them, too. This one needs treatment. We'll see about the others."

Fairleigh's nose wrinkled as he caught the smell, but he glanced at the purser, unctuous and insistent, and said: "Can't it wait? I'll have a farrier meet the ship in Wellington."

"Not while I'm responsible," Chink said.

"But can we get someone down here? Do you know a man?"

Chink said: "When I take your money, Mr. Fairleigh, I'm your man." He walked away from them, Fairleigh, the purser, Lewis from the stable, and the other passengers.

On his way back on board, Chink passed the captain, talking with the midshipman Pietr.

"A minute," Pietr said. "He want to say no delay. We leave."

"Does the captain speak German?" Chink asked.

"*Ja*," the captain growled. He had a big, fierce grey head and very heavy brows. "*Und so?*"

"In twenty minutes," Chink said in German, "please come to the van. I'll have something to show you."

He got pinchers, a rasp, and the leather apron from his duffle bag. Back in the stall area, he opened the veterinary box and found a can of Coppertox. Then he went to the carpenter's shop, to which he'd recently returned the wrenches, got a hammer and a small cold chisel, and found what he hoped would be there, a can of Stockholm tar they had on hand for caulking. He wrapped the things in the apron, so that he could carry them with one hand, went to the galley, where he asked for and got a pail of warm water and detergent, and a small scrub brush.

He passed the captain again on his way back down to the dock. The captain was glowering.

By the van, Lewis was still holding Rebel Deb, and there were more spectators. The new ones were seamen returning from shore leave.

Chink put on the apron. He'd have preferred to start with Vasco, but he had a point to make. He picked up Deb's infected foot, cradled it in between his thighs, and started chipping with the cold chisel and hammer to find the cleated ends of the horseshoe nails buried in the sides of the overgrown hoof. It took more than the twenty minutes he'd mentioned to find all the nails and pry off the shoe. By the time he had it, the captain was on hand, staring, his jaw clenched, his hands made into fists, knuckles pressing into each thigh.

Chink put Rebel Deb's foot down, and held out the horseshoe.

The captain had thought of an English word: "No," he shouted. "No, no." His right hand came off the thigh; the index finger came out of the fist and slashed toward the *Vesterålen*. "Yess."

Chink carried the horseshoe to him. "You have a wooden deck," he said, in German.

The captain glared at the bow of metal. "Ahhhr," he yelled, took the horseshoe, and threw it violently across the dock. They could hear it splash in the oil water of the empty slip. "Take the damned things off, all off," he yelled in German, and stomped away.

Chink took care of Rebel Deb's thrush next, trimming and cleaning her hoof, washing it out, using the Coppertox and then packing it with tar. It would take some time for the frog to heal, but only one hoof was affected. He checked her ears and saw that she had mites, but he could treat those on the boat. He began to do her next foot.

The two De Kalb men said they were going aboard to rest. One of the wives said she could hold a horse if that would help.

Chink thanked her and accepted, and kept working.

Fairleigh said it was getting on, perhaps he'd take the captain and the purser out for early dinner. Pietr, the midshipman, came and stood watching beside the teacher, whose name was Hildi. Pietr wasn't free to hold a horse because he was on watch and might be needed, but after a time Hildi held Sweet Lorraine, the bay. The sailors and the other wife left.

Chink worked on, wanting the horses on board before dark. His weight firmly into the rump or shoulder, poised for the horse to shift or strain for release, hoof and leg cradled, he tried to find the precise snap and exertion of the hand and wrist on the long-handled pinchers which would clip the edge of a hoof clear through, and the long, firm, quick stroke of the big rasp which would bite, level, and smooth, all at once. Finally, on Vasco's second hoof, it came. He could feel himself relax into sureness and speed, and with that came the relief of sweat. First it was a sense of lubrication of the skin and muscles. Then his pores came open, releasing bitter liquid, soaking the back of his shirt, the waistband of his khaki pants. In the drops of sweat, he seemed to feel the despair he'd held in him for the past twenty-four hours begin, at last, to leave his body.

Just before dawn each morning on the boat, he went to the horses.

In the first stall was Sweet Lorraine, the bay with the black nose, a gentle thing. Like Vasco, she'd been run as a two-year-old. Her wind would never be what it should be, but she had an affectionate nature, and had been made a pet. She was carrying her second foal. She was Chink's favorite among the mares, but he tried not to let the others know it.

Rebel Deb was next, the willowy grey with the bad foot, too tall for her weight, not a strong horse. Hers was the worst track record. She was picky and flighty, and the mare to watch most closely, for she was the only one carrying a first foal.

Piney Brown, in the third stall, was muscular, stubborn, a short, very dark bay with a white blaze. She'd run fairly well over distance, but hadn't had speed under a mile. She'd placed at five and six furlongs only when the tracks were muddy. She was an independent creature, a hard horse for Chink to like but easy to take care of.

Fourth was Franny Frisbee, almost black, with a white star and three white stockings, who had raced three inconsistent seasons of unexpected wins and inexplicable losses, and been pinfired. There was some glamor in her appearance, but she was a cowed, sneaky horse, and a biter, not an honest horse but one who had his sympathy. She and Piney Brown were third-foal mares.

And in the end stall was the big, boisterous young stallion, Vasco, a fine roan and a couple of hundred pounds overweight, but it was baby fat and would work off. He was a good-natured, animated horse, full of curiosity, not very sure of himself yet, and hadn't had time to develop bad manners. He wanted to play, and Chink enjoyed thinking of the time in New Zealand when, finishing this job, he would condition the horse. He and Vasco would be free to move together.

He wished he could have ridden them each, once or twice, to learn more than just their stable manners, and to gain not just control but trust.

"Lorraine." Going into the first dark stall, where the little bay's body heat would be working to cut the morning chill. "Hey, sweet girl." Stroking and patting her. She liked to have her muzzle rubbed. "What did you dream about?"

In the next stall, with the sky lightening behind the ship, blue-black to grey-blue to pale blue. "Debbie, you spook, settle down. It's all right, honey. Hey, we'll repack your foot today. Would you like that?"

And then on to Piney Brown. "What's your pleasure, hard nose? Want to go a couple of rounds in the gym, do you?" And Franny Frisbee. "Hold it now. You hurting somewhere, baby?" And finally to Vasco. Sometimes he pressed his cheek against the shoulder Vasco had lamed, feeling the pulse in it, hoping it had really healed.

Then he started again with Sweet Lorraine, feeding and watering as light came and the blue square of sky framed in the open doorway lost its pallor, checking the curved metal hayracks which showed him at a glance if a horse was feeding poorly.

He avoided turning on the lights, liking a natural dawn for the horses.

After the feeding, he haltered each horse in turn, put it on the crosstie in the alley while he cleaned its stall and shovelled in fresh sawdust. Then he groomed. On the first two mornings, he both washed and curried them. They all had bot fly eggs sticking to their hair, and he didn't see much point in producing a hatch of bots in mid-Pacific.

Like Rebel Deb, Sweet Lorraine and Franny Frisbee had ear mites to be got rid of, and he watched all the horses' feet carefully, because the sawdust Fairleigh'd bought was a little green, and wasn't going to dry out much in the salt sea air.

When he was done with grooming and treatment, he changed the halter for a lunging caveson and took each horse out in turn for half an hour of exercise, lunging it at a walk, letting it trot a few circles at the end as long as the ship sailed steadily. The horses' coats began immediately to respond to care, and Chink felt sure and calm, standing in the center while they circled, long rein extending twenty feet to the nose, whip end tapping lightly on the teak deck, seeing the hair gleam, feet lift, muscles ripple, tail stream, round and round against the larger circle of the sea as the sun came up behind to warm them.

He communicated, not always wordlessly, more with the horses than he did with the other human passengers in the first days of the voyage:

"The horse Father never forgot was black like you," he said to Franny Frisbee on the morning of the second day out, while he worked ointment into her ear. "His name was Pavel."

In 1920, Anton Petrovich Kovici, Chink Peters' father, was a twenty-two-year old lieutenant who had fought hard for the losing side in the Russian revolution, avoided capture at the end, and ridden east. In Irkutsk he signed on to join a commander named von Ungern-Sternberg, and became one of the five thousand horsemen who rode into Outer Mongolia to fight the Chinese occupation.

In November of the year, Anton was sent back to Irkutsk on a recruiting mission, then, with dispatches, in December, across the ice of Lake Baikal to a rendezvous in a fishing village on the eastern shore. He was there when word came that von Ungern-Sternberg's troops had whipped the Chinese and captured the Mongolian capital city, Urga. Anton threw a party for the Buryat villagers, with whom he was trapped by winter weather.

It was June before he was able to leave the village and start for Urga. On the way, half a day's ride behind Soviet army units he was trying to get around, he learned that his command had been defeated and dispersed by the Red Army vanguard.

He rode back to Lake Baikal to the Buddhist fishing village, and stayed only long enough this time to persuade Chink's mother to elope with him. She was Aksinya, youngest daughter of the Buryat headman's family. Anton and Aksinya left at night, Anton on a black horse, his fifteen-year-old bride on a shaggy pony that he'd stolen for her.

They rode all night. Sleeping the next day in a sheepherder's hut, empty in that season, Anton set himself to wake once an hour. In midafternoon, he had just climbed out of the ravine where the horse and pony were tethered, and was on its rim, when he saw a dozen horsemen go by on the road below. He scaled the next rock wall and watched them out of sight, to a place where the meadow between cliffs was narrow and they'd be likely to set up. At dusk, he and Aksinya tried to ride behind them and were almost past when a dog barked and a man cried: "There they go."

There was a volley from a wonderful variety of single-shot weapons—pistols, shotguns, even muzzle-loading rifles. Anton wheeled his horse and rode down into them while they reloaded, his sabre swinging in the half dark. Most of them scattered back, but one man rose up, his gun ready again, and fired it point-blank into the black horse's chest.

The man was wearing a fur hat. When Anton swung the sabre overhand and into the center of the thick hat's crown, he didn't know at first whether he had even got through all the fur. Then the man, Anton was never sure who he was, fell away, his skull cloven, and Anton leaped off the dying black horse, ran to the Mongol ponies hobbled together, freed them, jumped onto one bareback and with just a halter, dispersed the others, and dashed away from the second volley to where Aksinya was waiting.

They rode all night. They fled all summer. They were married at a Buddhist monastery one week and, a week later, married again by a Russian Orthodox missionary. They left the Buryat lands, but were still fugitives. Some of Anton's comrades were with the Soviets at frontier posts. Sometimes they helped; others were like Frog Frogovitch.

"Anton Petrovitch!"

"Ah, Frog. Old Frog, you're doing well."

"Embrace me, man, where's your bride?"

"Waiting outside."

"Yes, it's not bad here. But you must stop this filthy killing of filthy Mongols. It makes it hard for the rest of us. Have some filthy wine."

"It was only one Mongol, a Buryat. Her cousin I think. He killed Pavel, my black horse. You remember?"

"You're both well mounted now, my man says. He watched you ride in."

"Fat Sergei helped find horses for us."

"For a good price, unless Sergei has changed. Anton, now."

"What, Frog?"

"Why, now they have her. Stand and put your weapons down."

Anton stood and threw the cup of wine into his old friend's face across the little table, jumped onto it, kicked Frog in the head, and in a moment was behind the man, with a pistol in his back.

"Into the courtyard, Frogovitch. Tell your men to get new horses ready. Then they must run as fast as they can in that direction, while we ride in the other, or you're a dead Frog."

There were other fights, another man killed along the way. Sometimes Aksinya and Anton were hungry. The cold months were coming. They reached Vladivostok, where Anton Petrovitch was given a choice between detention and working passage on a shorthanded American freighter, sailing to Portland, Oregon. A number of this ship's crew had died of influenza on the voyage out. The ship was in distress. It had been denied landing permits in Japan and sailed north, looking for a port. In Vladivostok the new Communist authorities, brothers to toiling seamen, had let the ship in as a gesture, and were anxious to see it remanned and on its way.

The American second mate, a man of learning, was able to

explain to his boatswain that Anton stood for Tony and Petrovich meant "Peter's son."

"Father was not your textbook immigrant of the early twenties, dreaming of America," Chink told Sweet Lorraine, putting her back in the stall. "Get your black nose out of my pocket, dear. He was just a man running for his life, hand in hand with a little girl who must have looked something like an Eskimo doll.

"Fugitives, Deb. God, what are you sweating about?" He got a towel and rubbed Rebel Deb down. "America was just a direction of flight—he'd gone where his commander sent him, then where his horse took him, now where the ship sailed.

"Come on, Piney. No butting allowed unless you're really cornered. Father was fair-haired, so the American sailors decided he was some kind of Swede.

"Need more hay, Franny? Good girl. Mother had the only smile in the world that could turn back Father's. Her smile pulled the corners of her mouth down instead of up. Enigmatic. Maybe mocking. You could never be sure.

"Hello, Vasco. We're talking about Tony Peterson, the well-known Swede. You're restless? No, he wasn't. Finally beyond pursuit. 'He's some kind of Swede,' the captain told the immigration people, and the immigration people told the labor contractors in Portland, for a wink and two of the last ten gold rubles. So Father was sent to the woods, as a spar-tree trimmer. He was light and strong and not afraid of heights. Mother went along as a laundress. They thought she was something like Chinese. Are you afraid of heights? Not much, you clown. If we have to sling you onto a lighter when we get to Wellington, it'll be tranquilizers all around. You'll be goofy for a week."

He would go to his cabin, when the horses were settled for the morning, change from stable clothes to the sweat suit, still damp from being rinsed out the day before. Then he went to the cabin equipped as a gym for passengers and crew, in which there were a weight machine, two light punching bags, a heavy bag, a mat, and wall devices for calisthenics. The first morning he skipped rope for a while and then worked on the bags. Boxing was a skill he'd had as a younger man.

The second morning two crewmen joined him. One was Pietr, the midshipman. The other was a big kid from the engine room named Nils. They were carrying sixteen-ounce gloves.

"We box today?" Pietr said. "You like it?"

"Sure," said Chink. "But don't let me get in the way."

Pietr was pleased to have new talent in the room. He was blue eyed, pink cheeked, with unusually bright yellow hair, five ten, and a dancer. He and Chink weighed about the same, 135, but Chink was three inches shorter. This gave Pietr reach and, when they boxed, he turned out to have speed as well. Chink could hit a good deal harder, but missed a lot, partly because he was out of practice, more because he was holding back on his punches. They sparred for several minutes until Chink, his arms tiring, stepped back, dropped his hands, and turned the gloves over to Nils.

Nils spoke German, and had serious amateur boxing ambitions. "I hope to box for Norway in the Olympics," he said, lacing on the huge, padded gloves. "In the summer, I will attend boxing camp at home." Chink watched him lumber around the mat after Pietr. Nils was brown-eyed, brown-haired, and overmuscled from body building. Pietr could score points at will, but mostly danced away from Nils' power.

When Chink's turn came with Nils, he was curious and stood in to the big man, hitting him, as Pietr had, with ease. It took Nils about a minute to knock Chink down with a surprisingly good right hook.

"So many times he does this to me," Pietr said, laughing and helping Chink up.

"Good," said Chink in German. "That was a good shot."

"Now you tell Hildi how we beat you up?" Pietr had a good deal of boyish charm. "Okay?"

"Sure," Chink said.

Hildi was the schoolteacher. She and Pietr and Chink shared a table with the purser at dinnertime. Though Pietr was only twenty and Hildi eight years older, Pietr's admiration for the young women was quite clear. So was the purser's.

Chink skipped breakfasts, and went early to lunch. He was starting on a grilled Norwegian sausage of some kind when Hildi came into the salon.

"There you are," she said. "We never see you except at dinner."

She was square shouldered and deep bosomed, with a smooth, almost padded look about the way her skin fit, round armed with dimpled hands. She had a kind, husky voice with an edge of self-deprecation to it, thick, wavy, brown hair, and full lips which were habitually slightly parted. Only the eyes were out of tone with the general presence, which was one of amusement and curiosity; the eyes were slate blue, moved slowly, and seemed somewhat troubled.

Chink stood. "I do get here pretty early," he said. He enjoyed reading while he ate.

"The rest of us oink it up over the big Scandinavian breakfast," Hildi said. "Please sit down. You should try the herring and potato hash some morning, with a poached egg on top. Five hundred calories a bite."

"Perils of the sea." Chink smiled and sat, indicating the chair opposite. It was a mahogany chair and had arms. The tabletops were mahogany, too. The floor was parquet and well polished, giving the little room, curtained in red and fitted here and there with brass, a bright, luxurious look. "Shabby old tramp steamer," Chink said. "Will you join me?"

Hildi shook her head, but sat down anyway, across from him. "We don't get hungry for lunch until the last minute. Then we start pushing each other out of the way to get to the door before they close it. What are you reading?"

"A poem."

"Am I interrupting?"

"Quite a vehement poem, Hildi." She seemed uncertain whether she was welcome to stay, so he smiled and added: "It's called 'Riding Behind.' I think it's about a woman on a motorcycle, hanging on to a guy she doesn't much like, afraid for her life."

"Knowing she could drive better if he'd only stop the bike and switch places. That's one of Lydia Paul's. I went to a poetry reading of hers last winter." She mimed a pose of declamation.

"You follow poetry?"

Hildi signalled to the mess attendant that she didn't want to order. "Lydia Paul's all fire," she said. "She made me feel like a bowl of cold oatmeal."

There were a number of names on the dust jacket of the anthology. "Have you heard some of these other poets read, too?"

"Let's see." She held out her hand, and he slid the book across to her. The jacket was bright red and yellow, with a caricature wingéd horse prancing across the poets' names. "Lydia Paul's amazing on stage," Hildi said.

"Who else, Hildi?"

"I read something disturbing about her when we were in San Francisco."

She wasn't looking at the book. He took it back and closed it. "So did I, Hildi. Okay?"

The slate blue eyes found his, the lips parted a little wider. Then she said: "I'm sorry, Chink."

He tried to think of something else to say, and settled for asking if she was a bridge player. The foursome from De Kalb settled down to bridge every evening. He'd noticed Hildi watching, but the older people hadn't asked her to play. She loved bridge, Hildi said, and they agreed they'd sound out Pietr and the purser at dinnertime.

"Five dollar a corner?" the purser suggested. "To make us interested?"

"I haven't played in a dozen years," Chink said.

"Two dollars?"

"Let's just keep it friendly."

"Oh, good," said Hildi. "I'd be so nervous, playing for money with people I don't know."

Pietr protested: "Hildi, we are not strangers."

The purser said, "Tomorrow is for money, then. After Mr. Chink gets practice."

The purser knew bridge. He and Chink were partners by the draw for the first rubber, and won it in straight games. In the second rubber, playing with Hildi, Chink made a defensive trump lead which defeated the purser's plan to crossruff and set his slam bid in spades, doubled and vulnerable. Chink took the next game at three no-trump, with a good finesse, and though he and Hildi lost the rubber two hands later, their point score for it was higher than their opponents'. In the third rubber, Chink pushed Pietr into bidding a small slam in diamonds while the purser vengefully doubled, and Chink redoubled, holding long diamonds and a blank in hearts, into which the purser led and lost his first ace. It wasn't until two hands later that Pietr made game and rubber, and Chink had won all three of his corners on points.

The purser was stung, and wanted to play around again. Chink said thanks, but he needed to see to the horses.

"May I come?" Hildi asked.

"To the stall door," Chink said. And, apologetically: "Until they get to know you."

Pietr wanted Hildi to stay and play three-handed. Bernie from De Kalb called:

"Hey. Darrell and Mary Linda want to turn in. Two of you come play with us."

"Money?" asked the purser.

"You bet," said Bernie from De Kalb.

"Hildi, you watch now," the purser said.

"I'm going with Chink," Hildi said.

"I go, too," Pietr suggested.

"Come along," said Chink.

"We need you, Pete," Bernie said.

"Yes, Pietr," said the purser. It was a kind of command.

"Go ahead and play," Hildi said. "I'll see you tomorrow."

Pietr's features were still young enough to pout.

On deck, in the moonlight, Chink said: "The purser chose wrong. Pietr had luck, but you're a sounder player."

"You must have been professional," Hildi said.

"Not really."

"Tournaments?"

"Some."

"Duplicate, too?"

"Yes."

"If we'd played for money, you'd have cleaned us out."

"I had good cards."

"No, you didn't."

He smiled.

"Who was your duplicate partner, Chink?"

"I had a wife then." It seemed to be what she wanted to hear.

"Where?"

"It was in Virginia, years ago."

"Am I keeping you?" They had reached the stall door.

"I have things to do in there."

"I'll wait, if you'd like to talk."

"Thanks, but it's going to take a while," Chink said.

Next morning in the gym, Pietr expressed his displeasure, hitting his flurried combinations of light punches as hard as he was able. After a minute or two, when Chink stepped back and dropped his arms, wanting to rest, Pietr followed, pushed him, and said:

"Come to fight." Chink raised his guard and stepped back in. Pietr pushed Chink off the mat with his forearms. Big Nils, watching, said something in Norwegian and laughed. Chink hit Pietr in the chest with a left, hard enough to move the boy back.

Has to play King of the Ocean, Chink thought. Oh, well.

Instead of ducking away from the next rush, Chink set his right hand high, aimed it carefully, moved his left shoulder in through the flurry, and snapped the right into Pietr's nose, putting weight behind the blow. Even through the heavy padding of the boxing glove, Chink could feel his knuckles work at the end of the snap.

Pietr howled, and kept trying to come in. Chink pumped, set, and went to the nose again. Tears came into the youngster's eyes.

"Give it up, Pete," Chink said, stepping back off the mat and dropping his hands. He stood still and let Pietr push him once more. "I don't want to make your nose swell up."

Pietr, breathing heavily, snuffling a little, smiled a shaky smile, dropped his hands, and nodded. Chink smiled back. Nils stood up and held out his hands for Pietr's gloves. Chink considered the situation.

I suppose, he thought, I am about to do something stupid.

For a good three minutes, he ducked, wove, sideslipped, and let Nils chase him, watching the big engineer's punches get wilder. When Nils was out of breath and off-balance, Chink caught him, moving under a sweeping right hand, hitting Nils hard on the side of the head, using the engineer's own impetus to knock him down.

There was a good deal of indignant Norwegian spoken from the mat. Nils didn't want to accept the hand Chink offered to pull up on. Nils switched to German and said that Chink had tripped him.

Pietr laughed, and said, also in German, that Nils was wrong.

Chink shrugged, smiled, shook his head, and started to take off the gloves. Nils got up then, embraced Chink, and begged him to box a little more. Then he let loose a long right that caught Chink, still flat-footed, in the middle of the chest and knocked Chink down in turn.

Chink sat on the mat and thought about it for a bit, looking up, head cocked, lips pursed. Nils' face became expressively apologetic, even a little ashamed. But if Chink really had a legitimate knockdown, weighing 135 to Nils' 190, then the engineer's dream of boxing in the Olympics didn't amount to much.

What Chink thought was that he wasn't in the Scandinavian-dream-wrecking business himself, still he'd been sucker punched, and he didn't much care for that. He stood up and started to take his gloves off. Nils looked sorrowful and started taking his off, too. Chink showed bare hands, raised and lowered the hands in parallel, the traditional offer to wrestle.

Nils comprehended, smiled, went back to his gloves, dropped them; and Chink had the big fellow on his back with an ankle throw and a crossover five seconds later. In his teens, Chink Peters had won successive National Junior wrestling titles at 105 and 114½ pounds.

He could not have held the pin for a moment if Nils had tried to throw him off. Chink hadn't let himself realize, until he felt it under his own, how massive Nils' chest was, how big and powerful the arms and legs. But the rumble that came from the huge chest was the laughter of abasement, not a growl of aggression, and Chink rose to be embraced and congratulated by Pietr. Then, together, they helped Nils up and hugged him, too.

He went aft to cool off before his shower. He had moved a bale of hay over by the stern rail, and sat on it, thinking:

Father's idea of how to play with a baby boy was to poke and watch it try to fight back. I don't know what he would have done with one who cried, left it on a rock someplace, I guess. Mother said I never cried, but turned all red and banged away at Father's wrist, scratching and yelling. I must have had a fight every day of my life till I was six, except when Father was out of town. When I was six, Father had made me strong enough, taught me to hit and grapple well enough, so that I could sting and even sometimes tie him up. This pleased him tremendously, but after that we fought by rules instead of roughhouse: no biting, no kicking, butting allowed only when really cornered.

But what were the names of the bareback riders?

Mrs. Bernie from De Kalb was bold, smart, and inquisitive. She was a short woman, plump and firm with glistening skin and a round, red face.

Hildi said Mrs. Bernie was really an apple on a pumpkin, wearing a grey wig.

She was the wife of Bernie from De Kalb, a generally dour, self-absorbed man, retired early with his friend Darrell, with whom he'd been partners in the seed business.

"I've been called Mrs. Bernie for thirty-five years," she'd said, when she and Chink were introduced. "Since I got married at the age of eighteen and kissed the man off to war. My sister married his brother. She's Mrs. Ernie and I'm Mrs. Bernie."

She came aft in the late afternoon, with Hildi and Darrell's wife, whose name was Mary Linda. Chink was holding Piney Brown.

"I kept trying to ride for two years after the arthritis started," Mrs. Bernie said. "I had to quit, but I still can't stay away from horses."

"They know it," Hildi said. "The way they look at you."

"Who'd like to lunge Piney?" Chink asked. The afternoon circles were as much to air and entertain the animals as for training and exercise.

"Go ahead, Hildi," Mrs. Bernie said. All three women had had instruction the day before. Chink wanted the horses accustomed to the other passengers.

Mrs. Bernie and Mary Linda sat on the bale of hay. Chink stood beside them, watching Piney Brown walk dutiful circles around Hildi.

"I liked barrel racing best," Mrs. Bernie said. "It's fun. And I had one real good cutting horse. I suppose you think that's awful?"

"Cutting horses are great animals," Chink said.

"You eastern riders think we're all bumpkins, in your silly little stuck-up saddles," Mrs. Bernie said. "Did your wife ride?"

"I've worked cattle in all kinds of saddles," Chink said.

"Where? Not in Virginia?" She'd been talking, it seemed, to Hildi.

"Check her, Hildi," Chink called, seeing Piney Brown about to break into a trot. He flicked the deck with his whip to get the horse's attention. "Walk, girl."

The horses were already getting trained to his voice. He was considering the answer to Mrs. Bernie's question as to where he'd worked cattle, and thought he would mention places she might have visited in South America on her freighter travels, places she and Mary Linda might like to talk about, when Mrs. Bernie said: "Let her trot, Chink. Let her enjoy herself."

"She can't be allowed to break, Mrs. Bernie."

"You would any of the others. You're stricter with Piney Brown. Isn't he, Mary Linda?"

"Oh. Yes." Mary Linda was larger and softer than Mrs. Bernie, and had beautiful white hair.

"I didn't realize that," Chink said.

"You know why? Because she's just like you."

"Independent," Mary Linda said.

"I see." He adjusted his hearing downward, to the rush of water along the ship's sides.

"Where did you work cattle?"

"Excuse me," Chink said. "I'll get Rebel Deb out now."

There was no card game after dinner. Pietr had night duty, the purser was intent on buying Hildi brandy, and Mary Linda was a little seasick though the night was calm. Chink excused himself, and sat in his cabin, reading Runciman. Raymund IV, Count of Toulouse, had raised a large army of Provençals in response to Pope Urban II's call for the First Crusade, by the time the lights went out in the salon. Chink left his cabin and went aft.

By moonlight his bale of hay was chrome grey.

When Aksinya and Tony Peterson came out of the woods and applied for their first papers, he disdained being a fake Swede and shortened the last name to Peters. He was willing to renounce being Russian, too. No tsar, no Russia, and besides, things might be getting bureaucratic in Mongolia. Tony couldn't be sure that authorities over there might not be in touch with ones in Vladivostok, inquiring about a wanted man named Anton Petrovitch Kovici, about whom it would be recorded that he and his wife had been put aboard a North American ship. He understood perfectly that if news of that kind reached Portland, he and his Aksinya would not be allowed to remain in this big, loose, inviting country they had happened into.

When they were finished at the courthouse, they celebrated like Russians. They went that evening to a circus that had posters up in the shop windows and on the power poles of Portland, Oregon.

It was an agreeable, medium-sized circus, but the clowns were stupid and the bareback riders really scandalous. Their horses were slack and the two young women riders in ballet costumes seemed half trained and timid. Nevertheless, the older woman who directed them, their mother apparently, standing in the middle of a ring in a top hat, a man's tailcoat far too large, a long black skirt, and shoes instead of boots, was calling out commands in Tony's native tongue.

Next morning Tony Peters bought a pair of faun-colored britches and put them on, and with them the boots made for him five years before by a famous bootmaker in Omsk. He took a streetcar to the circus grounds. The bareback riders were Russian gypsies. The circus management had given them notice. The man of the family was doing a three-year sentence for larceny in Utah, and the act had gone bad without him. Tony offered to take charge. The top hat was Tony's size. The tailcoat didn't fit too well, but Aksinya Peters was wonderful with a needle.

They left Portland in the company of Hungarian acrobats, Japanese jugglers, and Mexican trapeze artists, and travelled south and west. There were high-spirited times:

One afternoon in Santa Fe, after the bareback act was done, Tony returned to the wagon in which he and his wife were living to find Aksinya and his cavalry sabre missing. He ran to the sideshow, knocked the ticket taker out of the way, and went in. There was Aksinya on a gilded stool, on a stand above the crowd. She was dressed in her fur hat and fur coat, with silk pantaloons showing under the hem, and fur boots, and the sabre was lying in her lap. A poster said she was the seventeen-times-great-granddaughter and only direct living descendent of Genghis Khan. The management had described this project to Tony, but he had misunderstood, thinking it was only the sabre they wanted to borrow.

There was calliope music from the carousel next door. To its beat, Tony leaped first onto the stand with the Strong Man and threw him off. He jumped next to the Fat Lady's platform, lifted and dumped her, chair and all, to show that he could do it. With the next leap he freed the Wild Man from his cage, which made the poor Wild Man, who was kept permanently drunk, break into tears of muscatel. Then, waving the sabre, grinning and yelling, Tony drove out the other freaks—the Tattooed Man, the Bearded Lady, the Genuine Hermaphrodite—and after them the cowboy-hatted crowd. Last there was the assistant manager who'd been conducting the tour and selling postcards. Tony caught him a broadside sabre slap on the rear that sent the man out gibbering and left the tent empty. Then Tony bowed to his wife, lifted her down, and to the strains of the "Minute Waltz," played by steam, danced her around and around. He was crazy about her.

He didn't want Aksinya to work at all, but Tony conceded an emergency when the wife of the old Hindu fortune teller ran off with an electrician in Dallas. Temporarily, Tony allowed Aksinya to serve as the fortune teller's assistant. One evening in Oklahoma City, after the circus turned north with spring, there was a drunk oilfield worker who kept paying admission, coming in, and trying to get the Hindu's turban. He wanted to wear it for his friends. The second time the bouncer was called to throw the driller out, there was a brief fight, the bouncer got the worst of it, and the manager was frantic. Tony Peters offered to put the turban on and take the old Hindu's place in the dim-lit tent. When the driller charged in, Aksinya got the crystal ball out of the way and Tony let the man get his hands into the turban.

With a loose end, Tony took a turn around the arms, then across the back, tripped the driller, and started winding. By the time the scuffle was over, Tony and Aksinya had the man rather neatly packaged in yards and yards of sequinned cloth, and rolled him out the tent door, Aksinya stepping out after him.

"She done gift-wrapped Henry," one of the driller's friends shouted approvingly, and Tony and Aksinya went away, out the back flap.

Aksinya was pregnant. The gypsy girls and their handsome mother, whose various individual lessons with Tony now seemed to require more privacy than they had during the winter, were behaving strangely. The mother threw hot water on one daughter. The other came after Tony with a knife one evening. Shortly afterwards, when the circus played Mexico, Missouri, an old breeder and dealer in horses saw Tony Peters, at the climax of the riding act, vault onto his knees on the powdered rump of a cantering horse, after the gypsy girls had dismounted, go into a handstand, and take three circles of the ring. The breeder knew exactly what kind of schooling Tony must have had. It was easy to hire Tony Peters away from the sullen gypsies, and employ him as a trainer of horses consigned to the east coast of America, where the gentry rode.

It was after a Missouri season, when their son was six months old, that Aksinya and Tony finally completed the three-year journey east, which had started on the shore of Lake Baikal, on a black horse and a shaggy pony, to its finish, riding in a Pullman car, with letters of introduction, to a great stone house, surrounded by woods and pastures, in New Jersey.

It would be nice to have a vaulting surcingle again, Chink thought. And teach a kid to use it, as Father taught the bareback girls, and later me.

"Good night, Vasco," he said.

When Chink came out of the gym next morning, where he'd been working out alone, Bernie, the dour man from De Kalb, was waiting, a tall, drooping shape in a bright blue tank top, widening into white duck pants against the pale, straight lines of the ship's rails.

"Hey, Chink."

"Good morning."

"Hey." Bernie lowered his voice and took Chink's arm. "I heard you knocked out a big guy from the engine room."

"No." Chink knelt and tightened a shoelace, freeing his arm.

Bernie produced a heavy, salesman's smile, the kind which went with winks and shoulder hugging. Chink straightened up and stood clear. "That's what I heard. Someone said he's Ingemar Johansson's kid brother."

"We were sparring, Bernie. He made a mistake and went down."

"With a little help from you."

"Then he got up and slammed me halfway across the room."

"Chink, can you help me? Darrell and I went out on the town in San Francisco, and I think I caught the clap."

"I guess they've got some there."

"Well, I think I did."

"Better see the medic, hadn't you?"

"I can't talk Norwegian."

"I imagine all you'd have to do is show him."

"I did see him, Chink. I guess I've got it all right. Well, I pointed like my throat was sore. You know, like strep?"

Chink waited. He was thinking about Rebel Deb. Her foot was much better, but he was worried now that she might be coming into season.

"Same medicine, see? But he wanted to give me penicillin. I'm allergic to penicillin and I couldn't explain it, and I got pissed off. Then he got pissed off. Chink, you've got medicine."

"Excuse me?"

"You've got medicine, haven't you?"

"Combiotic."

"Wouldn't that work?"

"Broad-spectrum stuff, Bernie. It's probably got ten kinds of penicillin in it." He was counting weeks, trying to calculate what might be happening with Deb.

"Don't you know? You're a vet, aren't you?"

"I'll get Pietr to talk to the medic for you. Pietr, the midshipman. You have any other drug allergies?"

"This thing will be all over the boat."

"You just going to forget it till we land?" Deb's pregnancy test had been positive ten days ago.

"We'll be in Hawaii soon. Will it get worse? I mean, Mrs. Bernie and I don't do much. I could probably get away with it, if it won't get worse." He sounded doubtful.

Chink could be pretty sure Deb hadn't aborted on board, and it wasn't likely she would have, unnoticed, in Visalia. But in the first hundred days, there was a chance of resorbtion in any of the mares. If Deb's foetus was resorbed and she came into heat, she'd raise a little hell and Vasco might raise quite a lot.

"What should I do?" Bernie asked.

There was a drug to suppress heat, and Chink thought he'd better use it if the signs got any stronger, though on principle he didn't like to. Suddenly he thought a dose of that for Mrs. Bernie might help with Bernie's problem, wasn't pleased with himself for the levity, but couldn't help smiling.

"Come on, Chink. What's the smile for?"

"Bernie, I'm no authority. My guess is, if you've got a mucous membrane infection, you ought to drink a lot of water, lay off the bran mashes, and keep your hooves out of your eyes. Try not to exert yourself and expect it to hurt like hell in the morning. . . ."

"Jesus."

"Stop being a damn fool and make peace with the medic."

"Will you do what you said, see him for me?"

"I didn't say that, Bernie."

"Please, Chink."

"All right. He probably speaks German. I'll explain it."

"Thanks a million. Hey, Chink, aren't you a vet? Veterinarian?"

"Just a horse medic," Chink said. "And the kid isn't named Johansson."

Then it was Bernie who handled the newspaper photographs of Mike and Wendy Diefenbach that evening. Hildi and the two De Kalb couples wanted to play poker. Chink didn't like the game especially, but the ship's officers were busy and Hildi at loose ends. He said he'd play, so that there'd be six hands, until the purser finished some accounts and could take Chink's seat.

Chink had laid out his billfold and was searching his pockets for change to buy chips with. The billfold was open. The clipping, folded inside it, slid partway onto the table.

Bernie, full of some nonallergenic drug by now, his usual self-confidence restored, certainly meant to be friendly when he reached for the clipping and unfolded it.

"What this?" he asked. "Hey, aren't these the kids that got murdered in New York?"

Chink held out his hand for the clipping. Bernie raised it for his friend Darrell, across the table, to see. "Remember? The day we left Frisco."

"Poor things," said Mrs. Bernie.

"It was horrible," said Mary Linda, and Hildi said: "Please, let's not talk about it."

"There had to be more to it than the papers said." That was Bernie's opinion. "I mean these two honeys knew the guy. It wasn't like he was some kind of stranger. A guy doesn't go crazy and do something like that, unless he gets some kind of come-on. . . ."

As steadily as he could, Chink picked up his billfold.

"We'll never know the whole story on a thing like that," Darrell said.

"Chink?" It was Hildi. Chink had stood up quietly and pushed his chair back.

"Hey," Bernie said. "I'm sorry. Here, you want this?"

Chink didn't try to answer. He left the salon, went up the companionway and onto the deck.

Bernie's voice came after him: "Aren't we going to play poker?"

Chink stepped into the night. The Pacific stars were brilliant, and the sea smooth and glittering. He walked aft, head down, passed the entry to the stalls, and went up along the port side to the bow, just trying to get his heart to slow down. When he started back down the starboard side and passed the entry to the salon, Hildi was standing there.

"Chink?" She moved in front of him. "Chink, here's your clipping." He didn't take it. He didn't want to push past her. "Did you know these girls?"

"I was a friend of their father's once."

"Don't you want this back?"

"Do me a favor, Hildi," he said. "Fold it back the way it was."

"I have."

"Fold it again."

"All right."

"Let the wind have it."

They were still three days out from Hawaii. He rearranged his hours. He started taking late breakfast in the crew's mess, and skipping lunch. In the evening, just before six, he would go to the galley and ask for a couple of the sandwiches they fixed for men on night watches, to take to his cabin. He finished reading about the First Crusade, and was learning about the organization of the Kingdom of Jerusalem, after the conquest of the Holy Sepulchre. He was able to stay out of the salon entirely, and for two days didn't see either of the men from De Kalb. Nils had found a new sparring partner his own size. Pietr still came gamely to the gym, and the women aft at four o'clock to help lunge horses. Chink didn't mind the women's company. He smiled, and made courteous replies. He watched hooves lift, curl, reach, and propel. He adjusted his hearing out to the rush of water, and his mind out farther.

Brigadier General Curtis Strawbridge III, Medal of Honor at the Argonne, eight-goal polo player, liked Tony Peters on sight and thought the little Mongol wife was cuter than a basketful of kittens. The General, who was called "Cap," born wealthy and a public figure, didn't bother to read Tony's letter of introduction.

"Do anything I can for you, son," he said. "Just name it."

Tony explained his background, and said he wished to be a U.S. Cavalry officer.

"Ram it through 'em, if I can," Cap Strawbridge said. "Know every one of those pencil pushers on the Selection Board. Went through West Point, Spanish-American, Mexico, and the Big War with 'em. But they're cuttin' down the forces, son. You're going to seem old to 'em for a shavetail, and they never heard of a real goddamn military education, like the kind you got."

Cap Strawbridge, a month later, hearing at home by telegram

that his candidate was unsuccessful, shouted for joy, drank a tumbler of prewar bourbon, squeezed most of the breath out of a passing chambermaid, charged out to his cherry red Pierce-Arrow convertible, and hurled himself into it without opening the door. He was a huge man and the car shook every time he entered it that way.

He drove into Princeton, where Tony Peters was working a school horse, at a place where Cap had got his man a temporary job.

"Great news, great news," Cap shouted. Tony dismounted, led the horse over at a trot, and came to attention. "The idiots have turned you down. Come on."

Cap Strawbridge took the reins of the school horse and handed them to a nearby child, picked Tony up in a bear hug, and flung him into the Pierce-Arrow. They sped out of Princeton. As they careened past the six-room stone cottage at the gate of the estate, Cap remarked, without slowing down, "There's your house."

They raised dust up half a mile of elm-lined lane, skidded behind the big stone Strawbridge mansion with its hundred glittering windows, cut across the back lawn instead of going to the next lane, and stopped against a white board fence.

"There's your barn, Tony."

It was all the command Tony needed to make him happy; a two-story barn, fieldstone like the house, with thirty stalls, four tack rooms, trails through the woods, three riding rings, a practice field for polo with a half-mile oval track around it where Tony's son Charles and Cap's boy Curt used to run, day after day, like a couple of colts.

Tony had two trainers under him, eight stable hands, and a retired carriage maker named Mr. Holmes, all of them quartered upstairs in the barn. There was also a grounds keeper who came in with his crew by the day, and there were always twenty-five or thirty horses and a kennel full of foxhounds for the local hunt. Cap Strawbridge was the Master, Tony the Huntsman, the terror and support of merchants who sold hay and grain, of veterinarians and blacksmiths, boot makers and saddlemakers. Even the tailors, who came to fit the Strawbridge family for riding clothes, had Tony to deal with.

Tony devised horse show strategies, and rode himself in the important classes that allowed professionals. He trained the neighborhood sons for polo, the daughters for equitation, and young horses for whatever they were fit for, racing, jumping, hacking, or dressage, and supervised the other trainers. One summer he and Mr. Holmes, the carriage maker, built a troika and trained three horses to pull it. Tony and Mrs. Strawbridge drove it in costume classes that fall for fun. Aksinya made the costumes.

In 1929 Tony's boy and Cap's boy were in first grade together.

"She slapped you where?" Tony asked, in Russian.

"Not just me, Father. She was hitting everyone."

"Yes?"

"She was crazy. She was hitting with a big ruler."

"A yardstick. Why was she crazy?"

"I can't tell you."

Mrs. Rice, Chink's kindergarten teacher, had gone wild when the children started saying *moo.* Mrs. Rice's Princeton-graduate husband didn't go to work on Wall Street in the morning anymore, she told them the first day, but she herself loved children and she was sure she could be a good teacher if they would understand and help her.

Mrs. Rice had a funny way of showing how she loved children, which was to say, "Shut up, oh, please shut up," sometimes, or hit someone and say, "Please. I'm sorry, but please."

Chink didn't tell that it was Curt who started everybody saying *moo.* Curtis Strawbridge IV lived in the big house, was almost six, like Chink, and Chink's friend.

Mrs. Rice asked Curt who the President was, and Curt said *Hoover,* and Mrs. Rice wanted the whole name, and said *Now Curtis, who?* and Curt said *moo.* But he smiled very nicely. Mrs. Rice asked another boy, Benjamin. Benjamin wanted to be Curt's friend, and said *moo* and laughed. Then most of the other kids started shouting *moo, moo, moo.* Chink didn't. Chink felt sorry for Mrs. Rice, and said *shut up* to Benjamin. Benjamin was scared of Chink, and stopped saying *moo.* Curt said *shut up* to everybody. Curt hadn't meant to start something like kids jumping up and pushing one another, saying *moo.* Mrs. Rice was crying and hitting with the yardstick. She was running around as much as any of them, hitting them, and Chink grabbed the yardstick away and broke it, and threw the pieces to Curt, who threw them out the window.

Then Mrs. Rice grabbed Chink's hair and slapped him a lot.

"You can't tell why she was crazy, all right. Now. She slapped you where?"

Chink pointed to his left cheek, then to his right cheek.

"Like this?" Tony Peters slapped his son's cheeks. There was nothing playful about it.

"Not so hard as that." Chink held back tears.

"And then you hit her how?"

Chink made fists and touched his father's thighs once with each of them. His father was wearing whipcord britches, with suede pads.

"How hard?"

Chink hit each thigh harder. The whipcord made his knuckles burn. His father hit him on the side of the jaw and knocked him down.

"So a man would have done," Tony Peters shouted, picked Chink up, turned him around, and said, "Stand still. Let your trousers down."

The belt was black with a yellow stripe. Chink's father had bought it in the boys' department at Wanamaker's, when they went to get Chink's school clothes. Tony took it off and thrashed Chink thoroughly on the legs and buttocks. Chink stood straight, and fought tears again. Then his father turned Chink to face him and said: "Now. Raise your trousers. When the principal called up, I explained to your mother, 'This is my fault, Aksinya. I haven't told the boy.' Now: A man never raises his hand against a woman. Nor against the man he serves until he means to kill him. Let's go riding."

He smiled, and of all the times Chink saw his father smile, he remembered best the brilliance of that smile, the sustained flash of teeth in the kite-shaped face, the pride in the hot, blue eyes. They ran together, up the lane and across the back lawn of the Strawbridge house to the barn, where the stable hands stopped what they were doing and stood straight, waiting to be spoken to.

I could probably wear the boys' department belt, Chink thought. I'd have to let it out a hole or two. Father was slighter than I, and his muscles were different. Ropy. Mine are like ropes with knots tied in them. I suppose Father tied the knots.

He was eating breakfast in the crew's mess when he thought that.

Mrs. Strawbridge, who was much younger than Cap, called Tony Peters "a remarkably handsome man." Mrs. Strawbridge, who was interested in art and said wonderful things about everybody, told Chink his mother was "a classic Mongolian beauty," which Chink didn't exactly understand. It puzzled but did not disturb him that his mother did not look like anybody else's mother.

Aksinya Peters was six inches shorter than her husband, less than five feet tall. She had a symmetrically wrinkled brow, and under black eyes, set straight across in the way Westerners call slant, was a slim, pug nose, like a Caucasian baby's, and the mouth that turned downwards when she smiled. Her skin was the tan which Americans, wanting to distinguish Indian from Negro, call red.

She was quiet, even noiseless, and, except to play cards, seldom left the house and garden where, in private, she was as completely in command as was Tony at the Strawbridge stables. She learned gradually to cook well, but it came slowly because she'd been raised a village headman's daughter in a household in which humbler relatives did the kitchen chores. She was marvelous at needlework. She made Chink's shirts, and embroidered high-necked blouses for her husband. She drank strong tea all day long. It came in bricks, which Tony bought in New York at an import store.

Aksinya Peters spoke rudimentary English, was fluent, ungrammatical, and functionally illiterate in Russian, but owned a small assortment of books in Buryat, a language written vertically. Some were Buddhist books, and one a long collection of tales, centered around a king named Vikram. She retold the Vikram stories in Russian to her son at bedtime, stories of sword fighting and magic, along with personal tales of the great home lake, the flight east, the north woods, and the circus.

She was dignified and deeply courteous. People like Mrs. Strawbridge understood their attraction to Tony, who was mettlesome, exuberant, and magnetic, but they could only acknowledge, without finding words for it, that there was something about Aksinya, too. She was an extraordinary card player, and what she had of social life developed from that gift.

There was a fad for contract bridge. Mrs. Strawbridge took lessons from a master in New York. Aksinya played on intuition and card sense. As partners the two were locally unbeatable, though other women mocked the accent in which Aksinya bid. "Tree dimus," she would say. "Fur harrs." Chink Peters and Curt Strawbridge learned the game at their mothers' knees.

Chink played cards, spoke Russian, rode horses, and learned the ways of fighting, but he inherited neither his mother's nor his father's looks, rather a combination of them confusing in a boy. Because his eyes were dark brown and shaped like his mother's, he was always called Chink, but the face was less flat and, in the way of Northern Europe, showed its bone. He had a wrinkled brow like his mother's, but his skin tone was nearly as light as his father's. He had black, coarse hair, and among his several scars was a long, wide one which showed white on the top, right-hand side of his head through the crew cut he generally wore. He'd got the scar when he was nine.

Cap Strawbridge banged on the door. "Come on, Tony," he said. "There's a bunch of vets camped down in the east pasture."

"We going to run them off?"

"No, Tony. They're veterans. They're marching to Washington. Make Hoover give 'em the bonus. Let's go palaver. Hell, maybe I'll march with them."

"They got campfires. The woods are dry."

"They're good men, Tony. Come on."

Chink went automatically, because he went everywhere on the place his father went. In front of the gatehouse, the Pierce-Arrow convertible sedan stood, showing its age. Cap Strawbridge had given up jumping into it over the door. It was about eight at night.

"Tony, you drive."

As they drove across the estate and passed the big house, they could see the fires in the east pasture, but before they reached it, there was a group of men, fifty or sixty of them, coming down the woods lane, towards the house. They were men with sticks, chanting in the night. The faces of the front rank were pale and angry in the headlights.

Chink's father stopped the car. "Let's get the boys," he said. He meant the stable hands. "I'll drop you at the house, Cap, with Charles, and get the boys."

"These men know me," Cap Strawbridge said. "I'll just walk out in front and give 'em a salute. You'll see."

He opened the left-hand door, and stepped out. In a moment the great, dark back showed in front of the headlights, one big arm waving, as Cap marched towards the veterans. There was no pause on the other side. The front rank came on, the sticks waved back, and the words of the chant came clear:

"Strawbridge. Rich bitch. Go to hell, Strawbitch."

Chink's father jammed the idling car into gear, and swerved it past Cap, clearing the men from that side of the road, as Cap went down under the sticks on the other. Braking, wheeling, ramming a tree, throwing Chink out of the rear seat, Tony zoomed the car into the crowd. Chink never lost consciousness. He didn't know his head was hurt. He got up and leaned against the tree, watching the veterans run, seeing his father haul Cap Strawbridge into the back of the car. Chink went over. They were alone.

"He's hurt, clubbed," Tony Peters said. "Charles. You're hurt, too. Get in. In front. They'll come back."

There was no second attack. Chink had stitches in his head, at the hospital in Princeton, and slept at home. Cap Strawbridge stayed at the hospital for a month, and when he came out was in the wheelchair in which he spent the rest of the waking hours of his life.

The estate was much quieter after that. The polo team was disbanded, so there were fewer horses. Tony Peters had to let some of the hands go. Though he still trained and gave lessons, there were fewer horse shows, and less riding off the place. People were giving horses away that year, which was how Tony came by Carlsbad, his steeplechaser.

For Chink and Curt Strawbridge IV, in their eleventh years, though, the big house was still a splendid place to play.

One rainy afternoon they were looking through a dog book, and found Curt in the color pictures. He was certainly an Irish setter. Then Curt found a basenji, and said, "Hey, here you are. You're an African dog."

They played dogs all over the house, hiding, jumping out at one another, wrestling, chasing. Curt was required to growl and bark when he heard Chink coming. Chink gave no warning sounds, because the book said basenjis didn't.

Running through the gallery where the Strawbridge art collection hung, Chink noticed the Seurat girl for the first time that day, *La Jeune Fille.* He skidded to a stop in his sneakers, amazed at the way the small canvas seemed to hold its own light. It was nine by twelve, in a white gold frame, a young girl's profile, made with pink, pale ochre, and a few blue dots. He looked, for some reason, from her to his hands, and Curt swept in, baying, caught Chink, and took him off his feet.

The painting was still in his mind at dinnertime, when his father explained that Cap's medical expense, the bad times, Mrs. Strawbridge's struggle to hold things together, meant some changes: The Peterses were now going to start making payments to buy the gatehouse; the east pasture was to be sold off, and the famous art collection, too.

But it was only the big, dark pictures that were taken. Many of the smaller, lighter ones remained, rehung now throughout the house, including Seurat's *La Jeune Fille.*

"We were not offered a very good price for it," Mrs. Strawbridge said. She had stopped by the gatehouse for a cocktail. Cap was not supposed to drink and, though he did so constantly, Mrs. Strawbridge preferred to keep the unconcealed part of the liquor supply with the Peterses. Aksinya didn't drink at all, and Tony, though he sometimes went on benders and got into brawls, wasn't a regular user. "Did you know it's Charles' favorite painting?"

"My Charles?" Tony asked. He actually went to look at *La Jeune Fille* next day and observed that Chink had picked a pretty girl. He probably conceded that girls were something of interest to boys, aside from their real function which was to fight and excel at sports. One of the stable hands Tony had kept was Tim Cassidy, who'd boxed professionally and who gave Chink and Curt lessons, off and on. Tony himself taught the boys fencing. Tim Cassidy said he'd have them ready for the Golden Gloves in a couple of years. Curt liked the fencing, but didn't care much for the boxing. Chink liked whatever his father liked for him. They were fourteen, ready for Chink to go to high school, and Curt to St. Nathaniel's Academy in Massachusetts, when Cap Strawbridge made an announcement.

"There's all kind of scholarships at St. Nat's," Cap said. The Strawbridge males, on their way to West Point, had attended St. Nathaniel's for four generations. "Got little Chink one. Told the Head he can learn anything from German to jujitsu, and I want the boys to room together."

In the first fall, when they were freshman, the older boys thought Curtis Strawbridge IV arrogant and his slanty-eyed roommate strange and surly.

A couple of juniors came in to take Curt to Kangaroo Court.

"Get out of our room," Chink said.

"It's all right," Curt said. "I'll go with the nice gentlemen."

"No," Chink said. "I told them to get out."

The juniors were sixteen. "What have we here?" one of them asked the other.

"A tiny li'l chinee muns?" Chink stepped in and hit the junior under the ear. They didn't scuffle long. Curt came into it, and the juniors weren't boys who'd been hit before. They went away and came back with enough of the school football team to smother the rebels, and shave their heads. Chink and Curt were outcasts then, and on probation because Chink had hit a proctor and blacked his eye.

It changed after Thanksgiving, when the first call for wrestlers came. Chink went out because Cap Strawbridge had hinted it might have something to do with his scholarship.

"I told the Head you could lick any kid in his school," Cap said. "Bunch of mama's boys they got these days."

The lettermen were there in the gym, lounging on one side of the mat in wrestling tights and special shoes. Chink and the other newcomers wore gym shorts and sneakers, and sat stiffly on their side of the mat, listening to the coach tell them that wrestling was a great sport, the only personal combat sport open to gentlemen now that the schools were giving up boxing. The coach said that strength and condition were basic, but take two strong, well-conditioned men of equal weight and the one who knew the skills would win.

"Which of you is Peters?" he asked. "Stand up."

Chink stood.

"You're supposed to be a scrapper, Peters. What do you weigh?"

"A hundred and six just now, sir."

"You're short. You'll wrestle at ninety-eight if you make this squad. Do you understand the rules?"

"Not yet, sir."

"You will. Shake hands with Dan Timrod. Dan's our ninety-eight-pound man. Just weighed in at a hundred and three. Want to wrestle him?"

"Yes, sir."

Timrod was a tall, thin boy, with long arms. He'd been one of the group that had shaved Chink's head.

"No hard feelings, Peters," he said, as they shook hands.

"No," Chink said, feeling a moment of uncertainty. But as soon as they gripped in neutral position, standing, hands under alternate elbows, the uncertainty gave way to surprise. Chink's hands told him he was a great deal stronger than Dan Timrod.

The coach said, "Wrestle," and almost without thinking, Chink heaved Timrod's arms up, went in under them, wrapped his arms around the thin boy's waist, lifted him, and threw him sideways onto the mat.

"Break," the coach said. "That's close to a body slam, Peters. Body slam's illegal."

"Good move, though," Timrod said, getting up, and a sense of confidence began in Chink that would last four years, through eighty-four matches in which he was never defeated and only once came close to it.

Eligibility rules prevented his wrestling except as a J.V., when they met other schools. J.V.'s from Andover, Lawrenceville, and other schools were no problem for Chink at any weight. As a sophomore, he began whipping their varsity wrestlers at a rate phenomenal enough to get sports page attention. St. Nat's was supposed to be a bit effete.

"The little Chink," a proctor named Buzzy Beanbrier said, "is putting us right in the middle of the great big map."

Chink was admired rather than popular that year, and, perhaps because of it, Curt's good looks and family pride were taken differently as well. By spring, both were included in the annual St. Nathaniel's Sophomore Zoo, in which the five outstanding members of the class were displayed to visiting alumni.

Buzzy Beanbrier must have put the zoo together, Chink thought. Buzzy was a senior, good at art and theatre, and five years later went down in a destroyer here, in this ocean, which was pretty theatrical if not very artistic.

First in the zoo was Amos Ames, with a shaved head and huge spectacles, billed as THE INCREDIBLE BRAIN, MAN OF THE FUTURE, ASK HIM ANY QUESTION. Only his head showed and there were flashes and crackles to distract the questioner, while Amos consulted his concealed reference books. There was MERMAN JONES, the swimmer, in a fishtail and flippers, lounging under running water in the shower room. Curt was featured wearing tails, with a champagne bottle, Petty girls from *Esquire* decorating his cubicle while he danced to a phonograph record with a fashion mannequin borrowed from a local store. STRAWBRIDGE IV, his placard read, daring for the 1930s, HEARTS BROKEN HERE, CAN V BE FAR BEHIND? There was a mathematical whiz, and then Chink Peters.

THE FEARFUL CHINK. TOUGHEST KID IN THE EAST. FEARS NO MAN. POSITIVELY CANNOT BE HURT. Chink was in a cage in wrestling clothes, with a boxing glove on one hand. There was a tackling dummy with an Exeter helmet, football pants, and jersey, so rigged that when Chink hit it, the head, arms, and legs fell off. Then Chink would pick up a cardboard core from a roll of paper towelling, painted steel blue, and break it over his head for them.

"Give him a real bar, Buzzy," someone said. "He'll never know the difference."

Wally Diefenbach, a St. Nathaniel's old boy in his senior year at Harvard, saw Chink in his cage that spring, and mentioned it when they met in Italy, five springs later.

He could just as well have seen me as The Brain, doing what Amos did. (This was not so much a present thought as the recurrence of a boyish one.) I never made anything but A's in that school.

He was shovelling sawdust when that thought recurred, and gave himself a punch on the kneecap for it, grinning at the shovel.

If Chink Peters' adolescence went well athletically and scholastically, he was, unlike Curt Strawbridge, thoroughly confused by girls. He didn't know what to expect of girls, or of himself around them. It wasn't one of the areas covered in Tony Peters' instructions to his son.

Summers were the worst time. There was always a group of Tony Peters' riding students, Chink and Curt the only boys, day after day around the Strawbridge stables. The students were girls who came to ride from neighboring estates, and though Chink went away to boarding school, as they did, the slim, brown-armed, articulate girls, with their penetrating voices and husky laughter, seemed beyond his powers to converse with, joke with, far less imagine touching.

At most he could instruct them in riding, quite severely, as his father's deputy, but once dismounted, and as soon as they felt confident of his shyness, the riding students tormented Chink merrily. Once five of them crowded him into the east tack room, and took turns kissing him.

"I want to French kiss him," Julie said, second time around.

They would say things like "We decided to take our shirts off and get tan all over today, Chink. Okay?"

When he couldn't answer, they would say: "Well, you're in charge. Is it okay?"

Curt Strawbridge could reply in kind: "Need help with the buttons?"

At fifteen, Chink sometimes got so embarrassed that he'd run. And sometimes he'd be chased.

"Let her catch you just once," Curt said, speaking of the one called Julie. "You might like it. She's nuts about you."

It took Chink a year to be glad that they liked him, and to learn to conceal his shyness with a studied, rather formal, affability. But even in the summer of his sixteenth year, when he was taking Amy, one of Curt's bold girl cousins, over the cross-country course through the woods, he was alarmed to have her rein up after a jump and say, "Chink, let's dismount and cool off. It's so pretty here."

They were in a dappled glade, out of the sun, out of sight, out of hearing.

"Whiskey doesn't tie very well," he'd said.

She was a moon-faced imp, with long blond hair. "Let him go. We can ride in double."

"You still have your weight too far back on the jumps," Chink said. "Watch me." He squeezed his legs into Whiskey and took flight through the timber.

"What are we going to do about you?" Curt asked. "Amy isn't made of dots like your little Seurat tomato. *La Jeune Tomate.* Amy's even got a body."

If it was Chink's function to protect Curt Strawbridge, sometimes, from the consequences of a conceit Curt was growing out of, Curt's contribution was a kind of teasing which prevented Chink from taking things too seriously.

In school, junior year, Chink won his first U.S. Wrestling Federation junior freestyle title. St. Nat's had never had a contestant in the big meet before.

"Note the small boys in this school," Curt said. "They are all wearing sleeveless sweaters in the Peters manner. They are walking like you, they are talking like you." Curt was lying on his bed, lazy, in the room they shared.

"Shut up, Strawberry," Chink said.

"That is, the poor little bastards think it's neat to scowl and not say anything at all."

Chink scowled, imitating the small boys imitating himself.

"Don't hurt me," Curt said. "Hurt me tomorrow, okay?"

Chink did hurt people sometimes. He'd injured a boy in an early round at the Nationals, during a hard takedown. The hold was legal, the injury, a shoulder separation, accidental. Chink had behaved properly, seeming sorry and concerned, phoning the hospital, asking for news from the boy's coach. But Chink had had to acknowledge to himself that he didn't really care at all. He recognized this as unspeakable, the first thing ever that he couldn't tell Curt Strawbridge.

Chink won a medallion as champion. He gave it to his father as an Easter present.

"At our school," Chink said, waiting for the record to change, "you get one of these when you win your third letter." It was March of his senior year, and his second trip away to the Nationals.

"Boy, that is nifty." She grabbed his hand. Chink might have felt wary if she hadn't been so short.

Barb was the name of the girl who thought the varsity ring was nifty. She was really short, bouncy, with fluffed-up, dark brown hair, cute, diminutive, enthusiastic. Barb's brother wrestled for the day school in St. Louis that was host for the meet. It was an accident, for which he felt slightly discourteous, that Chink found himself put up at the home of a kid he eliminated in the first round.

"It's all right with Fred," Barb said. "As soon as he found out he was wrestling you first, he said, 'Hooray, the season's over.' He's out guzzling beer with his friends, guzzle, guzzle."

"I know. He asked me."

"Why didn't you go?"

"My season's not over."

"I thought maybe it was because you wanted to stay and dance with me."

"I'd better get to bed. Two matches tomorrow, if I win the first." There were more records on the changer, but now she was making him nervous. "Thanks for the dancing lesson."

"Next time you have to ask me. That's part of the lesson."

He found the parents in their living room, visited politely for a few minutes, said good night, and went upstairs. He'd unbuttoned his shirt when the door opened and he saw Barb in the doorway.

"You're staying in my sister's room. Did you know that?"

"I didn't think the clothes looked like Fred's." It came out flirtatious, though he hadn't meant it to. It was just that the drawers of girls' underwear and stockings, the closet full of dresses and nightgowns, disturbed him. There was a permanent perfume in the air of the room, and in the bathroom was a laundry basket he didn't quite dare open. There was a satin coverlet on the bed, pale blue, and a big doll which had been set over on a dresser but probably belonged on the pillows. Even the doll, long-legged, short-skirted, with frilly underpants, was suggestive.

"Polly's away, but, boy, would you love her." Barb was now in short, yellow pajamas with a cashmere cardigan, worn open, instead of a dressing gown, and flouncy, high-heeled slippers. He thought she must be about sixteen, a year younger than he. He wanted to ask her, but she said: "Polly's a sexpot. Pot. Pot."

"Uh-huh."

"I said, I've got to get my English hairbrush." She came in and stood beside him at the dresser. He'd been trying, clumsily, to rebutton his shirt. She put a hand on his chest. "Boy, have you got muscles. Hey, take your shirt off?"

He didn't want to but couldn't say no. She unbuttoned the shirt and pulled it off.

"Boy. Rocks." She dropped the shirt on the floor, and ran the fingers of both hands up and down his arms, over his chest and back. It tickled, but not in a way that made him want to laugh. She pinched one of his nipples suddenly, and giggled when he jumped away. She took his wrist, raised it to her face, made a purring sound into it, and laughed. With her other hand, she picked up a hairbrush from the dresser. It had a black wooden handle and straw-colored bristles.

"I told you," she said, reaching around to tickle the hollow of his spine with the brush. He could see it moving in the mirror. "See? You had my English hairbrush, didn't you?" Then she started brushing his chest. "You haven't much hair on your chest," she said. She moved close to him, and let her arms drop to her sides. He could feel her breath on the skin over his collarbone. She raised one hand lightly to his waist, swayed into him, pressed and swayed away.

"You sound all out of breath," she said. "Why is that, Chink?" She moved the fingers of the hand at his waist. "I'm 'fraid somebody's got a dirty mind."

Then she smiled, stepped back, and pressed the hairbrush into his hand.

"When you hear Mom and Dad go up, you can bring me my hairbrush," she whispered. Then, reaching the other side of the room, she turned and said: "Right across the hall."

She closed the door after herself, and Chink was left there, holding the brush, flat-footed and inflamed. He moved finally, almost choking, to the bathroom, threw open the laundry basket, and at the sight and slight odor of a barely soiled pair of female underpants on top of the pile, touched them on the crotch and ejaculated.

Except as an ambiguous consequence of dreams, it was his first experience of orgasm. He had been told and believed that masturbating would weaken him.

He took off his clothes, except for the undershorts, and got into the shower. He found, when he reached for soap, that he was still holding the hairbrush. He finished bathing, wrung out the shorts and hung them on the shower curtain rail, carried the hairbrush over to the bed, and then, suddenly angry, dropped it onto the floor and fell onto his back on the bed, trying to relax.

He heard the parents go by and climb the stairs to the third floor. The hall light went out, but he didn't want to go to Barb's room. He was, he admitted to himself, scared, not of being caught, just scared. His genitals were stirring again, so he got up, took a cold shower this time, dried himself hard, and put on pajama pants. When he came out of the bathroom, the light had been turned off in his room and he could see Barb as a pale shape in the doorway.

"I found my brush," she whispered. "How come it got all wet?"

The pale shape was fading back. "I put it on your bed, Chink. Aren't you going to bring it to me?" She was gone.

He felt for the brush on top of the bed, found it, and the shape of the handle in his palm was immediately exciting. He went to his bedroom doorway. Darkness was helpful, but he'd begun to tremble, the way he did sometimes after a long, exhausting run in hot weather. The image of the bed behind him was wonderful, soft, safe. He could lock his door and go back to it. Instead he took one step into the hall, seeing Barb's door slightly open, opposite. Her room was lighter than the hall.

Chink took another step, to prove to himself that he wasn't really scared, promising himself that he could turn back after it. Then he took another step because he had to and, sliding his feet, holding his breath, entered her room.

"Close the door," she said, from her bed. "Come on, Chink."

At first she kept a pillow between them at the hips. Then it was just a blanket. When she raised the blanket and got him between the sheets with her, there were still pajamas, but after a time she slipped off her bottoms and then, incredibly, his. She spread her legs and pulled him over her. The coupling was difficult, for she was very small, but after a time she managed it, and after a time they both managed it again.

"And again and again, all that week," he said to Deb, leading her to the crosstie for grooming. It seemed certain this morning that Rebel Deb had resorbed her foetus and come into season. "I frankly lost count. I'd wrestle boys by day and Barb by night. It was a crazy week, but I damn near got licked in the semifinals. Serve me right? What'dya mean, sexpot. Pot, pot. Whoa. You're doing it to Vasco right now. You can't help it. He can't help it. I don't suppose little Barb and I could help it, though I didn't look at it that way then." He gave Deb a hug around the neck, and crossed under with the curry comb. The throb of the engines came rumbling up through their feet. "I don't think I'll tell you the rest of the story," he said.

The kid in the semifinals was from Oklahoma. He was hard and quick with good reach, a reddish-blond, long-jawed kid cowboy. His eyes were blue. He was a grinner, while he wrestled, and he started fast, shooting for the legs and taking Chink down for two points in the first two seconds. Chink let him control for a moment, then sat through and turned in hard, trying for a two-point reversal, but the cowboy slipped away and onto his feet, giving Chink only one point, for an escape. Chink went after him immediately, got in too high, scoring his own two-point takedown and then lost the advantage when the cowboy managed the reversal, got two more points, and deliberately let Chink escape again. They were tied at four to four, with thirty seconds left, too much action at too fast a pace for a single period, when the cowboy shot again, got one leg and lifted Chink off his feet, caught Chink's other ankle and took Chink down for two more points as the period ended.

"Slow it down," Chink's coach said, but Chink shook his head.

"Concentration," Chink whispered, behind six to four. He thought about the sleep he'd been losing, about Barb and her brother watching. There was a triple ring of spectators and he heard someone ask another, "Hey. Peters getting whipped?" as he trotted out for the second period.

It started in referee's position, with the cowboy down on his hands and knees, and Chink's advantage, above, and behind and planning. The referee said, "Wrestle," and Chink tightened his grip, took a wrist, and then let the cowboy sit out for a one-point escape. Chink went to the waist again, but he had his body position right this time, got the takedown and maintained control. That made the score seven-six, favor of the cowboy, and was half Chink's plan. The other half was to let the cowboy sit out again, thinking he'd be given a second escape, get a cradle on him and go for the pin. Chink had worked it before, but he underestimated the cowboy's strength. There were a wild final thirty seconds, during which they travelled all over the mat, Chink barely maintaining control, and wound up off the mat completely as the period ended. Chink was warned for roughness, and the cowboy was still ahead by a point.

In the third period it was the cowboy's turn to start on top in referee's position, with Chink on his knees underneath.

"Hope you had your Wheaties," the cowboy said. "Been wanting to see some of your famous stuff."

"Wrestle."

Chink moved out, knowing the cowboy wouldn't give him the escape, winning it anyway on straight muscle to tie the match. Then they were both on their feet, face to face, and Chink worrying about the roughness warning as they circled. He shot for the legs and missed, scrambled, shot again for the knees, trying to force the match, and the cowboy made a vaulting move, around and behind, for an unearned takedown and the lead, nine to seven.

There was applause, and shouts of "Hold him, baby," and Chink was forty seconds away from his first defeat. Probably the applause did it, cutting through the intermittent sense of general distraction which had slowed Chink's reactions, made him almost careless. He tucked his head, wrenched his shoulders, did a near somersault, and, in a furious flurry of arms and legs, had the cowboy turned and the shoulders going towards the mat. The cowboy was on the back of his head, Chink driving him, taking him sideways, when the buzzer sounded. It was a near fall, held for five seconds to win three points and the match, but Chink was instantly disappointed in himself for not having won by a pin.

Barb thought he had. In the car afterwards, her brother Fred driving, a teammate riding with Fred, Barb and Chink in back, she whispered: "I did, Chink. I got my gun, watching you press that boy down, the buzzer went off and so did I. Isn't that a scream?"

It came out wistful because Chink was clearly obliged to drink beer with Fred and his friends that night, and anyway Polly, the older sister, was home now, across the hall from Barb. Chink would be on a cot in Fred's room for his final night.

"Can I dance with Chink, just one record?" Barb asked, after supper, while the boys were getting ready. The record was of a song called "Moonlight Bay." They danced. Fred took Chink away on to the tavern.

Chink liked the beer pretty well, and didn't even feel guilty over breaking training for his spring sport, which was cross-country and which had already begun back at school. The male company, after the fevered nights and anxious days, was a fine relief.

He didn't see Barb next morning. He slept late. So did Fred. When they went down for breakfast, Barb had left for school.

"Thought your school had the day off?" Chink said.

"Sure. Barb doesn't go there yet. Mine's like high school."

"Barb's not in high school?"

"Nah," Fred said. "The little idiot's only fourteen, even if she does try to act twenty-four most of the time."

Chink couldn't finish eating. He couldn't think what to do or say. He was almost pleased when he found his varsity ring missing from the dresser top in Fred's room, knowing Barb must have taken it while Chink and Fred were still asleep.

It made the second thing he couldn't tell Curt. He wrote separate bread-and-butter letters to the parents, to Fred, and to Barb, but she didn't reply. He wrote again and got no answer. He settled into a baffled, outwardly courteous, secret misogyny, from which he was not released until, six weeks before his nineteenth birthday, during the Second World War, he shot a man dead in the water and realized his own death could be accomplished just as easily.

"And nobody ever called me 'a remarkably handsome man,' either, my dear," he said to Sweet Lorraine.

"Once though—be still, Franny—a woman told me I was gorgeous. Yes, you're gorgeous, too, and very, very fast."

Once again, he ran his hand back and forth along Rebel Deb's flank, feeling the hollowness. "Shot time coming," he said. "I'm sure you haven't aborted, just resorbed, but when it's daylight we'll dilate and douche you, anyway. Be sure there's nothing left to mess you up.

"And you're quite right, smarty," he acknowledged to Piney Brown. "The word she really used was *prächtig*. How would you translate it, if not gorgeous?

"Of course, that was in another country, boy," he said to Vasco, but did not go into the stall. "And the wench was daft."

He had to decide against taking Vasco out until he could clean off some of the scent Rebel Deb was throwing. The young stallion was quite upset. It was still not fully light outside. Chink used a flashlight to find the right-sized hypodermic, and to read the instructions again on the label of the heat-suppressant drug.

He led Deb to the crosstie and gave her the shot. She was good and stood for it. He put the caveson on and led her out for lunging, deciding he'd keep her out and away from the others until time for treatment.

Mrs. Bernie was standing outside, waiting, a heavy sweater on because the sun was not quite up.

"Chink," she said.

"Good morning."

"We'll be in Hawaii this time tomorrow."

"It should be a nice break."

"Chink, Bernie wants to leave the boat and fly home."

"Does he?"

"He almost got in a fight with the purser last night, about refunding our fare. Darrell and Mary Linda's, too."

"The purser's all business."

"It's not the purser's fault. It's you."

"I'm sorry?"

"Bernie says you won't speak to him."

"I haven't seen Bernie."

"You're avoiding him. He's sensitive. He knows it. He's been drinking. He's got us all upset."

"I'm very sorry."

"It's because he liked you so much. We all do. He says he'd apologize, but he doesn't know what for."

"No. I don't suppose he does."

"Please, Chink. Come and shake hands or something?"

"I have a rather busy morning."

"Please?"

"Well, then. May I join you at dinner tonight?"

"Would you?" Mrs. Bernie turned roguish in the dawn. "I'll say six chairs and I'll order wine. A chair for Hildi. She doesn't really like that Norwegian child."

Chink waited for her to bustle off before he patted Deb and said, "We'd better see that Pietr gets included. Come to think of it, we'd better see Pietr."

"Got half an hour for horse work, Pete?"

A wind had come up, an offshore breeze from the Hawaiians, probably, and the *Vesterålen* was rocking mildly. Pietr had a reason for liking to be asked: "Shall you get Hildi?"

"Not this morning," Chink said. "We're gynecologists this morning." He didn't suppose helping them douche Rebel Deb would be anything but interesting for Hildi, but felt some embarrassment on his own behalf and Pietr's. "We may have to use something called a twitch, Pete, to hold the mare."

It wasn't necessary. With Pietr at the crosstie, soothing her, Deb stood quiet while Chink put on the rubber glove and Vaseline, dilated her, and flushed the womb. It was clean, as he'd expected, and her temperature was already down from the shot. He was pleased. With Deb's foot healing up, he was going to have a sound mare to disembark when they reached Wellington.

He blamed himself for what happened next, for he knew Pietr's fascination with the size and strength of the stallion but hadn't warned the midshipman about Vasco's mood. He turned his head just in time to see that Pietr had opened the stall door, yelled, "Look out," and made a dive for the boy, knocking him out of the way as Vasco reared and plunged forward.

"Climb, Pete," Chink said, and moved forward, past the excited horse, banging the wall to attract Vasco's attention. He watched Vasco's front feet, ready to strike, jumped up, caught an iron pipe cross support near the ceiling, and swung himself past. He got to the big stall-area door, slammed it closed, and plunged into the feed stall, where he rolled himself up onto the sacks of grain and out of danger.

Vasco was watching him, half ominous, half playful, free now to roam the alleyway.

"Climb higher, Pete." Chink made his voice calm. "It's okay."

"I'm most sorry."

"Just get settled. It's okay. He'll go to the mare now."

"You saved my life maybe."

"Don't be silly," Chink said, watching Vasco try to figure out which mare. The scent to which the stud was reacting was general, was on Chink's shirt and in the water they'd been using. Chink stripped off the shirt and tossed it onto the gate of Sweet Lorraine's stall. Vasco went to it, reached his head in over it, and nipped Lorraine on the rear. Sweet Lorraine, who was eating hay, looked around, puzzled.

"Can you catch him?" Pietr asked, in a deep, strained voice.

"We'll wait him out."

Now Vasco minced over to Rebel Deb's stall. She was more interested than Lorraine had been. She reached her head out, and Vasco bit her on the neck. Deb squealed encouragingly, whirled, capered, and kicked the side of the stall smartly. Chink slipped off his perch and into his work space. He filled a metal feed measure with oats.

He heard the latch of the areaway door click, turned his head, saw it start to open, and cried out, "Don't come in."

Hildi's face, anxious, appeared and disappeared as she closed herself out again.

For twenty minutes, Chink and Pietr stayed pretty much as they were, while Vasco, not certain about Deb, ranged from one mare's stall to the next. Piney Brown bit Vasco before he could her. Franny Frisbee went around her stall at a frantic canter. Vasco tried Deb again, and the impeded courtship got quite active. When the mare finally moved away from the nipping, and Vasco lost interest briefly, Chink left his work space with the can of oats. He moved past Vasco's head, and knew the situation was nearly back in control when the horse turned with him. He poured the oats into Vasco's feed box, and climbed the metal slats of the front partition until he was three feet off the floor. Vasco came into the stall. Chink patted the flank as it went by him, watched the nose lower into the feed box, moved quietly out, and closed the stall gate behind him. When Vasco looked back, squealed, left the feed, and tried to storm the gate, it was too late.

"Okay, Pete, come down."

"Now I can thank you."

"Now we can let some air in."

He opened the big door to the deck, saw Hildi standing there, Mrs. Bernie beside her, and smiled at them.

"What was going on?" Hildi asked.

"A little merry-go-round," Chink said, and felt Pietr's hand on his shoulder.

"He saves me," Pietr said.

"Don't be an idiot."

"Yes, an idiot I was," Pietr said, in the same deep, strained voice. Chink realized Pietr must have been frightened the whole time.

"Hey, Hildi," Chink said. "Turn the man off, will you?"

"I've been trying to," Hildi said. "What do I have to do to get some help?" She gave Chink a level, almost an accusing, glance.

"Oh, Pietr." Mrs. Bernie reached her arms out. "Our poor Pietr." She gave him a hug, and pulled the young man's head down at least a foot to her bosom. "Oh, Chink."

Hildi nodded. "Chink." He wanted sarcasm from her, a mocking sigh, anything to deflate the situation, but all she said was his name, soberly.

At Mrs. Bernie's wine dinner there were seven chairs after all. Pietr was not excluded. Only the purser was eating by himself and looking quite irritated about it.

Bernie and Darrell, who'd become friends serving together in the infantry in the Second World War, were telling Pietr about Okinawa.

"It was rough, Pete," Bernie said. "I did things I can't believe."

"Bernie got the Bronze Star," Darrell told Chink. "And we all got a unit citation."

"That's pretty good," Chink said.

"Pete wasn't born, and you must have been a little kid," Bernie said.

"Do I really look that young?"

"Hey, were you old enough to get in?"

"About the age Pietr is now."

"Twenty?" asked Pietr.

Chink smiled. "I had home leave after two years, and still wasn't old enough to buy a drink."

"What branch?" Darrell asked.

"We were attached to various units," Chink said.

"Special Service," said Bernie. "I remember those guys. Great for morale, right? Pacific or what? You get overseas?"

Chink smiled. He could have named some odd places, but even after all these years, his training wouldn't let him, so he said Europe.

"But what'd you do?" Darrell pressed him. "I mean, I don't know what Bernie's talking about, Special Service."

"Who ever knows what Bernie's talking about?" Mrs. Bernie asked. "I'll bet it wasn't anything about morale."

Chink shrugged.

Darrell said the new volunteer army was really a deal.

Hildi said: "Wait a minute. Let Chink answer." Chink looked at her, and shook his head slightly, smiling, trying to dismiss it. "But you must. What was it you did in the war, Chink?" Now the mockery was coming, but it was too late for it to be welcome. "Something dashing and important."

"Sure," Chink said. "I was the only World War One aviator in World War Two."

"Charming. Elusive. Mysterious." She raised her wine glass to him. "What did you do in the war, Chink?"

"I killed people," Chink said, mildly irritated by her. It brought silence.

Then Bernie said, "Well, sure. That's what soldiers do, right?" And he was back on Okinawa again, in a foxhole with his M-1 and Darrell over there on the left, pinned down together.

"Oh, yes," said Pietr, relieved.

Chink knew that, across the table, Hildi was trying to meet his eyes. He turned deliberately to Mary Linda, Darrell's wife, on his right, filling her glass with German wine, asking for her impressions of the port of Bremen.

Silence and cessation woke him. He realized that the *Vesterålen* had docked in Honolulu. He got up, dressed, and went to the horses. It was three in the morning.

"It's all right," he said to them all, letting himself into the stall area, walking down the alley where he could feel more than see the five heads reached out towards him. "Seems a little weird, doesn't it? It's okay. I'll stay right here. It'll be light pretty soon, and you know what? This morning each of you gets a trot, we'll be nice and still, maybe even a little canter."

He went back to the first stall, feeling his way, and let himself in.

"Well, Lorraine. Well, Lorraine. It'll be nice here. I shouldn't have said to Hildi, but I had to turn her off somehow." Lorraine nickered, and he said: "Maybe you'd like the big door open. It's mild out there, and the land smells good."

He fastened the door open, and went on to Rebel Deb. "All over the nonsense, dear? We'll keep you on your drug until New Zealand, then we'll let you flow again. Breed you to young Vasco, there; you'll have his first foal ever, if the rascal's any good."

He spent a little more time with Piney Brown, who hadn't eaten any of her hay. "Suspicious, aren't you? And about the time you're used to being stopped, the boat will start again. What we've got here's the kind of situation you'd expect from humans. Young Pietr's one of the ones who's born to worship heroes, and the others are catching from him. Heroes are nothing but the worst of the good guys and the best of the bad guys, okay? You like that? Take the great Queen Richard the Lion-Hearted, better known in his time as Little Sir Yes-and-No. Hunted his father down until the old man died, turned on his brothers, turned on his friend and ally Philip, jilted his fiancée, and ran England out of money twice, once for a crusade, once for his personal ransom. Didn't spend more than six months of his reign in the country. Got himself killed squabbling over gold. He was forty-two, April 1199.

"You're not eating either, Franny? Pretty Franny. Speedy Franny. Do I dare go in to Vasco? So Richard never saw 1200, but he was the darling of the minstrel boys, and they gave him a hell of a press."

Vasco was off his feed, too, and listless. "Call it a dream, boy," Chink said. "It'll come true in New Zealand, but for now she's just another horse."

He decided not to go ashore on the first day of the stopover. He wanted to stay close to the horses, and he wanted to move all the baled hay out, into the sun and drier air, turn it daily, and stow it inside again before they left.

He was grooming an unusually nervous Franny Frisbee when she bit him, good and hard, catching the skin over his ribs through his T-shirt. The shirt tore away between her teeth, and Chink would have a bruise. It confirmed his feeling that he shouldn't leave the ship for now.

The foursome from De Kalb stopped by the stall area door to say that they were going to rent clubs and play golf at one of the hotels.

"Meet us for dinner there," Bernie urged.

"Thanks. I have an old friend in Honolulu." There was a man Chink had known and liked for many years, who taught oceanography at the university. "I'd like to stay free till I've arranged to see him."

Bernie didn't seem to take it as a rebuff, and there'd been no more talk of the two couples flying home.

Hildi came along while he was trotting Piney Brown. Hildi was dressed to go ashore, smart in white linen with her hair set and glossy.

"I have to ask you something."

"All right," he said.

"You were rude last night on purpose, weren't you, Chink?"

"I was truthful, Hildi. On purpose."

"Why? I mean, why did you make it sound so harsh?"

"I apologize if it seemed rude."

She was too willing to accept: "Whatever happened, it was long ago. Pietr and I are going to play tennis. Want to come?"

"Afraid I never learned the game."

"We could do something else. Do you like to shop?"

Chink said he was a nut for bookstores, but he guessed not today, and was ready to start Piney around again when Pietr appeared with tennis rackets.

"Tonight, we go dancing to the Navy Club," Pietr announced, dazzling in white flannels. "I have a guest card. You come?"

"Oh, yes," Hildi said. "Please?"

"I'd be in the way, wouldn't I?"

"Oh, no." Hildi was very emphatic.

"Please," Pietr said. "We will be honored."

"You can't keep saying no to everything."

"Thanks, then," Chink said. "I'd love to."

"Can we really count on you?" Hildi asked.

Chink smiled, and said, "Sure," mildly surprised at her asking. He always expected to be taken at his word.

The ship was emptying. His only other visitor was the purser, returning from shore at lunchtime, who came by to say, quite gratuitously, "Not any mail for you, Mr. Chink."

"I wasn't expecting any, thanks. Is the ship's phone hooked up to shore now?"

"Only for ship's business," the purser said. "Passengers are not to use."

Chink smiled.

At least, he thought, the purser's still being nasty.

Just past the middle of the afternoon, with the horses drowsing and the ship quiet, he decided after all to go ashore. What he needed was a run. He wore swimming trunks, shirt, and shoes. He stopped at a dive shop and rented a snorkel, flippers, and a mask. He took a bus out along one of the beaches to the end of its line. He ran on packed sand, past pineapple fields, along a fringe of palms, until he got to a place where cliffs came down close to the water. There were blackish, porous rocks, both on the beach and jutting out of the water at random angles, among which he could float, facedown, watching through the mask, breathing through the tube, seeing reef fish whose names he'd never known.

Just before reboarding the ship, he phoned his oceanographer friend. The man seemed delighted. Chink had dinner with the family, which included a western-dressed Japanese wife, a daughter, and two sons, the younger of whom shyly asked Chink for an autograph.

When he met Hildi and Pietr at a table beside the dance floor, they had news. The *Vesterålen* was to have its rudder bearings repacked, and would be in port three more days.

"We're all going to Maui," Hildi said. "Bernie arranged it." The passengers, along with Pietr, the purser, and the wireless officer, would be flying to the other island early in the morning to spend three days, two nights. "We made a reservation for you, but I don't suppose you can come?"

"I'd better stay with my beasts," Chink said.

"You allow me to stay with the horses?" Pietr offered. "So then you may go."

Chink said that was a nice offer, and he wished he could accept. Hildi said it was the sweetest thing she'd ever heard. Chink hoped silently that the excursion would settle the competition between Pietr, the purser, and perhaps now the wireless officer, too, for Hildi's shipboard affections.

The Navy Club was full of festive groups and couples, the women in long dresses, the men in and out of uniform, and though Chink didn't have much ear for music, it seemed to him that the band sounded quite a lot like the big dance bands of postwar times. So that it was oddly appropriate, as Hildi and Pietr got up to dance, to hear a man's voice call:

"Chink Peters!"

He looked up and to his right. It was a tall, slim man in a Navy Commander's uniform, dancing with a lovely, tall woman. Chink stood. "Sam?" he said. "Sam Lowen."

"My wife, D'Arcy," Sam Lowen said.

"I've heard about you," D'Arcy Lowen said. She had auburn hair and a caressing smile. "I never imagined I'd meet you."

"Chink, you're not alone?"

"The friends I'm with are dancing," Chink said, but they weren't. His shipmates were standing quite still, gazing and listening.

Please, dance away he thought, and introduced them.

Lowen glanced at the orchestra. A new tune had just begun. "Excuse me, darling?" he said to his wife. "Go ahead and dance, people."

"Of course," D'Arcy Lowen said. And then: "Chink Peters. Can you all join us for a drink, after you and Sam talk, Chink Peters?"

"Thanks," Chink said. "Won't you have one right here, now?"

She smiled and moved gracefully off by herself, the picture of an intelligence wife who knew her job.

"Pietr!" Hildi said. "Come on."

Sam took Chink's arm. "Let's sit. But all I want to say is, I'm glad you've come."

They sat, and Chink said: "Sam, it sounds like you're misapprehending."

"Sure. No question. Let me just be this indiscreet: There's no one I'd rather see right now than you." So. You want to run the story, fine. I believe it."

"There's no story," Chink said. "I wasn't sent here."

"Good. Look, I'm talking to your beer glass. This thing's too much for us. Or too different. We do fine on code busting and reading satellite photos, but local politics and this weird Philippine part of it . . ."

"Sam," Chink said. "Whatever it is, the beer glass doesn't want to know, either. I'm a civilian, passing through."

"Manila, I assume."

"I left the agency years ago."

"Sorry, I should know better than to make assumptions, shouldn't I? But let me give you my office number, Chink. If there's anything Naval Intelligence can do or needs to know, I'm in charge of it here."

"Congratulations," Chink said. He'd last seen Sam Lowen in the Virgin Islands, nine years before. "You'll make a nifty admiral, Sam."

"I admit I've started hoping for it."

"Sam, when I last saw you in St. Thomas," Chink tried again, "I'd been out of the agency two years, and mostly out long before that."

"I know. Then you turned up in that thing in Uruguay. I'm not questioning the way you people work . . ."

"Stop it, Admiral. Just stop."

"Of course. Sorry." The tune ended. "Your friends will be back. Can you get away to our table later for a minute? D'Arcy would love it. You're a legend to her."

Chink rose with him. "Sure. Sure, Sam." He wanted Sam gone before Hildi and Pietr came back.

"Excuse me?" In the orchestra's closing crescendo, he had missed Sam's last question.

"I asked if you might be going to Tahiti when it's over. Whatever it is."

"It's five horses," Chink said. "That's all. Going to New Zealand. No, I hadn't planned on Tahiti. Why?"

"Eve Shellcroft's in Tahiti. Didn't you know? Chink, you heard the terrible thing about Wally's two girls?"

No, Chink said, he didn't know. Yes, he said, he'd heard.

Eve Shellcroft was a woman Chink had been in love with in the Virgin Islands where he'd lived for a time after the breakup of his marriage.

Tomorrow or the next day, he thought, I will have to go to the public library in Honolulu and read about Mary and Wendy, all of the stories in *The New York Times*, but I would rather do that after the others have flown to Maui.

As for Eve Shellcroft, it was going to be a little hard to fall asleep tonight, back on the silent *Vesterålen*, with dance music in his ears, and a graceful woman's smile in his eyes, stars, soft wind, and the knowledge that he had been moving again through an ocean, towards an island where Eve was.

When he got back to the boat and checked the hayracks, he found that Piney Brown was eating again. Vasco was still off.

"Three quiet days, with the ship to ourselves," he said to the stallion. "Memory's the sixth sense, boy. What do you say to that?"

In June 1941, when he was seventeen years old, Chink Peters graduated from St. Nathaniel's Academy, winning prizes in German and Greek, and for the only time in his life refused his father something. It was an appointment Tony Peters wanted his son to accept to West Point, arranged for by Cap Strawbridge, still a genial and determined man, in spite of the decline of his body in the wheelchair and his fortune in the depression. Cap's son Curt was going to the Point, of course. Cap had always assumed the boys would go together, and Tony had foreseen his own frustrated military career realized by Charles, as aide or executive officer, perhaps, to the next General Strawbridge.

Young Curt supported Chink: "You're right, basenji. You're a linguist and you like history. Go to Yale."

West Point was free.

"Father," Chink said, "Mr. Spielberg at school has got Yale to offer a scholarship to pay part of it. Many other colleges will pay it all, if I wrestle."

"You are going to be in the war, Charles, not fighting other little boys." But Tony was confused about the war. Hitler and Stalin were suddenly no longer allies but enemies. He wanted England to make peace with Germany, and America to join them both in a fine war to win Russia back for the Romanovs.

The comfort and authority of Tony Peters' life in America were threatened by this confusing war, in which Tony himself was, unbelievably, too old to fight. He was, in any case, needed, and sometimes irksomely, to head both households in New Jersey, for Cap Strawbridge was staying permanently now in the hospital near Washington.

"I can take officer's training at any college," Chink said.

"You go where you wish. I can pay." Tony moved back to an area in which he was not confused. Scholarships were for the ragged children of the poor. The Peterses might be finding it a struggle to buy the gatehouse, might, now that the Strawbridge estate was much reduced, arrogate the use of other people's riding rings and pastures, but they were never ragged.

That year, Tony's horse was ready. The big steeplechaser, Carlsbad, qualified for the Maryland Hunt Cup and required an amateur rider. Tony had brought his boy and his horse along together, and Chink, having won the right to choose his college, agreed gladly to spend the summer at what was left of the Strawbridge breeding farm in Virginia. There his father schooled Chink and Carlsbad over timber, ran them successfully in hunt club point-to-point races and then in a couple of racetrack steeplechases. But in the big Cup race, running second at the fourteenth jump, Chink let his horse be crowded from behind. Carlsbad, taking off too late, crashed into the top rail and fell forward. Chink didn't try to get clear. He knew that if he held on to the reins, he could control the horse and legally remount after the fall. His left leg was broken that way. At least Carlsbad's legs were all right.

With his leg in a cast, Chink decided to delay his entrance to Yale, since he couldn't compete in cross-country or get in shape for wrestling. He returned to New Jersey, where he rested, healed, and read art books. He could remember, dimly, some of the great paintings which had been sold off from the Strawbridge collection, five years earlier. There were still the smaller paintings, the drawings and prints, and the books were full of reproductions. Mrs. Strawbridge tried to get Chink interested in music, too, but it didn't excite him the way paintings did.

By late October, he was out of the cast and on crutches. By mid-November, he was running again. In early December, the Japanese attacked Pearl Harbor. Two months later, on the morning of his eighteenth birthday, in February 1942, he enlisted in the U.S. Cavalry, which was getting rid of its horses and training its recruits in tanks. Learning this, Tony Peters realized he could not send his cavalry sabre off with Chink to Alabama, and had his blacksmith make the sword into a set of three knives.

They were throwing knives, double-edged and carefully balanced, with short, flat handles to fit the palm. At basic training, Chink kept the set in his footlocker.

One Saturday afternoon when there were no passes, he got out the knives as an entertainment for the training squad of which he'd been made acting leader. The squad found a discarded wooden door, meant for the camp dump, and propped it up against a tree outside their barracks. Chink borrowed chalk and outlined a figure on the door, arm raised in a Nazi salute with a swastika for a heart. They measured back twenty feet, drew a toe line in the dust, and took turns throwing.

The best at it was a hard, gangly southern mountain boy named Tenney. He and Chink disliked one another, but just before his second turn Tenney asked Chink quite civilly for the chalk.

"Like to do a little fixing on your picture," he said. "Now this going to improve everybody's aim."

He converted the Nazi's helmet into long hair, made circles on the chest with dots inside, erased the belt, and drew in curls at the crotch with a vertical line below them.

"Ain't she lovely?" He came back to the toe line, grinning, held out his hand for the knives, and threw them quickly, one after another. The first was off target, the second failed to hold, but the third whacked into the pine panelling, point first, held, and quivered. "Wowee," Tenney cried. "How many points for belly button?"

When Chink's turn came, he told the others to go ahead, he'd watch. It was a hot, early spring in Alabama. He sat in the shade, resting his back against the side of the wooden barracks building, disliking Tenney more than ever.

One of the knives was missing from Chink's footlocker in the morning. He looked across the narrow room at Tenney, lying on his bed barefoot, watching Chink close the locker. Chink nodded at him, opened the locker again and left the lid up. There were seven or eight other trainees lying around. It was Sunday morning. They were watching. Chink walked over to Tenney's bed.

"Looking for something, squad daddy?"

"Put it back in the footlocker, Tenney."

"Put *whut* back in the lock-fucker?"

Chink feinted a grab at the arm, locked his hands around the big, bare ankle, and heaved Tenney off his bed onto the floor. The handful of blanket the southern boy grabbed went with him. His head bumped the floor between his bed and the next, but even as it did, he was kicking free.

Tenney scuttled backwards to the wall and jerked up onto his feet, snorting and radiant, and Chink knew it wasn't the knife Tenney wanted but the fight. That was fine with Chink.

"What are you?" Tenney said. "Some kind of Chinese fart, pull a man off his bed on a Sunday morning?"

Chink smiled and waited out the insult ritual.

"I heard you put them choppie-stickers up your ass before you eat with 'em."

Chink kept the smile on his face, and said softly: "You've got dirty ears to go with that mouth, Tenney." He could have had the man between the beds, already down, a moment before, but he'd wanted room to swing and move.

"I believe you about half nigger anyway—which half? You daddy or you black-ass mother?"

"You going to talk or fight this morning, Tenney?"

The southerner looked five inches taller and forty pounds heavier, but Chink felt no fear of him. He figured Tenney for a country brawler, with the usual good right-hand punch. Chink could hit quite hard with either hand.

Tenney pushed off against the wall with one foot, and rushed. Chink let him come, went under the first big, wide punch to bang the solar plexus with four good jabs. The solar plexus was hard as Chink's fists.

Tenney grabbed Chink's shirt at the shoulder, spun Chink away, and caught him a blow on the side of the head. Chink went sideways, down, rolled, and was up again, smiling. When Tenney came at him again, he bobbed right, away from the right hand, and got Tenney's ear with a jab and a hook, pushed the head away, and hit the ear again.

Tenney yelled and wheeled, and Chink began to box carefully, thinking about footwork, circling, sideslipping the big punches, and countering with jabs. He got the ear again, very solidly, and saw it swell up quickly. He hit it again, switched to a right lead, taking blows on his shoulder to get the left into Tenney's face. He went back to the left lead and hooked into the nose, into the ear again, into the nose, until it, too, was swollen and bleeding.

Then Tenney grabbed for Chink's wrists, caught one, pulled, and had a knee between Chink's legs, so that Chink had to jump away to protect his groin, and Tenney came up with a big uppercut that could have ended the fight if it had got Chink's jaw. Instead it grazed and tore his cheek, under the eye socket. Again Chink had to go back, this time to prevent Tenney's getting a hug on him.

He sidestepped Tenney's next lunge, dropped to one knee, and went for the legs, got them, threw Tenney and reversed, and for an instant it was like a formal wrestling match. Then, as Tenney made it to his hands and knees and strained forward, Chink turned loose, pushed Tenney's face down to the floor, and whacked the hurt ear hard, with the heel of the hand and good body weight behind it.

Tenney bellowed, lurched away, and came up kicking. A kick at the hip sent Chink down, and he rolled away from the other foot but not before the heel got him in the head. He caught the next kick with both hands, and threw Tenney down. Then they were both on their feet again, and circling, Chink looking for a chance to hook the nose again. Tenney was bleeding, Chink shaking off dizziness from being kicked in the head, but neither was hurt enough or tired enough to quit.

Men had come running in from the drill yard, a crowd of them, pushing one another for position, closing in the fighting area. Tenney stood back against them, catching his breath and cursing. Chink didn't want him rested. He moved to draw Tenney forwards. Tenney came, crouching now to guard his legs, and Chink found that the crowd hadn't left him room to sidestep. He moved forwards, inside the next big punch, took a short left to the jaw which didn't have much to it, hit a good body punch over the heart, a couple to the solar plexus, which seemed softer now, and then missed one aimed at Tenney's throat and ducked back. He backed into someone who gave him a push forwards, towards Tenney, and the bigger man had enough speed left to meet Chink with a really good right, to the spot under Chink's eye. It knocked Chink partly down, into the side of their training sergeant. The sergeant caught Chink and stepped in front of him, staying there until Chink had his balance back.

"Sonofabitch, you're not going to stop the fun, sarge?" But Tenney said it between gasps.

"Enjoy yourselves," the sergeant said, and, to the crowd, "Move back. Give the boys some room. Move." The circle opened, and Chink decided that he had his man now. He feinted a high jab, took a blow on the shoulder, flicked the ear to roll Tenney back, crouched, and shot under again to get the legs, low. This time Tenney went down backwards. As he rolled to his stomach, Chink landed with a knee, hard, to the middle of the back, keeping Tenney flat, whacked the head, and then, with the crook of his left arm, went around and under the chin, and seized his own wrist. It was a choke hold nothing could break, and sent Tenney into writhing, dirty fingernails digging into Chink's arm. Limpness came and a squall of despair. Chink knew he could kill the man now, and it occurred to him that he wouldn't mind doing that, though he realized it was impractical. He considered what to do with the control he'd won, wondering how much fear and pain he'd be allowed to cause.

He released the choke hold, cracked the back of Tenney's head to keep the face on the floor, took a wrist, and brought it up sharply behind Tenney's back.

The sergeant was standing over them now. Chink forced the arm up high.

"Leggo," Tenney said, his voice full of mucus. "I was just joking you with your damn knife."

"Well, hell, that's okay about the little old knife," Chink said, imitating the drawl. "I'd rather break me your little old arm, any-how." He flexed the arm up slowly and three pairs of hands pulled him off and away.

"So, Lorraine. You know what they did after I fought Tenney?" He was checking her ears; the mites were gone and the tissue inside was a healthy, pale pink. "Hauled him to the infirmary, and transferred my little mad-dog butt out of that training company. There was always a transfer, after a serious fight, but usually it was the loser.

"So I languished, my dear," he explained to Deb. "Are you languishing? In a replacement depot? No, you're not, you fool.

"Piney Brown. Private Peters reporting. Yes, ma'am, I do speak Russian. Read it, don't write it very well. No, ma'am, Father's not a communist. He's the opposite. He would like to eat a communist. Some German. Not much French, ma'am. Eighty-four matches, thirty-seven pins. Classical, not modern. Expert with the forty-five, first try. But it may not have been the athletics or the languages so much as the liver-spotted hand of old Cap Strawbridge.

"You know the first thing they did to me in school, Franny? O.S.S. school, not St. Nat's, dear. Naturally, they had a man named Milliken steal my binoculars, and watched to see if I'd go nuts over it."

"What the hell do you think you're doing with my binocular case, Peters?"

"Admiring it, Milliken. Prettiest binocular case I ever saw in my whole, entire life."

"You givin' me a little who-struck-John, boy?"

"Why, no, Millie. You're lucky to have such a pretty case, you lucky thing."

"Listen here, boy . . ."

"Millie, tell the Captain I'd never in the world fight a lucky thing like you, okay?"

"Clean up the oats, Vasco. There are little horses starving in China. I didn't see through the next neat trick they pulled. They borrowed Randy Lyons from the navy for a couple of days. How could I have known the shrimp was a contender for the world lightweight title? Just my size and weight was Randy. Had him pick a locker-room fight, and beat hell out of me. Which he did without too much trouble. No more? I'll scrub out the feed box, maybe it doesn't smell right to you. I did give Randy Lyons just a little trouble, on the way to the showers. But I never saw the binoculars again."

Bought them in a pawnshop in Washington, he thought. German glasses, night glasses, beautiful.

From a place on the Egyptian coastline, not far from Alexandria, the British sailed small fishing boats to Crete, wooden boats with only sails for power, so that they would not attract magnetic mines.

There'd been troops left on Crete during the withdrawal. The small boats picked them up, in groups of three and four at night, guided by Cretan patriots, and took the men to Egypt. The boats carried knives and piano wire, also grenades, a Springfield, and a Bren gun, but the orders were to avoid firefights. The U.S. Army sent a few specialists, a token of regiments to come.

Warrant Officer C. K. Peters was one of the Yanks. He sailed with Subleftenant Marston Mooney as crew, navigator, and gunner. Mooney was nineteen, Peters' senior by a year.

Chink's weapon was the silenced Springfield rifle, with which he'd shot an actual perfect score in training school. He knew knife and piano wire work quite well. He knew the operation, maintenance, and repair of German and Italian small arms. He was okay on maps and celestial navigation, too, though Subleftenant Mooney could navigate well enough. On their trips out, Mooney taught the younger kid how to sail.

Chink fired his Springfield once in nineteen crossings. They had made their pickup in a cove, four Australians, one of them delirious from an old head wound, and started out, beating against an offshore wind before dawn. The sun came up. The wind went down. Mooney glassed the shore, and said, "No one looking. I hope. Break out paddles."

Chink and one Aussie paddled on the starboard side, the other two fit men to port, all kneeling, moving the boat along, with Mooney at the tiller. "If I say drop, it's flat under the gunnels," Mooney said. "We're showing more hands than a fisherman would carry, and ought to have a sculling oar."

As they came out of the cove, into open water, Mooney said it: "Drop." Then: "Too late," he said. "He's had a proper dekko. Right then, Chink."

Chink raised his head so that he could see over the gunnel. There was no one in sight on shore.

"In the water," Mooney said. "Five points off starboard bow."

Chink saw, just as it went down, a black bathing cap. "Bloody Jerry officer, out for his morning swim," Mooney said. "They go miles. He'll be up again at once. Can you get him?"

The range was easy, not more than fifty yards. Chink took the Springfield out of its waterproof case, adjusted the sights, shouldered the gun, and rested his elbows on the coaming.

The black cap came up, twenty yards farther out, and went down again immediately. The swimmer was going to go underwater if he could.

"Need to get closer?" Mooney asked.

"No. Keep the boat still," Chink said. When the cap showed again, the swimmer needed a deeper breath, and there was plenty of time. Chink squeezed off a single round. He thought the head might break open. Instead, the impact moved it in the water, as if the swimmer had made a little jump. Blood showed. After a moment the body rose, and the men cheered softly. They watched it floating for long enough to be sure, and paddled on to find the wind.

Chink had his first romance in Cairo, nights ashore, with a resigned, very cultivated young woman named Elena whom Marston Mooney called The Melancholy Baby.

"Have a go," Mooney said. "She can be nice to the troops, though she isn't glorious fun."

Elena was an elegantly educated Jewish refugee from Austria, whose immediate family, no others of whom survived, had owned factories. She had been in school in London when Austria was annexed, and come out to relatives in Palestine. The relatives were Orthodox, and very strict. Elena said they had cherished her only because, should Germany somehow lose the war, then she, Elena, might be rich. She had moved to Cairo, headquarters city for the Middle East, where the war and the men in it preoccupied her in a tragic way, for she thought the one was lost, the others doomed. She devoted herself, more in sorrow than in passion, to Marston Mooney and his friends, the young commandos.

Elena was a sales clerk in the haberdashery department of the British Officer's Store at the Kasr El Nil barracks. She was slim, with extraordinarily fine posture, an exquisite, high-chinned profile, and very short, dark, tightly curled hair.

Chink liked her very much, but it disturbed him to find her vulnerable and young, and at the same time loose, despairing, used beyond her years, which were twenty-four.

As Mooney had predicted, the tone of their times together was not cheery, only bittersweet at best. They would meet at Big Grappi's, a teahouse, for tea and ices, since neither of them cared a lot for alcohol. They would walk together in the Cairo dusk afterwards, speaking German as their intimate language. It was Elena who told Chink he was *prächtig*. She thought she might stop seeing the others, if they didn't mind. "For just now," she said. "For our own short while, you see."

Her accent in English was best-schools British.

They would walk to her apartment, which was strikingly furnished with French antiques her father had once shipped to Palestine, planning, before the trouble, to build a winter home near Haifa.

Elena was quite crazy in the brass-and-ebony Louis XIV bed, under the Fragonard engravings, tense and then abandoned, crying and then laughing, running away, careening back to seize and be seized. Chink thought of himself more as her comforter than her lover, as she must have thought of herself as offering nothing much better than comfort to himself and the others.

"All the little dead boys," she said. "How do you do, Charles? Good-bye, darling. Wear your overshoes."

"I don't mean to stop seeing you, wherever they send me next."

"We all say that, don't we? Ever so often these days. Shall we have a dance?"

One evening, when the moon was especially bright, she became a little gay and asked if they couldn't take a horse and carriage out to see the Sphinx. It was not a sensible thing to do at night, unless you knew a driver you could trust. Elena felt she did but, when they were on their way, admitted that she probably had the wrong man.

Chink wanted to encourage her impulse towards having fun. He pointed out how smart their carriage was. It was a tall, lacquered, closed carriage with clean windows and soft leather seat cushions, pulled by a well-fed horse. There were even flowers in the bud vase. But halfway out to Giza, the driver made a turn into the slums on the edge of the city and reined up.

Chink was out the door, up onto the driver's seat, and had pitched the man off, before his confederate with a long knife had even appeared from behind the tin shack they'd stopped beside. The confederate went for the reins, and Chink jumped down, kicking the driver in the head as he went by, and disarmed the confederate, a technique in which he had a lot of training. The confederate ran, but might be back with help. The driver groaned. Chink kicked the driver's head again, a studied, lethal kick. He had no impression of the man's age or of what his face looked like except as an indicator of the point of aim, just under the left ear. Chink called to Elena that everything was fine, climbed up, and drove the carriage back into Cairo. The horse was quite a good one, handy and well trained.

The driver died during the night. There was some local agitation. Chink had reported the episode, but his identity was said to be unknown, and the British sent him covertly off to demolition school in Aleppo, Syria.

"He's an old man," Chink said.

Major Diefenbach wore the kind of spectacles that magnified his eyeballs when you met his glance. The effect was comic, and he made use of it: "Old informers are so much less harmful than young ones, aren't they?"

Chink felt wary.

"It's the quality of their information, of course. They give such ancient information to such elderly Germans. Do you want help planning it?"

"Planning? I'm sorry."

"The trip for your old informer. This is Major Wally's travel bureau. Good morning. I think we can help." He sang: " 'Somewhere over the rainbow'?" His face expressed the question mark. "The all-expense package, don't you think?" He was a tenor.

"I hadn't got that far," Chink said.

"You hoped the others would see him off?"

"I didn't want to do anything, before I had to." Chink had come out of Yugoslavia by submarine the day before. On earlier trips he'd been taken to the British at Tripoli, but the war in Italy had moved north since last time. Yesterday's had been a much shorter trip to Bari, on the Adriatic coast, and then to this American headquarters at Castellammare. Major Walden Diefenbach was Chink's first American commanding officer. They had just met in the major's office in a big, stone building. The office had a marble floor and comfortable furniture.

"I wanted to check here first," Chink said.

The major was about twenty-six or -seven. He had wavy, light brown hair and very pink, smooth cheeks, a nice pair of shoulders, and good height and reach. He was snub nosed and dimpled, which made the glasses seem part of a costume, a clown-disguise. An ensign on the sub had called Diefenbach "the Great Horn-Rimmed Owl," and said he was rich in civilian life and ambitious in the military.

"How kind of you to think of us," Major Diefenbach said. "Name your complications."

"The old man, Tomajz, is my only Communist," Chink said. "The others are Chetniks."

"You know the overall situation?"

"Just the view from the cave."

"Your friends don't care to tell you any more than they have to. That's quite wicked and sensible of them." The major unrolled a map, and showed Chink where General Mikhailovitch was in the Serbian mountains, with what was left of the dwindling Chetnik army. Tito's Communist partisans, who hated Chetniks and called them fascist, controlled most of the rest of the country, between the sea, the Serbian rump, and Vojvodina where the Germans were. There were a few other Chetnik pockets. He pointed them out. The guerilla group, led by a man named Bozzo, to which Chink had been attached for seven months, was still fairly secure in one of the pockets.

"Even so, Bozzo says it's time to change caves again," Chink said.

"Our British cousins are getting ready to off-load the Chetniks," Major Diefenbach said. "You aren't part of their mission any longer, as a matter of fact. Which is why you find yourself with me, and I hope not too unhappily. The British want to tell Tito their mission's been reduced. Tito's getting pretty sassy. He doesn't seem to think he needs us. And perhaps he doesn't."

"Then Bozzo's keeping old Tomajz around for insurance," Chink said.

"To say nice things about you all when the partisans come."

"It won't work, Major."

"Make it Wally," Diefenbach said. "I've got twelve of you young ramblers out. You're the last I've met and the first to call me by rank. You do that out of contempt for the desk man?"

Chink smiled.

"Why won't Bozzo's insurance pay off?"

"Tomajz is a railroad man." It was Chink's test clue, to find out how well informed Major Diefenbach really was.

Diefenbach picked it up neatly. "A sentimental Communist from the twenties, then. Even the teens. Ideology all sweet and lacy, like an old-time valentine. So the partisans would laugh at Tomajz."

"He's used to being laughed at, anyway," Chink said, willing to confide now. "I'm afraid my guys are more cutthroats than patriots. Politics is a joke. They're country and small-town thugs, except for Bozzo himself. Bozzo's a city thug."

"Time in federal prison before the war? Regular crime, not political, of course."

"He was a career man in strong-arm robbery," Chink said.

"Standard profile of the idealistic underground leader."

"What Bozzo's bunch needs is a reputation," Chink said. Their little sabotage jobs had been too neat. If you didn't get caught, you didn't get credit. He pointed to Novi Sad on Wally Diefenbach's map. "This is the reason we have Tomajz."

"Rail junction. He marked the charts for you?"

"Otherwise, he's the cook. Bozzo wants the junction, so he got Tomajz." The idea was to do something impressive enough so that the partisans would deal respectfully.

"Do you need Tomajz any longer?"

"He's to help bribe. Otherwise, they all know the country. I know the junction."

"You've been to see it?"

"I counted trains there one night. There were lots of trains."

"It must be a two-day hike. You went alone?"

Chink nodded.

"Tell me, why would Tomajz put out the word on your friends?"

"Hates them. They ride the poor old guy a lot. And I suppose Jerry pays well."

"Looks like the cat's up the Christmas tree," Wally Diefenbach said, and looked across the desk at Chink with the magnified eyes. He was smiling. Wally's hand moved and settled on the strongbox that Chink had come to Italy to get. It held British pounds, German military scrip, and $1,500 in small American bills. They were captured bills, superb counterfeits manufactured in the German mint. "What were your plans for this box, Chink Peters?"

The pounds and scrip were for payroll, the counterfeits to bribe railroad guards, who were Croatian troops at the junction under German command, and a general called Nedić.

Chink said: "The box? Chain it to my wrist. Those guys are all money mad."

"Don't you think you might just chain it to old Tomajz, after payroll?" Wally asked. He cocked his head and smiled.

Chink thought a moment. Then he nodded and said, "That's smart."

"Of course, you'll have the box locked and keep the key."

Sirens sounded outside the headquarters building, and bells rang. Wally stood.

"If Tomajz tries to go off with it, Bozzo's boys will take him," Chink said, standing too. "Is this an air raid?"

"If Tomajz stays, he won't be doing any harm," Wally said. "Come on. You'll like my shelter. But afterward you may want to spare Tomajz the long walk back?"

It was a token air raid, small planes with light bombs, but once they reached the strong room Major Diefenbach used as an air raid shelter, he and Chink stayed awhile. The office day was over, and Wally kept ice in the safe and champagne on the ice.

"From Algiers," he said. "It's French, prewar, and legitimate.

Useful in some kinds of interrogation, nice for morale when one of you comes in. Or do you prefer the PX system out there?"

Chink thought it fine, sitting there secure, sipping champagne, hearing the muffled explosions of bombs and antiaircraft, outside, listening to his new commanding officer talk. Chink was in a clean uniform, he had had a real shower. There was even a record playing. It seemed perfectly correct, when they had finished the bottle, for Major Diefenbach to get out two more, hand one unopened to Chink, and say, "Raid's over. Come along, young Chinkie. Let's see what sort of dinner we can scrape up in Naples."

He had a Welsh driver, an open staff car, and friends in Naples named Anne and Bibi, from the bridesmaid-usher circuit in New England, he explained, just arrived with the Red Cross. What he managed to scrape up to eat, at a blacked-out restaurant on the Neapolitan docks, where the waiters were in evening clothes and the tablecloths were white, was baby octopus, noodles with fresh clam sauce, and roast wild duck. The salad greens were flown in from the Canary Islands. Wally had his own wine in the cellar, but the most exotic thing was to see civilian men and women dining quietly in a room in which Wally was the lowest ranked officer except for Chink himself.

Chink got half drunk, and worried for a while that he might not be able to keep the rich food down. That passed. There was a trio of violin, mandolin, and tenor, and he worried that the others would realize he was tone deaf and unable to enjoy the street songs as much as they did. Then he had a brandy, and stopped worrying about anything.

When they took their dates back to quarters, the one named Anne clung to Chink while Wally smiled benignly, and Chink nearly wept to see her go in.

"There'll be another time," Wally said. And then, briskly, when the door had closed: "So much for sweet smiles and tinkling laughter. Time for round arms and heaving bosoms," and took Chink and the Welsh driver off to an amazing brothel in a Neapolitan *palazzo*, which was like a fancy club and in which the madam was called "Contessa." At first Chink wasn't sure he wanted to accept Wally's final treat, but then he drank yet another brandy and saw no reason not to.

He drifted off to sleep in the back of the staff car on the way to

Castellammare, with Wally and the driver singing Welsh songs in front, thinking that the evening was the best time he had ever had in his life.

The next morning he woke feeling relaxed but not much like going back underwater right away. An orderly brought coffee and mail to him. Wally Diefenbach had sent a courier to the British Army post office at Bari to get Chink's mail.

There wasn't a lot: school alumni news, a letter from a friend in the Navy, one from a girl he didn't know very well, one from Mrs. Strawbridge, who wrote regularly to all the servicemen in her address book, and one from home. His mother couldn't write, of course, but dictated letters to Libby Strawbridge, Curt's younger sister, to which Chink's father would scrawl postscripts, in mixed Russian and English.

Chink opened the envelope addressed in Libby's handwriting first, expecting the stilted phrases into which a fourteen-year-old would transpose his mother's broken English, meaning to answer it before he went back in the evening to board the submarine at Bari. It was not dictated by his mother. It was from Libby Strawbridge herself:

"Dear Chink: Your mother doesn't want to tell you, because she says there is nothing to do about it, but I think and Mama thinks (my mother, that is) that you should know that they have put your father in jail. . . ." The rest was unspecific. He tore open Mrs. Strawbridge's letter, and felt frantically confused when it said nothing about jail, though it did explain that Chink's father had been in a tavern fight and hurt the other man, but things were going to be all right. Then he noticed that Mrs. Strawbridge's letter was dated a day earlier than Libby's. The police must have come for his father after the mother's letter was written and mailed. He went back to Libby's and gathered that Tony Peters had been booked for what was spelled "assalt."

As they were checking packs, Bozzo, speaking Serb, made a joke which Chink couldn't follow, and old Tomajz, waiting with the strongbox under his arm and chained to his wrist, turned away. His hair and mustache were yellow-white, and he had no upper teeth. He was a simple man. Chink liked him.

Bozzo's mustache was brown and bristly.

All the Chetniks laughed, and Bozzo repeated his joke in clumsy German: How can you tell which is the women's room in a Communist meeting place? It's the one without mirrors.

The scout asked Tomajz if he had his picture of Trotsky in the strongbox, and the others laughed again because the picture Tomajz kept by him and must now have somewhere in his pack was of Lenin, of course, not Trotsky.

Chink and the scout went out of the cave first.

The scout started down the trail between the big rocks, to where it entered a defile between cliffs. There was frost this morning, but no snow yet.

Chink stayed at the cave entrance, watching the eleven other men come out. There were a couple of riflemen, then the four with heavy packs of explosives. Then the machine-gun team, the gunner with the old air-cooled light barrel, breech, and stock, and two ammunition carriers, one of them with the tripod. Chink had trained them as well as he could, but they hadn't had much practice firing.

The last to come out were Tomajz with the strongbox full of fake money for bribes, and Bozzo, who had the only American M-1 rifle, and a dozen rifle grenades hitched around his belt. The group formed.

"You go walk with the scout," Bozzo said to Chink. "You know the maps better than he does." He winked at Tomajz's back. "I'll stay close behind."

Chink nodded. He was carrying a tommy gun and had the Springfield sniper's rifle tied across his pack. He moved past the men at a trot, and into the defile. It wasn't a large group, for the trouble they had made the Germans. He was proud of them. There were two boys, one nineteen, Chink's age, the other younger, whom they were leaving behind to clean out the cave and move their gear to a different one, to which they'd return.

Chink caught up with the scout, and followed him down the path through the defile. At the end of it they would turn northeast, across the top of a wooded slope. At the base of the slope was the road to town, eight miles off, where a German patrol was based, but as long as they went through the woods on high ground they could walk by again, as they had many times before, even if the Germans were on the road. They knew from people in town that the Germans were waiting for additional firepower, some kind of mortar group, to take their cave. There'd been a skip bombing while Chink was away. Chink wondered if old Tomajz knew where the new cave was.

The scout stopped at the end of the defile to look and listen. It seemed curious that the Germans hadn't set up to contain them, but the German patrol was undermanned and had other groups besides Bozzo's to worry about. It was first light as Chink came out into the forest, moving quietly, and the sound of birdsong was normal. It would not have been if there were Germans in the woods nearby.

The scout turned and started north. Chink took a step to follow him and paused, thinking back through the names, faces, and equipment of the men who would be coming along out of the defile, one by one. He pictured the first nine. Then his count stopped at Tomajz, with Bozzo close behind, and he thought that Bozzo was a scum. That he, Chink, was a scum. That Major Wally Diefenbach was a great horned scum. That Anne Goulay of the Red Cross was lovely. And that Bozzo could easily let old Tomajz run off, down through the trees, fire a useless round or two, and divide the money in the strongbox with Tomajz later.

Chink stepped aside. He stood behind a boulder, just south of where the defile opened, and set his pack down. He watched the explosives carriers file out. It was light enough to tell which was which now, the crooked pork butcher, then Tetracek the blacksmith, who could lift great weights, who sang, who had killed a priest once and had been an outlaw longer than any of the others. Milow the hunchback. They were all scum, and Chink loved them intensely. He watched the machine-gun team appear, one at a time, and turn north.

He waited. He looked at the barrel of the Tommy gun, and noticed that the drops of oil were still slightly congealed on it from the morning chill. There was a new scratch on the stock.

Tomajz came out. He didn't hesitate, or pretend to turn. One step out of the defile and the old man started running, straight downhill, the pack swaying, the strongbox under his arm. Chink had him in the gunsight at the first step, counted three slowly to give Bozzo a chance to shoot first if he was going to. When no shot came, Chink fired a burst into the old man's left side from twenty yards. As

Tomajz went down, Chink stepped out from behind the boulder and fired again, at the legs, and the body rolled a half turn.

Much too late, there were three shots from the M-1, and Bozzo walked out of the defile, grinning.

"Good," Bozzo said, in his terrible German. "You got him first."

The man with the tripod came running back to find out what the shooting was about.

"Chink got the rat, trying to run off," Bozzo said. This was in Serb, of which Chink, this time, could get the meaning.

"Tomajz," the tripod man said, and spat. Chink was glad the tripod man was there.

Chink knelt by Tomajz's body. This third man he'd killed was the first he'd known. He'd also known he would have to do it if no one else did, and expected to be upset. It depressed him to realize that he was almost indifferent. He unlocked the strongbox and took out the counterfeit bills. He knew Bozzo was watching closely, and was glad again that the tripod man had come back.

He stood and, quite deliberately, handed the bills to Bozzo.

"They'll be safe with you," he said, straight-faced. "We'd better move. There was a lot of shooting."

"Too much," Bozzo said. "I would have killed him with just one shot."

The tripod man was emptying Tomajz's pack on the ground, taking out British tinned cheese and biscuits.

"You want his ears?" Bozzo asked Chink, still grinning, showing his knife.

"Help yourself," Chink said. "I'm not hungry." He trotted off towards the head of the dispersed column, stopping off for a moment at each group of men to tell them what had happened. If Bozzo took off now, Chink thought, he could probably run the railroad job himself, though they would miss the rifle and the rifle grenades.

Bozzo didn't take off, and nobody ran the railroad job. They never reached the junction. They walked until early afternoon, slept, and started out again, walking the sidehill paths in the dark. By two the following morning, they were starting down, towards Novi Sad, and at three they stopped for an hour's rest. At five the column of eleven began to move again, first the scout, then Chink, then Bozzo, with the rest spread out behind over a half mile.

As dawn came a small valley opened out in front of them with a stream running through it beside which, under the brush along its banks, they planned to spend the day. They had used it before. It should be a safe camp.

The scout had stopped fifty yards up, to kneel and look into the valley. Chink stopped. Bozzo came up from behind and took Chink's arm.

"Listen," he said. Chink listened. "No birds."

"Pretty early."

Bozzo raised his arm to stop the man fifty yards behind himself, and said to Chink, "Let's climb up. You and I."

They scrambled upwards, climbing rocks, finding a small tree here and there to pull up on. The climb took twenty minutes, and the day grew lighter. They found a ledge with a good view of the valley, and stretched behind a big rock on its edge.

Their other men were all in view, now, below them to the right. Bozzo had field glasses and looked down at them.

"Stupid," he said.

"They're good men," Chink said, looking at them, too, through his own glasses, but Bozzo was right. Instead of staying dispersed along their line of march, waiting for a signal to close up, the men were continuing to walk until each arrived at where the scout had put his pack down. They were lighting cigarettes, visiting. Chink's comrades.

Bozzo screamed. It was a scream meant for the men below to hear. Chink turned his glasses out across the little valley and saw what Bozzo saw. There was camouflage netting along the brush line.

Then he saw the movement of men behind the netting. In about the same instant that it started firing, he located the first of two heavy machine guns. The second joined in, in a textbook cross fire. They were big, fifty-calibre, water-cooled guns.

"Bastard," Bozzo said. "Tomajz, the bastard."

Already the scout was hit and two of the explosives carriers. The riflemen had taken cover, right and left of the path, and were returning fire, and the other two explosives men, underarmed with old carbines, were prone and firing, too. Chink saw one of them get hit. Then he saw their own machine-gun team, behind a boulder, setting up the light thirty-calibre, but it wasn't going to do any good.

Chink unslung the Springfield. The range from high up was extreme, but he thought if he could set the scope up enough he could help. It wasn't until he had one of the people behind the net in the scope that he realized why Bozzo kept cursing Tomajz. The gunner on the other side wasn't wearing a German helmet. He was wearing a partisan cloth cap. Tomajz had got his message out, all right.

Bozzo, lying prone, ceased firing and fixed a rifle grenade to the muzzle of his M-1.

"Going down to the other side," he said. "You in range?"

Chink tried a shot at the cloth cap. "No," he said. "Too far. I'll raise up more."

Bozzo peered around their rock parapet, pointing to a ridge that curled towards the partisan position, over to the left. "I'll go there," he said. Their own machine gun was in action now. Sighting through his scope again, Chink thought he saw a partisan get hit and fall back. He fired another round and thought it reached the netting, but he couldn't be sure. He felt totally ineffective, and angered that they were fighting other Yugoslavs.

"I can't cover you," he told Bozzo, but Bozzo was already up and running, fairly well able to stay out of sight. Chink returned to his scope. They were five minutes into the useless firefight, and half their men were already gone. He looked down at the machine-gun team he'd trained. They were shooting singles and short bursts, saving ammunition.

He turned his eyes to watch Bozzo. Bozzo had slid and scrambled down already to where he could make his dash across the ridge line. When he made it, Chink would lose sight of him. Chink watched. Their own firing line was shooting quite deliberately now, and to some effect, but there was a change in the noise level. Chink saw Bozzo up, running, and over the ridge before he realized what the change was. Across the field, the heavy machine guns had stopped.

For a moment he felt exultant. He couldn't see how, but it seemed as if his comrades below had won an advantage and might, with Bozzo in position, at least gain retreating room. He put the ineffective Springfield aside, glassed the partisan position again, and had turned the objectives back on his own surviving six when there came a rending sound, followed by an extraordinary concentration of explosions at the Chetnik position and the six were gone, the rocks they'd been behind shattered, the whole position nothing but dust and smoke. He turned the glasses back towards the netting, and saw a bank of muzzles pointing upwards, rising together, and recoiling. There were flashes and the same sound of rent air, and the devastating explosions at what had been the center of their position. This time some of their own explosives went up, too, and Chink understood why the partisans were not bothered with trying to save the stuff for salvage. If they were getting equipment like Russian artillery rockets, they wouldn't care about the primer cord and dynamite in four field packs.

He was watching the smoke and dust clear, looking for any sign of survivors, when the last thing happened. There was a light pop, and then another. He looked at the partisan position, and saw yet a third rifle grenade go off in it. Bozzo had got close. Then he saw the rocket launcher reappear, swing, fire, and recoil, and Bozzo, somewhere behind the ridge, out of Chink's sight, must have been obliterated, too.

It had been quiet for half an hour when the partisans showed themselves, just two at first, running out, going prone, testing the situation. But there was nothing left of the Chetniks except the little, light machine gun down there, lying on its side.

Chink spent the day on the ledge, out of sight. In the late afternoon, he realized they had the ledge under observation. When night came, he left most of his equipment and spent a long time going down, not to where the Chetnik position had been, but to the ridge Bozzo had used; Chink crept east to the stream and north along it for a way before he started back, southwest, walking and often running out of Yugoslavia towards Italy.

The weather turned cold while he travelled, and on certain days he went without food. He had a fall and a slide one night that banged up his right shoulder quite badly, and his shoes wore out. If the remembrance of good men gone, the ones he'd lived and fought with, slowed him down, the need for news of his father got him going again. It took him twenty days to reach the coastal town where he'd formerly been met by submarines, and found the runs had been discontinued. He bought a boat, and sailed himself across to the Italian coast, five rough days and nights. At Bari he was able to requisition a motorcycle to ride to Castelammare, though the British captain, a man Chink had served under formerly, wanted him to stop for medical attention. Chink compromised with him on a night's sleep.

He was still extraordinarily tired when he arrived at eight on a cloudy morning, but convinced that it was very important that he tell Major Diefenbach about the kind of Russian equipment he'd seen in use by the partisans.

When he had, he said: "The rest of it's a pretty sad debriefing, sir. Can it wait until I see my mail?"

"Way ahead of you, Chink. Your mail's waiting, and so's a friend who's holding it for you."

He opened the door to a connecting office, and there was Curt Strawbridge, wearing first lieutenant's bars and infantry insignia, standing by the desk. Wally closed the door behind him, and Curt came forward. He and Chink hugged hard, and it was almost unnecessary for Curt to say:

"Your dad's dead."

"Yep." Chink felt tears in his eyes, and turned away to hide them. "And I'll bet he was wrong, too. All the way. Wasn't he?"

"Not according to the way Tony Peters looked at things. I got a copy of the police report."

"Yep."

"The guy he beat up was a local. Service manager at the Buick place."

"Foster, the fat man."

"Mother'd put the Packard up and bought a little Chevy to save gas. Foster kept finding stuff wrong with it, and charging like hell to fix it. Maybe he was right. Mother knows nothing about cars. I don't think your dad did, either. . . ."

Chink shook his head. "Just how to wreck them."

Curt had filled out. He still had his Irish setter look, but it was sleek and capable now, not puppylike. "Cap's in Washington, partly at the War Department, partly in the hospital. Your dad went down to see him, and then to check on things at the breeding farm. When he got back to Princeton, Mother told him about another big repair bill. Your dad was outraged that she'd paid it. He went down to the tavern where Foster hangs out to have a word with him, about crooked mechanics and helpless women. They were hot words, but it might have blown over. Except that Foster made a remark about your dad and my mother. I guess we both know there was something to it."

"Curt?"

"Not recently, but yes. I knew about it when I was a kid. I thought you did."

Chink could only shake his head.

"Your father had to fight for the lady's reputation, didn't he? Especially since the slander was true."

"Yep," Chink said.

"You want to hear it all?"

"Yep," Chink said.

"He bashed up Foster pretty thoroughly in the tavern, and a couple of bystanders, too, just for the hell of it. Then he went home. The police came for him next day, and I guess he didn't exactly go quietly. They kept him in jail overnight, waiting for Mother to get a lawyer down to negotiate about bail. First thing next morning, they brought your dad some breakfast and stuck it through the bars. He grabbed the plate and threw it back at the guard who brought it. It hit the bars and splattered the man's uniform. So then three of them came back with a mop, and told your dad to clean his cell. He waited until they opened the door, because the mop head wouldn't fit between the bars, and rushed them. He grabbed the mop and whipped them with the handle. I guess there were some others in the squad room. All the heroes who aren't in the army because they're local cops and wardens. He ran through, and they went after him with riot guns, sawed-off twelves. He was strolling down the courthouse steps by then, and they yelled at him to stop. He turned and charged back at them with the mop, Chink. They cut him down."

"Yep," Chink said. "Yep." He couldn't help it. He thought of Tomajz. He knew the old railroad man, with whom he'd lived, beside whom he'd fought, had not turned back towards him in the forest. He knew he'd fired a Thompson submachine gun, not a sawed-off twelve. But in that exhausted moment and for years, in waking dreams and times of pain, it seemed the other way.

"Father couldn't stand not being in this war," he said at length. "How's Mother, Curt?"

"Nobody can tell," Curt said. He was wearing campaign ribbons and a Silver Star. He'd been furloughed from West Point, gone through O.C.S., had an infantry platoon in North Africa and then the company. Now it was a staff assignment in London. When he'd learned of Tony Peters' death, he'd got in touch with Wally. When he'd learned of Chink's reaching Bari, he'd got a pass, and hitched a night flight to Italy. "Wally Diefenbach's working on getting a compassionate leave for you, Chink. Cap's after them in Washington. You'd better go see how your mother is."

He sat in the feed stall on the afternoon of his first day alone on the quiet boat in Honolulu, remembering the compassionate leave as the strangest time of his war. It was too hot to sit outside, and the heat was making the horses lethargic. He had closed *A History of the Crusades,* marking his place after the destruction of Conrad III's army by the Turks at Dorylaeum. He looked at the reproductions of drawings from the Ingres portfolio he had bought in San Francisco, now taped to the steel back wall. The wall was curved and gave the figure studies an odd additional dimension.

It had all been so familiar, he thought. So quiet and so altered by Father's absence, Cap's absence, Curt's absence, my visit to a world to which I might belong but with which I was so greatly out of phase.

His mother had been all right. Young Libby Strawbridge and her mother did Aksinya Peters' shopping for her. They drove her places now and then, visited often, played cards, and drank tea. After her son had been home two days, Aksinya had told Chink in her comfortable, grammarless Russian how she felt:

"Your father lived longer than such men used to, Charles. When I was a girl, they were always killing one another in duels. They had accidents on horseback. There were skirmishes and wars." Then she told Chink what she wanted: "I am ready to go home now, Charles." She meant to Lake Baikal, as if she had been away not for twenty-two years but for a month or two of touring.

Home was not a stone gatehouse in New Jersey, but the village of salmon fishermen where her father had been headman and her sisters still lived. Until the war they had written back and forth, several times a year in the odd, vertical Buryat writing. The village letter writer addressed the letters to Aksinya in Russian. Chink addressed his mother's replies in Russian and English. Photographs had sometimes been enclosed, and sometimes the letters had got through.

"After the war," Chink said. "Perhaps there will be a way."

"I have money from your father's life insurance. And there is some for you."

"You'll need it, Mother," Chink said. The allotment he'd already arranged to make her from his army pay would all have to go to meet the mortgage payments on the gatehouse.

When Aksinya went to bed that evening, Chink went over to the Strawbridge house to borrow books and see the pictures. His Seurat girl didn't seem to mind having been left behind with the other women. He stayed there in the library where it hung, looking and browsing for quite a while, until Libby Strawbridge came in to say that her mother was in bed, and Chink thought he'd better leave. Libby at fourteen was gangly and curious, blue-eyed, muscular. She was like the girl riding students of five summers past who had tormented Chink, the boy riding master.

She sat close, on the arm of my chair, he remembered. I thought of telling her about Anne Goulay, the Red Cross girl in Italy, but there was nothing to tell yet about Anne, and so I said good night, and I will go to the Honolulu library now before it closes.

He left the boat then, and went to read about what had happened to Wally's girls, in *The New York Times*. There were many stories, which he read in order, but learned nothing that he didn't know except that Mary, whom he'd called Mike, had been studying political science, and Wendy art. There was also a piece about the girls' father, under the heading "Man in the News," which said that Ambassador Diefenbach had, in recent years, been considered for appointment as Secretary of State by presidents of both parties. There was a picture of Wally. He looked distinguished. There was a picture of the Greenwich Village house, and one of each of the women who survived: Lydia Paul, Olive Dahlke, Vivian Martin, Susan McGrew, and April Dorsey.

A week after Chink returned to Italy, Wally Diefenbach asked him if he'd be willing to go into a prisoner-of-war camp, in the role of a Yugoslav fascist prisoner of high rank, to fight a German officer.

"He's a most ferocious colonel," Wally said. "He's got the other prisoners so scared, Intelligence can't get anything out of them unless you're fascinated by serial numbers. But if he should get whipped, man to man . . . he'd be in a punishment cell. You'd be locked in with him, being punished, too, unruly Croat that you are. No one could interfere."

"You want him beaten up?" It didn't appeal much to Chink.

"Would the arms of Judy Garland be softer?"

"Is that authorized?"

"That could happen."

The man was out of condition, twice Chink's age, and undernourished. Chink felt distaste for inflicting the punishment of an actual fight, and killed him quickly, using the carotid arteries, while men behind other bars screamed at him.

Chink was sent with some Sicilians to Sicily, to make sure of the assassination of a bandit who was said to be hiding German operators for pay. Chink did the shooting. He was guided behind lines on an errand of anticipation to Florence. In Dante's city he missed his shot, but one of the guides managed to get the target man with a knife, when Chink's second shot dropped the bodyguard. Chink took a couple of knife wounds himself in the melee, and did some hospital time, during which he became the author of a pamphlet on guerilla tactics in Yugoslavia, dictated to a severe young woman who was a WAC and seemed frightened of him. During convalescence, he requalified with a handgun, working at it until he was shooting Expert again.

Headquarters moved to Rome. Chink was in an advance party when the city was taken, charged with capturing a certain official wanted for questioning, but they got the wrong man. A few weeks later, wearing civilian clothes, Chink shot a man in the head at close range. This, too, was in Rome, and the man was pointed out for him. He didn't know who it was or why. Wally had loaned him to another program officer for it.

Anne Goulay, his dinner date on the long-gone evening in Naples, was in Rome. He got messages from Anne a couple of times, but didn't feel much like seeing her. He did his work, drank, whored sometimes, generally with Wally or with Wally's new aide, who was an ensign named Sam Lowen. The three had an apartment for weekends and Wally paid for the keep of a slim, tempestuous woman there named Filomena who entertained them variously. They had wild times, good times, until it was marred for Chink by the realization that it excited Wally to manipulate Chink into bar fights. One evening when Wally tried to start it, baiting an American Air Force captain, Chink said, "Fight him yourself, Major," and left the place.

It was after he walked out on the fight with the flyer that he called Anne Goulay, and asked to spend an evening with her. Anne was interesting-looking rather than pretty. She had straight dark hair, cut short and parted over a forehead disproportionately wide for her stature, which was small. She had heavy brows, brown eyes, a strong nose, and a very mobile mouth, so that the face was quite animated, but she would not have attracted the whistles of the servicemen except that, between an unusually small waist and slim shoulders, she had large, soft breasts, which were difficult apparently to confine, which would still have looked big on a larger woman, and which seemed almost to embarrass her.

She and Chink had been quite drawn to one another in Naples, but the evening in Rome didn't go too well. The intelligence and intensity she directed at him were focused in a way he didn't understand, so that he found himself resisting. They had eaten in an upstairs restaurant on the Piazza Navona, overlooking a fountain by Bernini, turned off in wartime. They were the last people there, sitting late over brandy.

"What's wrong tonight?" he asked.

"Nothing. Yes, there is, of course. Do you know the things they say about you?"

"Anne, I don't know what you hear. I'm not really allowed to ask you."

"They call you and Wally Murder, Incorporated," Anne said. "They call you Major Wally's Whizzbang. They say he loads you, aims you, fires you, and then the automatic takes over."

"They say, or Wally says?" Chink asked, saying too much.

"He gets the word around, in spite of the rules. You seem to know it. Rocks Rockne and the Gruesome Gipper. That's another one. You haven't heard it?"

"I suppose I have."

"Don't you care?"

"I don't think about it." But he did, of course. Wally's description went, *The devious mind and the steady hand, like coach and quarterback, we operate out of a balance of mutual disdain and grudging dependence.* He wished he could repeat it to Anne.

"Don't you care?" she asked again.

"Should I?"

"I've known Wally Diefenbach half my life," Anne Goulay said. "He's a brilliant, calculating, smirking, fascinating son of a bitch. When we were in college, we used to warn one another against Wally, not that that did him any harm in the sophomore dorm. But he used people. Endlessly. It amuses him. Do you like to amuse him, Chink?"

Chink stood. He'd learned that day that he was to be promoted. Wally was getting Chink a field commission, but Chink hadn't mentioned it to Anne and didn't plan to. "It's not a matter of choice, I guess. Thank you, anyway, Anne." She stood, too. He helped her on with her Red Cross uniform coat, and they went out to the jeep Wally'd got him for the evening.

"At least I feel safe with you," she said suddenly, seized his arm, and pressed close. "Chink, have you ever been really drunk?"

"No," he said. "Naples was about as close."

"I never have, either. Shall we?"

Anne shared a place with her friend Bibi. Bibi was away. Anne and Chink drank half a bottle of raw Italian brandy, and when it was gone, red wine. They got very drunk, and at some point took off all their clothes. Chink later had no real recollection of intercourse with Anne, but he could remember having his face between the disproportionately large breasts, and how thin her legs and hips were, and he remembered that, when he left her at dawn, she whispered: "Good night, Lieutenant," so he must have told her, after all.

Wally set up someone quite important in Corsica. The young aide from the Navy, Sam Lowen, was supposed to go along on the job, but hadn't the stomach for it. It was a botch. Chink shot the Corsican twice, in the head and neck, at some range with a sniper's rifle, but it took the man five days to die. He realized that there was word of that around Rome. He called Anne, but she asked him to wait.

"I can't decide about you," she said, and another time he talked to Bibi, who said Anne wasn't feeling well.

He worked on Corsica again. "Tell me, tell me," Wally said,

when Chink came back from that. It had been handgun work indoors, in an office into which Chink was introduced as a supposed customer for information, and left alone with his target. It had gone all right. "When you're face to face, and he knows," Wally said, "the tension, the trigger, the scream, the spurt, the sound . . . Ah, but you don't think it's good for me to know those things, do you, Chinkleberry?"

"I don't remember things like that," Chink said.

"So careful of my mental hygiene."

"Go to hell, Major," Chink said. He was angry because he had tried to call Anne again, had talked to Bibi again, and learned that Anne had started going out with Wally himself.

"Ah, but she chose me," Wally said. "She came forward. You won't believe it, but I pled your case, all the way to the bedroom. Miss Bibi speaks lasciviously of you, Chinker. Will you not have commerce with her?"

"I'd rather have the jeep," Chink said.

He was tired of Rome and the headquarters people. He drove to Pompeii and bribed a guard to let him take his sleeping bag into a far part of the excavation and spend the night. He made the first of several trips into southern France. Generally it was just to protect money and equipment being carried in, but sometimes other matters were arranged. He knew his colleagues were in awe of him, that some deplored him, some were even afraid of him. There were others who had similar assignments, but Chink knew he was the one who was talked about, and that Wally, and even Anne now, who was practically living with Wally, kept the talk going. Chink was well beyond caring. He spent his leisure time seeing what paintings he could, and visiting Renaissance and mediaeval buildings.

He was very pleased when they left Rome, finally, first for Marseille, then Vichy, where he got his head laid open, losing a fight in the line of duty, then Paris and beyond.

Early in January of 1945, he saw Marston Mooney again.

At a paratroop base in England, they made some practice drops with nineteen other men, American and British. They were not permitted to leave the camp. When they weren't training, Chink and Marston talked about the war. They had liked the Middle East, and talked about joining the Palestine Police, and Chink thought of looking out there for Elena, of whom Marston could bring no news, for she had left Cairo.

One night, late in the month, they put on white coveralls to match snow, strapped on chutes, got into a plane and were flown over Germany to the Schwammenauer Dam. They were supposed to capture the control house to prevent the Germans there from opening the sluices, letting the impounded water flood out in the way of the Allied advance.

Marston Mooney was first out the door. "See you downstairs," he said.

Three noncoms went, and then the Major in command yelled, "Stop. Stop. Abort."

The plane had got low enough so that the flight crew could see that water was already rushing over the fields where the drop point was. Men grabbed Chink, who would have been the next one out. He had heard the order to abort but was going anyway, after his friend and the three noncoms, white shapes dangling under white canopies, drifting down derelict in the cold night to drown. That was three weeks before Chink's twenty-first birthday.

Wally tried to use Chink sparingly in the closing months of the war. Chink was aware that it was partly because Anne Goulay, Wally's confidante and companion, thought Chink Peters a little crazy and possibly suicidal. She might have been right. Chink had an M.P. platoon for a time, and when they cleaned out German villages, behind the main advance, they were pretty bloody about it.

On the Monday before VE Day, Chink was assigned to a medical and military police force sent overland behind what little was left of the German line, to gather evidence and release any survivors they might find at an extermination camp which intelligence reported as inactive. The report was wrong. There were SS troops still there, and some resistance. Chink, on foot, followed a light tank through one of the side gates. He was carrying an ugly little stamped-metal submachine gun, a couple of grenades, and a sidearm. His M.P. platoon was with him, following the tank's slow lead, breaking off in groups of four to go into the empty barracks.

There were carrion dead in piles on both sides of the street. Gas from decomposing bodies stung their eyes.

The resistance here and there was dwindling away when Chink

branched off by himself. He went around one two-story barracks building and then another, off, away from the firing. He caught a glimpse of some sort of courtyard, went flat against the building to the corner, and there were German soldiers, eight of them, breaking down equipment, hurrying to get it out of sight. And a pile of new dead.

Chink started shooting. The men were twenty to thirty yards away. He fired from the shoulder, all fifty rounds, put in another clip, ran forward, and shot the wounded on the ground. He killed all eight, and could not have said whether any of them shot back. Then he ran into the barracks, threw a grenade into the squad room without knowing if there was anyone there, threw in his other grenade, and ran upstairs.

On the second floor was a locked office, with the word *Kommandant* and a name on the sign. He didn't hesitate to wonder whether whoever was in there meant to lock attackers out, or might himself have been locked in by troops who didn't wish to take his orders. He shot out the lock with his .45, kicked the door open, and saw, sitting behind the desk, a thin, grey man, almost the color of the dead, with sparse, pale, curly hair and one arm. His uniform was not SS but that of a German line regiment. There was no weapon in sight. Outside, the sounds of war had stopped.

The grey man spread his single palm out, and said: "*Bitte?*" Please? He was the last man Chink killed during the Second World War. Chink did not stop to wonder whether the grey man was asking for his life or for his death.

Chink was placed in custody. The medical colonel in command of the task force was horrified at him. The operations officer, an M.P. major, said the orders had been perfectly clear, to take all possible prisoners to give evidence. He wanted a court-martial.

Wally Diefenbach thought of something, took it over the colonel's and the major's heads, and, when Chink was released to him, had a tabloid newspaper in German lying on his desk in Strasbourg. Wally was smiling his owl smile, the one for which he used enlarged pupils, and his cherubic face had its pinkest glow of pleasure.

"Occupation time," he said. "You know the word *Fleischwolf*, Chinkle?"

"Meat grinder?"

"*Der Fleischwolf* sounds terrific, doesn't it?" He passed the newspaper over. There was a photograph of Chink, with his eyes narrowed and the word under the photograph. An account in German called his behavior at the camp a "number-one atrocity, a wanton, one-man massacre. . . ."

"It's only a proof," Wally said. "I won't let them distribute it without your permission."

The paper purported to be the work of a defiant German organization dedicated to resisting the occupation. It was to be circulated for purposes of intimidation. There were other horrid acts and scary people described and pictured in it, mostly fictional Poles and Russians and one monstrous-looking Frenchman on a motorcycle who was said to ride the black bike of death.

"I thought we were supposed to be anonymous," Chink said.

"Things leak, crevices appear." Wally smiled. "It's to help create docility in the populace, whom we will protect from you."

"*Der Fleischwolf* beats Major Wally's Whizzbang anyway, Major Wally."

"You like it. You actually like it."

"Makes me sound like a psychopath."

"It'll cost you a couple of medals, a *Croix de Guerre* for sure. Maybe something British. They don't decorate psychopaths."

Chink recognized the negative manipulation, and responded to it anyway: "Use the damn thing," he said, almost automatically. It became the origin of a rumor Chink heard about himself later, that he had turned down a British D.S.C. in bitterness at the death of Marston Mooney.

On the morning of the second quiet day in Honolulu, Chink made Vasco a bran mash, and was pleased to see the stallion eat some of it.

"You've been making my work too easy, boy," he said. "There's nothing to clean up in here." Wally's meat-grinder paper made a lot more mess, he thought. The military government people didn't want me around, and they thought Wally much too clever. They shipped us back to Washington, and we were both delighted.

There was still war in the Pacific, but Washington after VE Day was a soft, southern city of women and cherry trees.

"Think of me as your crown prince," Wally remarked to the city one morning, looking out over it from the balcony of an absent friend's penthouse, in which he and Chink had entertained a throng of people most of the night.

It had been a lazy, confused, festive week, during which Wally maintained that he was not promiscuous, it was true love every night at ten, and one night again at two A.M., when he got up for a glass of champagne, saw a fine brunette, and borrowed Chink's bedroom, leaving a fine blonde sleeping in his own. Chink hadn't found that sort of energy in himself. What he enjoyed that week was sitting up late, relaxed, returning smiles, hearing happy talk, pouring drinks, and knowing he was still alive.

"Everything I want is down there," Wally said from the balcony. "Yearning for me to have it. And what can we do for you, Chinkleberry, Captain?"

Moving to stand beside Wally, looking over the rooftops of the city, Chink said: "A couple of tickets to Vladivostok?" He was leaving at noon for New Jersey.

"One one-way and one round trip," Wally said. "Why not? And then, the Trans-Siberian?"

"To Ulan-Ude."

"Upper or lower berths, sir?"

"It's in the Mongolian People's Republic. It's where we'd be met, I guess."

"How good's your Russian, really?"

"Mixed accents. It worked all right in Germany, once or twice."

"It might be interesting for us, Chink. If we could get you and your mother on a Russian ship. And then again, it might not, but it would be nice for the Mommleberry."

It was a matter of repatriation, as Major Diefenbach worked it out with the Russians. He implied that the American son of Aksinya Peters, a Russian national, was trying to restrain that national, now prosperous and widowed, from returning home. Chink and his mother flew to Guam on a military flight. There were an admiral and his staff on the plane, who apparently concluded that Aksinya, with her escorting captain, must be somebody mysteriously important. The admiral invited them to sit in the front cabin, where Aksinya ran up an enormous score on him at gin rummy.

At Guam they waited for and boarded a slow Soviet freighter which had actually started off before VE Day, with a lend-lease cargo for Siberia.

During the three-week voyage that followed, and to an extent of which Chink was not then aware and at which he later marvelled, Aksinya Peters took her somewhat battered son in hand. Like the American admiral, the Russian sailors treated Aksinya as a great lady which, Chink came to feel, she might have been. Certainly she was a woman of intelligence and feeling, not nearly so unassuming and without self as he had thought. She talked to him, in an almost structured way, first about his father, whom she always called Anton, and with whom she had lived a life of fond forebearance, knowing everything and saying little.

Then she talked about Chink himself, as a child, a boy, and a young man, remembering with him, prophesying, long gentle talks full of reassurance and affection.

"It wasn't what she said," he told Sweet Lorraine, "so much as what she did. My mother mothered me, the way you will that foal. She was too good a Buddhist to like the life Father raised me for, but she soothed me and healed me anyway. And all the time she was showing me the strength in being quiet, and that the best life would be finding peace like hers. At which I cannot say I've had the best of luck, but it hasn't always been because I didn't try.

"I was a hundred when we left Guam," he told Franny Frisbee. "By Vladivostok, she'd got me back to twenty-one again.

"But I never set foot on shore, Piney." When they made it clear that she might board the launch, but I must not, he thought, we hugged, and I was sure I'd find a way soon. Japan would surrender, and the world go back to normal, and I'd visit the big lake, and see my Mongol aunts and cousins, go with Mother to places where the Living Buddha was still worshipped, see the house from which they'd started out, Aksinya and Anton, on a shaggy pony and a black horse named Pavel. . . .

We didn't know there'd be a cold war, he thought. The first

time that I crossed this ocean, the Russians were our dear, new friends.

"Mother may still be living," he told Rebel Deb. "Over on the side that we've been moving towards.

"Letters don't go through, boy, and I'll never get there. Not with the things I've done. Feeling better? Maybe a little? She may not have saved me from a life of folly, but at least she gave me back enough sanity so that I could say no to Wally's wonderful wonderful film deal."

When Chink returned to Washington from his journey to the edge of Russia, the war with Japan was all but over. Wally was well established in the capital with a staff job and permanent rank, Anne Goulay had returned and was working with him, and there was a captain close to them whom Chink hadn't met before, a moving-picture actor whose films Chink had often seen, growing up. The actor had commanded an army film unit in Italy, and been friends with Anne and Wally there.

Chink spent a couple of days, talking with people who wanted to know about the Russian merchant marine, before he met the actor for the second time in Wally's office one morning. The actor's name was Jim. It was the morning after the atomic bombing of Hiroshima. Everybody in Washington was talking about that, except for Jim and Wally.

"Hello again, Chink," Jim said. He was in uniform, but he wore it like a costume. He was a man of considerable charm and exceptional ease. "I've been hoping you'd be along."

"Thanks," Chink said. "Shouldn't it be the other way around?"

"Heard all kinds of wild stuff about you in Italy, and a few more items from Baby Face here."

Chink looked at Wally, grinned, and said: "I'd never thought of him that way before."

"Ever think of writing about the little secret war you two conducted?"

"It's classified stuff," Chink said. "Anyway, I see you have a sample of my prose there." It was the pamphlet Chink had dictated about the Yugoslav guerillas. The army had revised and printed it. "You find that forgivable, you're a kind man."

The actor smiled at Wally. "The voice is terrific, too," he said. "A genuine natural, if that's not redundant. Shall I leave you?"

Wally pursed his lips and nodded, and Jim left.

"What was all that?" Chink asked.

"Sit down," Wally said. "The war ends Monday."

"Make it Sunday if you want to."

"I've got the inside here on the system they're setting up for discharge. You'll be close to the first man out."

"We're required to stay in the reserves, aren't we?" Chink said. "To keep us under discipline. I signed something like that, long ago."

"I can get it waived."

"No need to."

"Good of the service. Maybe psychological grounds."

"Thanks, Major."

"I find this working title pretty awkward," Wally said. "But I haven't told Lord Jim, yet. *The Kid in the Nazi Nightmare*. Too literary, don't you think?"

Chink looked at him.

"Dreadful for a movie. It might do for the book. Then the movie could be called *Nazi Nightmare*. Better?"

"When you get done being playful," Chink said. "You'll probably tell me."

"He sniffs the bait," said Wally. "We twitch the rod."

"If it's writing, I can't. If it's telling tales out of Italy and Germany, it's all classified and I hope it stays that way."

"Parallel tales," Wally said. "Not literal. You've been in the papers here, Chinklebee, while you were gone. They picked up the *Fleischwolf* affair, with admiration. And people have been coming in from Europe with stories to tell about us." He smiled. "You and me. Their stories are mostly parallel, too," he said. "Jim's already got the money for a film."

"What are we talking about?"

"A film, young Chink. About our fascinating selves."

"There must be a way to stop it," Chink said.

"I don't think you understand. Jim wants to screen-test you. He loves your looks for it."

"Sure he does."

"He wants you to play yourself. The kid. The parallel kid."

"You do it, Wally," Chink said. "Let's get some lunch."

"I'd have to resign," Wally said, and for the first time Chink had to suppose that the whole thing was serious. Wally had been in the Foreign Service before the war and planned to return to it, but not before he could be on hand during the reorganization of their branch into a civilian agency. "Believe me," Wally said, "Jim wants the home run hitter, not the old, grizzled, double-talking manager. You willing to give this any thought at all?"

"Dream of a lifetime," Chink said. "I always wanted to be one of those actors who has to stand up on a box to kiss the leading lady."

"We're not talking about a career. At least I'm not. Jim is. Jim thinks you've got it, whatever it is that makes them sit in the dark and grow moist. I'm only talking about one book, one picture."

"Come on, Wally," Chink said. "I'm hungry."

"Hear me out and grow thin. First, you'd get some money. What you need to get moving with. You run with a pretty rich crowd, don't you?"

"I don't know who I run with, Wally, and if what I wanted to do was make a movie, which it isn't, it would be anything but the kind of film you're talking about."

"A little softening there? Flicker? Tiny sparks?"

"Nope."

"What movie would you make, for God's sake? *The Kid Who Went Back to St. Nathaniel's? The Kid Who Won the Big Horse Show?*"

"Maybe a nice comedy about grown-ups," Chink said. "I wouldn't mind growing up."

"You call me childish, I'll reassign you to Iceland for five years," Wally said. "In a childish peeve, okay? Or ram through that psycho discharge. Chinklebutt, I'm going to make a personal appeal. First, I guarantee the good taste of this. We'll have control. Why does it matter to me? Well, obviously there'll be a Diefenbach character in it. The kid's commanding officer. And friend? You know who plays him? Old Jim himself. The ticket buyers might not know who this major's based on, but here in Washington . . ."

"You're making it hard to say no," Chink said. "But it wouldn't be a Nazi nightmare, Wally. It'd be mine, with people paying to peep at it."

"You really feel that way?"

"I really do."

"Suppose it's a matter of duty?" It was Wally's last shot.

"How would that be?"

"There's people upstairs who'd like very much to have you do this. These are the people who are going to the executive and the Congress, about the new agency. We've been like the dear old British, the silent service. America works differently. A splash of glamor about a year from now would help."

"Then I'm sure they'll make the movie."

"It'll be much more authentic with you in it."

"I'm sorry," Chink said, and was. "I owe you a lot."

Wally gave up. "What are you going to do? Go to Yale, study old, forgotten things, and then what?"

"I'd like to have a family and some land," Chink said. "Someplace green and very quiet."

Wally smiled. "With grazing animals, and buildings so old there isn't any record of who built them. And people with manners so beautiful it breaks your heart to hear one say, 'Good evening.' If you find it, let me know. Next problem?"

"Lunch, I thought."

"Not the Strawbridge matter?"

"I guess I shouldn't be surprised at the things you know."

"Nor I at the things you try to keep to yourself," Wally said. "You wouldn't like a hand with the Strawbridges?"

"I've been trying to figure out what I could do. I thought I'd wait till I was out of uniform."

"No," Wally said. "Let's do it now. If you'll permit me. The Army's full of golden boys, but your friend Curt's got the karats. Our little agency that doesn't yet exist needs all the goodwill it can hustle."

"You saw Curt?"

"On his way to Okinawa. And you saw Mrs. Strawbridge over the weekend for a financial discussion, among other things, over cocktails."

"Sherry," Chink said. "I was actually shocked when she told me. I thought Libby was still fifteen."

Libby Strawbridge was, in fact, just seventeen. Her father, Cap, the old general, had died during the war, after a week-long, roaring celebration of the Normandy landings in his hospital room.

Libby was then sixteen and already, according to her mother, out of control. She had a friend ("a town girl," Mrs. Strawbridge said) with whom she would take the train almost daily, from Princeton to New York, and not be back until long past dark. The pair went to Central Park, Mrs. Strawbridge understood, where they met sailors. They went, too, to the Harvest Moon Ballroom, afternoons at first, where Libby ("I don't know where she learned how") won some prizes for jitterbug dancing.

In the fall, Libby refused to return to boarding school, but seemed otherwise to be behaving more suitably. She and her town friend began seeing Princeton undergraduates. These were either boys rejected by the draft or foreign students.

In the spring of 1945, the first of the veterans showed up at Princeton, men who'd been disabled and discharged. Libby's town friend found them scary, and the two broke up. Libby herself started going to New York again, sometimes with a patch-eyed veteran, sometimes with a wild group of undergraduates who seemed to be New York society homosexuals ("Nancy boys," Mrs. Strawbridge called them).

Libby learned to drink, and occasionally spent nights away from home. The only thing that kept her at all healthy, her mother said, was riding, which she did fitfully, expertly, and sometimes with a kind of desperation. But there was no hunt, and not much of a horse show circuit, and the people Libby could find to ride with were not the sort Mrs. Strawbridge knew ("people in the entertainment business, people who go to night clubs"). Early in her seventeenth year, Libby decided she was in love with the drummer in a celebrated swing band, crossed the country with the group, and spent several weeks in Hollywood, and Mrs. Strawbridge thought her daughter might have been pregnant and had an abortion.

There was, in any case, no question in the mother's mind that the brittle crowd Libby played with took some kind of pleasure in corrupting the little Strawbridge girl and, except for the elegant homosexuals, who were on the fringe of this crowd, encouraged Libby in making, just about VE Day, an impulsive marriage.

"I know hardly anything about the young man except his name," Mrs. Strawbridge said. "Eddie Venture. He's supposed to be a singer. Libby's still underage, Chink, and the lawyers say we can have the marriage annulled."

"I see."

"If Libby will cooperate."

That was what Chink knew from Mrs. Strawbridge, who was being protected from the other information Curt Strawbridge had given Wally. Libby had got a letter out to Curt through Eddie Venture's sister, who wanted to see Libby gone. The first time Eddie Venture had beaten her up, Libby had run away and been caught. Now she was locked in. Eddie Venture was teaching the Society Swing Queen the duties of a Catholic wife with his fists. When he went out now, he locked the doors of the Brooklyn row house on the outside, and the phone in a closet. Curt, with a single afternoon on his way between theatres of war, had got Libby's letter, gone to the address, and beat on the door. There'd been no answer.

Curt had left word of this for Chink with Wally.

"I wonder why he didn't just call the cops?" Chink said.

"Publicity."

"Never worried the Strawbridges before. Afraid Libby might get really hurt's more like it."

"Our man Eddie Venture's got one foot in the rackets and the other in his ear," Wally said. He had run a check. "Several cousins on the docks. One parent deceased, father, by gunfire. Nonmilitary. Don't know who deceased him. Making Eddie the head of the household, support of his mother, who probably bangs on Libby now and then, too. Eddie's a dresser, a dancer, a spender. Kid brother in the Army. It should be a cinch."

Chink waited. Wally had the mind for this kind of thing.

"The useful sister's set to let us know when Eddie's home," Wally said. "And what does it mean these days, if you have a relative in combat, and an Army car drives up, and an officer comes to the door? With maybe a noncommittal phone call first, terribly polite?"

"Yep, you're still the meanest man," Chink said, and it worked out pretty much as Wally had it planned.

Wally drove an Army sedan, and double-parked in front of Eddie Venture's house. Chink, in garrison uniform with ribbons and sidearm, got out, marched up the steps, and rang the bell. A dark, hostile, extremely good-looking young man answered the door. Behind him were untidy rooms, a smelly house. Libby's housekeeping, Chink supposed, and said, "I'm Captain Peters, Mr. Venture. You're expecting me?"

Eddie Venture grabbed Chink's sleeve.

"It's about my brother, Captain?"

"May I come in?"

"Please, please."

"I'd like to see"—Chink consulted an envelope—"Elizabeth Strawbridge Venture, please?"

"Her brother? Is that what?"

"I'm here because of her brother, yes."

Chink looked solemn, and the rest was simple. Venture pulled him inside, and called Libby downstairs. Libby was a shock, no gangly, coltish, mischievous charmer, but a pale, fat, listless woman, looking more like an abused thirty than the spirited, go-to-hell seventeen-year-old Chink expected. She was alert enough, at least, not to show she recognized him.

"Major Diefenbach has word for you, Mrs. Venture," Chink said. "He's in the car."

He was armed and ready for whatever Venture might do next, but the young man seemed merely confused. Gravely, Chink escorted Libby down the outside steps, handed her into the car, and closed the door. He walked slowly around behind, got in the other side, and Wally started up and drove slowly away, his face stiff, but singing, so that Eddie Venture could hear it out the open window, the martial music from the *Peer Gynt Suite,* "De-data-de-DUMP-DUMP, data-te-dee."

"Oh God." As they rounded the corner, Libby threw herself onto Chink and shouted, with something like the energy he expected: "Chink, Chink. I don't know whether to laugh or cry." But her voice was raspy, and she smelled stale. He kept himself still for her to crush against.

By Thanksgiving time, during Chink's first term at Yale, Curt Strawbridge was back from the Pacific. Chink visited him and Mrs. Strawbridge in Princeton. Tutoring had got Libby into a junior college in the South, and Mrs. Strawbridge said proudly that Libby had decided to stay at school during the short vacation and study.

It was a low-key visit. The big family place was up for sale.

Cap's lavish last hospital days and wartime inflation had used up a lot of capital. There would be some revenue from the Peterses' equity in the gatehouse for Chink to send his mother. Mrs. Strawbridge planned to keep a house in Georgetown for herself, and for Curt whenever he might be posted in Washington. Libby was to get the horse-breeding farm in Virginia.

"The place you love so much, Charles," Mrs. Strawbridge said.

"Hello, Chink."

It was Libby Strawbridge, sitting in the desk chair in his off-campus room in New Haven, on a late May afternoon when Chink got back from class. Sun through his leaded-glass windows lit her from behind. "Put down your books, and tell me I look nice."

"Libby," he said, somewhat astonished. "You look like yourself." The puffiness and pallor were gone. She had lost thirty pounds. Her eyes were clear, bright blue again, and her skin a lovely, healthy tan. She stood, and stretched back, leggy, high breasted, rather tall, with strong thin hands. Her face had not regained its girlish look, but it was still a face he'd always liked, high forehead, high cheekbones, a wide, rather thin-lipped smile, and marvelously even teeth. She had brown, artfully tousled hair, cut short.

"I've been riding and swimming," she said, pleased with herself. "Do you know what you did?"

He shook his head, but he could feel himself smiling back hard at her, delighted by the change.

"You. You sat cold and still. In that car, rescuing me from awful Eddie's place. I could feel you make an effort not to pull away."

"I'm sorry."

"It's never been out of my mind since, for a minute."

"You hardly seemed to be thinking."

"Taking it in through the pores. Hating it. Hating you. I swore you'd never want to pull away from me again."

"You win," Chink said, finally putting his books down.

"I decided to come be your prom date. I've never been to a Yale prom."

"I'm not sure," Chink said. "But I think the prom's next weekend."

"Of course it is. I wasn't going to take a chance on your already having asked some other dumb girl. Chink?" She crossed her hands at her waist. "I didn't run away to come here."

"Good."

"I'm here by permission, from school and mother. And Curt." She hesitated. "Do I need your permission, too?" She took a step towards him, looking into his eyes, and saw whatever she needed to see, for her arms came up and she ran at him laughing. "Bastard, bastard, bastard." She pummelled him. She kissed him. She pushed and danced, and finally was still enough for him to grab and kiss her, up on his tiptoes while she ducked into it.

The hard embrace turned soft and moved them towards the daybed. He thought of how much more experienced she was than he, though he was five years older. He heard her breathing quicken and knew his should, too. He thought it would in a moment, but that what was about to happen was too predictable. He had not thought of loving Libby Strawbridge as one of life's possibilities before, but now it seemed entirely expected, even the product of many intentions, as he gave in to it.

Her underclothes were fawn colored. She laughed because Chink was wearing olive drab undershorts. She ducked away. "We salute the uniform. Not the man," and stood at mock attention, saluting, in nothing but a garter belt and nylon stockings, outrageously waggling a neat, furry patch of pubic hair at him.

He tackled her and ruined the nylons, and thought, as they scrambled on the bed, that it was fun, that it was certainly possible to love Libby Strawbridge, and started to learn how.

Libby said: "You could have had me anytime from the age of three, you dope. Crush of my childhood, you're my absolute passion now. What took you so long?"

"Being a dope, I suppose."

"Wally Diefenbach wants you in the new agency. Curt says you could switch to regular Army, and get on a preferred list for Staff school. What are you going to do?"

"Learn something. Besides how to hurt people."

"In German, Russian, Croatian, Italian, and a little French," she said. He smiled and acknowledged that he liked studying languages and German mediaeval history. He told her about an offer he had had from the Secret Service, to become one of the men assigned to guard the President. He said he had so much distaste by now for anything to do with fighting that if he became a teacher, he wouldn't even want to coach a wrestling team.

On the *Vesterålen* in Honolulu he remembered talking with the Secret Service recruiter and thought that, in one way at least, his qualifications had been and continued to be perfect. Politically, he was utterly disaffected and totally committed. Raised to think Roosevelt a hypocrite, he had since thought Truman a clod, Eisenhower an ass, Kennedy a show-off, Johnson a liar, and Nixon a creep and would, without hesitation, had he hired on to do so, have given his life, he supposed, for any one of them.

"But speaking as your history teacher, Piney, *Was für Idioten*."

In New Haven, on a soft May postwar evening, Libby Strawbridge said: "I'm funny and sexy. You want to be serious and good. Maybe I'd better stay here and keep an eye on you."

They were married in Washington, between the end of spring term and the beginning of summer school. It was a large-enough wedding to express Mrs. Strawbridge's social self-confidence. Wally was an usher. Curt was best man.

"You do love my silly little sister, Basenji?" Curt asked the day before. They were in the Georgetown house, which was full of familiar furniture from Princeton now.

"I think I do, Strawberry. She keeps me loose, anyway."

"Did you fall or were you pushed?"

"I guess your mother takes credit, but Libby had something to do with it. Your dad wouldn't have permitted this, would he?"

"Why not? You were his other son."

"I was thinking about the Asiatic blood."

"There's a kind of snob so snobby that he knows he's got no equals, so he's democratic," Curt said. "That was Dad. He would have been more put off, I suspect, by someone like Wally Diefenbach because the money's new. As far as genetics go, you ought to see my Aunt Margot. Her father called himself a Creole. She looks like a Turkish harem guard."

Among the wedding presents was a check for $5,000, for which Mrs. Strawbridge must have had to sell a few more bonds. Curt gave them Seurat's little pointillist painting *La Jeune Fille.*

From the beginning, Chink Peters had a certain notoriety among his classmates at Yale. The release of the Nazi nightmare film, of which he was rumored to be the subject, intensified it. His marriage to a Strawbridge increased it even more. He found himself isolated from the life of the university, except in the classroom, until late in the fall when he was approached by some men who wanted to revive the university polo club. They were surprised to learn that he had no horses with which to play the game, but offered to mount him once they had seen him ride. He declined, but agreed to help coach, and he and Libby spent an exhilarating Christmas vacation in Argentina, commissioned to buy trained ponies for the group. During the winter Chink and Libby learned to ski, and loved it. In the spring Libby, who still had a fine dressage horse, moved the animal to a Connecticut farm where the U.S. Equestrian Team was getting organized for the resumption of the Olympic games the following year. There were good mounts in need of exercise and schooling. Libby and Chink rode there every weekend, and Chink was urged to try to qualify himself for the Olympics, in the modern pentathlon.

"I thought I was through with war and games of war, silly guy that I was," he said to Piney Brown. "But that military pentathlon intrigued me. It's a kind of drama, the things a young fellow might have to do to get the message to Garcia, or the good news from Aix to Ghent.

"Ride a strange horse over an unfamiliar obstacle course," he told that strange horse, Franny Frisbee. "Take a long run, and a swim. Shoot your pistol at silhouettes, and have a sword fight.

"They figured I could beat some people at riding, running, and shooting, Vasco. The sword fight was épée, which I'd never done, but I started working on it. I was no swimmer, but there was a coach at Yale willing to help out, and no one doubted I would make the team. I forgot I was already on someone else's team."

Chink had just finished final examinations at the end of his sophomore year when he was called up as a reserve officer, and sent to join Wally Diefenbach in Athens. Libby kept the apartment in New Haven.

A new war, which seemed to Chink politically boring and morally fuzzy, fought mostly by U.S. and Russian surrogates, was in its first campaign, in Greece. Some of Chink's old Chetniks, out of Italian exile, wanted another chance at Tito, who was supplying the Greek Communists. Chink spent the winter partly in the Aegean islands, partly in Macedonia, in and out of Turkey several times, mostly collecting information. In the spring he had a command on the Adriatic side, which penetrated and was withdrawn from Albania, without a fight. He was not directly involved, in fact, in episodes in which people got hurt, except for one bloody, unexpected incident on Corfu which turned into an intense, small-scale firefight. It was fought at night, with flares, small arms, and mortars, and left some dead on both sides.

It coincided, more or less, with the Olympic games in London, which Libby watched that summer, going over with their equestrian team friends. She saw a Swede win the modern pentathlon.

Wally, in civilian clothes with diplomatic immunity, was represented to be part of the U.S. economic mission, and worked out of an office building and a hotel suite. When Chink got in from Corfu, where they'd probably managed to prevent the establishment of a guerilla base, Wally tossed him a box with a Greek medal in it and said, "Next job's Berlin. Had plenty of time to polish your German up there, I'm sure."

"Aren't the Russians planning to invade New Haven?" Chink asked, and tossed the medal back. It was intensely disappointing to learn that he would not be back with Libby, nor in the classroom in September. He'd counted on both.

The Russians were planning a blockade of Berlin, Wally said. The U.S. was planning to meet it with an enormous airlift. Anne

Goulay, who was still attached to Wally, professionally as well as intimately, was there.

"Wally is way ahead of you, Chink," Anne said.

"As usual, you mean?"

"We can get Libby into Berlin," Wally said. "There's a job for her. I thought you might like to transfer for the year to the New University."

Chink was released, for reasons unspecified, from the Army Reserve, and became an employee of the new civilian intelligence agency of whose Berlin activities Wally was in charge. Officially, Wally was again in the Foreign Service, doing political liaison for the Embassy in Bonn. His actual assignment was planning and funding sabotage on the East side, and countering it on the West. There was the usual confusion and misdirection, occasional success and excitement, some incidental violence, and, after several months, an episode that showed the opposition had got Chink identified.

There was a student named Ulfert who was a member of one of several organizations which Chink, through intermediaries, kept supplied with operating money. Ulfert also attended the mediaeval history lectures for which Chink was enrolled. Ulfert was pale, intense, and intellectually arrogant, and had had dinner with Chink and Libby a couple of times.

One afternoon over beers, Ulfert said: "May I copy your notes, please, on the Frederick II lecture? I can't be there tomorrow."

Chink was flattered, said sure, and rode home on his bicycle. He used the bicycle and had got Libby one because there'd been an improperly armed car bomb in their car a day or two before.

Wally thought the bomber had probably chosen the car by mistake for another like it, which was shot up and had a colleague wounded in it, later the same day.

Starting off on the bike to the lecture next morning, Chink had got two blocks from their apartment building when he became suspicious. Ulfert wouldn't want Chink's notes. Ulfert would spit on Chink's notes. It was Saturday and Libby didn't go to work.

Chink wheeled the bike into a U-turn and rode back to their apartment building. Down the block was a Volkswagen, parked with the engine running. Chink turned into a side street, rode around behind the building, went into it by the back door, and ran upstairs.

At their apartment door, he stood against the wall with a drawn gun, listening. The door opened and Ulfert came out a step, looked right down the hall, and then left into the muzzle of Chink's gun. Chink had the index finger of his free hand held to his lips, and a slight smile on his face. With the gun he signalled the young German to keep walking. Pale Ulfert faltered, turned paler, and went forward. Next came Libby with another young man behind her, one arm crooked around her neck, the other holding a knife with its point in Libby's back.

Chink stepped behind the boy, hooking the knife arm and twisting it away, bringing a knee up between the legs and whacking the side of the head with his gun barrel. The second kidnapper dropped, and Chink ran Ulfert down, caught him on the stairs, and knocked him down the rest of the flight, which broke a couple of ribs. The Volkswagen driver got away.

"God, darling," Libby said, not quite tall, angular, mocking, tanned. She could take anything in her long, amused stride. "I thought it was going to be awful Eddie's all over again, but I knew you'd be there. I absolutely knew you would."

They took Ulfert and his partner in for questioning and detention, and went to see Wally, who said okay, it was boola-boola time and wished them a good trip home.

Chink was not permitted to resign from the agency, but he got indefinite leave and finally took his undergraduate degree from Yale at the end of the summer of 1949. He and Libby moved to the Virginia farm to breed and train hunter-jumpers. Chink had some money saved by then with which to buy brood mares. Libby bought some, too.

There were technical things Chink wanted to know. He commuted by car to Blacksburg, a two-hour drive each way, to take the theory and laboratory year of veterinary medicine at V.P.I. He didn't plan to take the second year, which was mostly clinical, economics, and small-animal work, since he didn't intend to practice. This was just as well. The Korean War pulled him out of school again.

He hoped Libby would want to stay on the farm this time, but she had loved the excitement of Berlin and wanted to go with him overseas.

"I adore being kidnapped," she said. "And I won't have you over there rescuing strange women." She also said that she'd been a spectacularly good girl in London during their last separation, in spite of the provocation of being surrounded by a dazzling, international collection of 4,030 male athletes, but shouldn't be left alone again.

He gave in easily because Libby's companionship had come to mean more to him than anything in the world.

They were posted to Thailand, a country which had token troops in Korea. Chink was set up as an exporter of handwoven silks. He felt completely ineffective, trying to work in a country in which he didn't speak the language. When they had been there ten months, Chink shot and killed a prowler in their house one night. Whether the prowler was an adversary or a thief was never determined.

A few weeks later he had to go, secretly and by himself, to Switzerland, where the Thai king was a schoolboy. He felt anxious about Libby. There was a British-educated Indian couple from Assam who lived next door, both physicians, whom Libby and Chink liked a good deal. It was arranged that Libby would stay nights with the Bhuyans.

Libby seemed a little off when he got back from a month in Switzerland, and continued unresponsive and low-key. He was able to account for this, when he'd been back three weeks, by her missing her period. They hadn't planned on having children yet, but he was elated. Libby was puzzled.

"I've done all the things, darling," she said. "I'll have Mike look me over. He'll love it and have to pretend he doesn't." Mike was the male Dr. Bhuyan, and an obstetrician. His wife, who was called Medha, was Libby's special friend and an anaesthesiologist. They were together every afternoon.

Chink went with Libby to Mike's office at the hospital next morning, waited, and was called in rather quickly. Mike was smiling.

"No baby, Chink," he said. "Too much chandoo stops menstruation."

"Chandoo?"

"Opium, darling," Libby said. "I'm afraid Medha and I have been having a perfectly lovely time."

When he realized that Chink was genuinely upset, Mike Bhuyan apologized. He didn't care for opium himself, but thought on the whole it was less harmful than gin, which he liked a lot.

"In Medha's family, they give a little opium to keep the baby quiet," he said. "She's had it all her life."

But he agreed that Libby didn't have Medha's tolerance. When Libby tried to stop and had abstinence problems, Mike and Medha hospitalized her to get her off the drug.

Chink cabled Wally in Tokyo, requesting transfer for urgent personal reasons.

In Tokyo Wally agreed that the Thai mission had been a waste of money.

"I want to leave the agency," Chink said.

"You can't resign. If I discharge you, it'll have to be for some terrible reason, like 'Wife has history of addiction.' "

"I didn't sign on for life."

"Go inactive," Wally said. "Work for us on contract when we need your specialties."

"Meaning?"

"Just language work. Translation, interrogation. Planning."

"I'd rather get out."

"Let's deal. No permanent posting, no combat zone, decline any job you don't like. The contract pay is very high. How long before that horse farm can support you?"

Chink agreed. He didn't want them living on Libby's money. Wally had a surprise:

"I know quite a bit about your horse farm, Chinklebutt. While you were out there fingering silk and shooting the maid's boyfriend, I got married and bought Water Mill."

Water Mill was the next farm over, a large, elaborate horseman's place, bigger and grander than the Strawbridge breeding farm.

"Married?" Chink said, shaking his head. "You and Anne finally did it."

Wally laughed. "I haven't seen Anne since before you left home, though she sometimes writes for money." Anne Goulay, after six years with him, off and on, had gone back to her first sexual preference, which was for women, a particular woman, actually, a writer of children's books who lived in Bucks County, Pennsylvania. Before informing Wally, however, Anne had got herself pregnant. She and the Pennsylvania woman wanted a child to raise.

"So, dear neighbors," said Wally to Chink and Libby at dinner, his chopsticks holding a bit of eggplant tempura raised halfway to his mouth. "When you get home, you will find the girl next door is Natalie Diefenbach, née Natalie Holly, Irish born, Boston raised, Bennington '47, and more your age I confess than that of her doddering, devoted husband."

"Wally!" Libby said. "You absolute sneak. Where did you find her?"

"I went over to Paris for a NATO meeting, and there she was, flinging her skinny body into the most atrocious poses, modelling high fashion."

"She must be lovely. Does she ride?"

"Ready to learn," Wally said. "As am I. I haven't since I was a kid. Will you help?"

"I'm so pleased someone we know has Water Mill," Libby said. "It's got the best trails and all the fox dens in the county."

"Take it slow with Natalie," Wally said. "I imagine she thinks of a den as a place where you go to mother Boy Scouts. At least she's got mothering on her mind. I left her with a little something in the tummy to keep her company."

Hildi said: "I didn't know whether you'd want to see it." It was late in the evening of the first day out from Honolulu. Hildi had left, in an envelope slipped under the door to Chink's stateroom, a copy of a poem she'd found in a New York paper called *The Village Voice*. It was by Lydia Paul, and Chink hadn't really wanted to read it. Its title was "Funeral Poem," and it began:

Mary, when I was sick you brought the book I loved,
Your journal. And I read it. I was moved.
Wendy, a silly picture that you'd drawn.
Dark are the brightest eyes, and the smiles gone.

"Thank you, Hildi," he said.

"I wasn't sure."

"It was nice of you." Hildi had found him standing aft, by the rail. There was a land mass a few miles off to starboard, a deep blue shadow against the dark sky, with a twinkle of lights over it, and clouds moving, their edges backlit by the moon.

"I know it isn't something you want to talk over."

"I was Mike and Wendy's riding teacher, when they were little," Chink said.

"You don't have to."

"I'll tell you what I can, Hildi, but it isn't much and it was long ago."

"I cried for them," Hildi said.

"Of course you did."

"When I realized you'd known them, I cried again. Will you be seeing their father, Chink?"

"I don't know. Things like that have a way of coming around again, don't they?"

She waited.

"He was my commanding officer during the war. We were associated for about ten years afterwards. When I married, my wife and I lived on a farm in Virginia. Wally and Natalie Diefenbach had the place next to ours. The two girls were born there, while we were friends and neighbors. Wally was away a good deal. Natalie, the girls' mother, wasn't very stable. So Mary and Wendy were at our place a lot. And often stayed with us. I drove them to school when their father was away. My wife and I were awfully fond of them. But I haven't seen them. Haven't seen them for eleven years."

"I'm sorry about my curiosity. I won't bring it up again."

"It's all right."

"You sit here every night, don't you?"

"Over on the bale, most nights. Till time to tuck the horses in. It's that time, now."

"May I go in with you?"

"I guess not. I'm worried about Vasco. He still isn't eating, and I want to keep him quiet. But come help lunge the mares tomorrow."

"I wish I had someone to tuck me in."

"Won't Pietr do?"

"Pietr's a child."

He hesitated. Then he said, softly, before he moved away: "I'd be a hell of a disappointment to you, Hildi."

That night he explained to Sweet Lorraine that Mike and Wendy Diefenbach were the closest he had ever come to having children of his own. "Libby and I were the world's least fertile couple. She'd got herself scarred up inside as a kid, and I turned out to have one of the lower sperm counts around. On the Strawbridge Farm we had the tillable ground and the good pastures. You never tasted such blue grass, Sweet Lorraine."

Natalie and Wally had the timber, he thought, and the big house on the hill. Libby hoped Wally'd sell to us sometime, and we'd put the land together. Old Wally had a different idea, of course. Our house was yellow brick, two stories, across a gravel road from the barn and buildings. Big kitchen downstairs, comfortable living room with a fireplace, and a nice spare bedroom with twin beds where Mike and Wendy liked to stay over with us, even when they were tiny. There were three big bedrooms upstairs. I turned the middle one into a great big bathroom. Libby and I had separate bedrooms because we kept such different hours, but sometimes we'd meet in that bathroom and have water fights. I'm sure that sounds stupid. Wrestle around soapy, and rinse off, and one of us would chase the other to a bed, laughing and yelling, but of course we kept the noise down when the little girls were visiting downstairs.

They were there the Christmas they were three and four. Wally was abroad. Natalie was nervous by herself, even with servants in the house. She brought the kids to our place Christmas Eve, and all their presents, but she hadn't wrapped them. Libby and I stayed up and wrapped them. And in the morning, I got to hand out the swag. Stuffed animals, music boxes. Pretty things.

"One summer, Debbie, I tore out the mile of fence between our place and Wally's Water Mill."

Rebuilt it all with rocks and rail. We could jump horses anywhere along the line, and the trail crossed back and forth, and I built jumps on it, piled logs, trimmed brush, made banks and ditches. We spent weekend after weekend with Natalie and Wally. Up at the

Ridge Club, or at our place or at theirs. Wally's chef was trained in Paris, and I used to like to watch him work. Learned to cook pretty well myself. I liked it. Libby didn't much. Anyway, we ate and drank, played with the kids, sat up, went to the club to drink and dance.

". . . I was running Wally's farm as well as ours, and, after a while, a dozen. Heck of a farm manager. I made some money, did some stuff for the agency, and was partners with my wife in the horse business. Long, full, good days, Debbie. Full, good years."

He told pretty Franny Frisbee that nobody ever looked smarter in riding clothes than Libby Strawbridge. "The only thing I didn't like about my wife was the way she sold horses sometimes. High-handed. She knew people liked to say, 'Libby Strawbridge trained it—of course, she's Libby Peters now.' Bam, she'd kick the price up high as it would go. I always liked to set a price and stick to it, tell the buyer what I knew. Libby might just hold back a little piece of information. Like 'Franny Frisbee's a biter if you don't watch out.' But Libby'd say, 'If they don't ask, I don't really care to tell them.' But she was lovely with the little girls, and they adored her.

"Piney Brown. You'll be disappointed to learn that I didn't whack anybody in the whole nine years, except the guy who tried to steal Mike and Wendy's collie."

Natalie phoned in absolute hysterics. I got in the car and picked the guy up when he drove by our place, ran him down, beat on him a little, and took them their dog back.

I forgot what trouble was. A little of this, a little of that, building up. I'd get up early, do farming in the morning, play horse with Libby in the afternoon, get supper, and feel like bed or reading afterwards. Made Libby restless. She'd look at a magazine, or the Washington papers, maybe challenge me to chess or backgammon, but she was rash and generally lost. We won at bridge, so that was better. She was great at playing the boards, see the unlikely chance and take it for extra points. But when I sacked out early, sometimes she'd go to the club to drink and visit. I got used to that. The club had golf, tennis, pretty good food, bar, and a dance floor. The Hunt was there and I was Huntsman. Wally wanted to be Master. He'd got to be a bold rider and had swell horses. Natalie was always timid on a horse. Anyway, that was another part of the trouble. I told Wally not to run for Master. Virginia monopoly. He tried to buy it with a hundred yards of eight-foot chain link fence for a dog run at the club. It didn't work, and he seemed to think it was my fault.

"I've never known when the affair started Piney. Maybe when Wally came back from Budapest. Natalie was halfway off her pretty rocker. Wally'd send for Libby that spring, or sometimes pick her up at the club late at night, to come help with the children when Natalie upset them. So they told me. Of course, another part of the trouble really was the two girls, because they were quite attached to us. And Wally was possessive of his daughters. A couple of times they ran all the way from their place to ours, to come to me or Libby. Anyway, there was that, and Wally and Libby having an affair, and *cherchez le cheval*, too, Piney. I had a little horse named Coker Wally coveted. My best friend Wally, the man from Budapest, seething, and the more he seethes, the less he lets you know it. So all he wanted were my horse, my farm, my wife, and his daughters' affections back. All right, my dear. Vasco's turn for a visit. I may not take him out tomorrow. What do you think? I'll go see him now. Good night."

The body of Vasco, the young stallion, shrouded in a horse blanket with a canvas hood sewn onto it, and weighted with anchor chain, was hoisted by crane and dropped astern the sixth day out from Honolulu.

The canvas for the hood was from the same piece Chink had bought from the purser to make a sling, trying to save the horse from a sudden, severe attack of equine encephalomyelitis.

The incubation period for the disease is one to three weeks, and Chink realized he'd had a feeling of fatality about this third week out of San Francisco, a low-key dread of its coming, since the day of loading. On the Tuesday morning of the week, when he got Vasco out of his stall, he knew from the way the horse led, before he could see him clearly, that the movement in the hindquarters was wrong. On deck, he released the halter and stood back a moment. The colt started forward, his front half working properly, trying to use it to drag his hind hooves along the deck. Then the hind legs crossed, the loin sank. Vasco got one hind leg uncrossed and, trying to move it forward, struck it with the opposite foreleg. Chink moved back to the colt's head, turned, and led him very slowly back inside. Already, Vasco was extending the forelegs in an exaggerated, painful strut, with the disoriented rear legs staggering after them.

Chink got Vasco into the stall, left him, and ran to the carpenter's shop, to which he had a key. He found the piece of heavy canvas, doubled it, riveted in a baton pocket at each end, cut and placed the heaviest dowel he could find in the pockets. He worked as quickly as he could, afraid that Vasco might go down before he could get the sling ready, but when he returned, the colt was still standing. Chink got the sling under the stomach, and ropes, fixed to the dowel ends, up over the steel beam above the stall. He was out of breath from scrambling overhead when he finished, but reasonably sure that Vasco would be kept on his feet. Chink took a little more time making a breast plate and breeching, using more canvas and Vasco's bridle reins, riveting these new pieces to the sling, front and back, so that the horse couldn't slip in either direction. Chink went around next to feel the rear fetlocks. They were very swollen, as he'd expected. Then he visited the mares, one by one, and found their feet all normal.

He got the ship's medic away from his breakfast, and borrowed a human catheter, which looked long enough. The medic came along to help. Cutting a slit in the sling to free the penis, and using warm, soapy water for lubricant, they catheterized Vasco and relieved his swollen bladder.

The urine was coffee colored, and the horse was now sweating heavily, but symptoms were developing so quickly that Vasco had needed no other restraint than to have a foreleg lifted for the operation. Vasco was resting most of his weight in the sling already, though Chink had set it so that it was an inch or two below where the stomach would meet it if the legs had held up.

Chink didn't need help, not even a foreleg up, to use the stomach tube with which he gave Vasco a drenching of saline mixture. Finally, he dosed with sulfanilamide, and had done all he could.

He was exercising Piney Brown when Hildi and Mrs. Bernie came along from breakfast.

"Something's wrong, Chink."

"I've got a sick horse in there."

"The medic told Pietr. Is it sleeping sickness?"

The women wanted to see Vasco, and Chink let them go in. In a few minutes, they came out again.

"The poor thing. The way his lower lip hangs down."

That was a new symptom, but Chink didn't say so.

"Wouldn't he be better lying down?"

"He might go into convulsions and bang his head around if he were down."

"Oh, Chink," Hildi said.

"We'll keep him up, and give him drugs, and hope."

At dinner, the purser presented his bill for canvas, and Bernie said, "People can get sleeping sickness from horses."

"So I've heard," Chink agreed.

"It's nothing to fool with, my friend."

"No."

"You'd better shoot him. We've been talking and that's what we think you better do."

"I see."

"What do you say, Chink? This is serious."

"I'll see, Bernie."

"What about us?"

"The horse still has a chance."

"I don't see that you get to decide," Bernie said. "It's up to the captain to decide."

"Oh, yes," said the purser.

"All right."

"Do we have to go see him? You come with us."

"No, thanks."

"Then Darrell and I and the purser will."

"When you talk to the captain, see if he can't do something about the mosquitoes," Chink said.

"What do you mean? What mosquitoes?"

Darrell said: "He's right, Bernie. That disease, you've got to get it from a mosquito bites the horse, and then bites you."

"There aren't any mosquitoes out here." Bernie sounded indignant about the lack.

The next day, Chink and the medic had to catheterize again, but the penis wouldn't return to the sheath afterwards.

"The retractor muscles are gone," Chink said. "It's called

paraphimosis." He said "*paraphimose,*" hoping that was the German cognate.

In the afternoon, when the neck and pectoral muscles started twitching, and the paralysis was spreading into the forelegs, Chink began to think about the captain's pistol.

He had no drug in the veterinary chest designed to kill. He had seen an old Shetland pony once, its feet so bad they couldn't hold the body weight, dispatched by opening blood vessels. Chink believed the animal had felt pain and fear. He had seen too many other creatures shot to be able to persuade himself that there was any such thing as instantaneous death by gunfire. There would certainly be a fearful prior instant of blast and sear. There was no way to spare Vasco that, though he could, with a tranquilizer, slow the perceptions quite a lot. And then he thought that Vasco was perhaps so tired and had been so sick that, to whatever extent a horse could know of it, the colt might want to die. Vasco could not be imagined as knowing of death as a condition, but he would know about rest and an end to discomfort, and the promise of these might come to Vasco along with the noise.

Chink Peters got the pistol and shot the colt, holding the gun close, six inches above the eyes in the center. He had never had to shoot a horse before, but Hayes' *Veterinary Notes* showed, by a diagram, how to place the shot. Vasco dropped immediately, into the sling.

Darrell had offered to do the shooting. Darrell had worked in a slaughterhouse as a young man, and said he knew how. But it wasn't very complicated, and Chink preferred that Vasco's final image, if the eyes could see and the small brain still register, be that of a face of which the horse was unafraid.

After Vasco's body sank out of sight, Chink Peters went into the stall area, closed the compartment door behind himself, and took down the Ingres drawings from the curved steel wall of the feed stall. He took them down carefully, and replaced them in order in the portfolio. He put the recollated portfolio in the veterinary medicine chest to keep it clean, since he did not wish to go out on deck to put it in his cabin.

Natalie Diefenbach said she didn't feel like riding.

"Please, Mommy," Wendy said. "Coker's such a smooth horse."

Natalie smiled. It was late afternoon in the Peterses' paddock. Chink had brought little Coker, his personal horse, out under saddle. Coker was fifteen hands, almost black, with impeccable gaits. Chink had agreed to teach Natalie to jump that spring, and been working her on Coker over the cavalletti. She was now about to take her first small jump.

"Darlings." Natalie smiled at her daughters. She was a willowy, fey, ash blond woman with a flickering smile and eyes so large as to seem eerie sometimes. "Your silly mother had a drink for courage and turned into peepee pudding instead."

"Aha," Wally said. "Yes, indeed. We enjoyed putting on the beautiful canary breeches, and our lovely custom-made black boots with the brown leather tops. Yes, we did. And our new silk ascot from Paris, with the periwinkles winking . . ."

"Listen to your father being helpful," Natalie said.

"Tell the photographers she's ready," Wally said. He turned to Libby, who was sitting on the paddock rail. "Is her makeup right, Flash? Should she hold the lustrous hunt cap or wear it? Think we'll get a cover?"

"You see, girls," Natalie said, "your father had a drink with your mother, but I think he may have had some others, too, don't you?"

"You'll love jumping," Mike said, seriously. She was nine, and her face a darker, more serious version of her father's, pug-nosed and open. Wendy, a year younger, looked more like Natalie, but Wendy was a young sprite, freckled, healthy, and giddy, her mother a slightly ravaged one.

"We'd better get this horse out of the picture," Wally said, walking over to Chink at Coker's head. "He'll ruin everything. You know how horses are."

"Why don't you come over in the morning, Natalie?" Chink said. "We'll do it without the audience."

"A sweet, solemn suggestion," Wally said. "From a strong

man, for a lovely lady. Come on, Libby. Let's take the girls and leave our mates to their tender lessons."

Libby slipped down off the rail. "Let's all go make a bowl of rum punch. It's been a day."

"I'll put Coker up," Chink said.

"Rum punch," Natalie said, "will really bring out Wally's charm, don't you think?"

"Piteous creature, married to a sullen drunk." Wally shook his head. He'd gotten a little heavy as he passed forty. His saddle was on the rail, near where Libby had been sitting. It was a new Kieffer. He walked to it, and started working off a stirrup leather. His feet were too big for normal stirrups. "Wait, Chinklebird."

"What, Wally?"

"Let me show this virtuous lady how her inebriated husband can take the little black horse over the big white jump."

Mike and Wendy had started to leave the paddock with Libby, moving towards the yellow brick house across the gravel road. They stopped together, outlines softened by the dust motes they had raised in the slanting beams of early evening sun.

"Sorry," Chink said, as softly as he could.

"What?"

"You're a big man. This is a boy-sized horse."

"You ride him. Libby rides him. Natalie, of course, rides him best of all."

"We could ride him," Wendy said.

"Darling, your mother is about to scream," said Natalie.

"I weigh a hundred and thirty-five," Chink told Wally.

"And I'm the great, fat camel who's going to break the fragile little straw back? I see it. I see it." Wally had one stirrup leather off, and turned to the saddle to get the other one. "I'll diet fiercely. Water for dinner, one glass only. Lose ten pounds, twenty, thirty. Roadwork." He began jogging in place. "Huff, huff, huff. Rubber suit. Up to my neck in the manure pile. Chink, let me just get on and demonstrate that I can ride the straight line, so the woman will stop laughing her cruel, beautiful-woman laugh. . . ." He was at Coker's saddle now.

"I'd rather you didn't," Chink said, still very softly, but he supposed the women heard.

Wally stopped, turned, and stared at Chink. Wally wasn't wearing his glasses, and the naked eyes were pale blue. Wally pursed his lips, nodded, turned back towards the paddock rail, crossed to his own saddle, and with an appearance of immense concentration replaced the stirrups, picked up the saddle, and left the paddock.

"Come on, girls," Libby said. "Let's be soothing."

By now Natalie's oversized eyes had tears in them, though she wasn't sobbing. "I wish he'd just beat me, like other men," she said. "Do you beat Libby, Chink?"

"I'll put the horse away now," Chink said.

"Maybe you should," Natalie called after him. "With your eyes closed, of course, to keep it sporting."

Chink didn't see or hear from Wally again until the middle of the week. It was a relief. Wally'd been petulant all spring. There was the matter of the Hunt election Wally'd lost. There was another, about a horse, an Irish hunter Chink had located for sale, intended to buy, and mentioned one Saturday night at dinner. Wally bought the horse himself on Sunday without telling Chink first, paid too much for it, and then blamed Chink for the price. There'd been an elaborate weekend party at Water Mill in March, for Washington people, to which Libby and Chink were not invited. Chink was pleased. They'd had the girls as weekend visitors, which he preferred, but he supposed Libby minded.

"I think it's the state Natalie's in," Chink had said. "When we're around she feels free to be erratic."

Libby had smiled, kissed Chink, and said: "You never miss a chance to take care of me, do you? We could have gone."

Chink saw that she and Wally must have talked it over.

When Chink did hear from Wally, during the week after the incident with Coker, it was by phone and on business, an offer of a week's work for the agency in Santiago, Chile, which Chink accepted. They needed the cash, but it was a waste, really, from the government standpoint.

The air attaché, who was Wally's man in Santiago, thought he had a defector, a Russian sailor who'd jumped ship in Valparaiso. Chink was sent to interview, but it was all too simple. He and the Russian had known one another on opposite sides, years before but unforgettably. They met in a hotel room in Santiago, both tensed up.

Each recognized immediately who the other was and relaxed. They exchanged smiles and handshakes, and Chink asked the man out for a sandwich and a glass of wine. The air attaché was furiously disappointed. He wanted his defector. He tried to insist that Chink could be mistaken.

"There's only one mistake," Chink said, surprised that Wally could have made it. "And that's spending a couple of thousand bucks to bring me down here." There was a long file on this particular Russian. Chink could have made the identification from a photograph and voice tape without leaving Washington.

When he got back, it was the weekend of the Ravensburg Horse Show, the first big show of the season.

Chink's little horse Coker won it all at Ravensburg, everything he was entered in, dressage, all the jumping classes except open jumping. Libby had Coker in the classes restricted to amateur riders. He was close to perfect. As for open jumping, in which the jumps were raised each round, Chink disliked it and wouldn't enter Coker.

"Change your mind once," Libby said. "Show them, Chink. The horse can do it."

"He's not ready for it."

"Will you let me try him in it? No, don't answer. It's not fair for me to ask."

"Thanks," Chink said to his wife. "Thank you, Libby."

At the end of the first day, Wally said: "Let me buy him now, Chinkster, for Natalie. A month from now he'll be worth all the oil in Saudi."

Chink smiled, embarrassed as he always was at the thought of selling a horse to a close friend, but of course the offer was rhetorical. Coker's value would increase greatly with each successful show.

Wally was genial during the second and final day at Ravensburg. He did well on his new Irish hunter in open jumping, taking a red, and was even nice to Natalie. Libby, who'd finished behind Wally on a grey she was bringing along, seemed pleased for him. There were some resentful people around, though, one blond man in particular whom Chink had never seen before. The fellow might have been a little drunk. He was more than a little unpleasant.

When Chink came out with a blue on Coker, in a class which had some children in it, the blond man, standing near the show-ring gate, said loudly, "Whose little boy is the slanty-eye? Looks like one of the ringer family."

And later, after dressage, as Chink went out to a fair amount of applause, for the horse had been beautiful: "Ding dong, for Christ's sake, ringer. Ding dong."

Chink ignored it. It was hard to make out who the young man was with. Perhaps he was a disappointed father. Chink had in mind asking Libby, who knew a lot of people, but she'd left the show early. Then Chink forgot the blond man, because when he went to pick up his gear and load the trailer, after the final class, his dressage whip was missing. It was one he'd ordered from Austria and waited three months for, and he minded losing it. Some larcenous kid, he supposed.

At the Ridge Club, after the show, the Peterses and the Diefenbach family celebrated with an early supper. Mike and Wendy had won minor equitation ribbons. Natalie had been quite calm in seeing them through. Libby had had a good day, Wally his important red ribbon; and Chink's day had been superb. Coker looked like a sure ten-thousand-dollar sale by fall, maybe twice that.

Wally toasted: "To a season we'll never forget," he said, and Chink had his glass of beer half drunk when the waiter came up.

"There's a gentleman outside to see Mrs. Peters."

"Did he give a name?"

"No, sir. He seems mad."

Libby looked surprised: "To see me?"

"I'll see what he wants," Chink said, and excused himself.

Libby followed him onto the clubhouse porch. Wally, Natalie, and the little girls came as far as the doorway.

Standing at the bottom of the steps was the young blond man from the horse show. He was swishing Chink's Austrian dressage whip back and forth.

"I'm Chink Peters. You wanted to see my wife?"

"Hello, Ding Dong." He didn't seem drunk now, so much as reckless. Chink estimated his weight quickly at a hundred and eighty. Late twenties and fat. Chink saw that there was another man, twenty steps back and watching. "I don't want to see her, exactly. No."

Chink heard either Mike or Wendy say to Libby: "Who's that man?"

Chink waited. Finally, he said: "You seem to have my whip."

"I do see her, don't I? I see a thief, Ding Dong. She sold my dad an unsound horse."

"What horse was that?"

"Never mind, Dong." He kept swishing the whip.

"If what you say is true, you'll be repaid."

"Too late for that. We shot the goddamned horse." His speech was from much deeper in the South than Virginia. "I'm here to whip a thief."

Behind Chink, Libby gasped.

Chink turned his head to look at her. "Do you know this man?"

She shook her head. "I haven't sold a horse since fall."

"You seem to be mistaken," Chink told the man, trying to keep his voice even, though the swinging whip infuriated him.

"The thief's callin' me a liar, I believe. That might be two whippings. Why don't you stand back, Mr. Peters? Just let me have her down here."

Chink moved then. He was quite confident. He was bound to get the whip in the face once, but it wouldn't be more than once. He watched it flick left and keep going. He had just time to realize that the blond man had tossed it away, and that his own eyes had followed, when the first blow caught him, a left lead to the right side of his head. Chink Peters ducked then, but he was too late and off-balance. He ducked into a short, stiff, precise right-hand punch, moving up from the man's chest, which hardly needed the unnatural weight it carried in it to break Chink's jaw. Chink went down and out, trying to swallow a scream, which he heard with embarrassment as a ridiculous caterwaul, following him into unconsciousness, along with three pieces of knowledge: that the man was professional, that a weapon was involved, something like the conventional roll of nickels clenched in the fist, and that Chink had been set up for him. There were some people around, he guessed, who might have wanted to do that.

What Chink Peters came to think of as the red summer in his life began late at night. The hospital corridors were dark when Natalie Diefenbach came into his room. His jaw was wired and hurting so that he couldn't sleep. He was not right in the head, and took Natalie for the night nurse.

"Chink, are you awake?"

The second time she asked he recognized her.

"Hello, Natalie." He couldn't talk very well.

"Were you sleeping?"

"We don't sleep much in here." His voice worked better than he thought it would.

"What are you going to do?"

"Lie here and heal up. I guess." It certainly sounded strange. He hadn't really tried to use the voice before. It was interesting that he could.

"I mean about Wally?"

"What about him?" He mustn't let the jaw move much.

"Chink, he hired that man with the whip."

In the moment it took him to think it over, Chink realized that what Natalie said must be true, curious, and upsetting, and that actually he had known it all along.

"No. Natalie," he said.

"I sat there and listened to him telling Libby. As if I hadn't been there at all. He was very angry with the man. You weren't supposed to be injured."

Finally Chink said: "Yes. That's hard to control. Sometimes."

"Do you know why?" Natalie said.

"Sure." He didn't, but he didn't want to hear about it, either.

"So that Libby would see you fail. And the girls."

Chink said: "They saw that. All right."

"Even if I hadn't heard it, I'd have known. I know the things Wally does."

"Me, too," Chink said. "Best in the business."

"That was last night he told Libby. With me sitting there. It was part of his plan to tell her. I'm sure it was. She called him a skunk. Then he kissed her and she laughed."

"Kissed her."

"I left this morning and drove to Washington. Then I decided to drive back and tell you. You won't tell I did? It's two A.M."

"Libby and Wally."

"I'm afraid of him, Chink."

"Yes."

"They're going to get married. I know he's been asking her, but you're not supposed to know that. Not yet. She had to see you fail. And the girls."

Chink felt his teeth go together, against the wire that held his jaw, and his hands shook, under the covers. He managed to say, "I see," as if he did. Then, he added, knowing it was not quite relevant: "She always did want to put the farms together."

"She wants the money, Chink, and the first-cabin jet rides. She wants servants, and those awful parties and the clever, dressy people, along with everything else."

"Sure," Chink said.

"What are you going to do, Chink? You're not the kind of man to take something like this."

Chink supposed that was a compliment and said: "Thank you, Natalie."

"What are you going to do?"

Chink said: "Sleep. If I can." Then he added for clarification: "I'm very tired."

"You've got to punish them. When you have a plan. If I can help? We could stop it, Chink. Otherwise, he'll fight to keep the girls. He'll say I'm crazy. Tell me what to do."

Chink thought about that. "If you see a nurse on the way out," he suggested politely, "tell her I'd like a little codeine, please."

When Libby came to the hospital in the morning, he didn't want to use his new ability to talk, and let her think he couldn't yet.

"Chink. How are you feeling?"

He nodded. He noticed she hadn't used an endearment, or tried to kiss his brow. He thought she looked wonderful.

"Well. We gather that the beans are spilled."

Wally would have had Natalie watched. Chink didn't bother to nod.

"It's so indecent this way. Damn Natalie. He wanted you to heal and be feeling yourself."

He lay still, looking at her. She was wearing a white shirt, and a blue cashmere sleeveless sweater with her boots and britches. She was so slim.

"Wally would like permission to come and see you. There was an awful mistake. He wants to explain things."

He felt himself smile.

"I told him it wasn't a very good idea, unless he wanted to wear a bedpan for a collar. Chink, I hate this. It was all going to happen, anyway, but not like this. I'm so desperately fond of you. You've been my life for thirteen years. But stupid me. I'm in love with that monster."

Best in the business, Chink thought, but he kept the smile fixed.

She chose, this time, to misunderstand the smile. "There's something we want you to think about. It's going to sound strange, but you're the kind of man who could do it, and it's really right for all of us."

Everybody seemed to know what kind of man he was.

"I want you to have the breeding farm, Chink. The Strawbridge place." They had been putting joint earnings into the mortgage, and she said: "I'll sell my share to Wally, and he'll deed it to you. I've made him agree to it. We're going to be away a lot, after this summer. You'll have your place, and there'll be Water Mill to manage and your other farms. You'll have the horses to yourself and see the girls a lot. I know how much that means to you. The only difference is, you won't have me underfoot, making deals you don't like, getting in the way. I'm sorry for all that. The little girls aren't tainted for you. They love you, Chink."

He wanted to say that her deals hadn't been so bad, only a little careless sometimes, and might have said it if he hadn't thought of something quite different. What he thought of was that he had always been out front for somebody, his father's son, Curt's squire when they were boys, Marston Mooney's little Yank, Major Wally's Whizzbang, Libby's protector. The new appeal was unexpectedly strong and simple. He would be out front for Mike and Wendy, while they were growing up and going to school. Except that looking at Libby, he felt a little like crying. He had learned to love her a great deal.

She was talking on. He wished she wouldn't, or that he could stop listening. "I'm going to say good-bye for a day or two, and let you think. Call me when you can talk, and feel like it. You have the fairest, strongest, most generous mind of anyone I'll ever know. The love games may be over for us, the boy-and-girl part. It has been for a while, hasn't it?" Dumb Chink hadn't realized that. "But I admire you more than anybody in the world."

With that, she did lean in and kiss his brow, and he held himself as still as he could, not wanting her to feel his withdrawal. They were in the Army sedan, leaving awful Eddie's. He kept himself rigid. He didn't think she'd sense it this time, but there were tears in the corners of her fine blue eyes when she straightened up.

"Oh, Christ, I hate myself," she said, in a tone almost of meditation, looked down at him gravely, turned, and left the room, her head unnaturally high.

Three weeks after his beating, he left the hospital. Libby had phoned and offered to come by for him at noon. He had thanked her, but at ten o'clock he got dressed, wrote a check for the hospital bill, got the nurse to call a cab for him, and went out to the farm.

There was no one there when he arrived. Libby was staying up at Water Mill.

He packed his clothes and his few effects in a large suitcase and a small one, and put them in the back of his Plymouth station wagon. He backed it around to the one-horse trailer, which was his, too, and hitched on. He loaded Coker. He went to the tack room and got his personal tack, a Hermès saddle, his boots, stirrups, and leathers, a mohair girth, a crop, Coker's bridle, and a halter. Weirdly enough, the Austrian dressage whip which the blond man had used was there. He left it. He also left a Spanish Riding School saddle which Libby'd bought him for his last birthday. It was an expensive thing, hard to come by. He'd enjoyed having it.

As he was putting the Hermès in its canvas cover on the backseat, Libby arrived. She was wearing a natural linen dress, with bone buttons.

"Chink, I've been to get you from the hospital."

"Thanks," he said. "No need."

"Are you leaving? There's no one staying here now."

"Better get someone," he said.

"We can't persuade you?"

He smiled.

"Where are you going, Chink?"

"Out the driveway and turn left."

"We have to be in touch. It's important. Curt wrote from Germany. He's very upset."

Chink nodded. He had heard from Curt, too.

"Curt said you wouldn't stay. He feels you should be paid for the work you've put into the place, as well as the money. We'll get an accountant. Or you do. Your own man, so that we can settle it fairly. Please?"

"No need," Chink said. The heavy wire in his jaw had been replaced by gut pins, which would have to stay in awhile. His jaw felt loose. "Been a pleasure," he said. "Shake hands?"

He offered her his hand.

"Damn it. Oh, damn it. I knew you'd be this way."

"Don't care to shake hands?" She took his hand with both of hers. He shook the one whose palm met his, as if the other were not there, disengaged, smiled, and got into the station wagon.

"Chink. The little painting. *La Jeune Fille*. Curt said it's yours."

"You want it?" When she shook her head, he said, "I picked it up. I'll get it appraised and buy your half."

"No. It's all right."

"I'll get it out." He started to open the door.

She pushed the door closed against his hand. "Please don't. Please, Chink?"

"All right."

She looked into the back of the station wagon, and said: "Your other saddle. The Spanish Riding School saddle. Aren't you going to take it?"

He started the motor, put the car in reverse, and started maneuvering the trailer.

"Let me get it for you?" she called.

It was a rather heavy saddle, suede, something like a stripped-down Western. In his last look at Libby at the Strawbridge farm, she was standing in the tack-room doorway in linen, holding the big tan saddle out towards him with some difficulty, as he finished backing his trailer into position, saluted her, and drove away.

The first thing he told himself, saying it aloud, was: "You didn't have to do it that way, did you?" And silently replied: *I couldn't help it*. During the red summer, he did a number of things he couldn't help.

He drove first to the place of a man he knew in West Virginia, arranged to board Coker, and rented himself a cabin nearby. Then he drove on to Washington, because there was his reputation in the collegiate world of the agency and its men. He had no intention of continuing to work with them, or even of seeing them again, but he wouldn't be able to help acting to restore the reputation before he abandoned it.

At the agency his clearances were still in effect, the files were open to him, and he had no difficulty finding the blond man in one. He was a New Orleans man named Jolliver, part of someone's Cuban informer network. Not Wally's, of course. Wally would have researched independently, just as Chink was doing.

Jolliver would have to wait until Chink's jaw was stable again, but Chink made Xerox copies of what would be needed from the file. There was information on how to get hold of Jolliver, who his associates were, and what his price was. Chink estimated it had cost Wally seven hundred dollars plus expenses to get Chink's jaw busted by mistake. Jolliver had gone to Duke for two years on a football scholarship as a defensive back, and had been thrown off the team for disciplinary reasons. He was half Cuban, in spite of the blond hair. He often spent evenings at the Bourbon Street bars, hustling tourists. He could generally be found at an oyster house in that area, late at night, eating oysters after work. Chink drove back to West Virginia, and tucked the Xeroxes on Jolliver away.

It was mid-April. He spent the next six weeks schooling Coker for the kinds of jumping classes he disliked, the five-bar, the touch-and-out, classes won by the horse and rider clearing the highest jumps in the shortest time. Those were events for world-class horses and riders, not for amateurs with unconditioned animals to ruin. In addition to schooling Coker, who took to it briskly, he trained a rider.

On a mountain patch farm near where he was staying lived a towheaded child named Nanny Dell Harmon, whom Libby Strawbridge Peters, Diefenbach-to-be, along with everybody else in the horse show world, found insufferable. Nanny Dell was now fourteen, but from the time she was nine West Virginia owners had used her to show gaited horses, walkers, and saddle breds, and she generally turned in winning rides. Since Nanny Dell was slight and fierce, her winning had always amused Chink, even when it was Libby who lost a blue, but it wasn't the losing that bothered people. It was that Nanny Dell was revoltingly sassy. Once, when Libby had been asked to present the ribbons for a five-gaited class, and paused to greet an acquaintance in the ring, Nanny Dell had come up behind, snatched Libby's wrist, and wrested the blue away, saying, "You gimme my ribbon, lady."

"She's strong as a snake and just as mean," Libby told people. "God help us all if she ever learns to jump." This now struck Chink as an interesting suggestion, particularly as word came back that Wally Diefenbach was doing very well in the early season on his big Irish hunter.

Nanny Dell Harmon had grown up riding anything that would stand still long enough for her to mount it, including her family's dairy cow. Until people had started mounting her in shows, she had never used a saddle, and preferred a halter and rope to the mule bridle her departing father had left behind. She rode with her legs, had an extraordinary bareback seat and the lightest hands Chink had ever seen, and was totally fearless.

She lived with her mother, a handsome, slovenly, good-hearted redhead named Lornelle, in a two-room unpainted wooden house with its yard full of ducks. The cow and mule, like the husband, were gone. Lornelle rented out her forty acres, and used her share of the corn to make a little moonshine to sell to neighbors, along with plum brandy in season.

Chink bought Nanny Dell boots and britches to replace other children's castoffs, a saddle that fit, stirrups, gloves, a hacking jacket, and a hunt cap. Nanny Dell hated the cap, but he wouldn't let her ride without it. He spent five and six hours a day until the end of June, pleading, commanding, demonstrating, yelling at her sometimes until screams came, to get Nanny Dell's heels down.

He was dismayed at himself for the way he treated the child, but kept at it anyway. Lornelle the mother watched, most days. She was ambitious for her daughter, and backed Chink with a good deal of scornfully good-humored energy.

One night when they had worked late, Chink took Nanny Dell and Lornelle out to dinner before driving them home. When they got there, Nanny Dell went immediately to sleep and didn't even wake when Chink pulled her boots off. He covered her, blew out the kerosene lamp, heard a deep, suggestive chuckle, and looked up to see Lornelle standing in the doorway to the other room, one hand on her hip and the other holding out a quart mason jar of moonshine. Though she wasn't tall, she had a broad forehead and attractively craggy features which made her seem large, and her strong sexual appetite was much discussed, generally with enthusiastic confessions of desire. Men liked Lornelle. Now she tossed her head back, the wild, carroty hair flipping, in a gesture of demand. It occurred to Chink to decline, but it was part of the red mood of the summer to go after her, kick the door shut behind him, and roll down with Lornelle onto a corn-shuck mattress, where he took all he could handle of what she offered. He had neither touched nor desired to touch any woman other than Libby in almost thirteen years. He found the change pretty exciting.

By the Fourth of July, Nanny Dell's heels were right and they began campaigning, first in small shows, sometimes two a week, the three of them going from town to town in the station wagon with Coker and Lornelle's milk goat in the trailer behind. Nanny Dell loved goat's milk. Occasionally, Chink took Coker on his rounds in the competitive jumping events, but Nanny Dell did most of the riding, and they both won consistently. They became an attraction. Show committees would track Chink down by phone and ask him to enter his horse and rider. He said yes to all he could. They began to meet and beat Wally and Libby, whom Chink would greet civilly and try to avoid, out of the ring. Wally wasn't trying to push the acquaintance either. Wally'd had some points accumulating for his Irish hunter as Horse of the Year, and while Coker had started too late to make it, they were going to be in time to deny Wally both the award and the importance in the world of horse people which went with it.

Chink was standing with Nanny Dell at a hamburger stand on a showground in Maryland one afternoon when Libby walked by close behind him, and paused long enough to say, "Wally can wait, Chink."

"Hello, Libby," he said. "Have you met Nanny Dell?"

Libby nodded to the girl and went on.

By the end of August, there was a good deal of speculation about whether or not Coker would be for sale. People knew Chink didn't have a stable any longer.

"You getting ready to auction, I guess," one acquaintance asked, an old Virginia horseman on the circuit.

"When the price is right," Chink said, making it public, "I'll make a deal."

"What would the price be? Fifteen, maybe?"

"I haven't set it yet." Fifteen thousand was a lot for a hunter-jumper, but horses had sold for more than that.

"You coming to the Hunt Club after the show? Need a guest card?"

"Thanks, I've got one," Chink said.

"You come down. Bring that good-looking hillbilly woman, she might like it."

Chink was always invited to the clubs and private parties. He rather enjoyed going because Lornelle revelled in them. She was an enthusiastic drinker and a tireless country flirt. She was boisterous, impulsive, and genuine, and Chink wanted her and Nanny Dell to have friends around the circuit. Wally and Libby, he noticed, stayed away from those parties more and more.

The bids were coming in for Coker by early September. There was an insistent, wiry woman from Wisconsin who had already offered twenty thousand dollars. She had taken to standing by the show-ring gates, and would wave her checkbook at him as he led Nanny Dell out or rode out himself, the woman shouting, "Let's do business, Peters. I want that horse."

It didn't take Chink more than a couple of phone calls to the Midwest to learn that horse people out there didn't know her, which made it fairly clear that she was Wally Diefenbach's agent.

Harrisburg, Pennsylvania, was a big fall show. The first day, he sat quietly in the grandstand and watched Mike and Wendy on their Connemara ponies in the equitation classes, and thought they were both riding quite nicely. Mike won a yellow and Wendy a white in the good hands class for the youngest children.

The next day the people of the horse show circuit saw Chink Peters, in open jumping, win a jump-off, taking his ex-wife out at five feet and her new husband, on his big Irish hunter, out at five and a half. Peters then requested that the bars be raised to six feet and sent the horse around with a fourteen-year-old girl up, and without a fault.

There was cheering around the outlet gate when Nanny Dell finished, and many hands to reach for Coker's bridle when Chink lifted the girl down. He sent Nanny Dell into the ring for the cup and ribbon, took the bridle, and led Coker away past people who said, "Is he for sale now, Chink?"

"What about it? Can we talk some?"

The wiry woman from Wisconsin was among them, tagging along, chattering persistently until, on the way to Coker's stall, she and Chink outdistanced the rest.

"Mr. Peters. Chink. Tell me one thing. Have you set your price?"

"I'm sorry," Chink said. "I have a buyer."

"Who?" The woman was indignant.

Chink shook his head. The buyer was one he'd intended all along. He was called Choo Choo Calloway, a West Virginia miner's union official who had made a fortune in insurance, and who showed Tennessee walkers. He was ready for jumping horses, he had told Chink, eager to sponsor Nanny Dell, admired Lornelle. Choo Choo Calloway, with his union background, thought of the Diefenbach family, who had coal mine interests, as lifelong enemies.

"I heard twenty-seven thousand," the woman said. "I'll pay thirty. If it takes more, I'll get more."

"Tell Wally Diefenbach," Chink said, "that he couldn't buy five minutes on Coker's back for everything he's got."

While he was washing Coker down, Libby came. She was stunningly handsome, he thought, admiring her deep tan and the muscle cords in her arms.

"Well, Chink."

"Hello. How are you, Libby?"

"What can I say to make you change your mind?"

He smiled and shook his head.

"It's the end of Wally and horses. He won't go through another losing season. It's the end for me and horses if he's lost interest."

"You'll be around."

"Where? At the children's classes, with the girls? A horse show stepmother." Chink looked past her and saw that Mike and Wendy were there, on the other side of the paddock fence, standing together on the first rail, their stomachs pressed against the top one, watching. "Is that what you had in mind, Chink?"

"I just needed to beat a man at something," Chink said.

"All right. You have. Will you let Wally buy Coker now?"

"No," Chink said.

"It's not like you to be vindictive."

"He wouldn't be buying Coker, Libby," Chink said patiently. "He'd be buying me." Then he said: "Tell you something?"

"Please."

"I won't be around anymore at all. It's all yours."

She ignored it. "The woman. That was a good shot, Chink."

"Excuse me?"

"You know what people say? And how they do love to say it. That you left me for that wonderful, crude haystack of sex and partying. That part's been fun, too, when you flaunt her and the other men crowd around."

"I didn't think it would matter," Chink said, and he hadn't. He hadn't anticipated, either, that Lornelle would have hysterics as she did when Chink told her he was going to travel on when Coker was sold. He hadn't anticipated that Nanny Dell would comfort her mother, saying, "We don't want him, Mama. He's mean and poor and he's selling the horse and ain't got nothing for us, anyway."

"I'm sorry it bothered you, Libby," he said. "No. I won't change my mind."

"I wish you would," Libby said. "Not for us. For you. Come on, girls."

She started towards Mike and Wendy. Mike said: "Uncle Chink? You didn't, did you? Sell Coker to someone?"

"Yes. I did, Mike."

She was trying not to cry.

"Your father's too heavy to ride Coker, Mike. It wouldn't be right for the horse."

"But he was buying him for me," Mike said. "And Wendy after. So we could be like Nanny Dell."

"Uncle Chink?" Wendy said, putting her arm around her elder

sister. Then Libby reached them, and gathered them in, and Chink still couldn't change his mind. It was the last he saw of Mike and Wendy.

"Old, unshapely things, Piney," he said. After Vasco's death, he talked to rough Piney Brown more than he did to Sweet Lorraine and the others. "It's not the lumps you get, but the ones you give that won't go down."

"Chink, may I come?" It was Pietr.

"What is it?" Chink stood in the doorway, the horses behind him. He did not move aside.

"Just if you are all right?"

"Sure." He was managing pretty well not to see his shipmates, except for the ones in the crew's mess who gave him sandwiches when he asked. He stayed in the stable area, sleeping on a horse blanket on baled hay. Sometimes Hildi and Mrs. Bernie came when he was lunging the mares. He waved to them, and didn't offer to let them help. Otherwise, when he did go out, to his cabin to shave, or to the gym late at night to skip rope, he was able to keep to himself. He was, he knew, a little out of his head.

"Hildi and I, we worry," Pietr said.

"Uh-huh. Well, thanks. How's all that going, anyway?"

"Without change. It's you she likes, I think."

"She's an idiot, Pete. So are you. That makes three of us." He started to close the door.

"Then what are you doing now? All day and all night . . ."

"That's pretty good English," Chink said. "Love is making a linguist out of you."

"But how do you do?"

"No. 'What are you doing?' was better. Trying to swallow lumps, Pete. Got some hot advice on that?"

After Harrisburg, it was time to see young Mr. Jolliver in New Orleans.

Chink flew to Atlanta, and took the bus from there. When he arrived in New Orleans he was wearing a soiled shirt, a shabby sweater, and a frayed red necktie. Over them, he had on the shiny remains of an old, drab suit, and scuffed shoes, the clothes assembled at the Atlanta Goodwill store and soiled in the yard of his motel. He was also wearing a wig he'd bought in Washington that showed baldness and wispy grey, and a drooping grey mustache, and he walked with a cane. He checked into a run-down hotel at the end of a streetcar line, paying in advance for a single room.

The mirror in the room wasn't very good but he thought, looking at himself, that he looked about fifty. He reinforced the lines in his face slightly, using white powder over the lines, and then wiped the powder off. He thought he probably looked sixty now, which was about right. He tried a seedy, fake-Panama hat as part of the costume, and decided against it. It undercut the effectiveness of the wig. He picked up the cane, enjoying the feel of it. It was sharpened and weighted at the ferrule end, and the bend of the crook wide and reinforced with steel.

He went out to locate Jolliver's favorite oyster bar, ate there, went to a movie, and returned at midnight. Jolliver came in about one o'clock. As soon as he did, Chink left, and stood across the street. Jolliver came out, walked a block, and went into a small, working-class tavern where he stayed for twenty minutes. Jolliver came out again. Chink made no attempt to follow him. Instead, he went into the same tavern himself, after Jolliver had left, and drank a glass of beer.

The second night, Chink repeated the series of moves, except that when Jolliver came into the oyster bar, Chink preceded him to the tavern and was there when Jolliver arrived.

The third night, his man must have had some luck with a tourist or a girl. He didn't show.

By the fourth night, when Jolliver came again, Chink, waiting across the street, felt sure enough about the pattern not to go to the oyster bar at all but directly to the tavern.

For the next several nights he was there, a glass of beer in his shaky hand, spilling a little of it into his yellow-grey mustache, each time Jolliver came in. Chink would be on the same stool near the door, and he wanted to sustain this long enough so that Jolliver would both recognize and dismiss Chink as a regular. Chink also bought a half pint, each evening, from Rory the bartender, which he would throw away on his way home, so that he could be seen in conversation with Rory at times.

He had arrived in New Orleans on a Saturday. On the following Saturday night, he got up and lurched out of the tavern just after Jolliver did, turning in the opposite direction, then leaning, head first, against the side of a building to watch his man go just one block and turn into a side street.

Chink shuffled down in that direction, and reached the corner in time to see that Jolliver went into what seemed to be a rooming house, most of the way down the block. Chink was pleased to note that, even on Saturday night, the side street was quite deserted by this hour.

On Sunday night, Jolliver didn't show. On Monday, Chink was in the tavern early, and thankful to be, for Jolliver came in early, too, just after Chink did.

Walking with his cane, Chink went to the men's room, passing Jolliver, who was drinking shots at the bar. A couple of minutes later, Chink came back by and stumbled into Jolliver, making the man spill what was left of a shot. For this Chink got shoved almost off his feet and called a disgusting, pissy-faced rumhead. Rory, the bartender, gave Jolliver another shot on the house, as Chink went muttering back to his own stool. He drank half of another beer and waited.

Jolliver got up then, told Rory the bartender he'd see him tomorrow unless something softer and furrier came up, and left the tavern. As he went by, he gave Chink a clip on the shoulder, making Chink spill the rest of the beer, and laughed.

Chink waited half a minute. Then he got up, went out of the tavern, and was just in time to see Jolliver turn his corner.

"Hey, mister, Mr. Jolliver."

The man looked back, gave Chink the finger, and continued around the corner. Chink hobbled after him, and when he himself had turned the corner called to Jolliver's back, "Hey. Rory said you left your money. Your change."

Jolliver stopped and turned towards Chink. Chink now had a ten-dollar bill, a couple of ones, and some silver in one hand, and the cane in the other.

Chink kept moving. "Don't you want your change?"

"I didn't have change. Rory must be drunk."

"Okay, okay, I'll keep it," Chink cackled. "You want me to keep it, huh, huh?" They were ten feet apart now, the street deserted, Chink holding the money out. He closed his hand on it, and started to withdraw the hand.

"Give it here, rumhead."

"You said I could keep it."

"Come on. You'll get yourself hurt."

"Well, here." Chink threw the money forward, onto the sidewalk.

"Well, I'll be a son of a bitch. . . ." Jolliver had got that far, eyes down, legs moving him forward, when the ferrule of the cane drove into his solar plexus at the end of a fencer's lunge. It doubled and, for a moment, paralyzed the man.

Chink hit him a sabre stroke next, with the weighted end of the cane, just under the left ear, and, as the blond man went sideways, reversed the weapon, caught Jolliver's ankle with the crook, and jerked. Jolliver now went backwards, down onto the concrete and half conscious. Chink whacked his chest, to keep him from getting air, and rested the ferrule in Jolliver's right eye socket.

"Put your hands out flat. Quick." Chink used his normal voice for the first time.

Jolliver did it. He was wide awake now and frightened.

"Just lie still," Chink said. "If you want to keep your eye. And keep those hands out." The hands were spread flat, palms up. "That was a pretty good right-hand punch you broke my jaw with, Mr. Jolliver." He took a quick, short step and broke the right hand with the crook end of the weighted cane.

Jolliver yelled, thrashed away, and turned over. Chink hit him once more, across the back, and watched him roll and hitch into a sitting position, holding the right hand now with the left.

"This is Chink Peters." Chink wrenched off his false mustache and tossed it into Jolliver's lap. "Here's a mustache for you. If you want to find me, I'll be in St. Thomas, in the Virgin Islands, Mr. Jolliver. Care of a man named Shellcroft."

Making this little speech was, again, something he couldn't help doing, not something he was especially pleased about, later on.

He turned and walked away, not looking back until he reached the corner. When he did it appeared that Jolliver might have fainted from the pain.

Falling in love with Eve Shellcroft was the last in the sequence of things Chink couldn't help doing that year. He fell in love with Eve instantly, totally, and on sight. She was a full head taller than Chink, perfectly gentle, perfectly beautiful, and had been married to and deserted by the brother of the man Chink went to work for in the Virgin Islands.

Chink had, during his time at Yale, thought he might someday like to try teaching.

Taylor Shellcroft, his employer, was a British schoolmaster from Bermuda, who had started a day school in the Virgin Islands, where the dollars were. Chink hired on by mail to teach American history and German, and to help on the playground.

"Some of your American games the little rotters want," the headmaster said. "Like your famous football and baseball."

Chink smiled. He had never played any of those except in pickup games, but there were books, just as there were books for periods in history he hadn't learned yet.

Taylor Shellcroft was tall and fair, with a big, fine, imposing nose, disdainful manners, and brusque intelligence. Taylor was an outspoken puritan and parsimonious. Pierce, the departed brother, was said to have been, just as arbitrarily, a spendthrift and a rake.

In the first week there was a reception for the new instructor in the School Hall, to present Chink to the faculty.

Chink was chatting with the French teacher, a chic woman with very little English, about surf and beaches, when he heard Taylor Shellcroft say:

"Get Mr. Peters some cake, Eve. His plate's as empty as your pillow."

"Yes, Taylor." The voice was gentle, almost meek.

Chink turned, expecting to see an abject woman, someone with the bearing of a bully's victim. As he turned he said, putting an edge on it, "Thanks, Taylor. The cake's good but I've had plenty."

Taylor raised his brows and walked away, and Chink was facing a woman tall enough so that, although she was sitting, she had hardly to raise her head to meet his look.

"Thank you, Mr. Peters."

He smiled.

"I'm Eve Shellcroft."

"I know." She had been pointed out to him in the schoolyard, and he had thought her formidably lovely. Now she seemed lovely, but still and self-contained. The effect of quietude came from the pigment in her eyes, which were blue with no trace of green, and hardly any radiating flecks of white.

"Thank you for speaking up. But I'm afraid that goes on all the time."

Chink was having trouble with his composure. It had never occurred to him to pursue a woman before, but there was an urgency he'd never known in his response to Eve. He managed to ask, "In public?"

Softly, she mimicked Taylor's voice: "Isn't that precisely the point?" Her finger touched Chink's wrist, and he realized the urgency was there for Eve, too.

He said, just as softly, and astonished at himself: "Have lunch with me tomorrow."

She smiled, shook her head, and whispered back, "It wouldn't be wise."

"I'm sorry." His palms were hot. "I shouldn't have asked."

"No. But I'm glad you did." She held his eyes with hers for another moment, and then looked down at her teacup. It was a flared, octagonal cup of thin white china, with a delicate blue rim, a thin blue stripe around the inside, just under the rim, a pattern of stylized bluebells, lightly done, and a prettily recurved handle. He left the reception as soon as he could to go away and think about her.

What he thought was that Eve Shellcroft was beautiful in the way some individual animals are beautiful, and remembered, of all things, not Reynolds' women or Gainsborough's, but a Jersey heifer, light-boned and fawn-eyed. This cow had been a fine, sentimental old farmer's last animal, and from the velvet cleft of her lips and creamy lashes to the gleaming whisk at the tip of her tail, she was a perfectly lovely cow. Eve had that best-of-breed look. She was golden blonde with exceptionally clear skin, and one of the things he came to find endearing was that, while she stood and walked gracefully, she was quite awkward when she tried to move athletically. Hers was a still, often a sad beauty, but it quickened to a brave, restrained glow when Eve got excited, as she did quite easily. The glow could, almost too obviously, begin whenever, during the next few weeks, they met casually, and Chink needed all the discipline he could find in himself to concentrate on learning his new duties at the school.

Eve had been left with two boys, half grown, free students now at their uncle's establishment, which gave Taylor Shellcroft more license than he needed to be rude to his brother's ex-wife. Chink thought it clear that Taylor, who was married to a drab woman with capital and pretensions, was harsh to Eve out of repressed desire.

He learned that she was Bermuda British. Her father had commanded a sub-chaser during the war, while Eve, still a child, was sent to relatives in the United States. She'd romanticized her father and gone to find him, after the war, a savage drunk who talked constantly of bloodshed; terrible stories, she told Chink later, about tracking submarines until they had to come up to recharge their batteries, when Eve's father and his men would slaughter the crews, here in the calm of the Caribbean, under the palms.

Very young and confused, she had married Taylor Shellcroft's brother, Pierce, and with him joined, for a time, that group of people who drift, in well-bred poverty, into the playgrounds of the world when seasons end. They are mostly a gentle crowd, expatriated, living on remittances and alimonies, who come to rest at Teneriffe or Port-au-Prince, Andros, Mallorca, set in motion by drops in the exchange rate. When vacation time is gone they come to rent the playful, vacant houses and take care, not wanting to attract attention or cause trouble, though they do, sometimes, among themselves. Pierce had abandoned Eve in St. Thomas, one of those places, during Eve's second pregnancy. To win an education for her children, Eve stayed, taking abuse from her brother-in-law, working part time as an information clerk at the tourist bureau.

Chink and Eve had known one another six weeks when he found her one day, sitting on a white towel on the beach, watching her sons play in the surf. He knelt on the end of the towel. She turned her head and their eyes locked.

"I forget my manners, Eve," he said. "I couldn't wait for you to ask me to join you."

"I forget mine, too," she said. "I nearly called out to you, and everyone would have heard."

"Can we ever see each other?"

She surprised him. "We have to. Shall I come to your house after dark tonight? Taylor and his wife are cruising, and the boys have a party."

Theirs was a totally secret affair of infrequent meetings and absorbing emotion. They were not often together, for discretion was always Eve's first thought. The tension between meetings could get painful, its release so great as to be almost painful too. At the end of the first school year, Chink would have left and taken her away, had Eve been willing. She wouldn't interrupt her children's lives.

It continued into a second year, and Chink stayed only because of Eve. Teaching, he'd found, was not his kind of work, and he was not at all flattered by the way Taylor Shellcroft asked him to return a third year as assistant headmaster:

"The boys do follow you about so. I suppose it's because you're such a muscular specimen. They make up Mr. Peters stories."

During the long summer vacation, Chink went to London to see the Tate and National galleries, and to think about Taylor's offer. It was beginning to be difficult for Taylor to keep his staff. Racial violence had begun in the Virgin Islands, and people were frightened by it. By the time Chink returned, there had been an incident in which one of Eve's sons was hurt, though not badly. Still, it affected her a good deal.

"I can't make love," she said when they were alone. "Dear Chink. I'm sorry. I really am. But I feel so guilty about keeping Kevin and Tommy here now. It was all so quiet and safe before."

"Let me help in any way I can," Chink said. "I'll leave after fall term. May I find a place for you to bring the boys and join me? I'd like us to be married."

Eve demurred but did not decline. They were together more openly, now that they were no longer secret lovers, and the tension between them was high. They both enjoyed cooking, and had one another to strangely elaborate meals. Now and then Eve would grow passionate and they would come together for a frantic hour, after which she'd be upset but couldn't tell him why. Eve needed money, would not accept it from Chink, and increased her working hours at the tourist bureau. It was as if they were waiting for what happened next. It came in October, when the Caribbean area went through the tension of what was called the Cuban missile crisis.

The agency's man in St. Thomas was Sam Lowen, supposedly representing the Navy in the harbormaster's office. It was the same Sam Lowen whom Chink had known slightly as one of Wally Diefenbach's young ramblers in Italy, years earlier, and would see again years later at a dance in Pearl Harbor, from whom he would then hear that Eve was in Tahiti.

In the Virgin Islands Chink and Sam Lowen saw one another socially from time to time. Sam was, like Chink, divorced, and, like Chink, an admirer of Eve Shellcroft. Chink supposed the agency connection still existed for Sam, but there'd been no reason for them to discuss it before the crisis. Now Sam phoned.

Chink told Eve: "I'm going to be away for a few days."

"I wish I were surprised," Eve said.

"You do?" Chink hadn't told her of the work he'd left behind.

"Do you remember someone called Anne Goulay?"

"Of course. She was close to a man I knew very well. They were almost married."

"She came into the tourist bureau one day," Eve said. "She's the social director on a cruise ship, and wanted help arranging shore things for her passengers. I spent some time with her."

"You didn't tell me."

"She asked me not to. The day she came, she was at my desk when you stopped to see me. Her back was to you, I suppose. I came to the counter, and we talked a moment, and you left. And then she asked me if that could have been Chink Peters, and I said yes."

"I wish I'd known."

"Did you really know her in Italy, Chink?"

"Yes. First. She was in the Red Cross then."

"I couldn't believe the things she told me," Eve said. "I didn't want to."

Chink hesitated. Then he said: "I wish I'd seen Anne. I don't know what she said, so I don't know what to say."

"She didn't want to see you," Eve said.

"Had I offended her?"

"She said she was frightened of you in Italy."

"Once in Rome she said she felt safe with me."

"I gather it's women she feels safe with now."

"Maybe that's just a lurid rumor, too."

"Anne wanted to be intimate with me." Eve had a somewhat stilted way of talking about sex though she was not inhibited in bed.

"Perhaps she wanted to discredit a rival, then."

"That's what I told myself. Now there are Russian ships out there. It's a strange time for you to be going away."

"I guess it is."

"Can you tell me why?"

"No, Eve."

"I didn't think you could."

There were five days of crisis, and though Sam Lowen and Chink, and a third man he knew named Randy Allstine, were in a watch-and-watch situation all through it, there was nothing really for Chink to deal with. Sam and Randy received messages on kinds of electronic gear for which Chink didn't have clearance. Chink stood by.

When he saw Eve again, she was pensive.

"I don't suppose you can tell me what you were doing?"

"Nothing very useful."

"I'll tell you what I've been doing, then. Thinking about the boys. And about my father. People killing and being killed for politics."

"I've been away from that for years."

"But you go back. You just did, Chink. And two years ago—did you go to the Bay of Pigs?"

"I don't want to lie to you, Eve, but there isn't much I can tell you, either."

"Were you there?"

"No."

"Where were you?"

"I'm sorry."

"Chink, you've hurt people. A lot of people. I couldn't believe it of you."

"Not since the war. No, that's wrong. I shot a prowler in Thailand, at the time of the Korean War. He was armed, and on his way upstairs, where my wife was sleeping."

"But you kept on working for that agency," Eve said.

"She was right. Temporary assignments. It was my profession."

"After Thailand, did you ever . . . have anyone hurt?"

"No, Eve."

"Suggest it at a meeting? Help plan it?"

"I did a lot of what you're doing now. Interrogation."

"Helped plan someone's death? Or let it happen when you might have been able to stop it?"

"It's not that clear-cut."

"Which?"

"I might have let it happen. There's a lot of talk about those things, but generally something else is done instead. And when it does happen, perhaps one or two people know for sure. I've not been one of those who knew for sure since Thailand."

They were in the living room of the house he rented. It was an airy room with big windows, looking over the harbor. On one wall Seurat's *La Jeune Fille* was hanging, next to it a framed reproduction of a Rousseau painting of mustached Frenchmen playing rugby. She stood, walked over, and looked first at the painting, then at the reproduction, which she had given Chink, before she looked back at him and said, "Wherever you were, how did you feel about the Bay of Pigs?"

"I felt badly. We got licked."

"But we were in the wrong."

"Maybe, Eve. One reason I was glad to leave the agency was that I stopped believing there was any right or wrong in politics. It's like being chosen in a game, for one team or the other. It's not till you're on a side that you're loyal to it, and then just because it's your side."

"That's terrible."

"Yes. It is."

"Chink, isn't that why you're really here? Because there are two sides here now. Before you came, those things didn't happen."

"What things, Eve?"

"The violence. People leaving. My friends. My boy. It didn't used to be this way."

"Eve? Do you think I was sent here?"

"Sometimes I think you were, and you can't tell me. And even if it's true, you have to say it isn't. And sometimes it's more superstitious, and I wonder if there are people trouble follows, and violence, all their lives."

"I wasn't sent."

"Could you tell me if you were?"

"No."

"While you were gone just now, I imagined so many things. Fins and scuba gear and ships. Like my father's frogmen stories. Landing on some island with guns . . ."

"Eve. The agency has people here I know. Old comrades. They asked me to sit through this missile thing with them. That's all."

"They'll ask you again."

At the end of his third year's contract, Chink left teaching and the Virgin Islands. Eve and her children were already gone.

"Eve and the boys are in Nairobi," Sam Lowen called up to tell Chink.

"I don't want to know that, Sam. It doesn't please me much that you know it."

"It's an assignment, Chink. Keeping track of you and yours. You know that."

"I suppose."

"The agency doesn't lose sight of you. Your folder was here when you arrived. I know your wife married Wally. I know you whacked a guy in New Orleans. I knew about you and Eve from the first night."

"Isn't that wonderful?" Chink made himself a promise, in memory of Eve, never to have anything to do with the agency again, in any way. He hung up telephones, and threw letters away unread.

After the islands, he tried conscientiously for a career in open law enforcement for a while. He commanded a unit for the U.S. Border Patrol, left to organize security on a hundred-thousand-acre ranch in Texas and New Mexico, and accumulated a couple of new knife scars. He managed the ranch for a year afterwards. He was asked by the police commissioner in an Arizona city, a man he'd known in Berlin, to direct a civilian investigation of police corruption, as a special deputy commissioner. There were threats on his life, but no damage done. He finished that, and invested his savings in a cattle partnership which went quite well for a time. When his partner wanted to expand, hire a foreman at the ranch, and switch Chink to running feed lots, Chink cashed out. He knew by now that what he really wanted was land of his own, again, and Eve Shellcroft to share it with, but that seemed quite impossible. He supposed another woman might sometime take Eve's place in his imagination of a life to lead, but was not searching.

He had a letter once from Libby, asking, because she was having disciplinary problems with her stepdaughters, in particular Mary, if Chink would write to the girl. He tried. His letter was so stilted he was almost ashamed to send it. He yearned to sign it "Love, Uncle Chink." Not knowing whether that would be acceptable, he made it "Affectionately, C.K. Peters" but Mike's reply confused him. It was prompt and effusively long, but in a tone he took for snippiness. It seemed to challenge him to endorse her defiance, and he supposed his own letter must have made her scornful of him. Not long afterwards, he heard that Libby and Wally had separated.

He went to Venezuela to supervise a cattle-breeding program. He was in his late thirties by then, and what followed were his wildest days. It was as if he'd never really been a kid, and had some hell-raising to catch up on. He got into a bunkhouse brawl at the cattle station one evening and got fired, as he deserved to be. He went to Caracas, and got a job as night manager of the good, secure little hotel where the airline stewardesses stayed. He offered them protection, in that oil-boom atmosphere, from insistent Venezuelans and from the passengers who sometimes took them to dinner, and wanted to come to the hotel afterwards. Some were welcome. Chink got rid of the ones who weren't.

He was earning quite good wages, but couldn't take the money seriously. He spent it carelessly, loaned it freely, seldom got repaid. His salary was gone a day or two after he was paid each month, and his savings began to go, too. He knew his friends on the Carribbean flight crews of various nationalities worried about him. He drank with them late, tending the hotel bar, and knew for the first time in his life a situation in which he was going casually to bed with any woman, in a large and shifting group, who might make herself available. Whatever restraint he might have felt about it was removed, though he did not understand why, when he read one day in the English-language newspaper that Colonel Curtis Strawbridge IV, one of the Army's bright young stars, was dead, victim of pancreatic cancer. Two months and many women later, Chink became friends with a reprobate former airline pilot, a younger man, and went with him up the Orinoco River to the diamond and emerald fields. That ended in a jungle camp fight, when Chink's friend got into more than he could handle alone, and it turned out to be more than he and Chink could handle together.

There was a hospital stay. During it, he wrote to Libby and to old Mrs. Strawbridge about Curt's death. Libby replied very briefly, Mrs. Strawbridge at length. Curt was survived by a wife and four children. Libby and Wally were now divorced. Mrs. Strawbridge said she hoped Chink would visit her in Washington, and suggested he might like to become reacquainted with Libby. Chink smiled at that.

He went to Mexico, to take charge of fieldwork in a vampire bat control experiment. Mexican cattle ranchers ran his teams out.

Passing through Washington, he saw Sam Lowen again. Sam, still unmarried then, had actually followed Eve to Africa, and said, "No soap for me, friend. But she's herself again; she'd got so overwrought in that St. Thomas situation. Woman seems to think she did you wrong, damn my luck. It must be love." Chink wished he could believe all that, but Sam had always been a blind and stubborn bearer of glad, unlikely tidings. Chink went to Uruguay.

"You like it out on that rancho?"

The vice-president of a hide exporting firm had just turned out to be the agency man in Montevideo. He was supposed to be a very able young man in the hide business.

"I'm thinking of buying into that rancho," Chink said.

"I wouldn't."

"Is that right?"

"I gather you're eager to keep away from us."

"Yep," Chink said.

"I'll do you a favor. We already own that place. So you'd hardly want to buy in."

"Nice favor."

"Because of the border land, with Brazil. You used to be with Wally, didn't you?" The second generation was always curious.

"Diefenbach."

"He just got divorced again. Third time."

Chink didn't know there'd been a third wife, but he said: "How fascinating."

"Come on, Mr. Peters. Wally's our great man."

"What do you want? I came here thinking it was hides. Which we have."

"You're needed, Mr. Peters."

"No, I'm not."

"I told Washington I was going to try to reach you. Want to see the okay?"

"No. I've resigned, been discharged. I've torn up paychecks. And I'm going now." Chink stood up.

The young man behind the big desk said, "You're needed."

"What have you got, action? I don't do it. I don't do anything anymore."

"Why do you think it's action?"

"If it weren't, you'd have made it clear first thing."

"That's probably true."

"I'm moving along towards fifty. I haven't got the legs. I haven't got the wind. I haven't got the speed. And I wouldn't do it for you if I did."

"You just don't like us."

"Do me a real favor. Send in a fitness report. Lacks heart. Lacks judgment. Lacks balls. Okay?"

"I need you."

"You've got people. If not here, you can fly some in."

"There isn't time, Chink. It's tonight."

"I'll be back on the ranch tonight. I expect I'll be packing, damn you. I really liked the place."

"You know what this is about, don't you?"

"No. The kidnapping?"

"The federal cops are going to storm a house tonight. The ransom's been paid. Now the kidnappers say they want more."

"Good. Give it to them."

"You know what these kidnappers are like? They're not the

tough, radical pros. We can deal with them. These are middle-class, educated kids. Intellectuals. Amateurs. I doubt if they even know any proletarians. They're trying to turn the country upside down, and nobody even understands what their program is."

"Infiltrate, buy in and write one for them," Chink said. "Goodbye."

He'd got as far as the office door, when the young man said, "They'll hurt him. They might kill him tonight, if they haven't already. You probably saw in the paper, his wife's come here, with their children. She tried to negotiate."

"He's an oil man, isn't he? Or I suppose that's his cover." Chink was getting a little angry, and stepped back towards the desk. "Jesus, can't the agency take care of its own anymore?"

"It isn't a cover. He isn't with the agency. That's the trouble."

"Then what's the line about the Uruguayan politician offering to take his place? And the kidnappers saying no deal, we've got just who we want?"

The young man sighed and shook his head. "Chink, he's one of those damn fools who's been working overseas for years. Different places. One of the ones who likes to drop the hints at the cocktail party, that he's with us. Glamorous stuff, isn't it? To be precise about it, I guess the kidnappers are convinced he's me."

"That's very neat. You'd better go rescue yourself."

"You know better. I'm still under orders. Anyway, I'm a lousy shot. Bad eyes."

"I'm sorry to have wasted your time, Bad Eyes," Chink said. "Good luck."

"It's interesting that we've created a world of frauds who want to be taken for us. Frauds with wives and children." The man got up, and came towards Chink. He was tall and slim, with a pleasant, thoughtful face and thick glasses, a blond young man. "If they'd really snatched me, Chink, there'd have been a team here by now. Money, firepower, leverage. All this poor creep's got is me and you. And I'm officially restrained."

"He's got the Uruguayan police."

"They want an observer. They want somebody who can yell instructions in American English. The creep's in a bedroom on the second floor. He speaks Spanish, but he'll be scared. They want someone there to talk him through it, when the door goes down. If you won't do it, it won't get done. You can go in unarmed, if you want."

"How about blindfolded, hands behind my back?"

The Uruguayans gave him a pistol, a flak vest, and an hour on their indoor range. Then he borrowed an empty cell in which to sleep for a couple of hours. He'd left the ranch very early.

What disgusted him was how comfortable he felt, once the thing started. It was just after two in the morning. The house was isolated in a big yard in suburban Montevideo. The sentry was also the police informer, and the rest of the kidnappers were asleep. The informer let Chink, a lieutenant, and five more police in, and at first it looked as if the rescue might be made without a shot being fired. Otherwise, there were enough weapons trained on the house to have levelled it.

Two of the police were tying up and gagging the informer to support the appearance of his having been overcome, when a voice from the interior of the house called out in Spanish, asking who was there. Chink knew the floor plan, and had his assignment. He moved immediately in the dark, down a corridor which led past the dining room, into the kitchen, to take the back stairs.

There was someone coming down the corridor as he moved, but no disturbance yet. They brushed against one another in the hall, and the voice he'd heard asked sleepily who it was. Chink muttered, "*Esta bien,*" and kept going. He tensed for a flashlight to pick him up, ready to go flat under the beam, roll, and shoot if necessary, but the man went on towards the sentry post at the front door. Then Chink heard sounds of others moving, elsewhere on the first floor, and sprinted for the back stairs, figuring their noise would cover him. He reached the bottom step as the first shot was fired. There was a flurry of shots behind him, a lot of yelling, and he hoped the police who were supposed to block off the front steps were in position.

He ran upstairs and got to the back landing as searchlights went on outside, and there was brilliant, uneven light to show him the upstairs hall, weird and remote from the crack of guns below. No police appeared at the top of the front stairs. They hadn't made it yet. Chink located the door of the bedroom where the captive was, but didn't move towards it. He heard shouts from other parts of the house, threats to kill the captive, demands that the police withdraw.

He moved back to a position where he could command both back and front stairs. The firing stopped for a moment. House lights were on downstairs, and there was tear gas being used somewhere, probably the west wing where most of the kidnap squad was known to sleep. Shots started again, more shots than before, all across the front floor, and a shadow rose quickly on the wall opposite the front landing. The shadow turned into a slim kid in jeans and beret, with a submachine gun, who turned and fired a burst down the stairs.

The kid whirled, then, and started for the bedroom door. Chink aimed carefully, shot at the legs, dropping the kid with the first shot, firing again immediately, twice, into the chest, then stepping quickly in, holding on the head, firing the finishing shot and getting back fast to the head of the rear staircase. No one else appeared for a minute or two. Then Chink saw shadows again, turning into Uruguayan policemen, coming up in front, and called out his name to them. The firing below ceased all of a sudden. The Uruguayans and Chink met at the bedroom door, Chink stepping over the kidnapper's body.

The door was locked.

"It's the police," Chink called. "Can you hear me? You okay in there?"

"My God," a voice said, inside the room. "Oh, my God."

"We've got control. We're going to shoot this lock off. Get way over against a wall, out of line, and lie down."

More Uruguayans, including the lieutenant to take charge, arrived in time to blow the lock. Then they all went into the room, turned on the lights, and found the American all right, getting up off the floor by the wall. He looked thin and dirty and smelled awful. He embraced Chink and the Uruguayan lieutenant. There was a tremendous rolling of shots outdoors, someone making a run for it. The rest were dead and captured now.

"We lost one man, and have two wounded," the lieutenant said.

"How about the kids?"

"I don't know yet. We had to kill plenty."

"My God." It was the only thing the American seemed able to say so far. Then he managed, "My God, but I'm glad to see you."

Chink was partly supporting the man, who could walk and seemed sound but was doing a lot of shaking.

"Let's get out of here," Chink said.

Then there was a cry from one of the policemen in the hall. "*Por Dios, es mujer.*"

"What did he say?" The American screamed it. "He said a woman."

"He said a woman. Take it easy." But Chink had started to shake some himself.

"*Paca.* Oh, God. Oh, my God. She was my friend. Paca." The American was hitting Chink, weak blows on the arms and chest. "She was coming to let me out."

Chink left the man and stepped into the hall on numb legs, to look at his victim, and it was so clear now, seeing her lying there, that he could not understand why he hadn't realized it was a young woman.

There was nothing more to remember now, or to tell Piney Brown or Sweet Lorraine, only that he had left Uruguay soon afterwards for northern California where, in the three years just past, he had lived quietly alone, and reestablished himself as a horseman. At the end of a fortnight in San Francisco, just after his return, he had conceived and carried out an act of contrition.

On the second Friday morning, he unpacked the Seurat painting, *La Jeune Fille*, which had travelled with him everywhere, stored carefully when he was in the field, hung in the places he had got set up. He looked at it for the last time, rewrapped it neatly, and took a bus out to the San Francisco Palace of Fine Arts, where a guard stopped him on the way in and asked that the little package be checked.

"It's for the museum," Chink said. "Perhaps you can call someone?"

The young man who arrived was dressy and indolent. "Hello, hello," he said. "If it's a gift, I'm pleased to see you. Or at least I might be. Unless you painted it yourself, of course. If it's something to sell, we've miles and miles of red tape."

"It's a gift," Chink said. On a card he had written:

La Jeune Fille by Georges Pierre Seurat, 1887.
Oil on canvas. 11″ x 14″.

The young man read it, drew back his head, and looked at Chink with a playful smile. "Good heavens," he said. "What a marvelous hoax. It's really an eleven by fourteen bomb, isn't it, and you've come for our Rembrandts?"

"Read the back of the card, please," Chink said. On the back he had written:

Formerly in the Strawbridge Collection, this painting was a wedding gift to Mr. and Mrs. C.K. Peters. She was Elizabeth Strawbridge. It was acquired by Peters in a property division, preceding divorce. It is offered as an anonymous donation, provided the Museum will agree to maintain confidentiality and to notify the former Mrs. Peters, recently Mrs. Walden Diefenbach.

To this Chink had signed his name. Now he offered the not-so-indolent young man his passport, for identification.

"This simply can't be happening," the man said.

"It's authentic," Chink said. "You'll know immediately when you open it."

"But . . . do you know the value of this? That's an insulting question, please forgive me. May I really open it?"

"I'd just as soon you waited till I'm gone."

"Mr. Peters. Good heavens. Please come up. Let me get the director. I'm dithering, I know. . . ."

Chink smiled. "It's okay. Take down the passport number. You'll have to check. And take my address."

"But you'll want an assessment. For the tax ogres. I mean, we have all sorts of marvelous forms."

"Never mind," Chink said. "If you'll just ask your director to write me, accepting the conditions, I'll reply, confirming the gift."

"Of course. But well. I don't know what else to say. Just to hold it. And see it. Oh, there'll be such a splash when we announce. I think I can promise you a special gallery for it, for a month at least. Next time you see it, there it will be, Mr. Peters. In the most absolute splendor. And there ought to be a press-and-patrons party, and you can come in disguise or something, would that be fun?"

"Here," Chink said, handing him the package. "I'll be waiting for the letter."

Adieu, jeune fille, he thought. *Adieu, toutes filles, jeunes et vieilles,* blue, pink, and ochre girls, you're nothing but a bunch of dots, good my ladies, and I am dottier than any of you.

He left the museum and walked out to Seal Cliff, where he stood for more than an hour, watching the sea break, grey-green water curling white over grey-green rocks.

"Here I am again," Pietr said. He said it in excellent German. "It's sad about the horse, my friend, but must we lose you, too?"

Standing in the doorway, Chink replied: "I've barely heard you speak German before, Pete."

"It's English I need to practice. This time, please let me come in?"

This time Chink stood aside. "Maybe that's been your mistake with Hildi. Maybe you should have been speaking German to her."

Pietr stopped. "Do you think so?"

"She knows a little. In German, you'd be the grown-up, she'd be the child."

"How obvious," Pietr said. "It may be too late. Shall we sit on your hay?"

"Wherever you like." Chink tried to smile and found he could. He let the door swing closed. Pietr had sat down.

"Hildi believes you are a clinical case of melancholia. I said 'misanthropy,' though that is not a disease recognized by psychiatry."

"German, and now psychiatry."

"Look at Sweet Lorraine, Chink."

Chink glanced over at the little bay. Her head was down. She was sleeping.

"All your mares," Pietr said. "How listless they are."

This time Chink's smile came without effort. "You think they're catching melancholia from me, Pete? Or, sorry, misanthropy?"

"Dogs reflect their owners' moods. Not horses?"

"Lorraine, wake up." He went into her stall. "Lorraine, have you girls caught the blues from me?"

Sweet Lorraine nuzzled him, raising her nostrils into his chest and moving him back a step.

Pietr changed to English. "Now you see very well. She smiles."

It made Chink laugh. He rubbed the horse. "Pietr, you're marvelous. You and Hildi. Go talk some German to her."

He felt now like having the door open, taking the horses out for a second time, into the afternoon sun, and did it. He thought it would be nice to eat hot food in the evening, and pleasant to have a glass of beer with the people.

Chink Peters didn't go to Tahiti. Eve Shellcroft, as she later said, knew quite well he wouldn't.

It was by personal communications from Commander Sam Lowen, CIC Naval Intelligence, PFHQ, Pearl Harbor, that Eve learned that Peters was in the hemisphere and might make contact.

Chink was at the rail of the *Vesterålen* beside Mrs. Bernie, watching Wellington, New Zealand, grow solid in the dawn, when he saw that Eve was there, on the dock. She was unmistakable to him at fifty yards, the height, the grace in standing, the ineffable shine of the blond head, the pearl glow of the upturned, searching face.

At fifty yards he said: "Eve."

Mrs. Bernie said, "What?"

He heard Mrs. Bernie but didn't exactly understand her question.

She repeated: "What, Chink?"

"I'm sorry." He felt an indiscreet sob in his throat, and his eyes were moist. "A friend is here. To meet me, I think."

Mrs. Bernie didn't speak again until they were much closer, ten yards off and moving in. Then she said: "So that's what she was up against."

Chink held out a hand, palm down, in benediction. Eve held out a hand, palm up, receiving it.

Mrs. Bernie said: "You don't play fair. You could have told her."

"Told?" He didn't look away from Eve.

"Told Hildi. About that one."

"About Eve?"

"Whatever her name is."

Chink's face felt contorted, out of control. He closed his eyes, wiped them, opened them again, and Eve was still there, arms at her sides now, head slightly to one side, face raised and smiling the question his own face was so busy trying to answer.

Yes, I am glad to see Eve, he thought. What am I going to tell her?

The whole day passed before they were alone. A cheery young trainer drove them, following a horse van, out to Fairleigh's ranch, where Chink unloaded and said good-bye to Sweet Lorraine, Rebel Deb, Piney Brown, and pretty Franny Frisbee. He liked the place for them. The grass was beautiful. He trusted the young trainer, who said right away that he would keep the mares on hay for a while, turning them out to grass only for half an hour or so at first.

"We've room for you, if you'd like to see to them yourself for a bit," the trainer said.

Chink thanked him. Without Vasco to be conditioned, there was no reason for Chink to stay.

He and Eve were driven back to Wellington, where he checked into her hotel. They had a drink in her room, kissed tentatively, and went down to dinner. In the lobby they saw Hildi and Pietr and the four ate roast beef together and drank strong beer.

After dinner Eve asked Chink back to her room. She had some cognac there. She sat on the bed, looking as lovely, speaking as gently as ever, and asked Chink if he was free to come back to Tahiti with her.

He sat in a desk chair, turned in her direction.

"What's it like there for you, Eve?"

It was, she said, like so many places, slow paced, bypassed, with a few people there she'd known a long, long while, around the beaches of the world. And others like them. It was lively sometimes, but more often dreamy. She thought Chink might enjoy the tourist game of looking for Gauguins.

"Is getting married ruled out?" he asked.

"I haven't let myself think about it much," she said. "Do you want it ruled out?"

"No."

"What is it you'd like, Chink?"

He told her about a place in California, far north of San Francisco, which he imagined buying, a place for horses and sheep with a fine, clear stream running through woods and pastures.

Eve smiled. "I'm not a rider, you know," she said.

"You might like the sheep. They're quiet animals."

"I might."

"I haven't really given up wanting children, Eve."

"And mine are grown."

"I've thought about adoption."

"Does it all have to go together for you?" Eve asked. "The land, the woman, the livestock, and the family?"

Chink nodded and drank off the cognac.

"I remember how we used to cook," she said. "Do you still?"

The short order man and the salad girl, he thought, but he said, "Eve, I've been celibate for three years. Longer, really."

She walked over and kissed him on the neck, under the ear. "I haven't been very wild either," she said. "Do you want more cognac?"

"It might help."

"I thought . . ." It was hard for her to say, but she did it: "Maybe we'd start by making love, and see what happened."

"That would be the nicest way, Eve, if I could." He finished the second glass of cognac, and poured a third.

"It sounds like some kind of vow."

"It is, in a way." He was going to have to tell her about Paca now. He finished the third drink, and said slowly: "I was living on a ranch in Uruguay." He didn't mean to spin it out, but it took him time to get to it. By then, Eve was kneeling on the floor with her hands on his arms, and when he said, "It was a girl I killed. About eighteen," Eve's face went down into his lap and her arms went around his legs.

She straightened herself up, and said: "You're shaking," and put her arms now around his waist. "It doesn't make any difference, Chink. Dear Chink. What else could you have done?" But he was a little out of control by then, and talking wildly about Mike and Wendy Diefenbach, as if he were not just Paca's killer but theirs as well.

Eve put him to bed quite drunk from stronger spirits than he was used to, and exhausted by confession.

In the morning, when Pietr, full of apology, found them at breakfast, bringing the cable from Wally, it was as if Chink had known there was such a cable all along.

"It came to the ship," Pietr said. "Even before Hawaii. So I didn't understand, but gave it to the purser. I thought ship's business and for him. But it came first to me, not you, because we have the same name. Pietr, Peters. I didn't think at all, I am so sorry."

"It's all right, Pete. Everything's all right." Chink and Eve were holding hands, rather sadly, under the table. They'd agreed, without great hope, to stay in Wellington a day or two. "Come on, Pete. Help us with the bacon and eggs."

What the month-old cable said was: *Please phone soonest. Diefenbach.*

THESE BLUE GIRLS

When Chink Peters got back to San Francisco, the fog was still in the streets, so that he felt as if he had not really left.

He was on his way to New York, but there were a few things to arrange on the way through, and the mail to get.

"What seemed simple and terrible has got complicated and terrible," Wally Diefenbach's voice had said, on the radio-telephone, in the American consular office in Wellington. "If you have no commitments, please come, Chinkleberry." The silly word had arrived wanly over a few miles of line and five thousand more of microwaves.

The mail in San Francisco didn't amount to much. A couple of requests for him to judge horse shows, now past. A dude ranch scheme, proposed as a joint venture by a couple he knew. An offer of an agricultural management job in an African country, which really meant, between the lines, commanding mercenaries. A note from a realtor in Eureka saying that the price was likely to rise on the property Chink had described to Eve.

The fog was still thick when he left the branch post office, and seemed almost comfortable to him, as if he had been too much in the sun and exposed by it. Though he had travelled far, the momentum of his urge to go to Wally Diefenbach's assistance seemed to have been waiting here for him like the fog.

He took a cab to the Bay Equestrian Club to leave his duffle, gear, and books with the steward who had charge of his other things. The steward was Hungarian, an escaped freedom fighter with a thin face and green eyes.

"Not staying here now, Mr. Peters?"

"I'm afraid not, Paul."

"There's been some people asking for you."

"Give them my regrets."

"Maybe you'll like to translate now?"

"Maybe."

"Take the book?" Paul had written, in Hungarian, a book on advanced dressage. He had had to leave Hungary without a copy, then come upon one in a foreign-language bookstore, infuriatingly translated into Russian, which let the reader assume that the author was Russian, too.

"Not your only copy."

"I've got Xerox now." He pronounced it *sea rocks.*

"All right," Chink said. "I'll take that."

"Some address for you?"

"I hope to be back soon. If I'm not, I'll call in."

He went to the bank and withdrew $2,500 from his savings account. It left him with a net worth of $19,500, all of it savings except for perhaps $500 worth of luggage, clothes, and saddlery.

He had arrived from New Zealand before dawn. He was at the airport again in time for a one-thirty P.M. United flight, and was at Kennedy in New York just over five hours later. With the time difference, that made it nine-forty-five at night.

Wally Diefenbach's chauffeur met him, a slight, fierce-looking Turk, wiry and quick handed, with a black mustache and a gun in his left armpit.

He took Chink's suitcase in one hand, and with the other offered Chink a pen and a sheet of paper.

"I'm Frank. You Captain Peters."

"Just Mr. Peters, Frank."

"I recognize you all right, you mind to write your name for me?"

The signature seemed to check with one Frank had, and they walked together out through light rain to a government limousine with diplomatic plates, parked by a NO PARKING, NO STANDING sign. An airport policeman was directing traffic around the car.

The Diefenbach apartment was in a vast, new white brick building complex in the East Seventies, with views of the river and several entrances. The doorman at the entrance at which Frank stopped the car was black, and looked like a light-heavyweight fighter. There was another man, even bigger, backing him from the elevator control panel. They wore white leather, rubber-soled shoes with their uniforms.

Frank, the chauffeur, introduced Chink, who was passed on up to the twenty-fourth floor, where a husky, quiet-spoken man in a grey glen-plaid business suit let Chink into the apartment, saying he was Wally's secretary.

"Ambassador and Mrs. Diefenbach will be back about midnight. Can I get you something?"

"I'd like to change clothes and run," Chink said.

"There's a gymnasium on the roof."

"Open?"

"I'll have them open it."

When he returned from working out the stiffness from sitting still on airplanes, Chink drank a glass of milk and looked through back copies of *The New York Times* filed in Wally's study.

The study had a blue and rose Chinese rug, and antique walnut furniture. There was a pair of Eakins' paintings which Wally had inherited and Chink remembered, scenes of oarsmen on the Schuylkill. They had been at Wally's house in Virginia.

On one of the *Times* society pages he found an account of Wally's third marriage to Adrienne Howard, a clothing designer. There was a photograph of the couple, about to board a plane for Europe. It was a reasonably clear photograph. She was tall and dark haired. Wally looked pudgy. A color studio portrait of the same dark-haired woman stood, framed, on Wally's desk. Her skin was strikingly white and the photographer had lighted the hair so that it seemed to ripple.

On intuition, Chink opened the upper-right-hand drawer of the desk, and found two more framed color studio portraits in it. They were of Mike and Wendy. He sat down with them in the leather desk chair.

Mike had had brown hair, too, but lighter than her new stepmother's, and high, dark color to her skin. She was not smiling in the photograph. The pigment of her eyes was very light, like her father's. He wondered if she had worn glasses, and thought, yes, she must have. Her expression in the picture was grave. She looked as if she were about to ask a question.

"Hello, Mike," he said, because he had to say something. Then he said, "Hello, Wendy." From the picture Wendy smiled at him. She was fairer than her sister, the hair streaky blond and feathercut, and her eyes a livelier blue. Chink thought of Natalie, née Holly, the girls' mother, and remembered that Wendy, as a child, had inherited the airy, wood-sprite look that had made her mother somewhat famous as a fashion model, long ago. Wendy in the recent picture still had freckles. Natalie, long ago, would have been freckled, too, except that she wore hats and did not stay long in the sun.

Hello, Mike and Wendy, he thought.

He put the photographs back in the drawer. He did not like to do it, but turned them facedown as he'd found them, and closed the drawer.

He tried to think of something else but, for a time, he couldn't. Then he tried wondering if Wally had a picture of Libby somewhere, but he didn't look for one. He left the study and went to lie down in his room.

Adrienne and Wally Diefenbach, who had taken some Gabonian diplomats to the theatre, came in about twelve-fifteen. Chink heard them and went out to the living room. It was quite stately for an apartment room, its floor tiled in black and white marble squares, formally furnished, and big enough to entertain a crowd in. The new wife looked much as she had in her photographs, but not so fresh-skinned. Her face showed anxiety under the makeup, and the interesting pallor was a little blotchy. She wore an accordion-pleated, off-white, floor-length dress, with a gold belt and gold evening bag. She put the bag down and seized both Chink's hands when they were introduced, bending her knees slightly to come down to his height, and thanked him for coming with an unaffected sincerity which he had not expected.

Wally himself had changed in appearance, though not beyond easy recognition. He was flushed, very worn around the eyes, and heavy. He no longer used the thick-rimmed, comical glasses, but slim ones with slightly harlequinned rims which matched and blended with the grey at his temples. Elsewhere on his scalp was the same light-brown, curly hair, and if a certain jowliness made it unlikely that anyone would call Wally Baby Face again, the pug nose and dimpled cheeks still gave an agreeably mischievous look to the face when he smiled.

Almost immediately, Wally excused himself to get out of the dinner jacket and black tie, leaving Adrienne and Chink together.

"I don't know what it may have been between you two," Adrienne said. "Your wife, of course. I know about that." There was a return of artifice to her voice and manner now. It seemed to be her way of gaining self-possession. "But I don't think anything in the world could mean more to Wally than having you back as a friend."

"How is he, then?" Chink asked.

"I don't really know. I don't get through to him. We'd been married . . . only a few weeks when it happened."

"I know."

"He treats me like a guest. He's, I think he's well. 'A stranger and afraid . . .' in a world he helped to make?" Her voice rose and brightened as Wally returned. "You'll excuse me if I leave you to talk? I'm playing tennis early with one of Wally's Gabonians. He said, 'Den afterwurrs, I will like to haff you for breakfuss.' Oh, dear. You don't suppose he's a cannibal? Anyway, good night, darling." She kissed Wally, and said to Chink: "I'm so very glad you're here."

Wally watched his wife out of the room, before he turned to Chink and said: "You're so tanned and hard. It makes me want to kick you in the head." He was wearing a tan cardigan now, over his evening shirt.

Chink smiled. Then he said: "All right, Major. Okay," and stepped forward, and the two men hugged hard for a moment.

Wally said: "Let's sit in the study and trickle something down our dusty throats." His way of talking hadn't changed, but it lacked some of the old energy.

In the study, Wally poured himself quite a lot of scotch into a brandy snifter, and got Chink a bottle of beer. They sat in leather armchairs, and Wally said:

"So you didn't go to Tahiti."

"I don't think I would have. Anyway, I got your cable."

"What's she like?"

"It doesn't matter, does it, Wally?"

" 'One of the world's loveliest people,' to quote Sam Lowen. Chink, the apartment Mike and Wendy lived in is empty now. I've kept it that way, waiting for you to get here."

Chink Peters felt a chill between his shoulder blades, stared at Wally Diefenbach, and didn't want to hear him say the next thing: "Would you be willing to stay in it for a while?"

"Ah, Wally. How could that help?"

"There are five other young women living in the building. I feel responsible for every one of them."

"But the killer's dead."

"Let me tell you about him." Wally drank part of his scotch and poured some more into the snifter. "I do a lot of this, late at night these days. After Adrienne's in bed. Three or four drinks and take a pill. Then I can sleep. Well. He was using the name Manuel Carbajal. He came from Colombia to Puerto Rico, on a forged U.S. passport worth two thousand dollars, and then on to New York. The police found the passport in his room. It took us a while to get it from them."

"Us? The agency."

"Such profound love in your voice when you say that, Chinkle. Yes. The day I cabled to ask you to call was the day the lab people figured out who made Carbajal's passport. It was made in Japan by some bad little boys who've made passports for half the terrorists in Europe and Asia."

Chink closed his eyes, and opened them again.

Wally said: "There's a place where they train these friendly creatures in Colombia."

"I've heard of the place."

"And someone was keeping Carbajal in funds here. He called himself a folksinger, but he wasn't looking for a place to sing."

"You think your girls knew all that, Wally?"

"That's one of the questions that keeps me up at night." Wally sighed, a long, despairing exhalation. "I have to think they knew. I wish I could learn that they didn't."

"You think the five girls in the house . . . we're supposed to say women, aren't we? Think they could answer your question?"

"Some. Not all the women, probably. Maybe not all the questions."

"April Dorsey, twenty-three, actress?"

"You've been reading the papers. I don't know about April. But Lydia Paul, twenty-five, poet. She was very close to Mike. She lives in the second-floor apartment with Vivian Martin, who's another actress. And was another of Mike's friends. On the third floor is Sue McGrew, who teaches preschool. She was closer to Wendy, I think, and a little like her."

"Living alone?"

"No. I'm sorry. I left out Susan's roommate, Olive Dahlke, who'd belt you out for calling her a girl."

"Olive handy with the dukes, is she?"

Wally smiled a little at that, and Chink asked: "Another teacher?"

"Executive training. In a company I direct, as a matter of fact, though I don't know Olive well. She was Wendy's friend, and had just moved in."

"Mike and Wendy had different friends?"

"They weren't much alike, though they were very close. I imagine the friendships shifted around."

Chink made up his mind. "Wally, you could put someone down there who'd be better at gaining these women's confidence than I would. A younger guy. Another woman. A couple might be best."

Wally was shaking his head.

Chink said: "Investigation wasn't my kind of thing even when I had a kind of thing."

"I've got no one to put, Chink. We don't do those things any longer. The agency only works abroad."

"The New York cops. The F.B.I."

"They think it's done with."

"You want it that way, don't you? Because of which one, Wally? April? The other actress? The one with the dukes?"

"Look at the knight jump, Mommy. Two squares straight and one square sideways."

"Going to tell me?"

"All right. It's April. Or it was briefly, Chinklenoninvestigator. What do I owe you for your trip back to San Francisco?"

"No. You're letting me have that too easily. What am I missing, Wally?"

"Let's talk about terrorists," Wally said. "You never dealt with that kind of slime, Chink. They kill strangers to get attention."

"Not always."

"No. Not always. Sometimes they pick people out. That's my other awful question. I'm a hard-liner on terrorists in the U.N. I've made some tough agreements. Did they pick the hard man's daughters?"

"They'd let you know it, wouldn't they?"

"Not if it all went wrong. Not if their little trained maggot was supposed to do it clean and went off his sleazy head when he found himself alone with a girl." The aging, cherub face grew dark with rising blood. "Wendy." And Chink was on his feet, a hand on Wally's shoulder, saying sure, he'd move into the apartment in the Village.

It really wasn't at all a matter of investigation, Wally said, when he recovered. Just a presence there, possibly protection. Because if there had been a plan gone wrong, there could be other maggots hatching in the slime.

"Eustace Martin has your keys," Wally said, at breakfast. He looked less tired.

"Who's Eustace Martin?"

"You don't know the name?"

Chink shook his head.

"Father of second-floor Vivian, the other actress. But you must have heard of Eustace."

"I'm afraid not."

"Basically, he's a jazz clarinet player," Wally said. "Traditional musician, not as well known as he used to be. But he's also a clown about town. And he has a pretty good jazz club a couple of blocks away from your new house." Wally was in good control this morning. "I've known Eustace quite a while. Libby liked him. We helped him start the club." Chink was about to ask how Libby was, and where, but Wally went on. "Eustace is a kind man. He was nice to the girls. He's been a help to me. Want to see him?"

"I guess I'm going to, when I get the keys."

"No. I've got some tapes." Eustace Martin, Wally said, was often a guest on television talk shows, welcome for being somewhat eccentric. Wally had a television tape player in the study. "I use it for work. We keep the current tapes from the U.N. closed circuit. All those glutinous speeches. But it's more fun collecting Eustace."

He got a tape cassette from a collection on one of the bookshelves, put it on the machine, and turned it on. Almost instantly, to the sound of studio audience applause, a tall, bony, thin-haired man with a mournful face appeared on the screen, slouching but still a head taller than the natty talk-show host. The host was clapping loudly, his hands stuck up in front of Martin's face. Martin was watching the hands with distaste, but after a moment moved his head back away from them and covered his ears. The audience laughed. The host led Martin to a chair between two other guests, into which the long man lowered himself, his lined face settling into a sad-hound expression.

"The unpredictable Eustace Martin!" said the host. "Say something unpredictable, Eustace."

Eustace Martin looked away.

"You're not talking tonight?"

Martin looked back at the host, and shook his head, no. But this was a *talk* show, the host pointed out. Eustace Martin opened his mouth and closed it.

"Was that supposed to be a view of the cat that's got your tongue?" Laughter. "Here, kitty, kitty, kitty." Laughter.

Wally said: "Eustace was doing this to promote the club. I'm afraid it was a bit rehearsed."

Now Eustace opened his mouth again, and took a reed out of it, held the reed up, reached down as if to scratch his ankle, pulled up the pant leg, and revealed, as the camera panned down to it, the pieces of a clarinet taped to his shin. There was prolonged applause as the host insisted that Eustace had promised not to bring his instrument, and Eustace put the thing together. He made a couple of rude sounds on it in the host's direction, and then began to play something unexpectedly slow and soft, a kind of meditation. Chink thought it was probably quite nice.

"It's called 'Do You Know What It Means to Miss New Orleans?' " Wally said, and let the tune finish. After it, Eustace smiled and invited the host and everybody else to visit him at his nightclub. "Featuring a little music, and a lot of overpriced booze," he said. The delivery was slow, country, and lugubrious. "And the worst hamburgers in the city of New York."

"They can't be that bad," the host said.

"The other night I saw the cook out in the alley, trying to feed one to a hungry dog," Eustace said. "Poor dog took a sniff and couldn't believe it. He took another and sat down and started to howl."

Wally interrupted the scene and advanced the tape. "Watch this one," he said, his finger on the hold button. "It's spontaneous. But I wanted you to hear him play." The next was a recording of a different sort of show, a panel during one of the moon shots. "Eustace writes comic space songs sometimes," Wally said. " 'My wife's got eyes on her fingertips, so I never cheat on Mars. When I want the bliss of a ten-lip kiss there's lots of other stars.' " Chink smiled. "This panel was called 'The Moon in Pop Culture.' "

An announcer's face appeared and asked for opening statements. There was a science fiction writer who wanted it acknowledged that he'd invented moon shots accurately in a novel thirty years earlier. There was a professor of astrochemistry, who wanted to explain that while the moon was not a place where life could evolve, moon shots illustrated the possibility of forms of life inhabiting spatial bodies through immigration.

Eustace Martin said he'd immigrate on past the opening statement. This seemed to pique the others. It was clear that neither the writer nor the astrochemist, and not the moderator for that matter, was aware that Martin was chiefly a musician, nor even that the songs he'd written were satiric.

"Is this moon business causing a revolution on Tin Pan Alley, Eustace?"

"No barricades going up last time I looked," Eustace said, in his slow, gravelly way.

"Do you tunesmiths still feel the same about rhyming 'moon' and 'June,' for instance?"

"Maybe 'tycoon.' Would that be better?"

"In my novel *The Crater Dwellers,*" the writer said, "there is a tycoon, as a matter of fact, who finances moon development."

"Surely you didn't indicate that there were creatures dwelling in the craters?" the professor asked.

Eustace nodded. "Gibboons?" he suggested.

The moderator, trying to get back in control, looked at his notes and read, quickly: "Now Shakespeare, in his famous play *Romeo and Juliet,* speaks of the moon as 'inconstant,' and therefore inappropriate as a lovers' pledge. Was Shakespeare right, Eustace Martin?"

Eustace thought it over. " 'Spittoon'?" he inquired, and began to push himself up. He was leaving the table, the conversation, and the suddenly flurried camera.

" 'Saloon,' " they heard him say decisively, as the long shambling legs filled the screen for a moment.

"He walked out on it?" Chink asked.

"He said it was a swell conversation but it made him thirsty," Wally said, turning off the TV. "Not that it takes much to make Eustace thirsty."

"Show him Vivian, too." It was Adrienne Diefenbach, who had come into the study and stood watching.

"Hi, darling," Wally said. "How was tennis?"

"Brutal. Everything he served was a double fault or an ace. Good morning, Chink."

"Good morning."

"I want Wally to show you his tape of Eustace Martin's daughter, Vivian." Adrienne said. "I love it because people think she and I look alike, and she's so stunning."

So there was a final tape showing, this last of Vivian Martin, the young actress living on the second floor of the house downtown, who had been a friend of Mike Diefenbach's, though older. The tape was of an episode from a soap opera, in which Vivian played the visiting sister of a man in coma in a hospital. Her resemblance to Adrienne was not close, but they were the same physical type, tall women with dark hair and fair skin. Vivian's features, Chink thought, were larger and more definite, and like her father she showed her bones. Her movement was quite graceful in a practiced way.

In the scene there was discussion of turning off the coma victim's life-support machinery. Vivian, as the sister, was against it. In a low, vibrato voice, she refused to leave the hospital room. The machinery, she objected, could be turned off without her knowledge.

"Don't you trust me?" the sincere young interne asked.
"I've trusted men. I even trusted a doctor once, Doctor."

"I love that intensity," Adrienne said.

"Ah, Vivian," said Wally.

On the screen, the doctor left the room. Vivian plumped her brother's pillow, and was telling him something, a family secret perhaps, which Chink understood no better than the brother could be supposed to.

"So get well. Come to, Bradley. Please come to before Saturday
—or *I'll have to do it myself.*"

The camera moved to the light which showed the life-support machinery turned on, and then to a switch beside it.

"I think I'll do it myself," Wally said, and turned off the tape machine. The grey-suited secretary Chink had met the night before came in a moment later to say that the ambassador was wanted on the communications room phone.

"Well," Adrienne said. "Were you ravished?"

"By Vivian? Sure."

"I was rather jealous of her when Wally and I were first seeing one another. Even though she's young. Or maybe because she is. I thought he was seeing her, too, and so he was but not romantically. It was a different sort of courtship."

Chink supposed he wanted to know whatever it was she was getting ready to tell him.

"Wally didn't know his daughters very well. They'd been away at school, and with their mother. With your Libby, sometimes, even after the divorce. Will you be seeing her?"

"I don't know," Chink said. "Is she in New York?"

"Long Island, since her mother died. Wally sees her sometimes. On business. Financial business. I gather she can be difficult."

"She didn't used to be. About money, anyway."

"The girls liked her. Mary was quite hostile to her father, really. She took her mother's side, and Libby's too. Wendy was sweet to everyone, but distantly sweet to Wally. When he found they wanted to come to New York for college . . ."

"Excuse me," Chink said. "Were they in the same year?"

"Yes. Mary had spent a year out of school. She and Vivian Martin went to Ireland and France, while Wendy caught up. Wally wanted the girls here with him. Mary said a flat no, and Wendy a sweet no, I suppose. So Wally and his friend Eustace Martin found that house in the Village and Wally bought it. Vivian was mad to move in, and helped persuade the girls. The idea was to make it a little community of interesting women."

"Vivian found the others?"

"I'm not sure. But she's nice. A little overpowering but nice. I can't stand her roommate, Lydia. But that's not your worry, is it?"

"It may be," Chink said. "Wally's asked me to stay down there for a while."

"He what?" The splotches on her cheeks changed color. "Wally didn't tell me he was going to ask you." The complexion went back to normal. "Well, he doesn't tell me much of anything, as a matter of fact. I don't suppose you will, either."

Though it was a dozen years old, the Guggenheim Museum had been built since Chink Peters' last visit to New York. In the afternoon he walked over to it, twenty blocks or so from the Diefenbach apartment, spent an hour there, and found, towards the top of the great, caracole ramp, the original of the Rousseau painting of Frenchmen playing rugby of which Eve Shellcroft had once given him a reproduction. At the desk downstairs, he bought a framed copy of the same reproduction, and asked that it be sent to him at Wally's address.

At about three, he left the museum and started walking downtown. Wally had said that Eustace Martin, from whom Chink was to get his keys, was hard to track down during the day but ought to be at his club shortly after five, for the cocktail trade.

It was quite a cool, late summer day. Chink walked down through the park, then along Fifth Avenue, past the great department stores, enjoying the frivolous look of women's clothing in the windows. The faces of people on the street, responding, he thought, to the washed air and crisp weather after a night of rain, looked open and relaxed.

At Brooks Brothers, on Madison Avenue, where he hadn't been for twenty years, Chink stopped in and bought some shirts and a couple of neckties. He couldn't remember the last time he'd bought a new necktie. The two he chose were striped rep, a black and red one and a tan and green. He thought of going next to the Yale Club, to have a beer there, but found no sense of connection in himself with Yale any longer. He paid, asked to have the clothing sent, and walked on down to Greenwich Village.

It was just after five when he came to a sign on West Twelfth Street: EUSTACE MARTIN'S. The sign had a blue background on which tubular orange light outlined a clarinet, crossed with the owner's name in script. Under the sign was a short awning, and under that a half-glass doorway. There was a blue velvet curtain across the glass, inside, and a poster between glass and curtain to tell anyone considering going in the names of the trio and the intermission pianist currently appearing.

Inside, the place was barely open. There was a long bar on the left, with blue-plastic-covered stools along it, blue-seated booths on the right, and a double door, standing open, leading into a second room where there were tables and chairs and a small bandstand. There were no customers, only a bartender on hand, an ambiguously dark-skinned young man, with glossy black hair, a pencil-line mustache, and a very white smile.

"Yes, sir?"

"I'd like to see Mr. Martin, please. My name's C.K. Peters."

The smile went away and was replaced by a theatrical rendering of confusion. "Ees no coming no tonight, Missa Martinna."

"Is that right?"

"I teenk tomorra maybe he go out fum town. . . ." The hands spun.

Chink said in Spanish: "I'm not a bill collector."

"I used to talk funny, too," the bartender said.

"You Cuban?"

"I'm American, born in Cuba. What about you? Navy? C.I.A.?" He made his guess. "Federal marshal, ex-Army."

"Civilian. For a long time now."

"It's the way you wear your clothes."

"I see."

"I used to see them trying to look civilian in Miami, growing up. I could always tell."

"What do you do? Besides tend bar and always tell?"

It made the bartender smile again slightly. "Help Mr. Martin. And I'm a medical student. What do you want to drink?"

"Draft beer, please. I do need to see your boss. For Ambassador Diefenbach. Does that help?"

"I know the name. Diefenbach. He comes here for the music sometimes."

"I understand he's part owner."

"You understand pretty good. What's your name again?"

"C.K. Peters. Is Eustace Martin here someplace?" Chink supposed there must be an office in the back.

"You think I'm lying, Mr. Peters?"

"I teenk tomorra Missa Martinna maybe go out fum town."

"I told you I help Mr. Martin. What's it about?"

Two men came in and up to the bar. Chink said, quickly and quietly in Spanish: "The ambassador asked me to move into the house where Vivian Martin lives."

The eyebrows went up. "Number One apartment?"

Chink nodded. "Eustace Martin has my keys."

Suddenly the bartender's smile was dazzling again, and both hands came across the bar to seize Chink's hand and wrist. "You are? Yes? My name's Leon. Leon Quiroz, at your orders. Let me explain that Eustace isn't here yet. But come on. Enjoy your beer. Allow me to get it. Eustace will come."

"Hey, guys," one of the customers called. "How about less Spanish and more alcohol?"

When he came back, Leon Quiroz was still beaming. "Let's continue to speak Spanish if you enjoy it," he said. "You have that nice Argentine accent."

"Thanks," Chink said. "Uruguayan. Are you a friend of Vivian Martin's?"

"I know all the young ladies," Leon said. "Charming, brave, wonderful girls. So brave, but I'm glad there's to be a man there. Anytime. If you need assistance, please call here. I can get there in two minutes."

It was nearly six. Eustace Martin had not arrived. There were a dozen cocktail customers when the two young women came in. One was slight, blond, and absurdly young-looking to be entering a bar. She had a brown paper sack of groceries in her arms. The other seemed older, mid-twenties, with dark, ivory-shaded skin, dark red hair, curiously bulky shoulders. She carried a briefcase. The young one wore a white sweater and a blue skirt, the older one a tailored pants suit.

"Leon," the one in the suit said. "Is Eustace here?"

"Hello, Olive. He's not here yet. Hello, Sue."

Chink knew the surnames and the occupations: Olive Dahlke, executive training. Susan McGrew, preschool teacher.

Susan, the blond one, was wispy and very light on her feet. "We need Eustace for an escort, Leon." She said it gaily, with a smile and a small toss of her head.

Leon's voice was doting. "You want to have a drink and wait for Eustace, Susan?"

"Or if you could come?" She reached across the bar and touched Leon's wrist lightly.

"To leave here right now is hard."

"Leon." Now Olive Dahlke spoke, clearly and slowly as though to a child. "There is a man asleep, blocking our doorway. We can't get in."

"He looks like a very large man," Susan said, still lightly, mocking Olive's severe tone. "As seen from well across the street. Which is as close as we strong, liberated women dared to get."

"A nigger man?" Leon grew agitated. "They get drunk, they sleep anyplace."

"Probably," Olive said.

"He doesn't have to be black," said Susan. "Anyway, we didn't get very close and he's got his arms over his face."

"We didn't get very close." Olive repeated Susan's remark.

"I don't think he's hurt," Susan said. "He looks all curled up and peaceful."

"The light must have been in his eyes," Olive said.

"I'm calling the police." Someone down the bar was tapping with an empty glass, trying to get Leon's attention. "They'll put some light in his eyes."

"Why don't we have a margarita?" Susan's voice had a pretty lilt to it, and it was clear enough that she wasn't actually a child, but a young woman who would look like one for a while. "Let the poor man wake up and move on."

"Good. Two margaritas?" Leon asked.

"No, thank you." Olive's ways were not as pleasant as Susan's, a little grim even. "We want to go home."

"Please don't call the police," Susan said. "If it's a black man, he'll get in trouble."

"What's wrong with a little trouble?" Leon finished making an old-fashioned for the impatient customer.

"Oh, Leon, stop it," Susan said. The bartender smiled, delivered the drink, and returned.

"May I walk over and see about it?" Chink asked.

"Sure." Leon was pleased. "Sure. Good idea. You want to?"

"Who are you?" Olive didn't sound as if she really wanted to know.

"Sure," Leon said. "Sure, this is Mr. Peters. Your new roommate."

Olive stared at Chink. Susan seemed startled.

"I'll be the tenant in the ground floor apartment," Chink said. "At Wally Diefenbach's request."

"The ground floor," Olive repeated, and Susan said, "Oh. Oh, really."

"He's waiting for Eustace, too," Leon said. "To get his keys. So let him walk with you."

"I think we might have been asked," Olive Dahlke said.

"Oh, Olive!" Now Susan smiled. "Hello, Mr. Peters. I'm Susan McGrew." She offered her hand. "Dangerous Sue McGrew."

Her handshake was a brief, warm squeeze, Olive's, when she introduced herself, firm enough to be a challenge.

Susan allowed Chink to take the grocery bag.

"Oh, Susan!" It was Olive's turn to scold.

From the club on Twelfth Street they went a long block east, turning downtown on Seventh Avenue, and then east again at the corner of Tenth Street. Susan chattered, and Olive grew friendlier. She'd been coming home from work, she said, couldn't wait for a shower and slippers, and saw Susan standing across from their house, some distance from the man in the entryway.

"She was waiting for me or one of the others," Olive said. "So she could run over and try to wake him, but I wouldn't permit it. Someone like that can be shamming."

"Well," said Susan. "He's still there. Or his feet are, anyway."

Partway down the block Chink could see a stoop rising to a brownstone front with a set-back entry. The feet stuck out of the entry. One had its shoe partly off, as if, in his sleep, the man had pushed at it with the other foot. The shoe was a moccasin, a very large one, even seen from forty feet away, and the sock maroon. As the angle opened Chink could see that the man, partly curled up with his arms over his face as Susan had said, was wearing a white shirt and no tie under a tan wool jacket. The pants were dark and showed the grime of the entryway.

"He's a white man," Chink said, seeing the hands.

He started up the steps, inhaling, smelling for alcohol, and there was some of it in the air though not as much as he expected. He could hear deep, slow breathing, an easy half snore at the beginning of each intake, reassuringly even and healthy, and before he'd reached the top of the steps and uncovered the face he felt quite sure that the man would be the one he'd been waiting for, Eustace Martin, passed out at his daughter's front door at six-twenty-five on an August afternoon.

"Overloaded," Eustace said. "Six tons on a five-ton truck."

They had got him to the third floor, to Susan and Olive's apartment. It had been difficult to wake the tall man and walk him indoors and up two flights of stairs. Now he was stretched out groggily in a green chintz-covered armchair, but his head seemed clear.

Susan brought Alka-Seltzer in a cocktail glass.

"Sue McGrew," Eustace said. "My love so true."

"I'd have floated a rose petal in it, if only I had a rose."

"A dozen a day for the rest of your life," Eustace said. "If only I had a flower shop."

"What do we tell Vivian?" Olive asked, smiling.

"Tell her her old man drinks too much. It'll come as a great surprise." He finished off the Alka-Seltzer, made a face, and said, in his slow way: "I can feel every little corpuscle fizz inside. Was coming to see Vivian. Fell in with evil companions." He sighed. "Got here and reached in my pocket, and found a key about the size of a telephone pole. Well, I couldn't locate a place in the door big enough to fit a thing like that. So. I sat down to wait for the key to shrink, and pretty soon, along came Sleep. 'Howya been, big Eustace?' says Sleep. 'Kinda lonesome for you, old friend,' Big Eustace said, and out he stretched his big, long, weary bones. . . ."

Chink liked listening to the man talk. He asked, during a pause, about his keys. Eustace said they were at the club, but the power wasn't on in the ground floor apartment. They'd get it reconnected in the morning.

Susan said she thought she heard the door open and close down below, went away, and came back with Vivian.

"Daddy!" Vivian was more sweepingly dramatic than she'd

seemed on the television screen. "You are not too big to spank." It was a strong, warm voice that filled the room with energy. "Incorrigible." She threw her arms around her father's head and squeezed it, released him, glanced at Susan for confirmation, and extended an arm and hand towards Chink. "And this is Mr. Peters?"

"Maybe he's incorrigible, too," Eustace said hopefully. "He's called Chink. That's a bad sign, isn't it?"

" 'Chink' Peters?" Susan said. "Are you Chink Peters?"

"He is. He must be," Vivian said.

"I have a picture of you," Susan said. "Because I'm a horse nut. Oh, I feel so stupid. Look." She darted off into another room.

Olive said, "I'm afraid I can't play this game, Mr. Peters."

"Good," said Eustace, morose again. "She never heard of you in her whole, entire life, and she is an intelligent, well-informed, and popular young woman."

"Do shut up, Daddy darling," Vivian said, and Sue McGrew returned with a photograph in a glass-and-leather frame. It was very old, from the cover of an issue of *The Chronicle of the Horse,* a professionally taken picture of himself on Coker, jumping.

> *"Chink" Peters on Coker. A good bet for Horse of the Year—next year*

the caption read.

"Yep," said Chink.

"And you were on the Olympic team, too," Susan said.

"No."

"You helped coach it, then."

"How do you happen to have this?" Chink asked, and was sorry, for the answer was predictable.

"Wendy gave it to me," Sue McGrew said. "Mike kept threatening to make me give it back."

"We talk about them, Chink," Vivian Martin said. "All the time. I don't think any of us could stand it if we didn't."

When Chink got back uptown he found that Adrienne Diefenbach was in for the evening. She was wearing a black and orange striped housecoat, and black sandals. She was the kind of woman, Chink thought, about whom you would always notice what she was wearing.

She had a glass of champagne in her hand when she let him in, said that Wally and his secretary were at an evening meeting and that she'd sent out for Chinese food.

"Much too much of it. I couldn't stop ordering. I hope you haven't eaten?"

"I tried," Chink said. "At Eustace Martin's club. They think food's some kind of joke there."

"Those awful hamburgers. They're for the drunks, and very expensive, aren't they?"

"Mine was on the house, but it didn't do much for the flavor."

"Let's sit in my studio," she said. "You haven't seen it. Would you like champagne?" She picked up the bottle and an extra glass, and led him into a north-lit room with a drawing table, swivel stools, a heap of fabric samples, a light sofa with a caned back, and Adrienne's fashion sketches pinned up around the walls on corkboard. She drew nicely, an easy flowing line.

"Wendy came and drew with me one day," Adrienne said. "Those were hers. She had a flair, didn't she?" Chink looked at a group of half a dozen drawings, different in style, the line more dashing, the figures interestingly angular. "Never mind. Here." She handed him a glass and filled it with champagne. "We'll finish this bottle and open another. Tomorrow let's make Wally take us to Twenty-One."

"I've never been there," Chink said, still looking at Wendy's drawings. "She had some strength."

"She kept it hidden. Mary was openly strong, and much harder for me to get to know. Would you like to sit?"

"Thanks." He sat on the sofa. Adrienne remained standing, looking down at him now, the bottle held out with its bottom against her hip.

"Have you seen the apartment?"

"Not yet. I've been in the building."

"I hope it's all right. I did the decorating. Not a very happy task, but Wally didn't want a stranger in there. Did you meet the girls, then?"

"Susan and Olive. And Vivian."

"I know Viv, of course. And I've met Susan. A kind of Tinker

Bell type, isn't she? I don't know Olive but she works for Wally's company."

"The packing house?"

The champagne was French and vintage. Chink was thirsty and drank it off.

"W.C.I. Western Construction Industries. It's a conglomerate. One of the things it owns is the old Diefenbach meat business."

"Wally's mentioned being a director."

"Pretty much *the* director. The conglomerate bought Diefenbach Packing with stock, as I understand it, and our friend sandbagged them. He and Libby were quietly putting all her money into more W.C.I. stock, and they got enough to control. Here." She handed him her own glass, and then refilled both his and hers when he held them up. "Tell me how the girls are down there now."

"A little spooky."

Adrienne took the glass and sat down, close enough to him so that their hips brushed. She put the bottle on the floor. She moved her shoulder back, so that her face turned towards his, and asked: "Is it going to be hard for you?"

"Excuse me?" He kept his voice stolid.

"Being surrounded by all those girls?"

"I hadn't thought about it."

"What an odd man you are, then." She smiled slightly and swayed back a little, then stood, drank off her champagne, leaned towards him to pick up the bottle from the floor and to fill her glass again. She moved off a step or two, turned, and said: "Wait till you see April. She looks like a schoolgirl. A naughty one. They all do, don't they? Not naughty, but. Not Vivian, of course. Chink, did the girls you met, the Olive . . . Oh, my. I'm not sure I ought to have more champagne, but I shall. What did you talk about with Olive and Susan? You haven't met Lydia, either, but I simply don't care for Lydia . . . did I say that? Whatever did you young things talk about?"

Chink said: "Eustace Martin was there. We visited."

"About the other girls?"

"Not really."

"But you must have." Playfully, she stuck her chin out at him.

"I seem to be dying for some gossip. What did they say about, oh, April, or anybody?"

"I don't think her name came up."

It was as if he could see her giving up the idea of affecting champagne dizziness and some degree of flirtation, for when she sat down now it was at a more conventional distance, and her voice sounded normal. "I admit I'm curious. Wally more or less told me that he'd had an affair with April."

"It doesn't seem to be a secret," Chink said.

"But it doesn't make sense, does it? Wally Diefenbach is a subtle, sensitive man. But not even a very crude man would move his mistress in next door to his young daughters, would he?"

"I see what you mean," Chink said, and realized he'd been troubled by the same discrepancy.

Chink stood at the front door of the brownstone house on West Tenth Street with new keys in his hand. It was a bright morning and a dark, heavy door. The door was new, like the keys. There was a small, opaque window set high in it. The glass was certainly unbreakable and possibly bulletproof.

Beside the door was a mouthpiece, set in the outer wall. Visitors were to ring a bell, announce themselves, and be admitted by remote control of the door latch. There were four bells, arranged vertically with names beside them in small brass frames. From the top the framed words were: *Apartment 3, Dahlke and McGrew. Apartment 2, Vivian Martin, Lydia Paul. Apartment 1-B*, A. *Dorsey*. The bell for Apartment 1-A had no name beside it. Chink had one of Wally's cards with him. He got it out, wrote *C.K. Peters* on the back, folded it to fit, slipped it into place, and let himself into the house.

He stood then, for a moment, in the first floor hallway, hearing the heavy door close itself behind him. Helping Eustace Martin through this hall the day before, he hadn't paid much attention. Now he turned his head to see, as he'd assumed, that the glass window in the door, opaque from the outside, allowed a person standing inside to look out.

The hallway was wide and carpeted in green. The wall of the stairwell was papered in a lighter green than the carpet, with a thick and thin pattern of gold stripes. Just to the right of the landing at the foot of the staircase was a door with 1-B on it, in brass, and a peephole underneath the figure and letter.

In the center of the right-hand wall, opposite the stairs, was another apartment door which would be 1-A, but the lettering had been removed and the door was being sanded. A workman had left his tools, a sander, brushes, cans of varnish, stain, and thinner, neatly placed on a folded dropcloth beside the door. When the workman returned, he would presumably finish sanding out some words which had been painted on the door. Chink went close to try to make out the words, but couldn't.

" 'Pat and Mike.' " It was a distant, inexpressive female voice.

He turned. The speaker was standing in the doorway to 1-B, holding the door slightly open behind herself.

"Excuse me?"

"It said 'Pat and Mike.' It was a joke because Mary was called Mike, but Wendy was never called Pat. Wendy painted it there for some reason, just before they were killed." All this was said flatly, almost recited, as if the words were both true and without meaning.

"I see."

"Wally Diefenbach called me. You're Chink."

"And you're April Dorsey."

She looked at him without nodding, but it was possible the whole body inclined slightly in his direction, signifying yes. She had brown eyes and straight, sandy hair, cut short. She was wearing penny loafers, panty hose, and a chino skirt about the same shade as her hair. She had on a man's T-shirt which said: "Property of the Athletic Department, University of Maryland." She was conspicuously buxom and wore no brassiere. Her complexion was smooth, a little sallow, but fresh enough looking. It was a pleasant appearance, still somehow unformed, youthfully pretty without being striking and quite out of tone with the disengaged way she spoke.

"Not working today, April?"

"I'm an actress. Sometimes I work."

Chink wondered why Adrienne Diefenbach thought April looked "naughty," and supposed that, since there was none of the energy there of being mischievous, Adrienne saw something suggestive in slackness.

Chink glanced away, at the apartment door, and then back

again at April. She stood well. Her full figure could be dressed and lit to be quite voluptuous on stage, and her expressionless young face made up to look like anything required. She was just about his own height or a little shorter.

"I'm going to be living here," he told her.

"That's what Wally said." It didn't seem to interest her any more than the other things on which she'd commented.

She continued to watch him in her disassociated way, through the brown eyes, under the shell of sand-colored hair. He turned away, put in a key, and opened the partly sanded door. He stepped in without looking back again at April.

The carpeting, drapes, and sofa in the high room he entered were new. The walls were freshly painted. Adrienne had chosen quiet, warm colors, brick and light ochre, with bone white walls and blue accents, here and there, for contrast. It was a decorating textbook room, with no look of ever having been inhabited.

He lifted the phone and heard a dial tone. He tried a wall switch, and the lights went off and on. He thought it might be possible to stay here.

The left wall at the rear of the house was mostly glass, French windows opening into what seemed to be a small garden. There was an empty fireplace opposite the front door with brass-knobbed andirons, and, on the right, doors to the rest of the apartment.

He unlatched the French windows, stepped outside, and stopped short. There was a small door over to the left, going into what had been a one-story addition to the main house, possibly servants' quarters once, now April Dorsey's studio apartment. The other two garden walls were translucent, corrugated fiberglass, light green. They were covered with bright bursts of spray-can painting in a cheerful hodgepodge of styles, friendly blobs of color and squiggles, figures of animals and children crude and gay, flower shapes, balloons, and words: *Love-Love, Rabbits Keep Right, Viva Peace, Please and Thank You, God, Pardon My Kangaroo,* and the name *Wolfe Tone,* with a wreath around it. All Chink could do at first was try to concentrate and fail at remembering who Wolfe Tone was.

Then he gave in to the scene those walls implied of girls at play, on a sunny afternoon, Coca-Cola, sandals, shorts, potato chips, and cold white wine.

"I need the purple, don't be piggy." Was it Sue McGrew?

"I'll paint a purple pig," Wendy cried, spraying Susan's foot.

"I've got her, help. Susie, grab the paint." Vivian, taking charge.

"Here, Sue. Use red," said Mike. "Get her with red."

"Wolfe Tone. Save me, Wolfe."

"Paint your toenails, Miss?" And down go two or three in a squealing heap.

"Keep right, rabbits."

"Pardon my kangaroo."

He made himself stop. He didn't really know how young women sounded, frolicking. But was April there, and solemn Olive, too? The laughter was still there, frozen in color, and ghost voices in the August sunlight. Shaken, Chink Peters went back into the immaculate living room.

He found himself staring at the new sofa, polished wood and raw silk, knowing that it replaced a yellow velour one which, the newspaper had said, was so covered with blood as to turn its cushions orange. He went quickly into the next room, which was a small dining room. Beyond it, with grilled windows opening onto Tenth Street, was a kitchen. He supposed the dining room furniture and kitchen appliances to be unchanged.

There was a hallway from the living room down the center of the rest of the apartment, its door next to the dining room door. The bedrooms opened off the hallway, to the left. Their closets were empty. The beds were freshly made with new linen. A bathroom connected the bedrooms. He went into it, and knelt by the tub. After a time, he pressed his forehead down against the cool white enamel of the rim, and allowed sobs to come.

Then he went slowly back into the living room, knowing that he must complete his reconstruction now or he would not be able to come back here.

He sat on a corner of the new sofa, in front of the empty fireplace, as he imagined Wendy must have sat on the old sofa, in her dressing gown and bare feet, waiting her turn to bathe. He thought she might have been reading.

There was a mahogany coffee table now, between the sofa and

the fireplace, with carved legs and brass claws for feet, holding clear glass balls.

The ceiling was high, and the plaster had been maintained in a false-dome look, with dart-and-egg molding in the plaster outlining the illusion.

Whatever the other changes, Wendy had been sitting under the same ceiling. He supposed a knock at the door.

He supposed Wendy rising to let Manuel Carbajal in. Chink stood and moved towards the door.

Hello, Manny. Was she surprised, or was Carbajal expected? Was he challenged or welcomed? Chink, standing, stared into the fireplace, and had a sense of conversation, its content without dialogue, in which, growing alarmed, Wendy asked Carbajal to leave. Lines came into Chink's mind:

"Manny, it's so late. Come have breakfast in the morning."

"No."

"Waffles, Manny?"

Carbajal was a trained man. He knew the disabling blows. He had struck her with something, probably stunned her, and begun to stab. Then the blood must have excited him, there was so much of it. Exposed now, Chink was Wendy, hurting, but couldn't be, of course. That was the horror. He couldn't hurt for her, any more than he could come in, smash Carbajal, subdue him. He could only hope that the man's first, surprise, stunning blow had been a swift one, powerful and accurate, taking Wendy out of knowing. *Please and thank you, God.* But he had seen too often how bodies kept fighting to live, even when consciousness is gone. Then, the butchery of the corpse—Chink's eyes were blurred and his body jerking. Only gradually was he able to contain the spasms. When he did, he thought he could leave now, and had better. It was going to be harrowing, always, to stay here, but he might manage it, if he stayed out of the garden, now that he had made himself imagine fully.

He opened the door, and pulled it away from the burring of the sander he'd seen earlier. A workman, leaning into the sander, half fell towards Chink, stopped himself, and said:

"Hey." He was a blur of a pale, middle-aged workman in overalls, with lank white hair. "God, you scared me."

"Sorry." Chink heard his own, choked voice.

"Hey. I didn't know there was someone in there."

"Tenant." Chink was having trouble getting his breath and focusing.

"Oh, yeah? You know what this place is, huh? Huh? I'll bet you do. The wife and I came down the next day, right after. We live on Fourteenth."

Chink walked into him, shoved the man aside, and lurched down the hall. He still hadn't recovered his normal balance by the time he reached the street door, pulled it open, and went out. On the steps, moving aside quickly to let him pass, he might have seen a small, grey-haired woman, but as soon as he was by her and down the steps he could not have said that she had actually been there. He turned west, towards the river, going the way Carbajal had gone, down two long blocks and a short one, to the warehouse fronts where the street was cobblestoned.

Over to the right across the street was a space between two warehouses. Chink went to it and saw the pier out which the killer must have gone to drown himself. Chink moved on slowly, onto the heavy, lateral planks, past the creosoted posts to where the structure ended, and stood for a time looking down into the oily water, as if Manuel Carbajal could still be seen floating down there, just under the surface, wavery and pale.

I can't stay long, it's too damn hard, he thought. A week, only because I said I would.

He sent for his things in the afternoon, and moved in, unpacking as he might have in one of the forgotten hotel rooms in which he'd spent so many of the nights of his life.

He had shopped. He was sitting in the living room in the twilight, drinking a bottle of German beer, hoping still that Adrienne Diefenbach might call to say that Wally had agreed to take them out to dinner. It no longer seemed likely that she would.

The German beer label had reproduced on it, in blue-green and yellow, a Gothic-style engraving of the landgrave's palace at Wartburg, the castle where Walther von der Vogelweide sang for Hermann of Thuringia.

He wondered if he wanted to call some one of the people he

knew in New York, but thought that if he had no more in mind than to avoid spending this evening here alone, it would not be fair.

He was pleased to hear a knock on the door, and opened it to Susan McGrew.

"Hello." She bit her lip, smiled, swallowed, and said, all in one breath: "If I beg and plead and pout and throw fits, will you come up and have supper with us?"

"I'd love to see you do all that," Chink said. "What time?"

"We might be ready in an hour, if we concentrate like mad."

"What may I bring?"

"A sunny disposition, oh, I'm sorry. It's what my father would say, but it came out cheeky, didn't it? But Olive's being grave tonight, and Vivian's being dramatic, and Lydia never knows the difference between interesting and quarrelsome, so we do need you."

Chink smiled and said he'd be along in an hour.

He asked himself what the kindly, middle-aged bachelor neighbor role required, candy, wine, or flowers? He decided on flowers and went out to shop for them. There were handsome chrysanthemums. He amused himself getting the florist to mix two dozen, straw yellow for Susan's hair, yellow-brown for April's, and a red that was almost brown for Olive Dahlke's. He let the darkest orange stand for Vivian, though of course her hair was black, and added five flowers that were nearly white, having, he thought, no idea of Lydia Paul's appearance.

About that he was wrong. When he knocked at the door of Apartment 3, it was opened by someone oddly familiar, a short, trim, frowning young woman with an oval face, unplucked brows, large dark eyes, and hair that had already gone pepper and salt.

"I'm Chink Peters," he said.

"I know. You nearly knocked me down this afternoon."

"Excuse me?"

"That's what you should have said this afternoon."

"Wait. Were you—was that you? On the steps when I came out of the building?"

"You looked like the fiend was riding on your shoulders. Susan? Susan, come here. Your sexist brute has come with flowers."

"Oh, look. Look!" Susan came dashing to the door, her right hand full of silverware, and Chink could see past her to Olive, coming more decorously out of the kitchen, wearing a striped apron over the skirt and blouse of a business suit. Susan seized the flowers with her free hand, and said: "They'll make me beat you up for bringing these."

"Hello, Chink." He was a step inside the apartment when Olive arrived to greet him. "They're lovely."

Chink smiled. "I don't have to take them back?"

"Try and get them," Susan said, kissed his cheek, and danced off, asking what to use for a vase.

"I brought French whiskey and Scotch wine," said a droll, mournful voice. "My wholesaler's special. Do you think I got a kiss?"

Now Chink saw that Eustace Martin was stretched out in the green chintz armchair, with a glass in front of his face. "That's Lydia Paul you're fighting to get past," Eustace said. "You never would have guessed."

Chink smiled at Eustace, shook Lydia's hand, and said: "There was a fan of yours on a boat I took not long ago."

"Really?" She sounded sarcastic but not displeased.

"She was using some of your poems to teach English to a young ship's officer."

"I'm glad they're good for something. I assume you'd like a drink." There was no grace in the way she said it.

Olive said, "Please sit down. What will you have?" Susan's word for her was right. Olive was grave, until suddenly she smiled and said: "Flowers. I don't suppose anyone in this house has had flowers since Vivian's first night."

"I'd like beer, please, if you have it."

If Lydia heard, she paid no attention, returning from the kitchen a moment later with an Old Fashioned glass full of ice and pale liquid.

"That's scotch," Eustace said. "If you can't use it, hand it over."

"It's fine," Chink said.

"I always like to have one at bat and one on deck," Eustace said. "And nobody out."

"Don't you want that?" Lydia asked.

"Have we any beer?" It was Olive.

"This is fine," Chink said, and took a sip.

"I knew you'd be that way," said Eustace. The way he said it made Olive laugh, but not Lydia Paul. "What have you hussies done with my daughter?"

"She's dressing," Lydia said.

"She's always dressing."

"Daddy, you shameful old rummy, I am not." Vivian swept in and across the room, looking taller and more commanding than ever, dressed for the evening in red. "I'm exactly on time."

Managing it effortlessly, swinging it in front of her as if she were waltzing with it, she held a wooden bowl full of salad greens and vegetables.

Chink had risen, and Vivian said: "Chink. Our lovely new friend. How are you tonight, Chink?"

"I am not a rummy," Eustace muttered. "I don't like rum. I'm not even a wino. I'm a whisker."

"He is standing when a lady enters the room," Lydia Paul said. "That's how he is tonight."

"Don't pay any attention to my roommate. She is not a possible person." Vivian raised the gleaming salad bowl towards heaven, and swung it down in a long curve into Olive's hands. Then she spread her arms to include everyone in the room. "We are none of us," Vivian said, "possible persons."

"Yes, we are," said Sue McGrew, finished with arranging flowers and lighting on the arm of Chink's chair. "We're all wonderful. I'm pretty and charming. Vivian's a great actress. Lydia's published three books already, and Olive won a silver medal at the Pan-American games."

"Susan!" Olive said. "Mommy strangle."

Her embarrassment seemed genuine, and Chink, who'd known that kind of discomfort, tried to help. "Is April a great actress, too?" he asked.

"April?" Lydia said.

"April does not worship at the shrine of Thespis," Vivian declaimed. "April does not suffer immolation in divine flames."

"Jesus Christ," said Eustace Martin. "What have I begat?"

"You really don't know, do you?" Ignoring the affectionate tone of the exchange, Lydia attacked him. "You ought to sober up long enough to find out about your daughter sometime, Dad. She works at acting every minute of her life."

"She might let it go until after dinner," Eustace suggested.

"She's up at six doing dance exercises. She makes every casting call there is. When there isn't one, it's acting class, or voice lesson, or music, or fencing, or rehearsal, or sight-reading group. Or she's seeing a play. By herself. Or watching someone else rehearse. I have to do lines with her every morning at breakfast. Weekends, she has Sue come down to play piano accompaniments, and makes me fence with her."

"Are you a fencer?" Chink asked.

"I'm terrible, and I hate it. It hurts my back, if you want to know. Olive could learn, but she won't. How about yourself? An eminent swordsman, I suppose, but terribly, terribly busy."

"I used to be fair with foils and good with sabre," Chink said. "I was just getting started in épée."

"My Lord Peters." Vivian dropped to one knee in front of him, one palm up in supplication. "Say you will? Fence with me? Tomorrow morning?"

"Sure," Chink said. "I'd enjoy it. Anytime."

"Not right now, please," Olive said, from the kitchen doorway. "The chicken's done."

"Foils," said Eustace, in a dark mutter. "All right. Foils if you must. I don't want you whacking her on the head with a sabre. Her brain's loose enough already."

"Can you see your little friend April working like Viv does?" Lydia demanded.

"I've only seen April once," Chink said.

"April goes to acting class," said Sue McGrew.

Vivian rose, let her eyes glaze and became unemphatic. "April is lazy. April is hazy." The mimicry was quite accurate.

Still perched on the arm of Chink's chair, turning her head to defy the others, Susan said: "Oh, we do disapprove of April."

"She's all right." Now Vivian became a peacemaker. "Sometimes I wish my father had taught me how to be lazy."

Olive, her apron off and fully with them for the first time, said matter-of-factly: "April's a mess. Let's eat."

Susan rose. "We're all just jealous because April's got half the men in New York lined up, waiting to take her out."

"April does?" Chink found the information surprising. He'd have supposed Vivian to be the belle, or pretty Susan, and was himself academically attracted to Olive.

" 'Two left feet, But oh so neat . . .' " Vivian sang it to her father, who didn't seem to be paying much attention to the conversation.

"Who?" Eustace asked, beginning to rise slowly out of his chair, glass first.

"Dinner. 'It's been said she knocks 'em dead,/When she comes to town. . . .' "

Chink recognized the words but couldn't have named the song.

"Listen to that." Eustace had his body erected now, and moved it along towards the dining room. "Would she sing it in G, like anybody else? No. She's got to have it in B and put me into C sharp. Every serpent's tooth in the scale."

Vivian and Chink, the last to start in, looked at one another, and Vivian said, softly: "You were expecting April to be here?"

"I assumed you were all friends."

Vivian raised her brows, pursed her lips. Then she slid her face into a different expression and said: "About Lydia and the fencing? Lydia's trying bravely to fill in for Mike. Mike fenced awfully well."

Sue's gay voice cried, from the other room, by the table: "If only Chink can play the piano. Can you? I'm so bad when Vivian wants to sing."

" 'But on modern dance,' " Vivian half said, half sang, " 'She wears the pants. Sweet Sue. That's who.' " Shooing Chink along in front of her, she added: " 'Sight-read quick, That's Susie's trick . . .' "

Olive seated them. There was white wine to go with Olive's chicken. Eustace had brought the wine from the night club. Chink, who had left most of his scotch behind, nursed a glass of wine, and noticed that Vivian did the same. Olive didn't take wine at all. Lydia, Susan, and Eustace pretty well went through two bottles. Susan got giggly, Eustace was unchanged, and Lydia turned unexpectedly silly and flattering.

Was Chink really a linguist? "I'd give anything to be able to read Pushkin in Russian," she said. "You make the rest of us look like utter fools."

"Nothing deceiving about appearance," Eustace said. "Not around this joint."

"And Rilke, too. I'd love to hear you read him aloud in German. You have that marvelous voice, maybe too virile for Rilke. But Heine. The *Nordsee* poems. Perfect."

On the whole, Chink preferred Lydia feisty, so he said, quite accurately, that he liked Heine's late poems better. It only made Lydia defer.

Before they were done eating, Vivian had excused herself and hurried away to an Off-Broadway opening, and as they finished there was contention over Chink's mild offer to help with the dishes.

"Let's get him cornered in the kitchen," Sue said, but Lydia pushed Chink away.

"I won't permit it. Not this time." She beat on his chest with the heels of her fists, driving him back.

Eustace resolved it: "Susan will wash," he said. "Lydia will dry, and I will drop."

Olive, for having done the cooking, was excused. She and Chink moved to the living room. It was a smaller, lower room than the one downstairs, and the casually assorted furniture showed a good deal of wear.

"Please sit," Olive said. "May I get you brandy?"

"Are you having some?"

"It's wasted on me."

"You don't drink at all?"

"The medal was for swimming. I never learned to drink."

"I noticed your shoulders."

"Not very delicate, are they?"

"They look like shoulders should."

"I was raised on Army posts. A long time on Guam. There wasn't much for a kid to do but swim."

"You missed the teen-age dances and the drive-in life?"

"I was very ambitious and very competitive. I wanted to go to the Olympics. I nearly made the team the first year I tried. I was fourteen."

"You must have been very good."

She smiled. "Dynamite." She grew pensive again. "When I was sixteen, I went to the Pan-American games. I qualified in freestyle and butterfly, but the coach wouldn't let me swim freestyle. She thought four hundred meters was too hard for my age. I wound up swimming butterfly in the medley relays."

"The next Olympic year you'd have been eighteen."

"Oh, but I'd rebelled. Didn't feel like doing the work anymore. Defiantly dating lieutenants who were too old for me, and nervous because they were in my father's command. I was a winner every weekend, I thought, until one bitter young West Pointer told me why."

"When you were nineteen, Olive?" He enjoyed drawing her out.

"Sick of myself, jaded with men, ambitious to swim again. But I'd lost my edge. You were on your way to being world class, too, weren't you? Susan showed me more pictures in her horse books. ' "Chink" Peters schooling Carlsbad over timber.' You look about twelve, but we figured out you were seventeen. About 1940? And then a picture of you and your wife in forty-seven, lined up with the Equestrian Team. The war came between, didn't it?"

"That was seven lives ago," Chink said. "I expect you know how it feels."

"Only a couple of lives for me. But they do seem distant." Then her sudden smile came again. He was engaged by the unstudied way Olive's moods switched so quickly, so differently from Vivian's controlled changes. "I can still break six minutes in the four hundred. That would be terrific time for 1910."

"Lydia Paul," Sue McGrew's flutelike voice announced, as she came out of the kitchen, wavering, giggling, holding Chink's Old Fashioned glass now filled again to the brim with scotch and, to judge by the color, very little water. "Lydia Paul, Yale Series Younger Poet, is writing an oral poem about you." This struck Sue as so funny that she had to stop walking. "It's a very stern, Russian-type poem, because it says that four foolish women invited you to dinner, when you were already a great swordsman and a famous chef, and you have . . ." She tried another step, teetered with the drink, and stopped again. "A French rapier for stirring ratat, ratatouille, and a Turkish . . . help me, Lydia, a Turkish what?"

"Scimitar for shish kebab. Seven swords and seven great white hats . . ." Lydia appeared.

"Yes. Tall, white hats, with, with . . ." Susan's laughing fit caught her again, and Lydia had to finish.

". . . the days of the week embroidered there in seven alphabets. And scabbards full of cinnabar and salsify."

"Cinnabar!" Susan gasped, tried to take a step, tripped, sprawled forward, and poured the contents of the glass into Chink's lap.

Chink's need to change pants, and Olive's to put dizzy Sue McGrew to bed, had brought the dinner party to an end.

Eustace Martin went with Chink, down to Apartment 1-A, lugging along a bottle of scotch, and asked if he might come in.

"You going to swill some of this malt beverage with me?"

The label on the bottle was decorated with musical notes, and read *High Society Scotch, Specially Bottled for Eustace Martin's Jazz Club.*

Chink got a glass with ice for Eustace, beer and dry clothing for himself. He sat in a butter-leather armchair, and they raised glasses to one another.

"Good health, friend," Eustace said. "All right if I talk about it?" There wasn't much question what he referred to.

"Yes. Of course."

"Haven't been in here since. Can't talk with Viv about it, or Wally. Or even Leon."

"Your bartender? I should think you could."

"You liked him? So do I. The trouble is, he's dippy about Sue McGrew. Anxious. Worked up. Calls here Sunday afternoons, they take walks and go to concerts. All very proper. How about that?"

"Nice," Chink said.

"He's glad you're here. So am I." Eustace sipped his drink. "Leon's excitable. He'll make a doctor, if he can keep the fire banked. The subject of Mike and Wendy drives him frantic. Drives us all frantic, in our various ways, I guess. But Leon and I were here."

"I didn't know that," Chink said.

"I don't know what you do know. April, next door. You met her yet? She found the girls, and called the cops. Olive and Sue were home and took April upstairs. Gave them something to do. Then Olive called me, because Lydia and Viv were both out. I closed the Club and Leon and I came over. Place was swarming. I told the lieutenant who we were and how we'd heard, and he let us in. Then he wanted us to. Yeah, confirm the identification. It was awful in here. Chink, Wendy was covered up, but the blood. They took the sheet down as far as her face, and I said yes, it was, and Leon started crying like a child and couldn't go in where Mike was. They'd lifted her out of the tub by then, and had her lying on the bathroom floor, on the mat. She looked so—exposed. I nearly started crying, too. Then the lieutenant said if I was a friend of their father's, would I be the one to tell him. Seemed like I had to say yes. I knew Wally and Adrienne were having people in that night, so I said I'd go. But first, we went upstairs, and halfway up Leon grabbed my arm, and said: 'Carbajal. Manuel Carbajal.' "

"He knew Carbajal?"

"We both did, Chink. Nervous, grungy little creep. Mustache. I don't know how Mike and Wendy met Manny. April knew him first, but they were all set on doing things for Manny. They got Wally to call me to let them bring him to the club to audition. He played clever guitar and had a hoarse little tenor voice, kind of charming and hysterical, but of course the music wasn't our style. I sent him on to a guy who has a folk club. Coffee house kind of place. Offered Manny a week, renewable. Manny accepted, and then never showed for it. Up to then, you see, he was staying with Leon."

Chink nodded.

"Sue set it up with Leon. Well, I helped. Chink, those girls all knew Manny Carbajal's passport was no good. The illegal stuff excited them, helping a fugitive. My man Leon didn't care for that part, but he couldn't refuse Sue, any more than Sue could Mike and Wendy. Leon could help Carbajal with the English. He took Manny in. It's on the Lower East Side, a kind of Cuban student block. They didn't get along very well, and after the auditions, Carbajal got a little surer of his English, and found his own room. I never thought about him. I guess Leon used to see him on the street."

Chink considered, and then said: "Wally says Carbajal was a trained terrorist."

Eustace frowned, and then nodded. "Well, he could have been. He could have been anything insane and bloody, couldn't he? When Leon said his name on the stairs, I thought he might be right. Leon wanted to go back down and tell the cops, but it didn't seem pressing like other things. There needed to be one of us with the three girls. The new women might say it wasn't necessary, but it was. Some kind of male presence in the night. And be there when Lydia and Vivian got home. Afterwards, they closed ranks and held on to each other, but not right then. Right then, they were shattered. Jesus, why wouldn't they be? And I had to get a cab and go up to Wally's." Eustace finished his drink, looked into the glass, and nodded. "What's the worst thing you ever had to do?" he asked, but not as one who expects an answer. "I got up there, and the guards didn't want to let me in the building. I got them to call, and Wally's secretary came down to see what it was all about. Slick little bruiser. So I said, 'Tell him Eustace Martin's in the lobby, and it's about the girls. It might be better if you'd bring him down here.' Secretary went back up, and ten minutes later he came down with Wally. Wally was about half bagged. Well, so was I, but mine was wearing off. Wally was smiling, and wearing big, funny glasses, and he said, 'Girlish capers? Wild oats tonight?' I took his arm and led him away from the secretary guy, to a marble bench, and he started to tremble. He aged ten years right in front of my eyes, and said, 'Are they all right?' I got him to sit down, still hanging on to his arm, and I just had to do it. I said, 'No, Wally. They're both dead.' "

At ten-thirty that evening, Chink offered to walk Eustace Martin back to the nightclub. Eustace had slept for a little while, slumped into the sofa cushions, waked up, and freshened his mouth with High Society Scotch. He seemed unburdened now, and wanted to talk about his own daughter, Vivian.

"I thought she ought to get out of here," he said. "I thought we ought to break the whole thing up, Chink. I didn't see how it could be good for them."

"They seem to care a lot for one another."

"It's family for them. Vivian never knew her mother." Eustace was still married to the mother, as far as he knew, though he hadn't seen her in years. The mother was a band vocalist and small-part movie actress whom Eustace had met when he was young and on the road. "She wanted to get married. She was older than me, and getting tired, I guess. Average swing vocalist, good scat singer. She kind of rested with me for a while, got pregnant, had the baby, and moved on out of sight. Maybe it kept me from dying young, being left with Viv. Got me off the road." His speech was thickening again, and he made a discernible effort at sobriety. "You were married to Libby?"

"Yes. You know her?"

"Nice lady. Knows some music. She was still Mrs. Wally when the club started."

"They put some money up, didn't they?"

"Know who really owns the club? It's in that conglomerate. Western Construction Industries. Suits me fine. It keeps the racket boys away. Hey, you know what? Lydia likes you. That's unheard of. Lydia doesn't like anybody."

He had just finished saying this when there was a light rapping on the glass of the French window, and a pale figure could be seen in the garden, trying the handle.

"Jesus!" Eustace said. "What's that?"

"It seems to be my other neighbor," Chink said. He'd been startled, too. "April, I imagine." He got up, went to the glass door, and opened it.

"Hello, Chink," April Dorsey said. She was wearing the same chino skirt he had seen her in that morning, but had changed the T-shirt for a light green sweater. It was an expensive sweater, cashmere, but stained and matted. "Do you have any ice?"

"I'm not sure." Chink stood aside to let her in.

"Hello, Eustace," April said.

Chink looked around to see his tall guest standing, clutching his bottle, looking almost rigid. "Ice!" Eustace said, as if it were an explosive word, and shocking. "Ice!" he said again. "I used up the ice."

"Oh, well." It was the vocal quality which had puzzled Chink earlier, as if April were really set apart in time from the situation, watching it from a minute ahead or a minute behind whatever she was saying. "They won't know the difference if their vodka's warm."

"Vivian's." Eustace had hold of the sofa back now with one hand. "There's ice at Vivian's. Upstairs. Vivian is out. Lydia is there."

April stared at him. The stare said she had no intention of going upstairs to ask Lydia for anything.

"Well, look," Eustace said. "Sure I will. Get it for you. Now."

He angled past then, quick, ungainly, and was gone.

"Were you talking about Lydia?" April moved into the room and looked around. "This is nice." It didn't sound as if she were making any connection with the last time she'd seen it. "I had to get away from the jokes."

"It's nice to see you," Chink said, wishing she'd leave. He was beginning to feel very tired.

"It's quiet here. Why do they want to laugh so much?"

"Your guests?"

"They say funny things and laugh. And then someone has to say something funnier."

"That doesn't sound so bad."

"I wish," April said. It seemed to be a complete thought. She was looking at Chink when she said it, and there was something more appealing in the look than what he'd seen in her in the morning, something both hungry and vulnerable. As before, she wore no makeup, but her sandy hair shone softly in the yellow light, and he noticed once again the exaggerated articulation of her waist and upper body under the blank, ordinarily pretty American face. "You ride horseback."

"The word seems to be around."

"Wally told me. I might make a movie."

The door swung open, and Eustace Martin rushed in with a tray of ice cubes. He put it down fast on a narrow, marble-topped refectory table against the wall by the door. "Night, Chink. April." He disappeared, leaving the door open behind him.

April paid no attention.

"I'm going to be Lady Godiva. The movie's called *Peeping Tom,* this man I know wants to make it, and sometimes I'd have to ride a white horse."

"I see."

"Could you teach me?"

"Have you ever ridden?"

She shook her head, and said, in her vacant manner: "Nude, you know. On a sidesaddle, with the horse just walking through some town. If William can raise the money. Peeping Tom is the hero. William says all men are peepers, but I'd have a wig to here." She indicated the bottom of her buttocks. "Not for rehearsals."

"If the horse were trained, you'd have very little to learn."

"I thought maybe you'd teach me."

"I'd be glad to help."

"And sometimes the wind?"

As April spoke, a young man with a handsome, discontented face appeared in the door Eustace Martin had left open. The new arrival seemed to be a very light mulatto with wavy hair, worn shoulder length and razor cut, and bright hazel eyes; he had found a tight, tailored V-neck sweater to match the eyes. Good muscle showed under the sweater. He wore no shirt, and there was a turquoise crucifix hanging from a short gold chain around his neck.

"Come on, April, darling, the ice," he said, and looked at Chink. "And good evening to you, sir."

April pointed to the ice tray Eustace Martin had left. "Take it, William."

William continued looking at Chink. "You'd be glad to help?"

"April was telling me about the movie. If you're the same William."

"May I ask your name, sir?"

"C.K. Peters." Chink offered his hand. The young man took it.

"William Williams, and seldom the same. One moment, your sparkling boy producer. The next, a foul procurer. House nigger, philosopher of course. I've mastered the existential paradox, Mr. Peters. If existence precedes essence, then simply change roles quickly and constantly, and you elude dull essence forever. Isn't that what you always say, April?"

"You an actor, too?"

"At the click of your Kodak carousel. It will be a very commercial movie, Mr. Peters. It's about peeping at April. All men want to peep at April, don't they, darling?"

"I guess so," April said.

"And since all women need to know what it is all men want to peep at, there will be lines at the movie houses. Lines segregated by gender, of course. Come on, April. You have eager boys waiting. Waiting each other out, poor fools."

"I have a headache," April said.

"These boys are two candidates for the lead in our movie, Mr.

Peters," William said, putting a hand under April's hair at the back of her neck, and squeezing with his thumb and fingertips. "One may get to be Peeping Tom himself. I shall wear a woolly wig, and do Peeping Uncle Tom."

"Please, William," April said.

"Hush, dear." He squeezed the neck again. "I'm explaining to your riding master. We have with us tonight, you see, a new candidate for Tom, whom April rather likes. Unfortunately, we also have with us a former candidate, who wasn't supposed to come along. He was last week's candidate, which was when April rather liked him. Tonight he's horned in, and I do mean horned, don't I, dear? He's a very old and rather hulking friend with a nasty temper, so I couldn't really refuse to let him come." This seemed to amuse William. He was now propelling April towards the door, but paused to add: "Tonight April rather doesn't like last week's Tom candidate very much at all."

At the door, he released April's neck. She turned her head. "Won't you join us, Chink?" There was some emotion in her voice now.

"Yes, come away, pray," said William. He picked up the ice cube tray. "Share the nice ice."

"Thanks," said Chink, declining.

"Watch the hulk sulk?"

"Another time."

Then Chink was alone and deeply pleased to be. He could give in, at last, to the emotional exhaustion of the day, the reconstruction of the murders, the visit to the pier, the carrying out of his promise to move in here, the survival of inspection by the young women, the acceptance of a share in Eustace Martin's sorrow, and the unexpected visit from strange April and her strange young man. It had all left him so drained of feeling that he couldn't summon much guilt at having resisted, just now, what seemed to be a mild appeal from April for help.

He opened another bottle of beer, and considered the one Eustace had left of High Society Scotch. He decided he would have a big drink of it, and did, almost half a tumbler. He could feel it, as he drank down his beer chaser, take immediate effect, and was grateful. It was decent to quiet down and cool out, at the end of such a day, with a providential bottle of whiskey, and no reason not to give in to the relief it offered from the pain of thought and the tension of social behavior. He had another fine, big drink, and kicked off his loafers.

The phone rang.

"Chink?" It was April's voice again. "Chink, please come over. Please?"

"All right," he said. "All right. All right, April." He sighed, hung up, tried to shake off a certain dizziness, and stepped into the hall in his stocking feet.

William Williams and a slim kid, a dazzling boy, blue eyed and very young with curly hair, were standing in April's doorway. The young one saw Chink, and held his hands up, palms outward. Then he moved them in imitation of an orchestra conductor for a few beats, swung the right arm in a circle and pointed at Chink with the index finger. Chink found this menacing, and stepped back.

William was looking back into April's apartment. "Come on, Jake," he said. "The cavalry's coming. There's other bitches around. Come on, now."

The young one became a galloping horse and rider. He knew how to do it without moving out of place. Chink grinned, and nodded approval.

A big, lumbering youth came out of April's place, turned as he crossed the doorstep, and spat back into the room. Then he saw Chink standing and watching, and the big fists closed.

"Well, Mr. Peters." William Williams made a small bow. "And was there a call for you?"

"What the hell?" said the big one. He took a step towards Chink. William caught his arm.

"It's all right, Jake," William said. "Forget it. That's her husband."

Chink nodded, willing to let William solve it.

Jake tore his arm loose, and hurled himself past Chink to the front door, the other two following. "Hey, husband." Jake moved aside, pushed the others out, and followed, turning to yell: "How does it feel to be married to the easiest lay in New York?"

Chink waited for the front door to close, and went to April's doorway. She was sitting on a daybed, looking fetching and undisturbed.

"They've gone," Chink said, wondering what he was doing there.

April smiled, a simple, friendly smile, put her hands behind her, palms down on the daybed, and said: "C'mon in," in a chirping voice.

Chink felt his genitals stir.

"C'mon, Chink." She patted the bed beside her, and he was there, and kissing her, before the door finished closing behind him, feeling intense, confused justification and no need to analyze it. The resolution of the confusion, it was clear, must lie in pushing his hand up under April's matted green sweater to feel a big breast and squeeze a corrugated nipple. To this she submitted and responded, pushing herself up at his hand, putting her arms around his neck. Then she slid her face aside, dropped her arms, and raised her torso so that his hand was stranded at her waist, and said, as if it were the next line in a conversation they'd been having:

"The young one was sweet, though. He's studying mime."

Chink removed his hand and pulled his head away, not sure whether he was astonished at himself or at the animation that had appeared in April.

"Actors. William has been my friend for ages, isn't he mean?" She gave Chink a little kiss on the cheek. "The young one was going to read with us tonight, but that awful Jake came, too." She put her hand on Chink's thigh. It tingled. "Can we go to your place? They didn't leave any vodka."

For a moment Chink felt clearheaded, but then the nice, fizzy feeling returned, and he said: "Got some scotch. Eustace left it."

She laughed, the first happy sound he'd ever heard her make. "He leaves it everywhere. High Society. But I hid it from the boys. It might have been funny. . . ." She laughed again. "Do you have any grass?" She stood, and pulled up his hand. " 'Mon. Let's go."

"No grass. Sorry," Chink said, letting her raise him to his feet, delighted with her, delighted with himself.

She pouted and sat down again. "I know why you want me to come over there," she said.

"Never mind, April," Chink said. It occurred to him that he'd been about to make an enormous error in judgment.

At that she smiled, cocked her head, and raised her arms, and he knelt into them, forgetting to feel anything but renewed enthusiasm. Her legs moved up onto the daybed and spread, under her skirt, for his trousered leg to move between, and they surged together for a time until Chink reached under to tug the skirt out of the way, and April said, "Wait." She pushed at him. "You wait."

He stood, panting, to let her up. She rose and turned her back to him, so that he could help her out of the cashmere sweater, and then undo the zipper at the side of her skirt. She leaned back against him but, as his arms tried to close around her, wriggled away, nude from the waist up, with the undone skirt hanging from her hips.

"I'll put on a record," she said, the tone of detachment coming back into her voice. "Jimi Hendrix? Why don't you fix yourself a drink?" As if there were liquor, after all.

She looked back over her shoulder, then, vacantly, down at the skirt, as if she were puzzled at its having slipped away like that. She twisted it around her hips. She was wearing shiny white underpants. She tugged the skirt zipper partway closed, without first getting the garment back up to her waist. Then she dropped her hands to her thighs and leaned towards him, and there was glitter in her eyes again. "I know. Let me get something to make us feel good."

She whirled and went to a small, mahogany veneer vanity table, pulled the center drawer entirely out of it, and offered it to Chink like a tray. In it were pill bottles, of many sizes and kinds. "I know some nutty doctors," she said. "What do you like?"

Chink had begun to feel a little dull. "No, April. Thanks."

She put the drawer down on top of the dressing table, picked out a particular bottle, and took out two tablets. "These are downers. They're nice." She swallowed a tablet, and held out the other. "Or if you're tired? There's speed. It's not strong."

He shook his head, and sat back down on the daybed. He had decided to leave, but couldn't keep his eyes away from the waistband of the underpants and the indentation in them of her navel. She had a very small roll of fat just above it.

She looked back at him, made a fist around the tablet she had chosen for him, folded her arms across her bare bosom sternly. He tried to smile, then sighed and rose to leave. At that she unfolded her arms, bounced her breasts at him, skipped halfway across the room to where he was standing, leaned in, pressing herself against him, and kissed him, sticking her tongue deeply into his mouth. He told himself this wasn't strangeness but some kind of dance he'd half forgotten, and gave in again to the excitement. He clutched her, felt her go soft against the length of his body and clutch back. Then she moved her face across his own, letting her nose rub his cheek, but instead of another kiss there came a whisper:

"Night, Chink. I'll see you."

He did the best he could with it. "All right, April." The welcome, unexpected physical response was subsiding into a regret with which he could hardly expect her to sympathize. "That's fine." He thought of hulking Jake, reminded himself that it was demeaning to be resentful. He walked to the door, not quite steady, still in fact feeling rather drunk, and had it open when he heard her voice again. "Chink?"

He paused. Her tone became one of undisguised despair. "Chink, don't leave me alone."

He turned once more to look and watched her loosen the skirt so that it fell around her ankles. "Turn out the light," she said. "By the door."

As he did, and started back across the room, he could see her sink onto her back on the daybed in the half dark.

He still had to take down the white underpants when he reached the daybed. April was lying so still that he hesitated, thinking the pill she'd taken might already have put her to sleep, but she murmured, "Oh, yes," when he hooked the waistband at her left hip, and she raised her buttocks so that the garment would slide off easily.

Nude himself in a moment, he knelt beside her, putting his hand between her legs and caressing as he kissed her. At that her tongue came darting into his mouth again, and out, leaving behind, at the back of his tongue, the pill she'd chosen for him.

What the hell, he thought. Let her win. Swallowed the thing.

There's too much death and despair in this house, he thought, with half-sober urgency, convinced now as he moved himself above her and between her legs, that to thrust into her was an act of life.

Waking at his own place next morning, he remembered that he had slept awhile, after prolonged copulation on April's daybed. He supposed the pill had caused the prolongation. They must have been at it, through two pairs of orgasms, for an hour, after which he had gone immediately to sleep. He remembered waking, after the induced sleep wore off, and holding April for a time, enjoying the animal warmth of a body against his own, and that she'd whispered fondly that he could leave now if he liked. He'd taken it as a request and complied.

He remembered next, back before that, an odd time, during the coupling, when, getting on top of him, she had turned on the lamp beside the bed, and said: "I love to see it go in and out of me." And he remembered watching her rapt face, looking down at the organs as she sat up, impaling herself, and then he had ejaculated upwards, into her, more satisfactorily than at the first orgasm, when he had been on top but unable to follow April's jerkiness and changes in rhythm.

He realized there was something else he was trying to remember, and went back to sleep for a few minutes. He had a pleasantly bewildered dream, in which Curt Strawbridge was still alive and Chink comfortable in Curt's command. He was reluctant to wake up from it. When he did, it was an abrupt, startled waking, and his mind was full of the recollection of a drunken night in Rome with the Red Cross girl, Anne Goulay.

Anne Goulay had chosen, or been chosen by, after that, Wally Diefenbach. Anne and Wally had been together, and carried on an intermittent affair for several years. Anne had left Wally when she was pregnant, to live with another woman.

April did not look like Anne Goulay, but their bodies were similar, both small-waisted, breast-heavy women, almost overbalanced.

They were both brown-eyed. He sat straight up in bed, staring at the wall, sweating, chilled, and felt appalled at what he'd done now, because it seemed to him quite certain that April Dorsey was Wally Diefenbach's eldest daughter, born out of wedlock to Anne Goulay.

It was a little after six. He tugged on his sweat suit, tied on his canvas shoes, and ran out into the streets of the city, wet with cool rain, but could not run off the feeling that he was guilty of betrayal, dishonor, almost incest.

At eight-thirty he phoned Wally's, insisted to the secretary that his matter was urgent, and got a sleepy Wally on the phone.

"Any extensions on this line?" he asked.

"Yes," Wally said. "Hang up, I'll call back."

When the phone rang again, Chink picked it up and said: "Wally. Is April Dorsey Anne's daughter?"

There was a fairly long pause before Wally asked: "Did she tell you that?"

"No. It's a bad guess, I hope."

"Good guess, Chink. Such a terribly, terribly good guess."

"She has a stepfather's name?"

"Anne never married. April made up her name. With an A for Anne and a D for Diefenbach."

"Where's Anne now?"

"Living in Spain, I think, with an Austrian woman. Chink, nobody knows I'm April's father, at April's insistence."

"Did Mike and Wendy?"

"No. She didn't want them to. Until they all knew one another. Then I was to be allowed to claim her. Has something happened between you and April?"

"Yep," Chink said. "And I'm sorry as hell. It won't happen again, but you want me out of here?"

"Oh, no. Chink. Stay where you're at. You're righter than you know about it not happening again." Wally sounded sad. "I'm afraid my daughter April's rather notorious as what's called a one-time Charlie."

"I've heard the term."

"And a tease, and even a *belle dame sans merci*. But she's very unstable. A couple of years ago I thought she'd gone to Spain with her mother. Then I started getting bills from a private mental hospital in Maryland. They were treating April for schizophrenia."

"Yep."

"Another little twinge of pain for Chinklepal."

"What happened?"

"They figured she could make it outside with some drug support."

"She's got a dandy pharmacy over there," Chink said.

"I know. I keep close track of April. Eventually, I suppose I'd have been told about your little visit, when, last night?"

"I suppose you would," Chink said. "You're sure you want me to stay here, then?"

"Oh, yes," said Wally. "I can't lose her, Chink. She'll get better. It's a matter of time."

"She shouldn't be here, Wally. She doesn't get along with the other girls."

"I know. But try suggesting to April that she move. Don't, of course. But if you did, she'd go blank on you and say, 'Why? I don't understand.' "

Just before nine that morning, Chink persuaded himself to knock, very lightly, on April Dorsey's door. He didn't quite know what he was going to say.

A moment passed. He started to back away, glad to be let off for now, when he heard the inner door lock click and saw the handle move. April opened the door. She was in the white underpants and matted green sweater, hair down over her eyes, having apparently pulled on whatever came to hand. She seemed unembarrassed by her costume. He was, to his dismay, faintly aroused by it.

Chink cleared his throat, smiled, and said, "Good morning."

"What do you want?"

"What's the matter, April?"

"What's the matter, April. What's the matter with April. God."

"Sorry."

"I'm trying to sleep."

"I'll see you later, then."

"Don't bother." At least she wasn't detached.

"All right," Chink said.

"You didn't use anything, did you?"

"No. I assumed . . ."

"Thanks a lot," April said, and whatever might have come next was interrupted by quick steps, coming down the carpeted steps. Chink looked up behind him and saw that it was Susan McGrew, dressed for work and scurrying towards him, with a clear line of sight into April's room.

"Hi," Sue called. "Do I feel dumb? Oh. Oh, I'm sorry." April's door was closing. Too late to avoid being seen, April had stepped behind the door and let it swing away. Chink hoped he didn't look as startled and guilty to Susan as he felt.

The guilt widened. He felt, as he went back into his apartment, that he had behaved dishonorably not just towards April and Wally, but to all the others in the house as well. With April, he had to suppress a little irritation, reminding himself that she was not sane. It was not a pleasant thought. Still, she had taken her pleasure with him. And with every other kind of pill at her disposal, she couldn't really lack the ones for birth control.

Anyway, he thought, I'm something of a birth control pill myself.

At ten, he remembered reluctantly, he had promised to go up and fence with Vivian. That was still an hour away.

In the front bedroom, which he wasn't using, was a set of bookshelves he hadn't looked at. He went in, and was pleased to find a full set of *Britannicas* on the bottom shelves. Unexpectedly, the next shelf up was all Tolstoy, the minor titles and some essay collections alongside *War and Peace* and *Anna Karenina,* and then Aylmer Maude's biography, and Troyat's. There was even a thin volume in Russian, a bound pamphlet by a man named Eichenbaum. He took it out, wondering if one of the Diefenbach sisters had been studying Russian, and found an inscription:

> For dearest Mike. I know you can't read this, and I don't even know which way is right side up. But it's supposed to be the last word on your troublesome hero. My own last word is
>
> Love, James.

Chink turned to the text, and read slowly through the first two paragraphs. There were critical terms he didn't recognize in the discussion of Tolstoy. He went to the bedroom in which he'd unpacked and got the Russian-English dictionary he'd brought along to use with the Russian version of his Hungarian friend's dressage book.

There was a pretty, cherry-wood escritoire in the living room. He took the books out to it, opened the writing leaf, and set them out. He read a little further in Eichenbaum, but it didn't mean much to him. He set it aside, got out a legal pad and a pen, and started in on the first photocopied page of the dressage book, reading and making notes.

He was nearly through the brief, official introduction, a clichéd exhortation to socialist sportsmanship, when the first knock came.

He got up, apprehensive, and went to the door. There was no one there. There was, instead, a second knock, and he realized both had been at the French door. He went to open it and there were April and William Williams in the light rain. April was laughing.

"You looked so funny," she said. "Going to the wrong door and throwing it wide open."

"Ready to face jealous giants," William said. "And it's just us peaceful pygmies." This made April laugh even harder. Chink thought he could hear something of Anne Goulay now, in April's voice. She and William were both dressed up, William in a suit and tie, with an umbrella, April in a tan raincoat with a rose jersey dress and stockings. Behind them, the spray can paintings were dim in the middle distance in the muted light.

"What are you doing over there, anyway?" April asked, her laughter starting to subside into giggles. "Are you writing something?"

"Or wronging something?" said William, which kept the giggles going. "I los' me some dang ol' glubbs las' night, Colonel Peters. Reckon they be lurking about in here?"

"Gloves?" It seemed warm for gloves, but Chink said, "You're welcome to look."

"Well, goodness," William said. "And gracious, too."

Burbling, April approached the desk. "Is that Russian?"

"No, but it's moving right along," said William, provoking April into outright laughter again. "And so must we, dear, so must we all. I'll just put my hands in your coat pockets as we go, and tickle."

"If you're that cold, I'll lend you my mittens," April cried. She went tripping back towards the open French window.

"Meet you in the hallway, Galway," William said, which made April, departing, laugh so hard she almost fell over the sill. "Isn't she wonderful today, Mr. Peters? All juiced up. You could tell her the house was on fire, and she'd shriek with laughter."

"It can't be very good for her," Chink said.

"April tells me you're working for a most distinguished man."

"No."

"Just good friends?"

"We're old associates," Chink said.

"From Boy Scout days."

"If you like."

"Oh, I'm easy to please," said Williams. "Do look." He pulled a pair of light grey mocha gloves out of the pocket of his suit jacket, and waved them gently back and forth, smiling. "There they were all the time. I just wanted to have a look at you in the morning light. The left profile's the better one."

"Shall we tell April that you had the gloves all along?"

"That's not the kind of information April's mind can handle," William said, gliding towards the door, still waving the gloves, smiling. He stopped. "Next, as your generation put it I believe, will come the beauty part, Mr. Peters."

To Chink's relief, Vivian called at five minutes before ten to remind him of their fencing appointment. He had been anxious about presenting himself, not sure of his welcome today. But as he went upstairs he realized that it was after all unlikely that the news of his being turned away by April in a state of undress could have got back, yet, from Susan to the others.

Lydia let him in and asked if he wanted sherry. He smiled and refused.

"You'd better have it for an excuse," she said. "Vivian's going to demolish you."

"You're planning to watch?"

"I'm the referee, sucker."

Vivian came out of the bedroom, in padded jacket and gauntlets, carrying her mask, and saluted with her foil. She looked splendid and formidable.

"Baron Peters, the Nun Duellist awaits your arrogant blade."

"Afraid I'll have to borrow one of yours, Nun," Chink said,

grinning, because Lydia and Vivian were, in spite of his apprehension, and each in her own way, cordial. He got into fencing gear, tested a foil, got the hilt tight against his wrist, and responded to Lydia's command:

"*En garde*, buddy."

Chink saluted and took the *en garde* position, and he and Vivian crossed swords, but what followed was no contest. She was practiced enough, and very graceful, but she had no speed and, he judged, poor eyes. He could wait for her lunge, make a circular parry, and touch her low almost at will. Some of her defense was all right, but she couldn't handle a beat and slide, close in. Still they kept working, both, he thought, enjoying the exercise, until Lydia said:

"Let her have a touché once, will you? I've got a meeting."

"I'm sure she'd rather earn it, next time," Chink said.

"You're on," said Vivian, saluting, and then lowered her foil. "You're marvelous. Give the man something to drink, Lyddy, while I take a shower."

Chink asked for milk, while he got out of the jacket.

Lydia came back from the kitchen with buttermilk, and said, "Jesus, were you a coach or something?"

"Lucky this morning," Chink said, accepting the buttermilk, which he liked well enough. "Vivian seemed slow."

"She was up late," said Lydia. "With her guy. Sorry to hear she has one?"

"I'd have expected it."

"And a big, big wheel he is, little man. There are two things your dopey friend Eustace Martin and I agree on. One is that Viv is wonderful and the other is her big, big wheel's an asshole. You'd probably love him." She was getting her raincoat on while she talked.

"Yep," Chink said.

"Broadway big. Viv wants to marry him. I want to eviscerate him. I don't know what Eustace wants to do about him. Cry, probably. You know who the big matchmaker is? Diefenbach. He brought them together. I've got to run."

"Good-bye," Chink said.

"What an original remark," said Lydia, buttoned the coat, and left.

The walls were covered with framed photographs, signed *Vivian*. They were a mixture of portraits and salon photographs, not very original but done with style. The pictures were hung in three even rows, but in the middle one, which included photographs of Lydia and Sue and Eustace, the spacing between pictures was wider than in the other rows.

"I took it down," Vivian said, coming in. "It's Mike and Wendy. I wanted to keep it up, but it made Lydia unhappy. You know what she's like when she's unhappy."

"I can imagine."

"She adored Mike and couldn't stand Wendy. Jealous of Wendy, really. As long as the photograph was up, Lydia would make unkind remarks about her, just as if she were alive. Would you like to see the picture?"

"If you'd like to show it to me."

"I would, please." Vivian, who was wearing a wrapper and had her hair bound up in a towel, still looked magnificent. She opened the top of a four-legged bench which stood in front of a spinet piano in the corner. The bench was full of sheet music. The photograph was under the music.

"I keep it hidden," she said. Then her voice, usually tuned to dramatize, became very simple. "Here they are, my very dears."

She handed the framed photograph to Chink. It was black and white, with great depth of focus, and had been taken in the little garden downstairs. In the foreground, Wendy sat upright, wearing a splotched, white, one-piece bathing suit, and Chink had to look away for a moment and compose himself, because Wendy held a spray can of paint in her hand. When he could look again, he looked at Mike, standing partly behind, partly beside her sister. It was Mike who was barefoot this time, wearing jeans and a man's shirt with the sleeves rolled up and the shirttail tied across her diaphragm. She had a hand on Wendy's shoulder. Both girls were smiling.

The photograph was full of sun, and behind the subjects a large part of the garden wall showed, freshly painted with the designs, the words, and the cartoons which Chink had seen out there. Buildings showed above and behind the wall, and over the buildings a bright sky.

"It was such a happy day," Vivian said.

"Who was there?"

"We all were. It was a party to welcome Olive when she moved in. We all painted and sprayed each other and drank wine."

"April, too?"

"Oh, yes. They were kinder to April than we've been since, I'm afraid. Isn't Mike lovely?"

She was. Chink had not seen a picture of Mike smiling before. It was a generous, open smile, and with it, even wearing glasses, Mike became the prettier sister, Wendy something more like the tomboy she'd been as a little girl. Neither, he thought, looked at all like April, yet had April been in the picture with her half-sisters, there might have been some kind of family resemblance in the way the faces were shaped, and the eyes set.

He could read the words behind Mike and Wendy on the garden wall quite easily in the photograph, including the name inside the wreath.

"Who was Wolfe Tone, Vivian?"

"An Irish martyr."

Chink recalled it now. "Was he the one who tried to get Napoleon to come help Ireland? Or was it the French revolutionaries? Anyway, the British hanged him, didn't they?"

"He cut his throat before they could. Mike had an Irish friend named James. Chink, would you like to have the photograph?"

"Thank you," he said. There was no way of refusing, and he didn't like her having to hide it from Lydia. He had another question for her. "Vivian, do you know an actor named William Williams?"

"April's friend? I thought he was a salesman."

"He seems to wear a lot of different hats."

"Actors have to. But it's odd, Chink. William called me this morning. I barely know him and haven't seen him for months."

"What did he want?"

"He works for a meat firm. He wanted to know who Daddy buys his meat from, for the club."

"He couldn't call your father?"

"Unlisted phone. I should have guessed about William. He looks actorish."

"I'm not sure what that means."

"Like me," Vivian said. "Not like the people in the photograph. They're natural and sweet, like grapes. I wish I were."

"They were younger, too."

"I've been a banana split all my life, three scoops, all different flavors. Three kinds of syrup and all that awful cream and nuts and marshmallow topping."

"You're hard on yourself."

"Somebody'd better be. Which reminds me to thank you."

"You're welcome. What for?"

"Not letting me score a point I didn't earn."

"You're welcome. It certainly made Lydia cross. Thanks for the photograph," Chink said.

She took his hands. "You're welcome, too, Chink Peters."

Just before lunch, Chink had a phone call from a secretary at Western Construction Industries, asking if Mr. Peters could possibly come by and see a Mr. Winkler in the afternoon.

"May I ask who Mr. Winkler is?"

"He's our executive vice-president," the woman said.

"I don't mean to be unimpressed," Chink said. "Can you tell me what it's about?"

The secretary didn't know. Chink agreed to go over to the W.C.I. building at three o'clock. Then he phoned Adrienne, and learned that Ted Winkler was the operating head of Wally's conglomerate, having been first with the agency, then on Wally's personal staff.

"What I want to talk to you about is a job," Winkler said. He was a calm, rather distinguished-looking young man, still in his thirties, with a high forehead, a thin nose, and a heavy Boston accent. "Might you be interested?"

"I doubt it," Chink said.

"May I outline it for you? It's a rather important job, here at this firm."

"If Wally's worried about me staying in New York, tell him to relax."

"No," Winkler said. "I'm discussing quite a challenging, high-level position here, which pays a good deal of money."

"Sorry. I'll do anything I can for Wally Diefenbach except put my name on his payroll."

"This is a corporation," Winkler said. "Obviously, Ambassador Diefenbach suggested we consider you, but we're far more interested in your experience and qualifications than in your personal associations." He smiled. "Though as a matter of fact, the board of directors to which you'd be responsible does happen to include your former wife."

"I'd heard that," Chink said, smiling. "I'm not sure I'd want to be on Libby's payroll, either. She's on Long Island?"

"Never misses a board meeting," Winkler said, willing to make use of Chink's show of interest. "And they're held once a month. As I understand it, the residue of her brother's and mother's estates were invested here while she was married to the ambassador. And there was further stock settled on her at the time of the divorce. She's our largest individual stockholder, and I wish some of the others were as active and as interested. Now, Mr. Peters. Before I get to other particulars, what I want to discuss would be based on a three-year employment contract, at sixty-five thousand a year to start with, and stock options. May I go on?"

"Please don't," Chink said. "I might be tempted."

When he got back to the apartment house, there was a note in the mailbox saying that Eustace Martin wanted to buy him a beer at the club.

Thank you, Eustace, he thought. I guess I'm tempted.

On his way to the club, he had time to stop at a supermarket to buy food, but he was still early. Sue McGrew was at the bar alone, leaning over it towards Leon, the Cuban bartender, licking salt from the rim of a margarita glass. Her tongue looked whitish in the fluorescent lighting. Chink was embarrassed.

"Hey," she cried, flying a curl and raising her glass. "To the man of the house, but I'm so sorry. I mean, about your pants last night. That is. Oh, Susan, Susan." She chided herself and tried again. "It didn't seem to be the right time to say it this morning. Susan! Oh, hell, let me buy you one of these."

"Don't cuss," Leon said.

She tossed her head at him, smiled, and turned back to Chink.

"I've been wanting one ever since Olive dragged us out of here the other day."

"It looks good."

"You want a margarita, Chink?" Leon asked.

"Beer, please. Are we expecting Olive?"

"Someone asked her out for drinks after work, not that she'll drink. I tried to get her to bring him here."

"Evil place for young girls," Leon said.

"I'm sure you and Eustace try your best to make it that way." Sue smiled. Leon smiled. Chink asked when Eustace was expected. Leon brought him a beer.

Sue said, "Every time anybody asks Olive for a date, I'm as pleased as if it were me."

"She doesn't smile enough," Leon said. "Tell her to cheer up."

"Maybe she doesn't have a lot to smile about."

"No more pictures in the paper in her bathing suit."

Leon's hand was resting on the bar. Susan spanked it. "You're awful. If you knew Chink had been a competition swimmer, you wouldn't think of him in a bathing suit. You'd say, 'Fine athlete, good man.' Wouldn't you?"

"She's raising me," Leon said. "Like one of her little kids. You swim big, Chink?"

"Very small," Chink said, and finished his beer.

As he set the glass down he heard a newly familiar voice say: "Lushing it up, Mr. Peters? Is that in character?"

It was William Williams. The look of pleasure left Leon's face across the bar.

"You want something here?" he asked.

"To see Mr. Martin," William said, putting a business card on the bar. "And a Coca-Cola, please, my friend."

Leon picked up the card, glanced at it, and dropped it on the floor behind the bar.

"You want rum in it?"

"Plain, thank you. Is Mr. Martin here?"

"Not here," Leon said. "Costs a dollar fifty with rum in it. Plain's two dollars."

"The two-dollar kind, please," William said. Then to Chink, and smiling at Sue: "And who is this?"

"She's a friend of mine," Leon interrupted. "Something else you want to know?"

"Susan McGrew, William Williams," Chink said. "Eustace is expected, William."

Leon put down a paper napkin, and on it a Coca-Cola. He kept one hand on the glass, and held out the other to be paid. William Williams thanked him, in a tone of normal courtesy, and handed Leon two dollars.

Three customers came in together. Leon paid no attention.

"That's for the first plain Coke," Leon said to William. "The second one costs three dollars."

"I really should see Mr. Martin, if you don't mind my waiting."

"Suppose I mind?"

"Well, I could wait outside."

"Good idea."

Susan flushed. "I'll pay for his next Coke, bartender. Whatever you want to charge for it."

"That right, Miss? Well, you can serve it, too, Miss," Leon said, pulling off his white jacket. Eustace Martin came in just then from the street. "Here, Eustace," Leon said. "Here's your monkey's coat. Some things I don't take."

"Leon!" Susan called after him. Leon pushed out the swinging door that led to the kitchen and was gone.

Eustace blinked his eyes. "What's that all about?"

"Oh, it's me," Susan said.

"He'll be back," said Eustace. "He quits once a week."

One of the new customers said, "Hey, what about a drink?"

Another said, "Jesus, let's go down the street."

They hadn't taken their coats off.

"I'm afraid it was me, this time," William Williams said, watching the three men leave. "I'm terribly sorry. Or not me, not even the dreadful company I keep. The company I work for. I'm William Williams, from Magnum Meat."

"Well," said Eustace, "your firm does have a winning reputation, but so does the firm I buy from. The sales pitch," he said to Susan and Chink, "is irresistible. Use our steak or be one."

"He still had no reason to be rude," Susan said.

"Do you and Leon know each other?" Chink asked William.

William spoke to Eustace: "Magnum Meats is trying to change the forceful image to one of quality and service."

"I book jazz," Eustace said. "I wouldn't mind dealing with a black firm. But you folks would have to fix it up with the Italian firm first."

"Of course," William said. "This is just a get-acquainted visit."

"I'm pleased to meet you," Eustace said. "But I'm afraid it's Leon who's usually here to see the salesmen."

"I wonder if I do know him?" William said. "What's his last name?"

"Quiroz."

"He certainly took exception to me."

"Maybe it's the price of meat in New York," Chink said, having just been to the supermarket. "Eustace, you want a slow, non-union bartender with fourteen thumbs?"

"You know the trade?"

"Done it before."

"If you could fill in? I call the employment folks, I've got an extra barman to pay when Leon stalks back in and says, 'What do you think you're doing behind my bar?' "

Susan said: "I didn't know it was meat. When I think he's being bigoted, I just flare up."

Chink, on the other side of the bar, put on Leon's jacket and asked if anyone had work for the new bartender.

"A Scotch mist, my man," said Eustace. "You may use the house scotch. It's excellent." There was a full row of High Society bottles, not just scotch but bourbon, blended whiskey, gin, and vodka, too, on the back bar.

Susan said: "I wish I could call him up. I've been so stupid. But he doesn't have a phone."

"He'll be back." Eustace was soothing. "Have another."

"I can leave a message with his father. It is Puig-Quiroz, Eustace?"

"Hector Puig-Quiroz," Eustace said. "I've got it written down somewhere, but you'll find it faster in the book."

Chink turned on the ice crusher to fill an Old Fashioned glass for the Scotch mist. The noise cut out whatever the next exchange may have been. He found he minded missing it, and switched off the machine. William Williams was in midsentence:

". . . any sort of advantage in expanding your menu, we'll be glad to send a consultant, and train your chef."

"That's nice," Eustace said.

Susan had put on her coat. "Good-bye," she said. "I'm going home and call. Nice to meet you, William."

They said good-bye and watched her leave. Chink held the Old Fashioned glass, half full of crushed ice, tightly, and waited.

William said, "The price situation isn't one they leave to salesmen, of course, but the grades are flexible. . . ."

Chink turned the machine back on, filled the glass with ice, and made Eustace his drink. A couple had come in. Chink took their order and filled it. When he got back to the center of the bar, William was saying, "Let me find out what can be arranged, Mr. Martin, and we'll talk again."

"Bye," Eustace said. "Nice of you to drop in."

William had pulled on the grey mocha gloves. He waved one to Chink, and left.

Eustace took a swallow of his Scotch mist, and said: "He knows I can't change suppliers. I wonder what he really wanted?"

"I think he wanted to train your chef," Chink said.

"My chef's the dishwasher. Or me, when the dishwasher's busy."

Chink nodded. William Williams hadn't touched his two-dollar Coca-Cola. Chink picked up the business card Leon had dropped on the floor. *William Williams,* it read. *District Representative, Magnum Meats.* Chink put it in his hip pocket, and went back into the kitchen to put the groceries he'd brought with him into the refrigerator.

After the cocktail rush, during which Chink and Eustace worked behind the bar together, there was a lull during the dinner hour, and then, for a time, no customers at all.

Eustace said: "At eight-thirty, we get waiters and a piano player. Nine-thirty, the band and the first show. I work the tables. 'Hi, howya been? Like the combo? Thanks, I'm glad. Haven't heard from him. Think he's dead.' Anyway. Mind if I sit down?"

Chink shrugged. Eustace went back around to the customer side of the bar and sat on a stool. "I owe more explanations in this world than I do money. That's a lot of explanations."

Chink smiled.

"Owe you one."

"Not that I know of."

"Ms. April Dorsey walks into your place last night. I turn zombie."

"I hear she has that effect." April was not really on Chink's mind for a change this evening.

"Not you too?"

"She's a strange young woman," Chink said. "Should Leon be back by now?"

"Okay, I won't pry but I want to tell. When you found me on the steps, out cold at teatime?"

"Was that April's doing?"

"I don't know what hell she gave me," Eustace said. "I'd got a certain amount drunk elsewhere, and thought she might be yearning for me. Phoned up, and she said, 'Not today,' but she and I had had such a lovely time not long before. So I said, 'How 'bout just a social call?' knowing she couldn't possibly resist a debonair and handsome fellow like myself in the firm, pink flesh, and I rolled in to see her. Reached for the lady, and she put a drink in the hand, and it seemed to me I knew what to do with one of those. Down the hatch, out the door, and away ran both my knees. I think it was the legendary Mickey Finn, whatever that is."

"Chloral hydrate," Chink said. "It's not hard to get."

"Now she scares the pants off me," Eustace said. "No. The other way around. Scares 'em on me. I wish Vivian would leave that house."

"Customers," Chink said, as people came in. "Excuse me, boss."

At nine, Leon was still not back. The regular second bartender, who stayed late, came on duty. Eustace came back again behind the bar, and Chink got his groceries and left. He hadn't eaten and was hungry. He'd bought a bottle of Pernod, something she'd mentioned liking, as a friendship offering to April.

There was a trio playing as he left the club, a soft piano and guitar, and a wistful-looking young woman vibraphonist who played with what he felt pretty sure was delicacy and taste.

He got to his apartment, made himself a fried-egg sandwich, sat the Pernod aside, and looked up Hector Puig-Quiroz while he ate.

He rinsed his plate, put it away, and dialed the number. The woman who answered was Leon's mother. They spoke in Spanish. She knew Leon had got angry and left the club. Others had been calling. A young woman? Yes, but a man, too. She thought her son was most likely at the medical school library, where he often studied. She said Leon and a friend had recently moved into an apartment on the Lower East Side with no telephone. She gave Chink the address.

He went back out onto the street and hailed a cab. It was a chilly night, and there was no one on the street in the block where Leon lived. Chink had the cab wait while he crossed the sidewalk and rang the doorbell for the apartment Leon seemed to share with someone called E. Quintanilla. There was no answer. There was mail in the mailbox. Chink added a note to the mail, asking Leon to phone him, and took the cab back home.

Just before eleven, he knocked on April's door to deliver the Pernod. She came to the door in her Maryland T-shirt, and the familiar chino skirt, and he found himself miserably excited at seeing her. She was pleasant, vague, and she thanked him for the Pernod. She stood aside for him to come in. He struggled against the invitation for a moment, then took a step her way, with which she said, "I don't think I'll ask you to come in tonight, Chink, okay?"

"Yep," he said. "Yep. Fine." He turned away, but back in his own quarters, he found it difficult to get to sleep.

Insomnia was unfamiliar to him. His mind went back and forth, from April to Leon, to the photograph he'd got from Vivian, to the man named Ted Winkler wanting to talk about a job, and settled on William Williams.

There's a vicious game men play, he thought. I was a player, and I think William Williams was playing it tonight.

A few minutes after six in the morning, he was on his way out of the building in running clothes when he heard someone coming down the stairs, and waited. It was Olive Dahlke, in a nicely tailored, sky blue sweat suit.

They reached the door together, and he opened it, saying, "Hello. Are you a runner?"

She looked at him without smiling. "Which apartment are you

coming from this time?" she asked, and then, withdrawing further, "Not that it's any big concern of mine."

"No."

She stood, hesitant, at the top of the steps while he closed the door. He watched her shoulders settle and her head move forward. Then she said in a low voice: "May I take all that back?"

He moved beside her. "Sure."

"I only run three blocks." Now she looked at him, her face apologetic. "From here to a health club on Fifth Avenue. Then I swim laps."

"I did some of that once."

"Want to try again?" It completed an apology.

"Do you swim every morning?"

"Almost."

"May I try tomorrow? I'll have to buy some trunks."

"You can go by the health club office later, and get a trial membership, if you like."

"Fine."

"Run me over, so you'll know where it is."

They went down the steps together and started to run at an easy pace. "I'd rather swim here than run," Chink said. "Even after a night's rest, the air in these streets is pretty tired."

"Wait till you try our chlorine," Olive said.

He left her at the door of the health club, to which she had a key. She acted as manager until seven-thirty, she said. If she heard the bell, she'd stop swimming and let people in, not that the bell rang very often.

He ran downtown a way, then east and over to Leon Quiroz's neighborhood. At about seven, he bought a paper and had coffee in a luncheonette. From seven-thirty to eight, he walked around. The shops were Spanish grocery stores and meat markets. Even the chain drugstore had its window ads in Spanish. There was a sense of neighborhood. Women were visiting as they came out to shop, children in bands going off to school, men greeting one another on the way to work.

At eight he returned to the tenement building where Leon lived.

The front door was open. He climbed three flights of narrow stairs and knocked on an apartment door marked L. QUIROZ—EDUARDO QUINTANILLA.

A dark, sleepy kid in pajamas came to the door, opened it, looked at Chink, and said, "Jesus, man. It's early."

"Is Leon here? I'm a friend."

"The bastard didn't come in," the kid said. "And he's got my physiology book in his locker at school."

"Could you tell him to call Chink? Chink Peters."

"Yeah. You left the note."

"Yes."

"Hey, Chink. You see him first, tell him to get the hell over here with the locker key. We got a test today."

At his apartment again, Chink took a shower, got dressed, and went to the refrigerator for milk. There was an unfamiliar package on the middle shelf when he opened the door. It was a white, rectangular box, a foot long, three inches high by five across, sealed with printed tape. The printing read, MAGNUM MEATS, SERVING RESTAURANTS AND INSTITUTIONS. He carried the box to the kitchen table, and cut the tape. Inside were six beautifully cut filets mignons, and a printed card reading, A SPECIAL WELCOME TO A VALUED NEW CUSTOMER.

He hadn't locked the French windows. Anyone who could get into April's apartment could come through the garden and into his.

He put the gift back into the refrigerator, and walked into the living room, thinking. The airy summer photograph of Mike and Wendy was lying on the open writing desk. He picked it up and carried it into the garden. He stood with his ghosts in the place of their gaiety, but the voice he recalled this time was Wally Diefenbach's, on the telephone, saying: "I keep close track of April."

Chink went back indoors, looked up W.C.I. in the phone book, and called Ted Winkler, the executive vice-president with whom he had talked the day before.

"I'm not calling too early?"

"I've been at this desk since eight," Winkler said. "Know what I'm doing? I'm writing you a letter about the job. Will you read it?"

"Sure," Chink said. "I'm going to ask a favor."

"All right. Are you at least curious now?"

"Yes."

"Good. What's the favor?"

"Information. Diefenbach Packing Company is a W.C.I. firm now. What about Magnum Meats?"

"That's a black firm," Winkler said. "We don't own it, but we put up the risk capital. It's a customer of Diefenbach packing, and we give it wonderful credit terms to keep it going."

"And you own Eustace Martin's Jazz Club?"

"Yes. For tax loss and cash flow."

"If Magnum Meats wanted the account, would they go to Eustace?"

"No. They'd go to our city investments group and try to make a case. It's nothing I'm specifically familiar with, Chink, but these things go by area. Eustace Martin's club is in an area served by an Italian wholesaler. Another Diefenbach customer."

"Your city investments group would arbitrate between the two."

"That's a civilized way to put it," Winkler said. "They'd knock some heads together and cool things down."

"A salesman for Magnum wouldn't take it up with Eustace on his own, would he?"

"Not unless he was a very dumb salesman. Has someone been hassling old Eustace about the meat?"

"Not exactly," Chink said. "I'll read your letter."

He could suppose all he liked that William Williams was Wally's means of keeping close track of April, but it didn't explain why William had come into the club with a flimsy story, or what that had to do with Leon's having spent the night away. It began to feel to him like a police matter. He decided to phone in to them about the disappearance, but he thought that first he'd better talk with Wally.

The door buzzer sounded. He went to the speaker and said, "C.K. Peters here," and, as if he'd already made the second of the calls he had in mind, a voice replied: "New York City police, Mr. Peters. May we come in, please?"

There were two of them, in plain clothes.

"I was about to call in," Chink said, as they showed badges and wallets. "I wonder if it's about the same matter?"

"What were you going to call about?"

"A missing person."

"Name?"

"Leon Quiroz."

"What else do you know about him?"

"Is it Leon you're here about?"

"Let's go in and sit down, Mr. Peters. Okay? You were looking for Quiroz last night and this morning. We want to hear about it."

They walked down the hall in silence, but at the door the younger of the two asked: "Is this the place, George?"

The older one, a heavy, bald man with a flowing mustache and a Greek name, Detective Sergeant Pappas, nodded.

Chink thought he might have read the name. With one hand on the doorknob, he asked: "The Diefenbach sisters?"

Detective Pappas nodded again. "I was here."

Chink opened the door and stood aside. "They weren't missing persons."

"I've been transferred and demoted since," Pappas said. "Okay?"

"Sorry," Chink said. "I couldn't help being curious."

"You see connections between the Diefenbach girls and the guy that's missing?"

"Only circumstances. Leon Quiroz knew them," Chink said. "He goes out with one of the girls who lives here. He's the bartender at Eustace Martin's, and Martin's daughter lives here, too."

"Yeah, the actress," Pappas said. He took a seat on the sofa. The younger one remained standing. Chink sat in the leather armchair. "Some woman, isn't she?"

"We talked to Martin already," the younger policeman said. "Boy, was he hard to wake up."

"He and the bartender came here the night the two girls were killed," Pappas said. Chink recognized the technique: Tell a man something he probably knows, as if you thought he didn't. "You were at the club last night, Mr. Peters, when Leon walked out?"

"Yes," Chink said, and started with the scene at the bar, speaking slowly into the younger detective's tape recorder, repeating the conversation as accurately as he could, spelling names and repeating addresses. "You may get a report of a cab going to Quiroz's address about ten-forty-five," he said. "That was me."

"His roommate gave us your note," Sergeant Pappas said. "You ever give evidence, Mr. Peters?"

"I've coached people for it."

"Lawyer?"

"I've coached on your side. I was a deputy commissioner for a while, out west."

"Can we check that?"

Chink wrote out a name and address. Pappas took it and put it away.

"All right, Commissioner. What for?"

"Why did I go over there last night?"

"You said you were worried about Leon. Why?"

"Williams was being too nice. Leon was very rude. He was trying to pick a fight. I'd met Williams. He can be nasty. He was holding it back."

"That's not much," Pappas said. "The girl was there, taking Williams' side. You were there. Martin came in. Williams was making points by holding back."

Chink told them what he'd found out from Winkler. "So Williams didn't really come in to sell meat."

"You think he was there for Leon. Why? Maybe it's the girl, or you, or Martin he wants to see."

"Maybe he was just thirsty," the younger policeman said.

"Maybe."

"I don't understand what got you going," Pappas said. "Hunch?"

"There's a game men play," Chink said, quoting a little of his night thought. "For politics. It's a lousy game, a kind of grown-up cops and robbers, with real blood. I used to be a player. Williams sounded like that."

The younger policeman said: "Bullshit. Who'd you play for, Notre Dame?"

Chink smiled. "A federal agency. I'm not allowed to talk about it."

"How long ago?"

"Sorry."

"That's where you knew Diefenbach?" Pappas asked.

Chink smiled.

"Can you give us enough to check that you were in it?"

"I don't think I can," Chink said.

"We get a need-to-know situation, you'll tell us?"

"Yes."

"Was Quiroz playing your game, too?"

"I don't think so. Leon was unguarded. I just thought he knew Williams, didn't especially want to greet him, and disliked him, which isn't hard to do. And I think Williams probably came in just to locate Leon, and the rest was playing around. Williams likes to play around. I can show you a sample."

Chink went to the kitchen and came back with the package of fillets.

" 'A special welcome to a valued new customer.' " He read the card and handed the box to Pappas. "It was in my refrigerator this morning. Someone brought it in through the French windows, I imagine."

"Williams? How'd he get in?"

"Across the garden." The younger policeman had gone to look out. "That door over there, right?"

"Leads into April Dorsey's," Chink said. "Williams is a friend."

"The other actress," Pappas said. "The little dolly one with the boobs. Can we take your steak?"

"Sure," said Chink. "What for?"

"You got a need to know?" the younger policeman asked. "You working on this? Pardon me, playing on it?"

"No," Chink said.

Pappas said: "It's okay, Mike. I thought we'd run the meat through the lab, Mr. Peters."

"There goes supper. All right."

"That other actress, April. Would Williams have a key to her place?"

"She's strange," Chink said, hoping they wouldn't question April. "Shall I ask her?"

"She's a pillhead," Pappas said. "Christ, she's got everything over there, with prescriptions to match. And I'll tell you something else. The papers had it wrong. They said she let us in the front door that night. Well, she didn't. The front door was open. So was that door there, your door. April was back in her own place, floating around near the ceiling. She never did make sense. Yeah, go ahead. You ask her."

He stood up.

"What do you think?" Chink asked. "Are the two things we're talking about connected?"

"No," Pappas said. "The murders're past history. I think the missing person is routine. He'll probably be back. I've got no reason not to think it."

"You go out and interview like this on routine cases?"

"No. We use the phone. Frankly, we're here because of where you're living, just for one thing. And there's some heat on this. First, the guy's family. They had three different phone calls from strangers last night. Two besides yours. They're scared. Then his roommate calls in about your note, and some book. Then we get the dean of the medical school. Quiroz didn't show for a big exam this morning. He's an A student, six months from graduation, and gets special federal aid. The dean's really after us. They want to show Uncle Sam they can make doctors, not dropouts. And finally some schoolteacher. I guess she's the girl."

"Sue McGrew," Chink said.

"Yeah. Kind of a flit, isn't she?"

"That's enough heat for two men to spend all morning?"

"You disapprove, Commissioner?" the younger policeman asked.

Pappas ignored it, and went to the door. "From our standpoint," he said, "there's no reason not to think it's the usual. Guy under pressure, big exam, girl and family and dean expecting big things. He walks. It happens a hundred times a day. You've been in this kind of work. How many times does someone with a small part in a big case turn up later in a little case of his own? Looks like connection, usually it's coincidence. You think Williams took Quiroz out, you have to tell me where and when and what for."

"I don't know," Chink said. "But I don't really understand why you're giving it your best attention, either."

"All right," Pappas said. "My guess is, you'd try it anyway. So I'll tell you: Phone Magnum Meats and ask for William Williams. Were you going to do that?"

"I hope I wasn't," Chink said.

"Go ahead," the younger policeman said. "Try it, Commissioner. Let's see how you work."

Chink got William Williams' card from the bedroom where he'd left it the night before, returned, and dialled the number. A woman's voice said, "Magnum Meats. May I help you?"

"William Williams, please. C.K. Peters calling."

"Is this the police again?"

"No."

She hung up. Chink looked at Pappas and shrugged.

"Williams didn't show for work this morning," Pappas said. "It's sales meeting day, they're not supposed to miss it. So we got a warrant and checked his apartment. Cleared out."

As soon as the police were gone, Chink tried to phone Wally, but was too late. Adrienne said Wally had gone to Washington for the day, but that dinner at 21 was on for the evening. Chink thought of phoning Leon's family again, to ask if there was any news, but it seemed an inhumane thing to do. Instead, he called Vivian, got Eustace's unlisted number, and tried there, but got no answer. He knocked on April's door, but there was no answer there either.

He tried to get his mind on the translation project. He couldn't concentrate. He walked over to Olive's health club and took out a trial membership, found a sporting goods store and bought swimming trunks, walked over to Leon's neighborhood again, but there was no one there at all in the apartment now.

When he got back to the brownstone house on Tenth Street, there were two pieces of mail. One was a postcard from Eve Shellcroft, forwarded from San Francisco. It said that she was going to be married again, to a French surgeon who worked in the government hospital in Papeete. The other, delivered by messenger, was the promised letter on W.C.I. stationery from Ted Winkler.

My dear Mr. Peters:

The position I want to discuss with you exists because Western Construction Industries, generally known as W.C.I., had its origins in real estate development and land speculation. In addition to the other sorts of enterprises now owned by W.C.I. (see list enclosed) we continue to have extensive land holdings. These include ranches, orchards, farms, vineyards, town and city lots, range, recreational, and timber land, and so on to the extent

> of about 1100 holdings and more than half a million acres, mostly in the West, some closer, some even abroad.

The letter went on to describe a job which was essentially supervising farm and land management, with decisions to be made about operation, production, and disposal. The man who'd done it had been hired away the year before, and W.C.I. had not found anyone to replace him.

> He now works for a West German outfit, and that would be the nature of your competition, along with American corporate farms, other conglomerates, the Japanese timber combine, Arab investors. . . .

It was a job, Chink thought, that he might be able to do. He didn't know row crops, except for feed grains, but he'd had experience with small grains and forage. He didn't know the oil and fibre crops at all, nor the fruits, but the letter assured him technical advice and research ("about on the scale of a small but extremely efficient agricultural college staff, right here in New York"). He knew livestock. What he didn't know was whether he had it in him to compete, under financial pressure, with high-powered businessmen, but, having always held them in a certain contempt, he thought he might like to try.

There was the postscript, apparently dictated by Wally, presumably over the phone from Washington:

> Don't take this casually, Chink. You're as good a man as I've ever known, and should be one of the good ones who helps to run things in this bad world.
>
> Wally (per T.W.)

Wally said: "Don't take it casually, Chink." They had finished dinner, and Adrienne was away from the table. "I won't say you'd be rich right away, but there's about twelve percent a year in bonuses and raises, depending on what you earn the company or save for it—that's up to the directors."

Chink smiled. Dinner at 21 had been exquisite. "Including Libby, I gather. How is she, Wally?"

"Lean, mean, and unmarried. You might enjoy seeing her. I won't say you'd ever be really rich, but you're a frugal guy, no family. You could look forward to putting your million away before retirement."

Chink saw Adrienne coming back towards their table, sinuous in silver, pausing here and there to greet people.

"That's Vivian Martin's friend, Henry Fumate, Adrienne's talking to," Wally said. "Wonderful guy. Want to meet him?"

"Wally, before she gets back. Did you put a kid named William Williams in at Magnum Meats?"

"We've got leverage at Magnum. I got him the job."

"Why?"

"He's a friend of April's, and needed work. It was that or invest in a silly film they wanted to make."

"What's he do for you, Wally, besides report on April?"

"April takes a lot of watching," Wally said.

"You pay him for it?"

"All right, Chink. Williams was in agency training but didn't finish. He works for me."

"If there's another side, he's probably a double," Chink said. "Is there another side?"

"There may be a dozen," Wally said. "You know that."

"The man's gone. He may have taken Eustace's bartender."

"Leon?" Wally said. "Why would Williams do that?"

Chink left Adrienne and Wally Diefenbach drinking cognac at 21 about nine o'clock and walked downtown, walking off the wonderful Malpeque oysters and Pouilly-Fumé, the Scotch grouse and Chateau Latour. He stopped and phoned Eustace Martin's Jazz Club on the way downtown, but Leon hadn't come in. When Chink got to Tenth Street it was ten. There was a figure in jeans and a pale jacket standing out on the stoop. He didn't know if she was waiting for him or not. He thought, with a rising heart because he wanted reassurance from her, that it was April, saw with a sinking heart that it was someone he liked better but wanted less to see.

"Hello, Susan."

"The police said they'd talked to you."

"They were here this morning."

"Do they know where Leon is?"

"No. I'm sorry."

"I called his parents again. Nobody's heard from him."

"Want to come in?"

When they were in his apartment, he asked if he could fix her something. She wanted a drink. He made himself tea. "The police talked about pressure," he said. "They thought maybe things were bearing down on Leon."

"They don't know him. He's a brave, intelligent man."

"I don't know him either, but I agree with you."

"Do you think he's all right, Chink?"

"There's no way of knowing yet. All you can do is the hard thing, Susan, wait."

"May I have another?" she asked. He poured her more scotch from the bottle Eustace Martin had left with him. "Will the police keep trying to find him?"

Chink hesitated, and then shook his head. "I don't think so. They have so many cases. Not unless they learn something new."

"Oh, Chink." She was trying not to cry. He let her hug herself against him for a moment, cradling her in his arms. Her bones were very light. "I'm sorry." She drew back, and drank down the scotch. "Thank you. I'm sorry."

He walked her to the door, with his arm about her shoulders, opened the door, and walked her to the foot of the stairs.

There was a note taped to April's door, in large handwriting: PLEASE DON'T KNOCK. I'M MEDITATING. He was pretty sure it hadn't been there ten minutes earlier, that April knew he'd come in, and that the note was meant for him.

Susan pretended not to see it. "Good night, Chink."

"Good night."

He gave her the bottle. "Have another drink and get some sleep."

She went up. Chink was furious at April. He'd meant to knock, of course, to ask her about Williams.

I know what April's victims feel like, he thought. Even out of contention, I'm getting the treatment, the beauty part, and it does work fine.

If he was not in contention, he asked himself a few minutes later, why was he standing here in the French doorway, staring at the light in April's curtained window across the garden, assuming she had a man with her and feeling stupidly jealous?

He slept off the jealousy, woke, thinking it was like any other poison. If it didn't kill you off, your system would get rid of it. He went swimming with Olive.

The swimming was excruciating. He did four lengths in fairly good style, able to keep up with the slow, smooth pace Olive set. In the middle of the fifth length, his arms began to tire, and he lost the sense that he could direct them accurately. He made the turn, seeing that Olive was, by now, half a length in front of him but swimming no faster. He tried to catch up, and after ten hard strokes was flailing, not swimming. He gave up on the crawl and finished the length in something he had learned as part of military training, called the resting breast stroke. She was sitting on the tile at the end of the pool, waiting for him, when he reached it and grabbed the edge.

"Are you winded?" she asked.

"No. My arms don't work."

"You're fighting the water. You're not using it. Take a rest."

He nodded and hauled himself out. In a minute or two, his arms felt all right again. He watched Olive, going smoothly up and back, relaxed and rhythmic, and wondered if he was too old to learn how again. In the pool at Yale, in his twenties, he remembered getting up to sixteen laps when he'd begun to train for the four hundred meters in the pentathlon. He did some push-ups, rested, dived in, and swam one more complete lap in a very slow crawl. The arms made it almost to the end before they began to flail again.

He found there was a weight room, went into it, and worked on his legs and back until he heard Olive calling, and went out.

"How many did you do?" he asked.

"Forty." She was breathing deeply, but not panting, and looked radiant. "I let myself off the last ten because I didn't see you."

"How long will it take me to get up to the first ten?" Chink shook his head.

"I'll watch tomorrow. Maybe I can help." She paused, and added: "If you'd like me to?"

"Please. I can get idiotically determined about this kind of thing."

"I'm glad. It's nice to have someone to swim with again."

As they jogged back, he asked how Susan had been after she left him.

"She started tearful, and then got a little drunk, and very cross at Leon for not sending word."

"That's a good way for her to feel."

"You think something's happened, don't you?"

"I don't mean to sound that way."

"They were looking at engagement rings. I suppose he ran out on Susie, though God knows, they weren't doing anything more than holding hands."

As Chink went back into his apartment, the phone was ringing. He picked the instrument up an instant too late, but five minutes later it rang again. It was seven-forty-five, and Adrienne Diefenbach calling.

"You're up early," Chink said.

"I've been trying to call since six. There's something I want to tell you before Wally wakes up."

"All right."

"The doorman had a message when we got in last night. It was for Wally, but Wally was full of cognac so I took it, and put him to bed, and then I read it. It's awful, Chink."

"Who from?"

"It was the late-shift doorman. He got it the night before, and, no, I'm sorry. That's not what you mean. The message was signed 'Double-double-u.' I shredded it, but I have it memorized: 'My Dear Ambassa dear.' You follow the spelling? 'Bye-bye. Ta-Ta. Toodle-Toodle. Oo-Oo. Why don't you pick up my dear little paycheck, and roll it up, and stick it up, and light it up? Might reach all that gas in there and blow it up. Whoosh-whoosh. Have a nice-nice, ride-ride, Double-double-u.' Do you know who it is?"

"Yes."

"Is it a man or a woman?"

"You don't have to play twenty questions, Adrienne. It's a man named William Williams."

"What is he to Wally?"

"It wouldn't mean much to you. A former employee."

"Wally gets lots of threats but this is so . . . I don't know."

"Peculiar," Chink said. "It's Williams' style."

"It's scary, oh, good morning. Give me a kiss. I'm talking to Chink. He called to say thank you. . . ."

"At this hour?" Wally came on the line. "Chinkle-twinkle, little star, go back to bed."

"Sure," Chink said, thinking that Williams' style was not unrelated to Wally's own, in a rococo sort of way.

"What have you achieved already today?"

"Went swimming."

"You did say swimming?"

"Yes."

"Splashing in the emerald waters."

April Dorsey appeared in the garden, wearing pajamas. They were white pajamas with tan piping around the cuffs and collar, and the legs were flared at the ankles.

"Yes," Chink said.

There was a set of underclothing April had apparently set out to dry, on the back of the garden chaise. The chaise had green plastic cushions and a design of white daisies.

"Breasting the waters by yourself, while the world slept on? Or were you with other dedicated fellows, breaking pool records?"

April pressed a thin, blue brassiere against her cheek, testing its dampness. She tucked the pajama shirt into the pants, undoing the drawstring. Then she pulled the string very tight around her small waist, frowning, and tied a bow.

"With Olive," Chink said.

"Oh, yes, of course. The swimmer."

April smoothed the pajama pants over her stomach, and went back into her apartment.

He waited half an hour, saw April return to gather up her underclothes and go in again. He gave her time to get dressed. Then, as he was about to get up and go to knock at her door, she appeared, rapping at the French door, dressed again in rose jersey. Chink let her in.

"Good morning, April."

"Are you through with your paper? I've got to look at the classifieds." The brown eyes were quite clear this morning.

"Sure. Take it."

She came in and sat down on the sofa. The newspaper was on the coffee table. April didn't pick it up.

"I have to find a job," she said.

"What sort?"

"Oh, anything. That's where William and I were going day before yesterday, all dressed up."

"Job hunting?" Chink took a chair.

"No. I mean it was my last time to get unemployment. So William was escorting me, wasn't that sweet? We had lunch afterwards. We had wine, and a boned rack of lamb, that's my favorite."

"It's very good."

"Every week, after unemployment, we cash my check and have lunch, and then we work on the script or casting or William takes me to see a backer."

"How long have you known William?" Chink asked.

"Very long. I don't sleep with him, if that's what you mean."

"No."

"I met him right after I came, and he wanted to be friends, but we really don't. Not ever. Of course, he might not want to." She giggled, picked up the paper at last, put it down. "Can I tell you something?"

"Yes, April."

"You're a nice person."

"Thank you, April."

"If I tell you, you won't tell the other women here?"

"No."

"What did the police want yesterday?"

"The bartender at Eustace Martin's is missing. A man named Leon Quiroz. Did you know Leon?"

"I've only been in Eustace Martin's once, weeks and weeks ago. Eustace brought me home."

"I see."

"I don't like places like that."

He waited.

"Did you call the police because I put something in your refrigerator? William made me do it."

"Is there something wrong with it?"

"Oh, no. I don't think so. He said it was a surprise, and so I sneaked in. You were asleep. You were snoring." She giggled. "I thought of giving you a kiss."

"It's a package of steak, April. Thank you."

"I'm so glad you didn't mind. I never eat meat."

"When did you see William, April?"

"You mean for lunch?"

"When did he give you the package? The surprise."

"About two o'clock, yesterday morning. Isn't that crazy? He called and woke me, and made me get dressed and meet him on Seventh Avenue. He had a car. I didn't know William had a car, did you?"

"No."

"Maybe he rented it. Once we went to see a little town, and he rented a car."

"What happened, April?"

"He didn't think the town looked right. I thought it was sweet."

"Yesterday morning, when you met William on Seventh Avenue."

"Oh, that doesn't matter. As long as you're not mad. But it was so crazy, going out on the street by myself at that time of night."

"He gave you the package of steak."

"I never eat meat, but he said you'd like it. So I came back, and sneaked in. You were snoring."

"I guess I do that."

"Well, you certainly do."

"Was William alone?"

"No. I was with him. But the little town didn't suit him."

"Yesterday morning, at two, when you met him on Seventh Avenue, April. Was William alone in the car?"

"I didn't know he had a car."

"April?"

"He had some man with him. He made the other two get out and go away, but the one in front was asleep. William waited till the two got in a cab and went away, and then he gave me the surprise and told me to sneak it in."

"Did you see the man in front?"

"It was pretty crazy, wasn't it? You were so sound asleep, I bet I could have got right in bed with you."

"Had you seen the man in front before, April? At Eustace Martin's club? Or here?"

"It was crazy, Chink. Do you think I'm crazy. Well, I am. That's what I wanted to tell you, because you're a nice person. Do you like me?"

"Yes, April."

"They say if you think you're crazy, then you're not really. But I was in a sanitarium for a year, a whole year before I came here, and I couldn't do anything but cry."

He fixed her some warm milk, and promised the police would not be back to question her, and after a time April seemed calm and said she would go back to her apartment and lie down.

He wondered how he could have felt lust, or jealousy, or anything but sorrow for Wally Diefenbach's eldest daughter.

Eustace Martin and Vivian stopped by.

"Speak to her, Chink, influence her," Eustace said. "The trollop wants to get married."

"That sounds quite wholesome," Chink said.

"Sounds weird to me. Whatever happened to being a bird in a gilded cage, anyway?"

"He's a wonderful man," Vivian said. "Oh, Chink. He asked me late last night. We'd had a fuss and I went to a play by myself. And then he was waiting in the lobby with orchids when I came out. I'm so excited." Chink was standing. Vivian threw her arms around him and kissed his cheek.

Eustace seemed rather pleased, actually, but he said: "Wait till Lydia gets hold of you. She'll bust you one in the chops."

"Poor Lydia," Vivian said. "Chink, you'll like Henry. He's someone Wally and Adrienne like."

"I'm sure I will."

"When he gets back to town. He had to go open a show in Philadelphia tonight."

"Lydia will open him and show him Philadelphia," Eustace said. "Chink, you got any of my High Society left?"

"Oh, come on up and help with Lydia, Daddy," Vivian said. "It's wall to wall scotch up there. Daddy's idea of how to raise a kid."

The phone rang.

"Excuse me," Chink said, and answered it.

"This is Pappas."

"Hold on, please," Chink said. Vivian and her father were at the door.

Vivian said: "Can you come up?"

"Thanks, not just now." Chink waited till the door closed, and spoke into the telephone. "I've been trying to call you."

"I know. Something new?"

"William Williams left town by car about two A.M. yesterday. April Dorsey saw him on Seventh Avenue, and brought the package of steak in here. She doesn't make complete sense, but she says there was a man in front who seemed to be asleep."

"You think it was Leon?"

"Yes."

"You think he was asleep?"

"No."

"Me, I don't know, Mr. Peters. You don't either, and you got a screwball witness. What I do know: Where I was when you called was the lab, waiting. Every one of those pretty fillets Williams sent you is loaded with LSD."

"Yep."

"You're not surprised."

"Surprised it isn't strychnine, I guess. Sorry that's a careless thing to say. LSD's not lethal, is it?"

"Probably not. This is a pretty hefty dose. Especially if you like your steak rare. You might have gone on quite a trip. Why, Mr. Peters?"

"I wonder, too."

"Something connected with your federal agency?"

"I doubt it. But you're right, the agency was how I knew Diefenbach. And later his two girls."

"I've got a great big need-to-know," Pappas said. "I'm recording."

"It'll take a while," Chink said, and began with his hearing of the Diefenbach tragedy in San Francisco. He told Pappas and the tape recorder everything he could about his being in New York. The only thing he held back was the information that Wally and April were related.

"Okay," said Pappas, when Chink finished. "So you're being some kind of watchdog or bodyguard. Now, William Williams, he's another watchdog, or at least that's what Diefenbach thinks. Why does Williams try to play the big trick on you with the meat?"

"Things we don't know yet," Chink said.

"Things Diefenbach knows. Sounds like it could be. Maybe he's got some other reason that he sent for you that's got more to do with Williams."

"He could."

"You find out, you let me know?"

"What are you going to do?" Chink asked.

"Right now? I still don't know it was Leon Quiroz in the car. But there's too much going on for missing persons, and not enough to take to homicide. What can I do? We hear you were a crackerjack commissioner. Transfer and demotions, right? We made a guess which agency, and found out you moved pretty good out of Washington in your time. You keep in touch."

"All right, climb out," Olive said. "Now show me your hand movement. No, that's wrong." She took his hands and moved first one arm, and then the other, through their strokes. "Now I want you to swim a length without kicking."

It was morning again, and there'd been no news still of Leon.

Olive met him at the far end of the pool. "I said no kicking. If you can't keep your feet together, we'll have to tie them. Pretend they're tied. Concentrate on it this time, so you'll really have to pull with the hands."

"Better," she said, after the next length. "But too much head movement. You don't have to burst out of the water like some kind of animated cartoon porpoise."

He thought she was terrific.

"You're coming along," she said. "You can rest and go play with the weights now."

On the way out she said, "Mike and Wendy used to swim here with me sometimes."

"For fun?"

"Wendy did everything for fun. Mike wanted to be coached. The man in her life was a swimmer."

"James? I saw an inscription."

"James. We were starting to have a little group."

"Where is he now?"

"Back home in Ireland, I guess."

"Why did you stay on, Olive?"

"I thought Susie needed me. But maybe I needed her. Things were lousy at work."

"At W.C.I.? How are things there now?"

"Lousy," she said.

At nine-thirty he phoned the second floor to ask if morning fencing was still on. Lydia answered.

"Baron Peters here. Is the Nun Duellist suiting up?"

"What are you talking about? Fencing?"

"Yes."

"You sound like Diefenass."

"Sorry."

"She can't fence today."

"All right."

"She went out with Adrienne. Shopping for her trousseau. Isn't that wonderful?"

"You sound upset."

"I was supposed to phone you about it."

"You won't have to now."

"I was coming down there, Peters. I'm still coming down. You stay there."

She hung up. When he went to the door and opened it, she was already on the stairs.

"Come in," he said, when she reached his door. "Would you like some coffee?"

"Whaddya want to drink that shit for?" Lydia said. She was carrying a thick, quarto-size, buckram-bound journal in front of her, arms around it, holding it to her thin breast. "Coffee sours your stupid stomach."

"I suppose," Chink said. "Come in."

"Look," she said, staying in the doorway. "You see Diefenass?"

Chink looked at her for a moment. Then he nodded.

"Well, give him this, will you? It's Mike's daybook."

"Excuse me?"

"Mary Diefenbach. What do you want, a singing telegram? Her daybook."

"I'm not sure I know what a daybook is."

"Like a diary, but not private. Mike kept one. So did I, and we passed them back and forth. Oh, Christ, you wouldn't understand."

"If I wouldn't," Chink said, "I'm sorry for it."

She was thrusting the book at him now. He crossed to the doorway and took it from her. "Did Wendy do it, too? Keep a book?"

"Wendy couldn't spell her name twice the same way," Lydia said. "She was a rotten painter, too."

Chink set the book down on the long marble table by the doorway. When she made no move towards turning to leave, he asked: "Was Mike a poet, Lydia?"

"Oh, Christ, just give her father the book, will you? He might learn something between lies."

"I'll find out what he'd like done with it," Chink said.

Lydia stepped in and snatched the journal up again. "You going to give it to him or not? You think I'd leave it here for you and the cunt next door to read aloud and giggle over? You think I'm stupid?"

"I think you must know some really neat people," Chink said.

As quickly as she'd picked it up, she slammed the daybook down on the table again. She was crying now, angry tears. "Read it yourself, you dumb asshole. You'll find your own name in there, but it isn't you, and I'm glad she didn't know. What you're really like." This time Lydia did turn and run to the steps, her whole, small body shaking with rage. From the first step she looked back and yelled, "I don't have to take all this bullshit," and ran on up and out of sight.

Chink closed the door and went to the phone. He hoped Susan might be home. She often had mornings off from the preschool.

He dialled the number, was relieved when the phone was answered promptly.

"Hello?"

"Susan? This is Chink."

"How flattering, you recognized my voice," Olive said.

"Olive."

"Second guess out of two possibilities. Very good."

"Olive." Now he hesitated. Susan would have taken a tirade by Lydia on the subject of Chink and April in stride. Olive might not, but he was too concerned not to say: "It's about Lydia. She just left here. She seemed close to hysterics."

"That's nothing new for Lydia."

"I thought someone ought to be with her."

"But she loves hysterics," Olive said. "All right. I'll go down."

"Thanks."

"She's reacting to the big news about Vivian, I suppose. You realize, of course, we're all to blame?" Olive chuckled at that. "We'll catch hell all week. I'll go get mine, but I bet I'll find her dry eyed, and prepared to make me feel moronic about something like Wallace Stevens' middle period. Did he have one?"

"Thanks, Olive," Chink said. "You're not at work?"

"What an opening," Olive said. "I think I'll be nice and not answer."

"Sorry," Chink said. "I'm not used to weeping women. Or funny ones, either."

"Aw shucks." Then she laughed, at her end of the phone conversation, and said good-naturedly: "I didn't tell you at swimming, because I didn't know. Office is closed today. Chairman of the board died. Diefenbach's uncle or something."

"That's been expected, hasn't it? He was old and in the hospital."

"Day off for me, anyway. I'll go see Lydia. Want to have lunch up here?"

"Yes," Chink said. "I'd love to."

> "There are worldly people, heavy and wingless. Their activity is on the ground. There are strong ones among them: Napoleon. They leave terrible traces among men, and cause a commotion, but it is all on earth."

So began the epigraph Mike Diefenbach, about a year before, had chosen for her daybook.

> "There are those whose wings grow equally and who slowly rise and fly: monks.
>
> "There are light people, winged, who rise easily from among the crowd, and again descend: good idealists.
>
> "There are powerful winged ones who, drawn by carnal desires, descend among the crowd and break their wings. Such am I. Then they struggle with broken wings, flutter desperately, and fall. If my wings heal, I will fly high. God grant it."
>
> *Tolstoy, 1879*

The handwriting in which the quotation was copied was formal and quite pretty, but not like Mike's, whose free, passionate, slanting script filled most of the volume. This was explained immediately:

> Thank you, Wendy light person, for the caligraphy. Now here is a poem for you and Lydia, made up from old Mr. Maude's translation of old Saint Leo:
>
> *Powerfully winged ones*
> *Drawn by carnal desire*
> *Descend and break their wings*
> *(And such am I.)*
> *Struggle with broken wings,*
> *Flutter desperately and fall.*
> *If my wings heal, I will fly high.*

Chink Peters' first thought was that it was an unexpected kind of sentiment for a girl of nineteen, which had been Mike's age when the daybook was started. His next thought was that he knew very little of nineteen-year-old girls.

He began to read. The book, apparently a gift from Lydia, had been started shortly after Mike and Wendy moved into the apartment. The religiosity lightened after a few pages, as Mike described herself as

> Recovered! Well again and straight in the leg, after Nantucket. Next time I find myself about to give in to somebody, I must remember to look at his feet and make sure they aren't cloven.

She wrote about love for several pages, and concluded that she hadn't really experienced it yet, after all. She reminisced a little about some weeks she and Vivian had spent in Dublin, and Chink smiled at the way she referred to her mother, since Natalie was, after all, Chink's age:

> Old Ma's old country—poets, hellcats, drunks, double-talkers, heroes, priests—I love them all.

Then there was a passage about April:

> With the new girl I begin a dozen different conversations in fifteen minutes. I am so puzzled by her. I thought I could talk with anybody. So much for pride. Wendy is better with April than I am. Lydia is awful and impatient (aren't you?), but April doesn't seem to notice. I think A. is lost and sad and I forbid anybody to be unkind to her!

Halfway through the daybook began to get political, and the writer to question Tolstoy:

> It is my 20th birthday, and I dedicate it to dear, bespectacled Petr Kropotkin. When I return the pearls to Father, I will use Petr's words, just now cribbed from the encyclopedia. They'd offered him a cushy job with the Imperial Geographical Society, but he said—and I say—"I had no right to those higher joys when all around me was misery and the struggle for a mouldy piece of bread."

> Lydia says we should take a piece of damp bread, and leave it out to turn moldy, and send it back to Father along with the pearls. All right, L., you're on, but I'll bet he makes one of his jokes about it. Silliness is Father's first line of defense.

Then the daybook quoted Wally's reply:

> I was right. I was right. I wish I weren't. Father phoned and said, "So thoughtful, Mary. A breakfast treat and it cured my strep throat too, dear." He's put the pearls in the safety deposit. (I'm going to get them back and sell them and the money will go to Dublin.)

Not long afterwards, James, whom Olive had called the man in Mike's life, began to appear:

> James says if I want someone to talk back to Tolstoy in Russian, to forget Kropotkin, who was dear, but simple, and read Bakunin. I don't have Bakunin yet. Back to the encyclopedia: "Real religion lies in political action and the social struggle." How now, Count Leo, it makes me weep to ask it, but how now?

There were several pages, then, which dealt with watching Vivian rehearse in an Off-Broadway play, and going to the opening night. James had been away. Wendy, Lydia, Susan, and Mike had gone, escorted by two unnamed young men, and had a glorious time as the Queen's court. April had declined to go. Then there was a long passage about Irish politics, and another about refugees, Palestinian, African, and Asian. There was, at the end of this, what might have been a reference to Manuel Carbajal:

> Better a refugee than a fugitive. A refugee remembers the lost home with longing, a fugitive bitterly.

Two thirds of the way through came another entry in Wendy's pretty caligraphy. Chink imagined her finding the daybook and writing in it, mischievous and unobserved:

To the Countesses Mary Mike and Lydia P.
(From *Trivia,* my dears, by Logan Pearsall Smith)

" 'And what do you think of the International Situation?' asked that foriegn countess, with her foriegn, fascinating smile.
"Was she a spy? I felt I must be careful.
" 'What do I think?' I evassivley echoed; and then, carried away by the profound and melancholy interest of this question: 'Think?' I queried, 'do I ever really think? Is there anything inside me but cotton wool? How can I, with a mind full of grey monkeys with blue faces, call myself a Thinker?' 'What am I, anyhow?' I pursued the sad inquiry: 'A noodle, a pigwidgeon, a ninny-hammer—a bubble on a wave, Madame, a leaf in the wind.' "

Chink began to have a sense of the bond between the two sisters by which Lydia must sometimes have felt excluded. The reply went:

No, Bubble and Leaf, you must not be careful. You must keep on loving everybody, as I wish I were good enough to do (but all I love is Wendy Diefenbach who is a nut, and who really loves her new Basque beret best, and when I borrowed it yesterday to go to the meeting, I loved it, too).

He had begun to feel he could hear those voices, and especially Mike's, when, startlingly, Lydia's half-forgotten taunt came true, and he found his own name:

Wendy and me telling Lydia about Chink.
Lydia: Ah, the white horse hero, but alas, the horse was brown.
Wendy: (Reasonably) Now Lydia, we couldn't help it if our Father's so rich he bought us our own Galahad to play with.
Me: Chink's picture was the icon of our adolescence.
Lydia: That's why all the Russian books and thinkers.
Wendy: (Who is getting terribly literary since the wavy-haired professor came into her Monday, Wednesday, and Friday life) He wasn't really Russian, Lydia. He was pure Carolingian.

There was a small break, and the next entry went:

> When I was 14, I asked Libby how she could ever have left Chink for Father. Libby laughed and said: "Your father is a marvelously interesting man, Mike."
>
> "Wasn't Chink?"
>
> "A simpler man, dear. Maybe a better one, but so rigid."
>
> If to be better means becoming rigid, freeze my bones to steel, O Lord, let my limbs stiffen and grow straight.

Chink read this with disbelief, trying to find ambiguity in Mike's feeling, but the next lines left no doubt:

> The difference between us was always clear: Wendy wanted to grow up and marry Chink. I wanted to grow up and be Chink.

It was all he could read. There had been an image in his head for eleven years of two little girls standing together on the first rail of a paddock fence in Harrisburg, stomachs pressed against the top rail, crestfallen and reproachful, saying, "You didn't? Uncle Chink?" That, and Mike's reply to his one letter in the interim, which, he realized at last, he had greatly misunderstood.

He put the book down, stood, and bowed his head, feeling shriven.

"May we talk about Mike and Wendy?"

Olive said: "I was wondering when we'd get to that." They had eaten tomato soup and watercress sandwiches. She'd made green tea.

"You hadn't gotten close to them, like the others."

"It was going to take a while. They could be reserved, each in her own way." She paused. Chink nodded. "They were close to each other, but Mike could get impatient with Wendy's light-headedness. Because it wasn't really light-headedness. Not like Susie. Wendy was terribly smart."

"Wendy?"

"Brilliant. The giddiness wasn't exactly a pose. It was a way of meeting life, and making people feel happy. Lydia, Vivian, and Mike were the serious ones. Wendy and Susie had a wonderful time being silly together, and I had a nice time with them. I thought Wendy was perceptive and talented and charming. I found Mike's mind a little scary sometimes, and never knew what she was up to."

"Are you talking about some particular activity you didn't understand?"

"That's a real cop question, Mr. Peters."

"Sorry. I suppose you got your fill of cop questions."

"Every girl does, sir."

"What am I being dumb about now?"

She hesitated, and then grimaced and said, "You're not being dumb. I'm being unfair. On the way to moving in here, I managed to get myself raped."

"Olive."

"It's easy enough to arrange in New York these days."

"Is it something you want to talk about?"

"You advertise your crummy studio apartment, because you've found a nicer place. A man phones and wants to see the apartment. He's probably been calling all the sublet ads, one by one, until a woman answers and says yes, come up, I'll show it to you. So up he comes and shows you something. His pretty new knife. Want to see a scar?"

Chink said, "I'd rather see the man with the knife."

She stared at him. "I wonder if you mean that? I suppose you do. He's safe from you in jail, Chink. Out of harm's way."

"I don't know if I meant it or not," Chink said. "I just had an image of coming into your studio apartment in time."

"No permanent harm done." Olive smiled at him. "Really not. Just another bad trip. Anyway, I was the hardship case around here when I moved in. Difference between them: Mike wanted to talk about violation and forgiveness. Wendy wanted me to forget it and have some fun. I preferred Wendy's approach."

"How did you meet them? I'm sorry, I don't know any other way to ask a question than to ask it."

"I was spending two weeks in the advertising department at W.C.I. Part of the training. Wendy came in with sketches. The art director was creaming because the name was Diefenbach. She bolted and told me to take Wendy to lunch. We had a nice time. Wendy told me about the apartment and Susie, who wanted a roommate. I hadn't thought I wanted a roommate, but I loved the atmosphere here. Things weren't very interesting at work and this house was so full of life and talk. And, of course, I met Mike. You know people whose laughter is contagious? Mike's seriousness was that way. She could get you talking about the most elevated things, without your quite knowing how and without your feeling silly and self-conscious about it."

"I'd begun to get that feeling about her."

"Begun?"

"I've been reading some things she wrote."

"The daybook? Did Lydia really part with it?"

"She practically threw it at me."

"That was the big scene. She wouldn't talk about it when I went down."

"Did you get Wallace Stevens?"

"Samuel Beckett. But I'm amazed. When I first got here, Mike and Lydia had been doing that for months, exchanging their daybooks once or twice a week. You'd see Lydia on the stairs, carrying the thing, so proud. She wanted all of us to acknowledge that she was Mike's special friend, and her having the book proved it."

"Is Lydia so religious?"

"More political. Her husband had left her. She was indignant at the world of money. Movies, really, and television. That's what he went off to. He's an actor. Lydia wrote a play."

"I didn't know she'd been married."

"It didn't last too long. Vivian took her in. They'd known one another around the theatre. In those days, Lydia resented Vivian's kindness. Now that Mike's gone . . ."

"Lydia tries to take Mike's place."

"Mike was our leader in all earnest matters," Olive said. "Vivian knew about the world. Wendy kept the party going. They were all powerhouses. We drank wine and loaned each other clothes for dates. We talked and talked and had silly nicknames that changed every other day. I used to look forward to getting home from the office. Maybe that's why they kept sending me around the training track at work, while the men got the promotions." She fell quiet. Then she said: "It was really quite a happy time."

Chink nodded, and was quiet, too. When it seemed permissible to speak again, he said: "Lydia was winning. Politics over religion, as I read the daybook."

"Not altogether Lydia. There was James."

"The man in Ireland."

"He's very nice. And Mike was already an advocate of the Irish cause, to the exclusion of pretty much all the other causes."

"Another cop question: Was there something going on with Mike and James, besides liking each other and talking?"

"Susie and I used to wonder. Vivian came up a couple of times and wondered with us. Lydia was probably in on it, if there was. I don't know how much Wendy knew. She never talked about it. She was loyal to her sister, but she seemed uneasy just before the end."

"Was Manuel Carbajal involved, do you think?"

"I think he must have been." She shook her head. "But I don't know how. Oh, I do know something else. Did you write a book?"

"Me?" Chink was puzzled. "No."

"Are you quite sure? Maybe a translation. Something published, anyway."

"The only thing I've ever written was years ago in Italy. A report about Yugoslavia. The army printed part of it as a training pamphlet on guerilla warfare. I'm sure it's been superseded many times over."

"Mike's book heist. I didn't connect you with it until Susie reminded me. Mike made a famous secret trip to Virginia, to steal a copy from her father's files in their house. She had to get the combination from her stepmother. That's your ex-wife, isn't it? It was half dramatic, half giggly. Sounded harmless."

"What did she want with the book?"

"You'd inscribed it. Susie remembered that, too. *To Wally. There are so many holes in this you could run it on a player piano. C.K.P.*"

He smiled. "Yes, I remember."

"It was for James. He had a going-away party, and there was a heap of foolish presents."

"The Irishman."

"You sound a little jealous," Olive said. "I'll be damned."

He smiled. "Yes. I remember."

"Which phantom are you falling in love with, Mr. Peters?"

"Let me up."

"Joan of Arc or Jenny-kissed-me? God, it's hard enough competing with the living in this world for a man's attention. Nobody has a chance against beautiful dead girls."

Since he could only reply to that by leaving or by kissing her, he stood up and moved around the table to where she sat. She raised her face, but when he lowered his, turned her cheek. Then, as he kissed the cheek lightly and straightened up, she reached for his face with both hands, held his cheeks, pulled his mouth towards hers, and kissed it rapidly, three or four times. She seemed to want to stand, so he moved back, pulling her to her feet, hands on her arms above the elbows, and they hugged. She started laughing.

"Go away, Mr. Peters," she said. "Scoot now, before I make you look at my rape scar."

In the evening, he stopped at the club to see Eustace. There was still no word about Leon. He ate alone, and went to a Russian movie, but the sound track was turned down so low he had difficulty understanding it.

He woke next morning with a feeling of anticipation which, for the first instant, he couldn't account for. Then he realized it was, of course, because he was going swimming again with Olive Dahlke.

He instructed himself, as he put on trunks and over them his familiar sweat clothes, stiff from the drier, to be realistic. He was almost twice Olive's age, and a battered man who had not behaved very admirably with another member of the household.

Still, he could not deny himself the pleasure of simply looking at her vigorous, sturdy frame as they met at the stairs with the new appreciation of a man for a woman who had, with a kiss, signified a willingness to let what has gone by be gone.

The care with which he tried to say, "Good morning," was probably betrayed by what felt like a rather goofy smile.

They reached the street, and Olive said, "Want to sprint?" and started away fast. He caught her with one short burst of running, went by, turned around, knowing how boyish he was being, and ran beside her backwards.

"Wait till I get you in the water," Olive said.

She unlocked the door to the pool and let them in. "Into the water, five laps, Peters," she commanded. He stripped off his sweat suit and obeyed. She gave him half a length before he heard her dive in after him. She caught him in the middle of the third length, swam with him stroke for stroke until they finished it and, when they'd made the turn, went over onto her back and swam along, a bit ahead of him, doing a tauntingly smooth back crawl. After the next turn, though he was tiring, he tried to imitate her, but his own back crawl was awkward and full of waste motion. Olive turned over again and went to butterfly, crossed into his lane in front of him, and splashed water in his face as she pulled easily away. Chink, feeling his arms tire from the effort of trying to keep up, went back to his old, military resting breast stroke, and a bell rang.

It was a very loud, startling bell, its peel ricocheting off the tiled walls. He stopped at the end, and saw that Olive had climbed out at the other.

"Someone wants to swim," she called.

It hadn't happened before. He got out, too, a little winded, and moved after her, feeling protective. It could be anyone ringing the bell, not a swimmer at all, but it was someone she knew.

"James!" he heard her call, the voice echoing back through the tiled hallway. "James, you're back."

"Yes, love." It was a light baritone. "Let me in for a bit of exercise, then."

They appeared, Olive and a stocky young man with bright blue eyes and black curls.

"Chink," Olive said. "It's James Ryan. The one who got your book."

"I've been hearing about you," Chink said, offering his hand.

James Ryan took it, with a flattering grin, and said: "No less than I about you."

"He'll put you to shame in the water," Olive said.

"But nowhere else, I'll vow," said James. He had a strong brogue. "I've read the book, too, I have."

"Heavy going."

"Why, it's a fundamental book," James said.

"James swam for Ireland," Olive said. "He's terrific."

"Did you?"

"I was on the national team, yes," James said. "Donkey's years ago." He was getting out of his street clothes, a cable-knit white sweater, brown herringbone trousers with the legs cut tight below the knees. He was wearing trunks under the pants. His chest was covered with curly black hair, and his body was the male counterpart of Olive's, the upper torso centrally divided, from the diaphragm up, into two powerful lobes, the shoulders deep and sloping, the waist solid, the hips narrow, and the legs long muscled.

James and Olive moved together to the edge of the pool, and stood side by side, poised to dive.

Olive looked back over her shoulder. "Swim with us, Chink."

"Next year," Chink said. "Go."

They went smoothly in and smoothly through a lap, while Chink watched. Then because he felt superfluous standing there, he got his things and left the pool, calling out good-bye, and ran for an hour. At his apartment, as he dressed for an early appointment with Ted Winkler, to talk about the land job, he found himself studying Eve Shellcroft's postcard from Tahiti.

By now she is married, he thought. To live forever in a distant, dreamy place.

The postcard showed a view of Lake Vaihiria with orange-flowered shrubs and screw pine in the foreground. The text on the back said that Lake Vaihiria was a high mountain lake, but Chink supposed Eve's days would be spent most often in Papeete, and he wished her pleasant hours and tender people. The place he'd told her of in northern California was high, with seasons of hard weather.

He smiled as he tied his tie, trying to imagine life with Olive on the California ranch, but did not suppose it would suit her, nor could he really see himself there with her. She was too perfectly a physical match for someone like James Ryan, and Chink felt, for a moment, thinking of them standing side by side at the pool, quite old and rather envious. He thought he would be willing to buy the ranch for them if they were to like one another and want it. He thought himself an ass for having had a thought like that. He went off to talk with Ted Winkler about management and money, old men's topics.

Chink and Ted Winkler got along well. Winkler was precise, idealistic, and well prepared. They started talking at eight. By nine they were going through files of land descriptions and operating figures. Chink found much of it familiar, all of it intelligible, and most of it fascinating. At ten Winkler had had his secretary cancel the rest of his morning appointments and was taking Chink from office to office to meet the technical and financial people Chink might have working for him. At noon they were back in Winkler's office, reading the proposed employment contract, which Chink thought very generous.

"We'd want you to take hold and do it yourself," Winkler said. "It's too various for the kind of executive who needs his hand held. You'd have your performance reviewed a couple of times a year in terms of balance sheets, not case by case."

"I'm surprised to find that I want to try it," Chink said. "Are you sure you want to try me?"

"We were sure of that before I got in touch," Winkler said.

"Agency files?"

"We know everything about you. We know stuff you've probably forgotten."

"This company agency funded?"

"I thought you'd ask that. No. There's interaction and cooperation, like any big company has with government. There are former agency people working here besides myself. But W.C.I. isn't a front and never has been."

Chink said: "It's all production. Growing, harvesting. I like that."

"You want to take the contract home?"

"I think I want to sign it. I'm not quite free to start." He felt bound to finish the translation he had started. He thought he could do it in two more weeks. "First of next month?"

"Wally's already signed it," Winkler said. "Copy for you, copy for us, and one for the files. You want a ceremony?"

"No," Chink said. "Just a pen."

He signed the three copies. They shook hands.

"Let's get lunch," Winkler said. "Company dining room's not bad."

It was in the W.C.I. company dining room that Chink, unexpectedly, saw Olive again. He was facing the cash register, across the table from Ted Winkler, when Olive got in line with another young woman, to pay her check. Olive showed surprise, then waved and smiled at Chink, and seemed about to come to their table when Winkler turned his head to see whom Chink was greeting.

Olive's face went stony. She returned Winkler's look with an expression of distaste, turned back to her friend in the line, reached the cash register, paid, and left the room without looking at Chink again.

"You must be the axe man," Chink said.

"You know our Ms. Dahlke? Of course you do."

"She tells me the gents get promoted while you keep her on the training track."

"It did happen. It wasn't actually her fault."

"What happened?"

"She was slated to go out of the management training pool to one of our companies that has a lot of army contracts. Account exec. The thought was that Olive knew that mentality. She was raised regular army. She has a law degree, and a good head."

"I didn't know about the law degree."

"Sometimes business is harsh. Her father's a retired brigadier. He was working for us as a consultant, and got hired away by one of the competitors."

"You retaliated against the daughter?"

"There's a lot of confidential stuff. Under the circumstances, I took it up with Wally. He thought we'd better hold off."

"Wally moves that way in business, too?"

"I tried to explain it to Olive," Winkler said. "Actually, I asked her to dinner. It was a bad scene. She said, 'The only secret I know is where the key is to the women's room, and they couldn't get it out of me with thumbscrews.'

"I said, 'Oh, come on, Olive. Let's have dinner at Lutèce. Something else will come along.' Olive said, 'Why, that sounds like a pass, Mr. Winkler. Do you take guys to dinner at Lutèce when you've got bad news?' She was really steaming. I tried to say that I really would enjoy her company, if she was free, and she said . . . Oh, listen, Chink, I don't want to go on with this."

"She said what?" Chink wasn't sure he wanted to hear it, but it was too late now.

"Olive said, 'No. I'm not free. I cost a hundred bucks, like any other businesswoman. Your office or mine?' I tried to calm her. She said, 'For a hundred, I could choose my own company for dinner at Lutèce.' "

"She's got a rough tongue," Chink said.

"Chink, I guess you'd better know. The girl went through with it. Not with me, I hope I don't need to say. There's a guy, one of our executives, who'd been trying to date her. She took his hundred, and made sure I knew about it."

"My God, why?"

"Self-destruction. Defiance. I don't know."

"You tell Wally?"

"No. Nobody. I'm not sure I should have told you."

"I guess I wish you hadn't."

"Well. Where you're living, what you're doing there . . ."

"What am I doing there?" Chink asked.

Winkler shrugged. "I'm not in on that."

"Was it a way of showing how she hated men or something?"

"Perhaps. Talk about binder twine?"

"Yucatán," Chink said. "Tons of henequen to the acre. African competition. Yes, that's better."

When he got back to the house there was an invitation under his door to preview a show of Vivian Martin's photographs at a gallery nearby, and he thought he'd go over. It was a bright day. He hung up his suit, put on flannels and a light sweater, remembering Winkler's last remark about Olive: "The legend is that a lot of women trick around New York offices," Winkler had said. "But I don't know of any others. And certainly not smart ones like Olive. She's still got a future here if she can stop defying us."

Chink supposed he was meant to pass that on. He opened the door to let himself out, and heard voices in the hall.

The first was April's saying, "How did you get in here?" It was toneless, April's emotional voice.

"And what's it to you, darlin'?" He had heard that lilting, Irish baritone a few hours ago at the swimming pool. "I wasn't planning to stop by for a squeeze and a tease, was I?"

"There's no one home upstairs."

"But I've Lydia's keys, you see. She's loaned them to me."

"I don't believe you," April said.

"Good-bye, April."

"Don't go up there," she said, as Chink stepped out. "Chink!" It was not a scream, hardly even a call.

James Ryan had gone past April, and was on the fourth step already. "Mr. Peters," he said. "We meet again so soon, sir."

"Hello, James." Chink's first thought was that he was pleased to see the young man.

"I've Lydia's key. She's asked me to fetch something."

"What's that?" Chink asked.

"Her pipe and slippers, for I'm a good dog, too, you see." With a flourish, James swung a ring of keys. There were far too many of them, and the shanks were much too long.

April said, "Lydia's out of town."

James said, "She's not, dear. Whatever she may have told you."

"She took a cab. She had a suitcase with her."

"I don't think you'd better go up, James," Chink said, as mildly as he could.

"Likely not, but then I shall, after all."

"May I go with you?"

"I shouldn't like that."

"I'll have to ask April to call the police." Chink had moved as close as he could to James without getting clear of the protective barrier of the banister.

"Ah, but that she won't. Not April." James was smiling. Chink was smiling. He moved around to the foot of the step, exposing himself.

"Nice set of passkeys," Chink said, and was ready for the leap, right foot first, that would easily have laid him out. It was a good kick, aimed at Chink's chest, with the compact, vaulting body behind it, but the target was gone, down, and rolling once sideways. James, passing by, lost balance and careened into the wall near April as Chink finished his roll, sprang up, pivoted, and struck from behind, two-handed, fists together, into the kidneys. He pushed James' head left, reached down, and hooked the left ankle and threw the man. He moved onto James, one knee in the small of the back, got the hammerlock, applied pressure, and said: "The keys."

James' hand opened, and Chink picked up the key ring. It was heavy. There were two dozen keys on it in several patterns with twelve-inch shanks. It would do for a sap, and he might have used it in the hot moment, but April's voice chilled him:

"Hit him, Chink," she said, faint and flat.

Chink sighed and stood up. "Lie still, James," he said, watching his man. "April?"

There was no answer. He heard her door open and, in a moment, close.

"Unpleasant child," James said. There was pain in his voice.

"Want to put your hands out flat?"

James complied.

"Want to explain?"

"Not in this position," James said. "With my back howling."

With the big key ring balanced in his right hand, ready to swing, Chink knelt and ran his left hand up and down each side.

"There's no gun," James said. "The knife's on the right ankle if you'd like it."

"No thanks," Chink said, but reached down to touch the sheath, under the sock. As he did, James rolled and kicked, catching Chink's shoulder, knocking him away, and closed to take a fierce headlock with both arms. Trying to twist loose and get his legs under him, Chink heaved them both half up, over, and down again, but couldn't break James' grip. The Irishman had weight and strength. Chink still held the heavy key ring. His arm was free enough to swing it and he knew what to do, flog the bruised kidney with the ring, smash until the pain made James turn loose or pass out. Chink realized, as the coarse wool of James' sweater punished his cheek, that he didn't want to swing the keys.

"No," he said, and tossed the ring away, down the hall. Immediately, James released him and moved back, kneeling.

"Why ever not?" James asked, hands ready to attack again.

It took Chink a moment to catch his breath. His cheek stung where the sweater had scratched it. "Seemed like a good way to get myself really hurt," he said, sitting up.

"No, sir. You never thought that."

"Absolutely," Chink said.

James smiled. "It was a hell of a shot you hit me in the back, it was."

Chink smiled back.

James said: "Well, then, shall we go along upstairs. What I'm looking for I meant to give you, anyway."

Chink stood up. "What is it, James?"

"It's a journal Mary kept. She called it her daybook."

"James. James. I already have it."

"Lydia gave it to you?"

Chink nodded. "You haven't talked with her then?"

"She won't see me," James said. "Gone off overnight to avoid me. Can't say I blame her a great deal."

"What about the daybook?"

"Have you not read it?"

"Not the last half."

"Will you? Today even? And then, will you talk with me?"

"Yes. All right, I will."

"I'll ring you up in the evening?"

"I'll be home."

"Sorry for the fight. I lost my head. So unnecessary."

"Most fights are. Or beside the point."

James nodded and stepped forward, and they shook hands. "I'm off then. It's been a great and painful pleasure seeing you again." When he got to where the key ring was lying, he paused, and looked back.

"Leave them, James. I have the daybook."

"They cost a deal of money."

"If you take them, I'll have to have the locks changed."

James nodded. "There's more keys, and more money," he said. "If it's wanted." And went to the door, leaving the keys behind.

Chink used a particular phone number. A woman's voice said, "Five-five-five, two-one-one-seven."

"For the ambassador."

"Name?"

"Grinder," Chink said.

"Meeting, Grinder. Shall I get him out?"

"Yes," Chink said, and gave a number he had copied from the phone booth at the corner drugstore.

He stood in the booth holding the disconnected phone to his mouth and ear, talking nonsense into it. He had a weight on the bar in place of the receiver. The weight was James Ryan's key ring. There was a blip from the phone box, and he had the key ring off, releasing the bar, before a full ring could sound.

"What's up, Chink?"

"Your man's arrived."

"What man?"

"From Ireland. James Ryan."

"How did you know I'd be interested?"

"He's a swimmer, Wally. You seemed interesting in swimming the other day."

"I hoped he wouldn't come."

"I suppose."

"Want to fill me in?"

"No. I want you to fill me in for a change."

"Ryan's the leader of something called the Bodenstown group. Do you know the name Wolfe Tone?"

"I've seen it recently."

"Eighteenth-century Republican martyr. He's buried at Bodenstown churchyard. It's a shrine. Ryan's people are fanatics, with European and Middle Eastern connections."

"What have they done?"

"A list of atrocious things. They exchange personnel with other groups. Hijackings, assassinations. All those things."

"And they're active here?"

"They raise money for the I.R.A., or steal it, or extort it."

"Does that bring us to Manuel Carbajal?"

"He was under Ryan's orders."

"What about William Williams?"

"It looks that way, doesn't it?"

"Why is Ryan here, Wally?"

"To have another try. At me."

"Is that what he and Carbajal were planning the first time?"

"It looks that way," Wally said again. "I'm afraid Ryan's coming back makes it seem rather certain."

"All right. If we can pick him up, I've got him for breaking and entering. With a witness. Detention and deportation."

"He broke in there?"

Chink described the encounter.

"Then April's your witness?"

"I wish she weren't."

"I'd like to keep her out of it."

"How can we?"

"Then let's make it stick, Chink. Let's do more to young Mr. Ryan than slap his wrist for a house call. He brought Carbajal in. We've got an accessory."

"I think he and Mike were in love," Chink said.

"Let's give him a long, long time in a quiet place to think about it. You'll be seeing him?"

"I'm not sure," Chink said slowly. He hadn't mentioned the daybook. "There's no guarantee of anything."

He finished reading the daybook. Towards the end, the initials J. and M. appeared quite often. Sometimes the names were written out, James and Manny. The prose became hasty:

> Wendy must not read this any longer. She still thinks it all quite playful, which is what we want her to think, but she nearly spilled a great, big bean. We were having duty drinks with Father, and W. said: "Our old friend Chink's a hero to the new warriors." Father said: "You mean like the Green Berets? Chink once wrote a pamphlet on guerilla action." Wicked Wendy Witch said, "More like the Basque Berets," and I was afraid she would go on and say something about the Irish, but she shut sweetly up. She approves of J. (or thinks she does).

The entry went on:

> We must write only on the second floor now, while Viv is away, and hide the book. M. is getting restless. He does not seem very

bright, but very intense and nervous. James keeps him calm. April upsets him but I don't know what to say to her about it. Anyway, it will soon be over.

What would soon be over began to appear in an entry two pages later:

We are planning it for Wolfe's birthday. Wendy will be in New Hampshire. I have agreed to go to the dance, and have already bought a gown for it, which, I admit, was fun. Wendy delighted about gown. She hopes I'm getting frivolous. Father and Adrienne hope so, too, and pleased with me, damn it. I hate the deception. Lydia says after we do it, I should be open about my role. No, Lydia, I can't. 1. James says better leverage, less confusion, if I seem to be a victim, too. 2. I believe in lies that are meant to spare people. 3. I can be careful and protective, especially keeping watch on M.

Chink put the daybook aside, looked up Wolfe Tone in the encyclopedia, and found that he'd been born June 20. He went out then to the branch library, and went through *The New York Times* for the previous weeks. He found an announcement of a UNICEF benefit ball for June 20, with Ambassador and Mrs. Diefenbach listed among the sponsors. He knew the date too well to have to remind himself that Mike and Wendy had been killed on the evening of June 18. He understood why Lydia had given up the daybook now. Furious because of Vivian's engagement, Lydia wanted to hurt Wally Diefenbach.

He returned to his apartment to wait for James Ryan's call. When, forty-five minutes later, a sharp knock came at his apartment door, he was briefly angry with himself for not having thought of the possibility that Ryan could have a second set of passkeys. He answered the door cautiously, pulling it open quickly and stepping aside, ready to move, but it was Olive.

He smiled. She looked at him in fury.

"You dirty son of a bitch," she said.

Reflexively, he caught the hand she swung at him, then made himself stand and let her hit him in the cheek with the other hand. It was a good crack. She was breathing almost too hard to talk.

"If you say . . . one dirty male word . . . or innuendo . . . to Sue or anyone . . ."

He let go her hand and shook his head. "I wish you hadn't thought I might."

She pushed into the apartment, her chest still heaving, face deeply flushed, and pulled the door closed behind her. "Once," she said. "Once because I was hurt and bitter and wanted to hit back at Winkler. And one more time to be outrageous and punish a man. Does that make me a whore?"

Chink walked away, to the French doors, and looked, frowning, out into the garden. Finally he said: "Probably."

She gasped. "Chink!"

He looked at her. She was sitting on the edge of the sofa, her hand to her mouth.

"Where would I get the right to let you off?" he said.

"Even when I hit you, I thought you'd understand."

"Once when I was a kid, I killed an Egyptian carriage driver who wanted to rob me. It was deliberate, unnecessary, and not even in self-defense. Do you have the right to tell me it wasn't a murder?"

She shook her head.

"Things get fuzzy when you don't call them by name," Chink said. "That doesn't mean you have to condemn people."

"Or yourself?"

"We all live with a lot of stuff."

She waited to see whether he would say something more. He looked at her, and thought nothing much beyond how young she was.

"Chink?"

"You're okay, Olive," he said. "You're fine. You're terrific."

"Have you known real whores? I mean full time?"

"Yes. And a few full-time murderers. They're subhuman, mostly, or psychos. The whores were sad, tarnished ladies, or sometimes fierce, stupid ones."

"I feel sad and stupid," Olive said, at which he found himself with a knee on the sofa beside her, holding her hands.

"You're young and lovely and twice as bright as anyone," he said.

"You're no Al Capone yourself," Olive said.

There was returning pressure on his hands, pulling him towards her. Chink stood up, releasing the hands.

"Yep."

"I wanted you to kiss me."

"I wanted to."

She stood and walked a step or two away, frowning.

"It's not because . . . ?"

"Of course not. Just scared to try, Olive."

"Of what?"

"I haven't been much use at getting into things, the past few years."

He couldn't have said what emotion her face showed then, but it was very powerful, making the mouth clench and the nose go thin and white.

"Did you tell April Dorsey that?" she yelled. She ran to the door and yanked it open. "You know what April did? She sold her baby. For ten thousand dollars. Maybe the next one she sells will be yours, Mr. Peters."

The door wouldn't slam for her. She was probably halfway up the first flight of steps before it finished closing.

"I've one hell of a bruise, up over me arse."

"Hello, James." He'd been sitting in the dark when the phone rang, and found it without turning on a light. "Sorry about the bruise."

"Finish with the daybook?"

"Yes."

"We must talk, then, mustn't we?"

"Yes. When?"

"I shouldn't like to come back there. Will you come out?"

"In the morning?"

"Ah, yes. 'Unless there are good reasons against it, daylight is the best time to negotiate. Rested men are reasonable. Tired men get emotional and stubborn.' There, you see. Those are your own words."

"It was Mike gave you my pamphlet. Her father's copy."

There was a pause, and then James' voice said, softly: "Oh, yes, she did."

"Where shall we meet, James?"

"Will you be swimming in the morning?"

"Let's not touch Olive with this."

"I'll swim elsewhere," James said. "There's a park by the gallery where Vivian has her photos."

"I haven't seen it."

"A bare, concrete park, without a tree or bush."

"All right."

They set the time for ten, when they wouldn't be conspicuous. Chink hung up, turned on the lights, and instructed himself to eat something. He had radishes, yoghurt, and a hard roll. It was nine-forty-five, too early to go to bed.

He had, nevertheless, unbuttoned his shirt when the phone rang again. He let it ring three times, composing his mind to answer whoever it might be, James calling back, Wally with a move to make. With a surge of hope that caught him by surprise, he thought it might be Olive and picked up the instrument.

"Hello?"

"You come up here, okay?"

He didn't recognize the slurring voice. "Who is it?"

"Boozy Susie. McGrewsie. Come on."

He heard Olive's voice then, indignant. "Susan. Who are you calling? Susan, you're not."

"Chink. Come up, Chink. . . ." There were gasps and giggles and the sound of a struggle for the telephone. "Chink, it's a . . ." Susan apparently lost the phone to Olive, for her voice was distant, breathless, laughing, as she shouted: "We're having a slumber party."

Then Olive's voice said: "Don't come up, Chink. We're in nightgowns."

"All right."

"Or do you want to?"

"Sure," Chink said. "But I'll put my shirt back on."

He felt exhilarated, trotting up the stairs. He wanted peace with Olive. He didn't want to miss swimming with her in the morning. Susan and Olive must, he supposed, have been talking about him, and Susan, who sounded as if she'd had quite a lot to drink, must have run to the phone and dialled.

"Said I was calling Vivian," Susan crowed, standing in the open doorway to greet him, wearing boys' pajamas and lambskin slippers. The pajamas were blue broadcloth. Susan was swaying slightly, and hanging on to the door, laughing. "Vivers getting married, so's said, let's haver up, tell her the bees 'n the flowers. . . ."

Olive's voice said, "Susie, Susie." He saw Olive then. She was barefoot and wearing a raincoat, buttoned and belted, over an ankle-length nightgown, its peach-colored hem showing below the coat.

"Poor Vivers got no mama to tell her." Susan wheeled away from the doorway, letting the door close as Chink went in, her short blond hair bouncing, her lithe body loose in the pajama top. She pounced on a glass she'd set down. It was clear liquor, vodka or gin. She took a big gulp and sat down abruptly in the green chintz armchair. "Sex ed. 'M a qualified teacher of sex ed, six credit hours. Yes, sir." This time she sipped instead of gulping. "Viver's my little friend."

"Your little friend's probably in the sack with her fiancé at the moment," Olive said. "Maybe there's still time to phone instructions."

"All a ruse, Susie's ruse." Susan stood up again, unsteady. "You two dumbbells kiss and make up."

Olive smiled a small smile at Chink. He smiled back.

"Go ahead, I won't watch," Susan said.

"I'll get you a beer," Olive offered, and went towards the kitchen.

"If you won't kiss him, I will," Susan called after her. She half circled Chink, paused, and pulled open the top button of the pajama shirt. "Topless."

Olive came back into the room with a bottle of beer and a glass.

"You watch me, Olive Dahlke," Susan said, and undid a second button, exposing no more than the swelling where her small breasts began. She growled.

"Go ahead," Olive said.

"Have to kiss him, first," Susan said. "Trouble with you, Olive. No sex ed." She eyed Chink, put her drink down on a side table by the chair, and then, breaking into laughter, threw herself against him sideways so that he had to catch her, reeled around, and planted a wild kiss somewhere near his ear.

"I like your technique," Chink said, feeling himself grin and holding her up, for she was more unsteady than he'd thought.

"What's the next move, Miss McGrew, please?" Olive asked.

One of Susan's arms slid around Chink's neck now, and he looked away from Olive into Susan's eyes. They were anxious eyes. She pulled his head down so that their lips met. It was a serious kiss on her part. He tried to respond lightly, raising his head after an instant, and saying, "More than flesh and blood can stand."

She tightened the arm around his neck, and pressed her face against his chest. Then her free hand went lazily to her bosom, with an intention which may have been left over from the moment before, and undid the third pajama shirt button. One side of the shirt fell away and bared a breast. Susan tipped up her face again, and smiled. Then she pushed herself away, saying in a strange, chokey voice, "She didn't think I would. She didn't." Her movements had turned slow. She saw the glass in front of her, and reached down, uncertainly, but couldn't pick it up.

She took a step away, and her knees wobbled. She took one further step, and then slid into a pile of cushions on the floor in a corner of the room. Sounds came, but it was hard to tell whether she was giggling now or sobbing. After a moment, whichever it was stopped, and Susan closed her eyes.

Chink looked at Olive.

Olive said, "That's the way she gets these nights. But she'll sleep now."

As if on command, Susan rolled most of the way onto her back, the shirt falling the other way now, baring the other breast. She sighed, and wrapped one arm around a pillow.

"Do we leave her there?"

"I generally get her to bed. You can carry her, unless you think you'll enjoy it too much."

Chink grinned again, crossed, reached under Susan at the waist and knees, and lifted her, crooking his arm so as to pull her shoulders into his chest. She was very light. The breast moved away, partly into the shirt again. "Isn't it against the law to have such pink nipples?" he asked Olive.

"Book her and lock her up," Olive said, and led them down a

short hallway to Susan's bedroom. There was a lovely, drowsy young smell from Susan's body, mixed with the sourness of the alcohol she'd had to drink. She was not completely sedated by it, though, for she stirred in his arms, and just as they reached the door of her room, her eyes sprang open.

"Where's Leon?" She said it quite clearly. The pupils of her eyes were very large. He shook his head, and the eyes closed again.

Olive turned on a light and turned down the bedclothes, and Chink settled Susan onto the sheets. At first the body flopped into total relaxation. Then it gathered some coherence and Susan's arms raised a little way towards him. Chink squeezed her shoulder and backed away.

"You'd better do the tucking in," he said to Olive, and left the room. In a moment, the light went off, and Olive followed him into the hallway, closing the bedroom door.

Without word or pause, they clung together, kissing, until Olive moved back just enough for him to undo the buckle of her belt and the buttons of her coat. They pressed together again more closely. There was no question of his not responding to the urgency of her lower body. She chided him, between breaths, pressing and whispering, "You understand . . . it's not because I like you . . . one damn bit . . . you and your . . . dumb old . . . senile challenges. . . . Makes a person horny . . . that's all. . . ."

"Olive," he said.

"So get on downstairs . . . and wait for me. . . ."

Susan's voice called out something from behind the closed door, and Olive called back, "Night, Susie, night," disengaged herself, and gave Chink a push.

Down he went, hardly believing that she really meant to follow, but by the time he was at his door she was beside him again, and they went in together and straight to the bed. In the scramble to get rid of their clothes and couple, he got overexcited. They had hardly begun before he had to lock his arms around her, thrust, shudder, and explode. He was aware that she had locked arms, too, shuddered, and thrust back, and as their bodies loosened she said, "Yes. Yes." Squeezed his upper arms with strong fingers. "That was just right. No technique. No style. Just . . . oooof."

He rolled to one side, clasped her shoulder, pulled her nakedness against his own, too gorged with affection to say anything at all. After a time she kissed his throat and asked if he was sleepy.

"Very wide awake. Very happy," he said.

"Then I'd like a towel and a bottle of beer," Olive said. "And I want to look at you."

An hour later they were still wakeful and happy, their heads together on the pillow. She asked if he was coming to work at W.C.I.

"We got an employment contract signed today," he told her.

"It's a bear of a job," she said. "It wrecked the last man who had it. You're probably tough enough."

"I like the difficulties," he said. "And I suppose it won't do me any harm to put some money away."

"You'll earn it."

"Will you stay at the firm?"

"No. Not after this. I've got offers. There's a good one on a magazine. I've been inert about it."

"Winkler says you have a future at W.C.I."

"Winkler can go *merder* in his pearl grey *chapeau*."

"He's not bad. He worries about you."

"I've just been staying there for stubbornness. But if you and I want to see each other, I'd rather be in a different office."

"We want to see each other," Chink said.

"May I ask you something?"

"Sure."

"Why did you come to New York? Are you investigating, or something like that?"

"No. Only waiting." That reminded him that he was to meet James in the morning. He realized morning had just come. "It's after midnight," he said.

"Am I a pumpkin?"

"Never."

"Then I'll go and let you sleep. Going to swim?"

"Yes."

She kissed him and sat up. "One more question. To help with Susie, because it breaks my heart to see her drink herself into a stupor, night after night. Is Leon Quiroz coming back?"

"I don't know yet. I may find out."

"Will you tell me when you do?"

He thought about it carefully before he nodded and said yes.

He went, right after swimming, to look at the park. It was, as James had said, bare concrete, without a tree or bush. It was marked off into playground areas, with gravel paths between, and surrounded by a heavy fence of iron pickets. There were benches.

He walked to a delicatessen, ate lox and a bagel with cream cheese, and phoned Winkler, to ask for the use of an office. The job excited him very much this morning, and he wanted to start learning it. He wanted a place in the world of business and money, because it was the world for which Olive had declared.

He returned to the park, and went up to the gallery where Vivian's photographs were showing. They were just opening. Most of the photographs were conventional, but there was energy in many of them. Vivian was good at catching things in motion.

"Is it art, Captain Peters?"

He turned quickly, feeling silly. It was James, of course, covering him with a pointing finger, only four feet behind him. "There, now," said James with a smile. "I did think you'd be early to have a look at the park. I'd have done myself."

"You should have whacked me in the kidneys," Chink said. "Then we'd be even."

"That from the man who wrote the book?" James shook his head. "Let's have no evens, no fair play, and no waste motion. Isn't that your teaching?"

"I hope not," Chink said.

"I've tried to learn it too quick, likely. I'm a soldier, Captain, not a bloody agent. But I was assigned this and mean to see it through. Do you know where I first heard of you?"

"Where?"

"From a man named Mooney. His brother was your chum."

"Marston Mooney was a brave man," Chink said.

"And yourself no less, to the brother's mind and mine."

A gallery attendant, a dark-haired woman without a smile, opened the door of an office and looked into the main room at them.

"Hello, there," James said. The sheer pleasantness of the way he said it brought some sort of light to the woman's face. "Afraid we're leaving, Miss. Or I am. Or are we?"

"We are," Chink said.

"Please sign the register?" She made a plea out of it.

"With pleasure," James said, and wrote, on the line below where Chink had signed earlier: *Marston Mooney, Bodenstown, Ireland.*

"Marston was English," Chink said, as he and James went down the stairs.

"Irish born, with an Irish heart," James insisted. "Only schooled in England."

"Is Marston's brother with you?"

"Never was. We only flew together."

"You're a pilot."

"Was. Flew the cargo ships, wherever the money was. That's to say a war. Congo, Lebanon, Biafra. Bags and bags of money. Lived like a millionaire. Didn't care which side."

"What changed you?"

"Biafra and the Jesuits. More brave men."

They reached the street.

"Shall we do the park then?"

"All right," Chink said.

"I'm here for Diefenbach, you know."

"Why tell me?" Chink asked.

They walked on across the street. The park gates were open now. There were two benches near the gate they entered at, one on either side of a forty-foot round sandbox. Young mothers watched young children from one bench. Chink and James took the other.

"Why tell me?" Chink asked again.

"Only that I'm sure Diefenbach has himself. And is it your job to kill me first?"

"Not my kind of work," Chink said.

"Ah, but it was, and you're spoken of with respect in many strange camps and dark rooms of the world. Then you're to be a shield, I suppose, or a target. To draw my fire, in hope that I'll reveal myself. And, of course, if the target should shoot back?"

"Hard to do without a gun," Chink said.

Abruptly, and in a different voice, James asked, "Do you recall a chap named Jolliver?"

"I don't think so."

"He broke your jaw, you broke his hand."

"Yes. I'd forgotten his name."

"And would you like to know how all that came about?"

"I think I do know it," Chink said.

"How could you, and be working again for Diefenbach?"

"I'm not working for him."

"Then what in God's name are you doing?"

"Being a target? You seem to know more about it than I do."

"And how do you like the job now?" When Chink didn't answer, James said, "How could you take it on, knowing about Jolliver?"

"It's too complicated."

"No, Captain Peters, for we talked with Jolliver."

"He on your side now? I don't care for the rank, James."

"Diefenbach used Jolliver against a friend of mine down south. We took Jolliver."

"Is he still alive?"

"That's a metaphysical question, isn't it?"

"I see."

"But he told us ever so many things. Pages and pages, poor sod. Everything he ever did for Diefenbach and the rest of your lot. So the Honorable Walden is your friend again, and you trust him? God in Heaven."

"They're not my lot, and I haven't trusted him or them for years. Nor do I you, my friend. Where's Leon Quiroz?"

"Now there's a name that I don't recognize. Or is it the bartender?"

"A man I did trust."

"I've never heard the name. Only that he was Puerto Rican."

"Cuban."

"Williams did him on the way to Canada, to change with me."

"Did him where, James?"

"I gather it was done here, the evening Williams left."

"The body?"

"Williams is a strange one, you know."

"Where's the body, James?"

"Williams said he kept it in the car to talk to, until he got just south of the border, in Vermont. The Canadian border, that is. And put it well out in the woods before he crossed, covered up with leaves and boughs."

"Then you met Williams in Canada, traded passports, switched the photos, and brought the car back."

"Williams went on to Libya."

"Training."

"This playground is for children." Two young mothers had arrived with three- and four-year-olds. "Don't you men see the sign?"

A metal parks department sign did set certain hours when the park was to be used only by children under five, and whatever adults had them in charge.

James recovered first, jumping to his feet. "Yes, yes, so it is," he said, with his marvelous smile.

Chink rose, too. "And we forgot our roller skates."

"They seem all right," one of the women said.

"It's because of perverts," the other explained. "And big kids crowding the little ones out."

"I do hope we're in your second category," James said.

"Are you Irish?" Now the first mother was disposed to chat.

"We must go," James said. "It's nice to talk with you."

"We come here every morning till it gets cold."

"I shall remember." James raised his brows at Chink. They moved off.

"You made a conquest," Chink said.

"Ah, but the other couldn't keep her eyes off you."

"Why Leon Quiroz?" Chink asked.

"He knew me," James said. "Seen me often enough with Carbajal and Williams, in what they call the barrio."

"Others could make the connection."

"Not many. Diefenbach likely. Lydia, of course. It was, in any case, Williams' judgment. He went to the bar to test Quiroz's temper, and judged it most unsafe to us. I don't know that I'd have done as Williams did, but he was on his own to clear the way here for me."

"You were counting on Lydia's still being with you?"

"Ah, yes. Last spring she was ready to go and have the training. Mike, too."

"I don't know whether I believe that."

"That's why you had to have the daybook," James said. "After I learned I couldn't count on Lydia any longer."

"But it was Lydia who gave it to me."

"A bit of luck. But shall you hear it now?"

They were walking on the east side of the street. "Let's cross over into the sunshine," Chink said. "Why should you still want Diefenbach? He's not young, James. He's not active in the field. After what happened to his girls, I don't think he's a very effective man."

"He owes us half a million dollars," James said. They'd got across the street by then and turned south. "It was the money that we needed to pay down to the Greek arms merchants, for the weaponry to capture Belfast."

He's mad, Chink Peters thought, but didn't say it.

"It's not hard to raise the small gold, from the little Irish American with his union dues or his plumbing shop. And there's many a solicitor or football coach who'll do a bit more. But there's wealthy Irish, too, who can do the big sums, and we were close to getting them. Diefenbach stopped that. The rich in your country listen to the other rich. The old wolf stopped it."

"I don't see how he could."

"My word he did. Found out who we were talking with, and stopped it so they'll not even say 'Hello there,' on the telephone."

"You were going to extort the money from Diefenbach, then?"

"You've read it in the daybook, have you not?"

"Not the details."

"Mike's plan, as much as anyone's. You've seen Diefenbach's chauffeur?"

"The little Turk with the big mustache?"

"Manny Carbajal was quite like him to look at," James said. "In a cap and uniform. In darkness." When Chink didn't reply, he said: "Mike Diefenbach and I picked Manny from a hundred photographs, would to God I'd never seen the things. Can we get a drink?"

"Mike picked him?"

"Can we not get a drink?"

"I'm surprised you're a drinker," Chink said.

"Ah, the father's voice. But I'm not, you see. Only when I need to steady myself, a stiff whiskey is the thing."

They were by a neighborhood tavern, a deep, narrow room with red paper streamers gathering dust in the front window, lit inside mostly by illuminated beer signs. The place smelled, as they went in, of last night's business. There was an elderly bartender with rimless glasses, reading a tabloid newspaper.

"Double whiskey," James said. "And a draft beer. You?"

"Is there coffee?"

"I'll make some," the bartender said, pouring the double shot and drawing the beer. James picked them up, and led the way to a wooden booth.

"Will you sit with me?" James asked.

"Yes," Chink said, thinking that there was no way he could take as young and strong a man as James Ryan by himself, and not much chance of phoning for assistance without James running.

"It was a simple enough scheme, really," James said. "And a good one. Mike pleased her dad by agreeing to go with him to a ball. Usually she gave him a good deal of back talk on such fancy matters. There'd be three, then, Diefenbach, his wife, and Mike coming out of it, late at night to get into the limousine. While they danced, Manny and I were to overcome the Turk and take his uniform for Manny."

"Kill the Turk."

"Whatever was needed. When our three came out, Manny was to be behind the wheel. I was to be hiding in front, on the floor, crouched in under the dash. There's bags of room. And so we'd have them. Six hundred thousand was to be the price, the extra to cover our expenses. I'd taken a flat. The transaction needn't have taken long."

"No," Chink said. "I suppose not."

"When you have the man who can transfer the funds himself, and that can be done by cable on foreign banks, to be picked up by your people abroad. And no one even to know that anyone is missing."

"Lydia was to be your messenger."

"Lydia and Williams, though she didn't know him yet."

"Do you want another drink?" Chink asked.

The bartender was coming with a tray, a glass pot, and a cup. "Thanks," said James. "I'll have coffee with you now."

"We'd like another cup, please," Chink said. When the coffee was poured and the bartender had left them, James said: "Let me have him, Mr. Peters. Let me have Diefenbach."

"You can't mean that, James."

"Only go away and leave him to us. He's badly frightened. It's only you who whistles back, when he's whistling in the dark."

"I was supposed to get a big dose of LSD and forget how to whistle, wasn't I?"

"We want him badly frightened," James said. "And then we'll find a way to take him, or his wife, and we'll have our money."

"And capture Belfast, and drive out the British. Make a home for the Palestinians, get self-rule for Puerto Rico, and win Japan and Italy for the patriots."

"You think me daft."

"The whole world, James."

"Will you not help? Let me explain, and then you'll think on it."

There came into Chink Peters' head, as James began to talk in earnest, the phrase Wendy Diefenbach had copied out: How can I, with a mind full of grey monkeys with blue faces?

James was eloquent. He made a sort of speech, and Chink could understand the effect James' passion and coherence might have had on Mike and Lydia, already quite disposed to be converted. The speech began with the great villain, Churchill, passing what James called "the Idiot's crown to old Truman," dealt with personages, countries, whole continents. It might have had the sound of a brilliant history lesson, to someone who shared James' commitment. "Do you not see then?" James leaned forward, across the table. "That it's we who've picked up where you left it, after Hitler? Can you deny that?"

Chink said, "It's a great lecture, James, but the student's dull."

"All right, then. I must tell you something more, though I've no heart for it, but perhaps it will help you trust me more when you know the thing I did."

"The coffee's bad," Chink said. "Can we go outside, in the sun?"

"Oh, yes," James said. "I'm shivering here myself."

A little wind had come up. They walked to the corner, and stood together in a protected place, against the wall of some large, institutional building.

"You can spare us both, James," Chink said, "if you keep it brief."

"Ah, no, I'll not," James said.

"It won't help you to tell nor me to hear it all."

"Shut up, Captain Bloody Peters, and I'll do it my own way, for I was there that night in the rooms you live in. And as I was approaching the damned house, who did I see, walking along the street with an odd-looking bottle in her hand, but April? It was a black bottle, shaped like some sort of bear, I suppose.

" 'Here,' says April. 'Are you going in to see Manny?'

" 'Perhaps,' I said.

" 'Give him this bottle, then. It's his.' Manny had been spending time with April, I knew that. Once I believe she'd had him to her bed, and he couldn't stop from trying to get back again. I couldn't understand at all what Manny saw in April, but then I was a man in love."

"Yes," Chink said.

"So I took the bottle. It was some swill called Pisco Manny drank. And stood talking there, in the warm night, with April. April says that Manny's in a rage, and so she's had to leave. She'd given him some Dexamyl, it was, and then he'd been swallowing down this Pisco, and got after her, and she'd run out, taking his bottle just to tease him more, and locked him in, she thought, behind her, not remembering the garden.

"So I said, 'Come along. I'll take Manny off your hands.' April and I went in together. I had a key to Mike and Wendy's place. As we came to the door, I said, 'Let's leave the bottle off. He's surely had too much by now,' and I opened up the door.

"And there she was, Wendy, lying in her blood. We've seen bad ones, my Captain, but never a one like that. A leg almost cut away, the stomach ripped. I cried out. Then I saw Manny. He was on one knee, over past the sofa, holding his knife and looking at me like an animal. Come back for that knife, I now believe, to go and butcher dead Mary in the bath, but then I didn't know that Mike was gone. I shouted again, and he came up and charged me, knife in hand, and

April shoved behind me, shoved me towards him, and ran back towards her place, moaning.

"Manny came at me with his eyes like pinwheels, and I stepped in and tried to get the wrist, but he knew what he was doing and gave me a good cut, he did, across the chest, and then was on his way out the door, yelling some hideous Spanish stuff, and I was after him. Shall I show you the sort of knife? It's what we all carry."

Chink shook his head.

"But you'll hear it now, and then you'll have it with you, as I do with me. I got my own knife out, and got out the door after him. I heard him thumping off in the dark, and could see him then, going along the street west, and ran myself. I'm fast.

"He went across the avenue and on along the street, and once I had him in my sight and at a distance, I slowed just a little to keep pace, knowing that I could catch him when I wished. I knew, too, that the houses would give out, down at the end of the next long block. And there'd be no one there to see us when we got there.

"He came to the cobblestones at the end of the street."

"I know," Chink said.

"He tripped and fell, got up again, and ran on. I closed the distance. Then he stopped and turned with his knife, and, seeing mine, threw his away, showed me at thirty paces that his hands were empty. So I closed up my own knife, and put it in my pocket, showed empty hands back, and went on towards him.

"It wasn't in the spirit of a duel, mind you; I was there to kill him, but I didn't need to let him know for sure until I had him caught.

"Just as I reached him, though, he turned and ran again. I moved to cut him off, so he'd not go back the way he'd come. He stopped. He ran the other way, and found the quay, and ran out on it. I stopped running then, and walked out after him. There was no way for him to go but into the water, and I didn't think then I wanted him to do that, so I started talking: 'Manny,' I said. 'Stay a minute. It's only James, isn't it?'

" 'I can't swim,' he said, or something like it, in his awful English. 'I no sweem, James, we get Diefenbach ourself . . .' he said. 'Okay? Okay?'

" 'Okay,' I said, and had him by the wrist, swung him around, arm up his back. Both wrists then and tripped him down—how often have you done it, Captain?

"Holding him then, with a knee in his back, and let go the right arm. 'Into the pocket, Manny,' I said. 'Get your capsule.' For we carry them, too, you know, just as you did. Many things we learned from you, and it's our rule, too, every man to have the capsule with him, so that he may kill himself in case of capture. Manny hadn't his, or I'd have stuffed it in his mouth. Manny cried then. He sobbed, and said he'd lost it. Bloody animal, afraid to carry it he must have been. Then he was pleading with me, thinking he was to be punished for this infraction of the rules. Only imagine. I held him there in the night, thought of giving him my own capsule, not wanting to kill him with the knife for they must think he'd done himself.

"And then I changed my mind, and raised him up, marched him to the end and gave him a kick into the water, let him splash."

"You watched him drown?"

"Would you have? No, you'd not."

"You took off your shoes and went after him. You drowned him."

"Too bloody true I did, and wish I could have him alive to drown again. He gave a frightful, coughing yell and fought at me with his hands, and I swam round behind and seized his hair and held him under, I did, until his struggling stopped. And only later did I know he'd done the same to Mike."

Both men were silent for a time. Then Chink asked: "Was it you who called the police?"

"I did after, and left the phone to dangle in a booth."

"I never believed it was April."

"No, not her. I wanted, then, to see Mike, of course, not knowing she was gone. Wanting to help her, if I could. I ran to the room we had, for dry clothing, and there were others there with the radio news, and so I learned the rest of it. Many of our group were there, William Williams for one. They stopped me then from killing myself. They packed me off home next day."

"You shouldn't have come back, James. Diefenbach knows you're here."

"From you he learned it?"

"Yes. If you're taken, you'll be tried as Carbajal's accomplice."

"But you've heard I'm not."

"I don't think you'd have much chance. Evidence can be forged. Feelings would be very strong against you. Diefenbach knows how to do those things."

"I'll kill him," James said.

"Go back, James."

"You could have taken me today."

"I doubt it. I considered it."

"Could have had men follow us from the park, but I made sure you hadn't done."

"No."

"Will you not let me have him then?"

"No, James."

"You'll stay on, in the middle."

Wally always has someone in the middle, Chink thought, and the thought startled him.

He said, "James." He paused, and felt certain. "How did Manuel Carbajal come to you?"

"It was as I told you. Mike and I went through many photographs."

"Where did the photographs come from?"

"We've people here, in touch with other people. William Williams brought that lot in."

"William Williams worked for Diefenbach then."

"What are you saying?"

Chink said, "I think you've got more revenge, James, than a man could want. I think Carbajal came in as Diefenbach's man, too. The pictures had to come from Diefenbach. And Eustace Martin was used. April was used. Wally Diefenbach put Manny in that house. It's the way he works."

"Good God above," James said.

"Go back to your war, James. Be a soldier."

"I'll need to think," James said. "I'll need to think most carefully."

"Good-bye," Chink said, and offered his hand. James nodded and shook the hand, his young face very serious. He started away, stopped, and called back over his shoulder: "Good-bye, then, Captain Chink. Good-bye, sir."

Chink Peters stood for several minutes where he was. He thought, for some reason, of the phrase from *King Lear*—"Poor Tom's a-cold"—though the sun was quite warm where he stood, out of the wind.

Wally phoned, during the afternoon, to say that Libby was in town. She wanted to see Chink, and Wally thought they might all get together for a drink. Chink said he wasn't up to it. They settled on lunch next day. Wally asked if Chink had heard from James Ryan. Chink said he wasn't up to talking about that today, either, he hoped Wally would excuse him.

Olive came down for supper. He hadn't cooked for anyone in a long time. He sautéed veal cutlets, and made béarnaise sauce for the first time in years. It turned out quite well. He told her that he had seen James Ryan and that they had said good-bye.

"Listen to the hearts break," Olive said. "Everybody here was mad about him except me. And I would have been if Mike hadn't seen him first."

He'd felt tired all afternoon, and even cold, but being with Olive rested him and raised his spirits.

"Party tomorrow," she reminded him. "Vivian's engagement."

He liked hearing her talk. "What else is going on?"

"The best thing is, Susie's got a new man. No, the best thing is, I've got a new man."

"But Susan met someone?"

"At a P.T.A. meeting after school this afternoon. He's a Pole, a count though I don't suppose he ever got to live that way. Exiled, rich, a widower, and very appealing, Susie says. He's got a kid in her school, and can't understand a word, but he made it clear enough he wanted to take her to supper. They're out tonight. Did you hear anything about Leon?"

Chink said, "He isn't coming back."

"Just as well, but it's a shame about his dropping med school."

"Yes."

"The count sounds better. May I read your contract?"

"Winkler tells me you're a lawyer," Chink said, getting the document from the writing desk.

"I haven't done the New York bar exam, but I'll have to now. Last week at W.C.I. I'm going to be in the general counsel's office at the magazine."

At two in the morning the phone rang and woke him. Olive had left an hour before. He realized the phone must have rung several times, and by the time he found it the ringing had stopped. He sat up, waiting for it to ring again, but it didn't until nearly five-thirty, by which time he'd gone back to sleep again. It was James.

"Did I wake you earlier?" he asked. "Very sorry. I was on the run."

"I thought it might be you. Are you safe now?"

"For the moment, but some of our people are in custody and the rest off to the winds. Our house is full of muckers. From Diefenbach, I suppose. Did you know?"

"No."

"I hoped you could call him off."

"You want to leave the country?"

"So I decided. I'm only sorry for him now."

"I doubt if I can call him off," Chink said. "He's bypassed me. And he never lets up. Can you get away?"

"By stealing a car to get back to Canada. I've no way of getting money now."

"The border'd be bad in a stolen car," Chink said. "Will you let me help?"

"Are you willing? Yes, I'll chance it."

"You have a safe place to spend the day?"

"Public buildings."

"There are things I'll have to show up for," Chink said. "To keep it looking normal. The house will be empty by six. We'll all be at Eustace Martin's for a party. I'll leave keys in my mailbox and the box unlocked. Wait for me here."

"Ah," said James.

Chink misunderstood his hesitation. "James," he said, "I think I know why I was brought here now. I think it was only to get you to come back."

"It did that," James said. "I left Ireland the same day Williams sent the word that you'd arrived."

"Come in quietly. Don't turn on any lights, and wait for me. I'll have a car. I'll take you to Canada, and bring it back."

"Yes, yes, I will," James said. "It wasn't not relying on you, only that house. To sit there in the dark in those rooms, waiting. Never mind."

"It's still light at six," Chink said. "I'll be back by seven."

"Yes, Captain," said James. "And will you be swimming now with Olive?"

"Yes."

"Would I could do it with you once again."

"I wish you could."

"Well," said Libby. "Look who's here."

He'd have recognized her anywhere, in any costume. Her hair was dyed, quite becomingly, back to its natural color, and she was still slim. There were some new lines in her face, but it was tan and taut. The smile was quizzical.

"Hello, Libby."

"I don't know whether to hug you or hit you. I guess I'll have another drink and think it over. You still take beer?" She signalled a waiter. The table at La Caravelle was for two.

"Isn't Wally coming?"

"He's got one of his operations going," Libby said. Chink nodded. "He said he'd see you this evening at the drunk club."

"Eustace Martin's. Are you coming?"

"I may. For God's sake, sit down."

"You look wonderful," he said, sitting. "Do you ride?"

"Not for years. You can count how many. I sail in the summer and skate in the winter."

He recalled that they had learned to ski together, and learned that she had taken it up again. They started eating. They talked about Curt's children. Libby said there was a real houseful of West Pointers and Irish setters, down in Washington.

Over coffee he asked why she had come to town today, and Libby said there was a W.C.I. board meeting.

"Is it true you're going to work for us?" she asked.

"Yes."

"I'm a little cross I wasn't consulted, under the circumstances."

"Would you have been against it?"

"I don't know. I'd have liked a chance to think about it. You may be just a little righteous for a businessman."

"I hope not."

"It's not all clear and straight and nice."

"Nothing is. But I don't feel compromised by the things I'll be doing."

"How about some of our other little activities? Eustace Martin's club, for instance. On the other side of the law, it's what's generally called a laundry."

"So I gather."

"You don't object?"

"If I were sitting on the board with you, I might."

"You think I should?"

"I'm not sitting on the board."

"Goddamn it, you haven't changed, have you?"

"I can't judge that, either."

"Wally and I used to laugh about you. So did Curt."

"Did he, Libby?"

"And Mike and Wendy. Except they didn't laugh. They just plain never forgave you."

"Could we get the check?"

"You seem to think I'm lying."

"I just think I ought to get our check."

"I'll take care of it."

"No, thanks, Libby," Chink said. "No, thanks."

"You're about as welcome as anyone else," Eustace Martin said. "Jesus, look at them."

The club, closed to the public for Vivian's engagement party, was already crowded.

"Theatre punks," Eustace said. For the first time since Chink had known him, Eustace had his clarinet with him, uncased and jointed up. He carried it carelessly, almost with disdain. "Also music punks. Please, Daddy, get some of your old friends and play for us.

And now I got a beer-drinking punk. What do you want to drink?"

Chink smiled.

"We got terrible champagne. I think they make it in Rhode Island, out of cranberries."

"I'll get something," Chink said.

"We got High Society Scotch, High Society Bourbon, and High Society Sterno for the musicians. Try the hors d'oeuvres, the dishwasher made them special. Cat food and mayonnaise on Ritz crackers."

Chink got himself a beer at the bar. There were platters of catered hors d'oeuvres, lavish and attractive. Susan was by one, nibbling, and with her a tall, emaciated young man in a pale whipcord suit of full, archaic cut.

"You haven't met Zygmunt," Susan said. "Isn't he beautiful? He doesn't speak a word."

"I speak a word," said Zygmunt, with a melancholy smile.

Chink shook his long, thin hand, holding it carefully.

"I just adore him," Susan said.

Olive was with Lydia at a table in the other room. Lydia groaned when Chink joined them.

"Here comes hot nuts," she said, addressing an imaginary companion. "Let's go and leave the young people alone." She stood up. "I think I'll go seduce Eustace Martin," she said. "And make it a really lousy day."

"Isn't she in a fine mood?" Chink said.

"She loves it," Olive said. "Wait till the happy couple enter. Then she'll really ride her broom."

"Is this Olive?" It was Adrienne Diefenbach, coming up with Wally behind her. Chink stood and made the introduction.

"May I take her away?" Adrienne asked. "I want to talk about the wedding. Lydia's no use and Susan has a young man."

Chink and Wally stood until they'd left.

"Well, Chinklebelly." Wally shook hands, and sat down. "Well, you really fixed things dandy, didn't you?"

Chink sat opposite. "What's the trouble?"

"What did you think of to say to our mutual ex-wife at lunch, little friend?"

"It didn't go too well."

"The job," Wally said, "is off."

"No," Chink said.

"There was a board meeting. I hope never to attend another one like it. She was pure fury."

"You control the board," Chink said. "Tell her I've got a contract."

"I can't use a fight. Not with Libby. She owns too big a piece of us."

"You proposing to pay off the contract?" Chink asked. "It's for a total of a hundred and ninety thousand dollars."

"You wouldn't take that money."

"No. I want the job."

"I want you to reconsider," Wally said.

"I don't think I will."

"I'm afraid you'll have to. There's no room to manoeuver with Libby. Unless you can apologize . . . What is it?"

A waiter had come and was standing by the table.

"Ambassador Diefenbach?"

"Yes."

"Telephone, sir. Over at the bar."

"Can you ask who it is?"

"It sounded like a child."

Chink and Wally looked at one another.

"April," Chink said.

"She isn't here?"

"I haven't seen her." Chink felt cold again. "Shall I take it for you?"

Wally was staring at him. "Where's Ryan?" he asked. "Chink, where's James Ryan?"

Chink pushed through the room to the bar, and reached for the telephone. "Hello?"

"Daddy?"

"Hello, April. It's Chink."

"Daddy?"

"No, April." Wally was behind him. "Here, I'll get over there."

Wally took the phone with one hand, and held on to Chink's arm, restraining him with the other.

"Hello, April." Wally listened, lowered the mouthpiece, and said to Chink: "She's never called me that."

He freed Chink's arm, and Chink went through the people quickly. He saw Olive's head turn, and saw her take a step to follow him. As he got to the door of the club, Eustace Martin and his friends had started to play "Do You Know What It Means to Miss New Orleans?"

He reached the street and started running. As he came to the house on Tenth Street, he could see from the sidewalk that there was a light on, somewhere in his apartment.

In the entry, his mailbox was open and the keys he'd left for James were gone. He used his spare key, and let himself into the empty hall. He ran to April's door, tried it, and found it locked. He went back to his own and opened it. By the door, perched on the narrow refectory table, was April in her rose jersey dress, her legs drawn up and the telephone cradled in her arms.

"April," he said. "Are you all right?"

"You're not my daddy." She said it in a high, little-girl voice. She wore no shoes or stockings, and her hair was mussed, but she seemed to be unhurt.

"April, is James Ryan here?"

She held the telephone away from him, as if he were trying to take it from her. She frowned. Olive came through the door.

"Stay with her," Chink said.

"Wally's coming," Olive said, taking the phone from April and hanging it up. "Hello, April."

"Go away," April said. Then, slyly, she reached over and got the phone again and held it away from Olive.

Chink crossed to the French window.

"Don't go there," April called. "It isn't ready."

Chink could already see James Ryan, lying in the garden, not far from the outer door to April's place. He turned the handle of the French window. She had locked it. He took the handle with both hands, twisted it and broke the lock, went into the garden and over to James.

Ryan was alive, asleep, drugged probably, facedown, and Chink felt tears of relief as he knelt by the young man. He took the wide shoulders gently, began to turn James onto his back, and saw that the face was mangled.

The nose was broken and askew, one cheek battered in, the forehead a mess of blood and pulp. He looked and saw a small, blue-enamelled iron skillet lying by the wall, where April must have dropped it. He could see blood on its bottom.

April's bottle of High Society Scotch, with its load of chloral hydrate, stood on a glass-topped, iron-legged table by the garden chaise.

Pardon My Kangaroo, said the gay, spray-paint graffiti. *Rabbits Keep Right.*

"Is it Ryan?" It was Wally's voice. Wally, holding April against him, stood in the French doorway. Behind him, Chink could see the Turkish chauffeur with a drawn gun, and Olive, watching.

"Yes," Chink said.

"This is April," Wally told the chauffeur. "Take April to my apartment, and we'll call the police."

"No, Wally," Chink said. There was no sign that April comprehended. "Do you want April out of this?"

"I've got to," Wally said.

"Do you want a contract to tear up?"

"Chink!" Olive said.

"Wally," Chink said, "get a doctor. Get this boy's face fixed up and send him home."

Chink Peters observed his fiftieth birthday on a ranch north of the Tagus River in Portugal, managing a cattle crossbreeding program funded jointly by a large U.S. foundation and the Soviet government. The Soviets had sent, for artificial insemination, the sperm of red steppe cattle, but there were half a dozen live bulls as well to breed with the Simmental cows.

The red bulls were murderous animals, best managed from horseback. There was a young man who rode with Chink, a Portuguese who performed in the bloodless Portuguese bullring as a *rojoneador*. He was fine young horseman, but there were still things Chink could teach him.

In the American Library at Lisbon, where they went once a month to spend the day, Chink kept track, through the accumulated newspapers, of some of his acquaintances. Wally Diefenbach was often involved in important negotiations. Vivian Martin, divorced within a few months after her marriage, was doing well on the West Coast in a television comedy series. Lydia Paul was poet-in-residence at a university in the southwest. Eustace Martin died of a liver ailment.

Deer hunters found a skeleton under the leaves in the woods in northern Vermont, he read once, and wondered if it might have been Leon Quiroz.

He did not read in the newspapers about Olive Dahlke, but had a letter from her and one, as well, from Susan McGrew. Susan was married, but not to Zygmunt, the Pole. Olive was making progress in her business career. Chink answered both letters, but he was not at ease in correspondence. His replies probably sounded stiffer and less inviting of further communication than he meant them to.